The Visioning
A Novel

by

Susan Glaspell

Double 9
BOOKS

The Visioning
A Novel
by Susan Glaspell

ISBN: 978-93-68093-49-7

Published by

DOUBLE 9 BOOKS
2/13-B, Ansari Road
Daryaganj, New Delhi – 110002
info@double9books.com
www.double9books.com
Tel. 011-40042856

ABOUT THE AUTHOR

Susan Keating Glaspell (July 1, 1876 – July 27, 1948) was a pioneering American playwright, novelist, actress, director, biographer, and poet, best known for her contributions to modern American drama. A founding member of the Provincetown Players, she played a key role in shaping the early years of modern theater in the United States. Glaspell's writing, whether in plays or novels, is characterized by her focus on complex, sympathetic characters and an exploration of the human experience. She often delved into issues of social and moral significance, using realism to portray life's challenges. Her work reflects a deep interest in philosophy and religion, and many of her characters are depicted as making principled stands in the face of personal and societal conflict. In addition to her literary work, Glaspell served as the Midwest Bureau Director of the Federal Theater Project under the Works Progress Administration, further demonstrating her commitment to advancing American theater. Her legacy endures in the richness of her characters and the depth of her exploration into the complexities of life and human nature.

CONTENTS

CHAPTER I

Miss Katherine Wayneworth Jones was bunkered. Having been bunkered many times in the past, and knowing that she would be bunkered upon many occasions in the future, Miss Jones was not disposed to take a tragic view of the situation. The little white ball was all too secure down there in the sand; as she had played her first nine, and at least paid her respects to the game, she could now scale the hazard and curl herself into a comfortable position. It was a seductively lazy spring day, the very day for making arm-chairs of one's hazards. And let it be set down in the beginning that Miss Jones was more given to a comfortable place than to a tragic view.

Katherine Wayneworth Jones, affectionately known to many friends in many lands as Katie Jones, was an "army girl." And that not only for the obvious reasons: not because her people had been of the army, even unto the second and third generations, not because she had known the joys and jealousies of many posts, not even because bachelor officers were committed to the habit of proposing to her—those were but the trappings. She was an army girl because "Well, when you know her, you don't have to be told, and if you don't know her you can't be," a floundering friend had once concluded her exposition of why Katie was so "army." For her to marry outside the army would be regarded as little short of treason.

To-day she was giving a little undisturbing consideration to that thing of her marrying. For it was her twenty-fifth birthday, and twenty-fifth birthdays are prone to knock at the door of matrimonial possibilities. Just then the knock seemed answered by Captain Prescott. Unblushingly Miss Jones considered that doubtless before the summer was over she would be engaged to him. And quite likely she would follow up the engagement with a wedding. It seemed time for her to be following up some of her engagements.

She did not believe that she would at all mind marrying Harry Prescott. All his people liked all hers, which would facilitate things at the wedding; she would not be rudely plunged into a new set of friends, which would be trying at her time of life. Everything about him was quite all right: he played a good game of golf, not a maddening one of bridge, danced and rode in a sort of joy of living fashion. And she liked the way he showed his teeth when he laughed. She always thought when he laughed most unreservedly that he was going to show more of them; but he never did; it interested her.

And it interested her the way people said: "Prescott? Oh yes—he was in Cuba, wasn't he?" and then smiled a little, perhaps shrugged a trifle, and added:

"Great fellow—Prescott. Never made a mess of things, anyhow."

To have vague association with the mysterious things of life, and yet not to have "made a mess of things"—what more could one ask?

Of course, pounding irritably with her club, the only reason for not marrying him was that there were too many reasons for doing so. She could not think of a single person who would furnish the stimulus of an objection. Stupid to have every one so pleased! But there must always be something wrong, so let that be appeased in having everything just right. And then there was Cuba for one's adventurous sense.

She looked about her with satisfaction. It frequently happened that the place where one was inspired keen sense of the attractions of some other place. But this time there was no place she would rather be than just where she found herself. For she was a little tired, after a long round of visits at gay places, and this quiet, beautiful island out in the Mississippi— large, apart, serene—seemed a great lap into which to sink. She liked the quarters: big old-fashioned houses in front of which the long stretch of green sloped down to the river. There was something peculiarly restful in the spaciousness and stability, a place which the disagreeable or distressing things of life could not invade. Most of the women were away, which was the real godsend, for the dreariness and desolation of pleasure would be eliminated. A quiet post was charming until it tried to be gay—so mused Miss Katherine Wayneworth Jones.

And of various other things, mused she. Her brother, Captain Wayneworth Jones, was divorced from his wife and wedded to something he was hoping would in turn be wedded to a rifle; all the scientific cells of the family having been used for Wayne's brain, it was hard for Katie to get the nature of the attachment, but she trusted the ordnance department would in time solemnly legalize the affair—Wayne giving in marriage—destruction profiting happily by the union. Meanwhile Wayne was so consecrated to the work of making warfare more deadly that he scarcely knew his sister had arrived. But on the morrow, or at least the day after, would come young Wayneworth, called Worth, save when his Aunt Kate called him Wayne the Worthy. Wayne the Worthy was also engaged in perfecting a death-dealing instrument, the same being the interrogation point. Doubtless he would open fire on Aunt Kate with—Why didn't his mother and father live in the same place any more, and—Why did he have to live half the time with mama if he'd rather stay all the time with father? Poor Worth, he had only spent six years in a world of law and order, and had yet to learn about courts and incompatibilities and annoying things like that. It did not seem fair that the hardest part of the whole thing should fall to poor little Wayne the Worthy. He couldn't help it, certainly.

But how Worthie would love those collie pups! They would evolve all sorts of games to play with them. Picturing herself romping with the boy and dogs, prowling about on the river in Wayne's new launch, lounging under those great oak trees reading good lazying books, doing everything because she wanted to and nothing because she had to, flirting just enough with Captain Prescott to keep a sense of the reality of life, she lay there gloating over the happy prospect.

And then in that most irresponsible and unsuspecting of moments something whizzed into her consciousness like a bullet—something shot by her vision pierced the lazy, hazy, carelessly woven web of imagery—bullet-swift, bullet-true, bullet-terrible—striking the center clean and strong. The suddenness and completeness with which she sat up almost sent her from her place. For from the very instant that her eye rested upon the figure of the girl in pink organdie dress and big hat she knew something was wrong.

And when, within a few feet of the river the girl stopped running, shrank back, covered her face with her hands, then staggered on, she knew that that girl was going to the river to kill herself.

There was one frozen instant of powerlessness. Then—what to do? Call to her? She would only hurry on. Run after her? She could not get there. It was intuition—instinct—took the short cut a benumbed reason could not make; rolling headlong down the bunker, twisting her neck and mercilessly bumping her elbow, Katherine Wayneworth Jones emitted a shriek to raise the very dead themselves. And then three times a quick, wild "Help—Help—Help!" and a less audible prayer that no one else was near.

It reached; the girl stopped, turned, saw the rumpled, lifeless-looking heap of blue linen, turned back toward the river, then once more to the motionless Miss Jones, lying face downward in the sand. And then the girl who thought life not worth living, delaying her own preference, with rather reluctant feet—feet clad in pink satin slippers—turned back to the girl who wanted to live badly enough to call for help.

Through one-half of one eye Katie could see her; she was thinking that there was something fine about a girl who wanted to kill herself putting it off long enough to turn back and help some one who wanted to live.

Miss Jones raised her head just a trifle, showed her face long enough to roll her eyes in a grewsome way she had learned at school, and with a "Help me!" buried her face in the sand and lay there quivering.

The girl knelt down. "You sick?" she asked, and Katie had the fancy of her voice sounding as though she had not expected to use it any more.

"So ill!" panted Kate, rolling over on her back and holding her heart. "Here! My heart!"

The girl looked around uncertainly. It must be a jar, Katie conceded, being called back to life, expected to fight for the very thing one was running away from. Her rescuer was evidently considering going to the river for water—saving water (Katie missed none of those fine points)—but instead she pulled the patient to a sitting position, supporting her.

"You can breathe better this way, can't you?" she asked solicitously. "Have you had them before? Will it go away? Shall I call some one?"

Katie rolled her head about as she had seen people do who were dying on the stage. "Often—before. Go away—soon. But don't leave me!" she implored, clutching at the girl wildly.

"I will not leave you," the stranger assured her. "I have plenty of time."

Miss Jones made what the doctors would call a splendid recovery. Her breath began coming more naturally; her spine seemed to regain control of her head; her eyes rolled less wildly. "It's going," she panted; "but you'll have to help me to the house."

"Why of course," replied the girl who was being delayed. "Do you think I'd leave a sick girl sitting out here all alone?"

Kate felt like apologizing. It seemed rather small—that interrupting a death to save a life.

"Where do you live?" her companion was asking. She pointed to the quarters. "In one of those?"

"The second one," Katie told her. "And thank Heaven," she told herself, "the first one is closed!"

"Lean on me," directed the girl in pink, with a touch of the gentle authority of strong to weak. "Don't be afraid to lean on me."

Kate felt the quick warm tears against her eyelids. "You're very kind," she said, and the quiver in her voice was real.

They walked slowly on, silently. Katie was trembling now, and in earnest. "My name is Katherine Jones," she said at last, looking timidly at the girl who was helping her.

It wrought a change. The girl's mouth closed in a hard line. A hard, defending glitter seemed to seal her eyes. She did not respond.

"May I ask to whom I am indebted for this kindness?" It was asked with gentleness.

But for the moment it brought no response. "My name is Verna Woods," came at last with an unsteady defiance.

They had reached the steps of the big, hospitable porch. With deep relief Katie saw that there was no one about. Nora had gone out with one of her adorers from the barracks.

They turned, and were looking back to the river. It was May at May's loveliest: the grass and trees so tender a green, the river so gently buoyant, and a softly sympathetic sky over all. A soldier had appeared and was picking twigs from the putting green in front of them; another soldier was coming down the road with some eggs which he was evidently taking to Captain Prescott's quarters. He was whistling. Everything seemed to be going very smoothly. And a launch was coming down the river; a girl's laugh came musically across the water and the green; it inspired the joyful throat of a nearby robin. And into this had been shot—!

Katie turned to the intruder. "It's lovely, isn't it?" she asked in a queer, hushed way.

The girl looked at her, and at the fierce rush of things Kate took a frightened step backward. But quickly the other had turned away her face. Only her clenched hand and slightly moving shoulder told anything.

There was another call to make, and instinct alone could not reach this time. For the moment thought of it left her mute.

"You have been so kind to me," she began, her timidity serving well as helplessness, "so very kind. I wonder if I may ask one thing more? Am—am I keeping you from anything you should be doing?"

There was no response at first, just a little convulsive clenching of the hand, an accentuated movement of the shoulder. Then, "I have time enough," was the low, curt answer, face still averted.

"I am alone here, as you see. I am just a little afraid of a—a return attack. I wonder—would you be willing to come up to my room with me—help make a cup of tea for us and—stay with me a little while?"

Again for the minute, no reply. Then the girl turned hotly upon her, suspicion, resentment—was it hatred, too?—in her eyes. But what she saw was as a child's face—wide eyes, beseeching mouth. Women who wondered "what in the world men saw in Katie Jones" might have wondered less had they seen her then.

The girl did not seem to know what to say. Suddenly she was trembling from head to foot.

Kate laid a hand upon the quivering arm. "I've frightened you," she said regretfully and tenderly. "You need the tea, too. You'll come?"

The girl's eyes roved all around like the furtive eyes of a frightened animal. But they came back to Katie's steadying gaze. "Why yes—I'll come—if you want me to," she said in voice she was clearly making supreme effort to steady.

"I do indeed," said Kate simply and led the way into the house.

CHAPTER II

And now that they were face to face across a tea-table Miss Jones was bunkered again. How get out of the sand? She did not know. She did not even know what club to use.

For never had she drunk tea under similar circumstances. Life had brought her varied experiences, but sitting across the teacups from one whom she had interrupted on the brink of suicide did not chance to be among them. She was wholly without precedent, and it was trying for an army girl to be stripped of precedent.

They were sitting at a window which overlooked the river; the river which was flowing on so serenely, which was so blue and lazy and lovely that May afternoon. She looked to the place where—then back to the girl across from her—the girl who but for her—

She shivered.

"Is it coming back?" the girl asked.

"N—o; I think not; but I hope you will not go." Then, desperately resolved to break through, she asked boldly: "Am I keeping you from anything important?"

A strange gleam, compounded of things she did not understand, shot out at her. To be followed with: "Important? Oh I don't know. That depends on how you look at it. The only thing I have left to do is to kill myself. I guess it won't take long."

Kate met it with a sharp, involuntary cry. For the sullen steadiness, dispassionateness, detachment with which it was said made it more real than it had been at the water's edge.

"But—but you see it's such a lovely day. You know—you know it's such a beautiful place," was what the resourceful Miss Jones found herself stammering.

"Yes," agreed her companion, "pleasant weather, isn't it?" She looked at Katie contemptuously. "You think *weather* makes any difference? That's like a girl like you!"

Katie laughed. Laughing seemed the only sand club she had just then. "I *am* a fool," she agreed. "I've often thought so myself. But like most other fools I mean well, and this just didn't seem to me the sort of day when it would occur to one to kill one's self. Now if it were terribly hot, the kind of hot that takes your brains away, or so cold you were freezing, or even if it were raining, not a decent rain, but that insulting drizzle that makes you hate everything—why then, yes, I might understand. But to kill one's self in the sunshine!"

As she was finishing she had a strange sensation. She saw that the girl was looking at her compassionately. Katherine Wayneworth Jones was not accustomed to being viewed with compassion.

"It would be foolish to try to make you understand," said the girl simply, finality in her weariness. "It would be foolish to try to make a girl like you understand that nothing can be so bad as sunshine."

Katie leaned across the table. This interested her. "Why I suppose that might be true. I suppose—"

But the girl was not listening. She was leaning back in the great wicker chair. She seemed actually to be relaxing, resting. That seemed strange to Kate. How could she be resting in an hour which had just been tacked on to her life? And then it came to her that perhaps it was a long time since the girl had sat in a chair like that. If she had had a chance, when things were going badly, to sit in such a chair and rest, might the river have seemed a less desirable place? She had always supposed it was *big* things—queer, abstract, unknowable things like forces and traits that made life and death. Did *chairs* count?

As the girl's eyes closed, surrenderingly, Katie was glad that no matter what she might decide to do about things she had had that hour in the big, tenderly cushioned wicker chair. It might be a kinder memory to take with her from life than anything she had known for a long time.

Katherine had grown very still, still both outwardly and inwardly. People spoke of her enviously as having experienced so much; living in all parts of the world, knowing people of all nations and kinds. But it seemed all of that had been mere splashing around on the beach. She was out in the big waves now.

She looked at the girl; looked with the eyes of one who would understand.

And what she saw was that some one, something, had, as it were, struck a blow at the center, and the girl, the something that really *was* her, had gone to pieces. Everything was scattered. Even her features scarcely seemed to belong to each other, so how must it not be with those other things, inner things, oh, things one did not know what to call? Was it because she could not get things together it seemed to her she must make them all stop? Was that it? Did people lose the power to hold themselves in the one that made you *you*?

What could do that? Something that reached the center; not many things could; something, perhaps, that kept battering at it for a long time, and just shook it at first, and then—

It was too dreadful to think of it that way. She tried to make herself stop.

The girl's face was turned to the out-of-doors; to a great tree in front of the window, a tree in which some robins had built their nests. Such a tired face! So many tear marks, and so much less reachable than tear stains.

A beautiful face, too. If all were back which the blow at the center had struck away, if she had all of her—if lighted—it would be a rarely beautiful face.

The girl was like a flower; a flower, it seemed to Kate, which had not been planted in the right place. The gardener had been unwise in his selection of a place for this flower; perhaps he had not used the right kind of soil, perhaps he had put it in the full heat of the sun when it was a flower to have more shade; perhaps too much wind or too much rain—Katie wondered just what the mistake had been. For the flower would have been so lovely had the gardener not made those mistakes.

Even now, it was lovely: lovely with a saddening loveliness, for one saw at a glance how easily a breeze too rough could beat it down. And one knew there had been those breezes. Every petal drooped.

A strange desire entered the heart of Katherine: a desire to see whether those petals could take their curves again, whether a color which blunders had faded could come back to its own. She was like the new gardener eager to see whether he can redeem the mistakes of the old. And the new gardener's zeal is not all for the flower; some of it is to show what he can do, and much of it the true gardener's passion for experiment. Katie Jones would have made a good gardener.

And yet it was something less cold than the experimenting instinct tightened her throat as she looked at the frail figure of the girl for whom life had been too much.

"I must go now," she was saying, with what seemed mighty effort to summon all of herself over which she could get command. "You are all right now. I must go."

But she sank back in the chair, as if that one thing left at the center pulled her back, crying out that if it could but have a little more time there—

The girl in blue linen was sitting at the feet of the girl in pink organdie. She had hold of her hand, so slim a hand. Everything about the girl was slim, built for favoring breezes.

"I have one thing more to ask." It was Kate's voice was not well controlled this time.

"You may call it a whim, a notion, foolish notion; call it what you like, but I want you to stay here to-night."

The girl was looking down at her, down into the upturned face, all light and strength and purpose as one standing apart and disinterested might view a spectacle. Slowly, comprehendingly, dispassionately she shook her head. "It would be—no use."

"Perhaps," Katie acquiesced. "Some of the very nicest things in life are—no use. But I have something planned. May I tell you what it is I want to do?"

Still she did not take her eyes from Katie's kindling face, looking at it as at something a long way off and foreign.

"I am not a philanthropist, have no fears of that. But I have an idea, a theory, that what seem small things are perhaps the only things in life to help the big things. For instance, a hot bath. I can't think of any sorrow in the world that a hot bath wouldn't help, just a little bit."

"Now we have such a beautiful bathroom. I loathe hot baths in tiny bathrooms, where the air gets all steamy and you can't get your breath. Perhaps one thing the matter with you is that all the bathrooms you've been in lately were too small. Of course, you didn't *know* that was one thing the matter; like once at a dance I thought I was very sad about a man's dancing so much with another girl, a new girl—don't you loathe 'new girls'?—but when I got home I found that one of my dress stays was digging into me and when I got my dress off I didn't feel half so broken up about the man."

An odd thing happened; one thing struck away came back. There was a light in the eyes telling that something human and understanding, something to link her to other things human, would like to come back. She looked and listened as to something nearer.

Seeing it, Katie chattered on, against time, about nothing; foolish talk, heartless talk, it might even seem, to be pouring out to a girl who felt there was no place for her in life. But it was nonsense carried by tenderness. Nonsense which made for kinship. It reached. Several times the girl who thought she must kill herself was not far from a smile and at last there was a tear on the long lashes.

"So I'm going to undress you," Katie unfolded her plan, encouraged by the tear, "and then let's just see what hot water can do about it. And maybe a little rub. I used to rub my mother's spine. She said life always seemed worth living after I had done that." She patted the hand she held ever so lightly as she said: "How happy I would be if I could make you feel that way about it, too. Then I've a dear room to take you into, all soft grays and greens, and oh, such a good bed! Why you know you're tired! That's what's the matter with you, and you're just too tired to know what's the matter."

The girl nodded, tears upon her cheeks, looking like a child that has had a cruel time and needs to be comforted.

Katie's voice was lower, different, as she went on: "Then after I've brushed your hair and done all those 'comfy' things I'm going to put you in a certain, a very special gown I have. It was made by the nuns in a convent in Southern France. As they worked upon it they sat in a garden on a hillside. They thought serene thoughts, those nuns. You see I know them, lived with them. I don't know, one has odd fancies sometimes, and it always seemed to me that something of the peace of things there was absorbed in that wonderful bit of linen. It seems far away from things that hurt and harm. Almost as if it might draw back things that had gone. I was going to keep it—" Katie's eyes deepened, there was a little catch in her voice. "Well, I was just keeping it. But because you are so tired—oh just because you need it so.—I want you to let me give it to you."

And with a tender strength holding the sobbing girl Katie unfastened her collar and began taking off her dress.

CHAPTER III

"Kate," demanded Captain Jones, "what's that noise?"

"How should I know?" airily queried Kate.

"I heard a noise in the room above. This chimney carries every sound."

"Nonsense," jeered his sister. "Wayne, you've lived alone so long that you're getting spooky."

He turned to the other man. "Prescott, didn't you hear something?"

"Believe I did. It sounded like a cough."

"Well, what of it?" railed Kate. "Isn't poor Nora permitted to cough, if she is disposed to cough? She's in there doing the room for me. I'm going to try sleeping in there—isn't insomnia a fearful thing? But the fussiness of men!"

They were in the library over their coffee. Kate was peculiarly charming that night in one of the thin white gowns she wore so much, and which it seemed so fitting she should wear. She had been her gayest. Prescott was thinking he had never known any one who seemed to sparkle and bubble that way; and so easily and naturally, as though it came from an inner fount of perpetual action, and could more easily rise than be held down. And he was wondering why a girl who had so many of the attributes of a boy should be so much more fascinating than any mere girl. "There are two kinds of girl," he had heard an older officer once say. "There are girls, and then there is Katie Jones." He had condemned that as distinctly maudlin at the time, but recalled it to-night with less condemnation.

"Katie," exclaimed Wayne, after his sister had read aloud some one's engagement from the Army and Navy Register, and wondered vehemently how those two people ever expected to live together, "Nora's out on the side porch with Watts!"

"Do you disapprove of this affair between Nora and Watts?" Katie wanted to know, critically inspecting the design on her coffee spoon.

"I distinctly disapprove of having some one coughing in the room upstairs and not being satisfied who the some one is!"

She leaned forward, pointing her spoon at him earnestly. "Wayne, they say there are some excellent nerve specialists in Chicago. I'd advise you to take the night train. Take the rifle along, Wayne, and find out just what it's done to you."

"That's all very well! But if you'd been reading the papers lately you'd know that ideas of house-breaking are not necessarily neurasthenic."

"Dear Wayne, lover of maps and charts, let me take this pencil and make a little sketch for you. A is the chamber above. In that chamber is Nora. Nora coughs in parting. Then she parts. B is the back hall through which Nora walks. C is the back stairs which she treads. Watts being waiting, she treads—or is it kinder to say trips?—with good blithe speed. D is the side door and E the side porch. Now I ask you, oh master of engineering and weird mechanical and mathematical mysteries, what is to prevent Nora from getting from A to E in the interval of time between the coughing and the viewing?"

Prescott laughed, but Wayne only grunted and ominously eyed the chimney place.

"There!" he cried, triumphantly on his feet before his sister, as again came the faint but unmistakable little cough. "A little harder to make a map this time, isn't it? Talk about nerve specialists—!"

He started for the door, but Katie slipped in in front of him, and closed it.

"Don't go, Wayne," she said quietly; queerly, Prescott thought.

"Don't *go*? Kate, what's the matter with you? Now don't be foolish, Katie," he admonished with the maddening patronage of the older brother.
"Open the door."

"I wish you wouldn't go," she sighed plaintively, arms outstretched against the door. "I do hope you won't insist on going. You'll frighten Ann."

"Frighten *who?*"

"Ann," she repeated demurely.

"Ann—*who?* Ann—*what?*"

"Ann *who!* Ann *what!* That's a nice way to speak of my friends! It's all very well to blow up the world, Wayne, but I think one should retain some of the civilities of life!"

"But I don't understand," murmured poor Wayne.

"No, of course not. Do you understand anything except things that nobody else wants to understand? Ann is not smokeless powder, so I presume you are not interested in her, but it seems to me you might tax your brain sufficiently to bear in mind that I told you she was coming!"

"I'm sorry," said Wayne humbly. "I don't seem able to recall a word about her."

"I scarcely expected you would," was the withering response.

"Tell me about her," Captain Prescott asked sympathetically. "I like girls better than guns. Has Ann another name? Do I know her?"

Katie was bending down inspecting a tear she had discovered at the bottom of her dress. "Oh yes, why yes, certainly, Ann has another name. Her name is Forrest. No, I think you do not know her. I don't know that Ann knows many army people. I knew her in Europe." Then, as they seemed waiting for more: "I am very fond of Ann."

She had resumed her seat and the critical examination of her coffee spoon. The men were silent, respecting the moment of tender contemplation of her fondness for Ann. "Ann is a dear girl," she volunteered at last.

"Having had it impressed upon me that I am such a duffer," Captain Jones began, a little haughtily, "I naturally hesitate to make many inquiries, but I cannot quite get it through my stupid and impossible head just why 'Ann' is hidden away in this mysterious manner."

"There's nothing mysterious about it," said Kate sharply. "Ann was tired."

"And why, if I may venture still another blundering question, was poor Nora held responsible for a cough she never coughed?"

Once more Miss Jones surveyed the torn ruffle at the bottom of her skirt. She seemed to be giving it serious consideration.

"I am glad that I do not live in the Mississippi Valley," was the remark she finally raised herself to make.

"One of Kate's greatest charms," Wayne informed Prescott, "is the emphasis and assurance with which she unfailingly produces the irrelevant. Now when you ask her if she likes Benedictine, don't be at all surprised to have her dreamily murmur: 'But why should oranges always be yellow?'"

"I am glad that I do not live in the Mississippi Valley," Kate went on, superiorly ignoring the observation, "because the joy of living seems to be at a very low ebb out here."

"Honestly now, do you get that?" he demanded of his friend.

"Ann and I had planned a beautiful surprise for you, Wayne."

"Thanks," said Wayne drily.

"To-night Ann was tired. She did not wish to come down to dinner. Of course, I might have told you: 'Ann is here.' To the orderly, West-Pointed mind, the well oiled, gun-constructing mind, I presume that would present itself as the thing to do. But Ann and I have a sense of the joy of living, a delight in the festive, in the—the bubbling wine of youth, you know. So we said, 'How beautiful to surprise dear Wayne.' In the morning Ann, refreshed by the long night's sleep, was to go out and gather roses. Wayne—"

"The roses don't bloom until next month," brutally interrupted Wayne.

"Of course, you would think of that! As we had planned it, Wayne, looking from his window was to see the beautiful girl—she is a beautiful girl—gathering dew-laden roses in the garden. Perhaps Captain Prescott, chancing at that very moment to look from his window, would see her too. It was to be a beautiful, a never-to-be-forgotten moment for you both."

"We humbly apologize," laughed Prescott.

"Hum!" grunted dear Wayne.

CHAPTER IV

She stepped out on the porch for a moment as Captain Prescott was saying good-night. The moonlight was falling weirdly through the big trees, stretching itself over the grass in shapes that seemed to spell unearthly things. And there were mystical lights on the water down there, flitting about with the movement of the stream as ghosts might flit. Because it looked so other-world-like she wondered if it knew what it had just missed. She had never thought anything about water save as something to look beautiful and have a good time on. It seemed now that perhaps it knew a great deal about things of which she knew nothing at all.

"Oh, I say, jolly night, isn't it?" he exclaimed as they stood at the head of the steps.

"Yes," said Kate grimly, "pleasant weather, isn't it?" and laughed oddly.

"It's great about your friend coming; Miss—?"

"Forrest." She spoke it decisively.

"She arrived this afternoon?"

"Yes, unexpectedly. I was never more surprised in my life than when I looked up and saw Ann standing there." Katie was not too impressed to resist toying a little with the situation.

"Oh, is that so? I thought—" But he was too well-bred to press it.

"Of course," she hastened to patch together her thread, "of course, as I told Wayne, I knew that Ann was coming. But I didn't really expect her until day after to-morrow. You see, there have been complications."

"Oh, I see. Well, at any rate it's great that she's here. She will be with you for the summer?"

"Ann's plans are a little uncertain," Kate informed him.

"I hope she'll not find it dull. Does she care for golf?"

"U—m, I—Ann has never played much, I believe. You see she has lived so much in Europe—on the Continent—places where they don't play golf! And then Ann is not very strong."

"Then this is just the place for her. Great place for loafing, you know. I hope she is fond of the water?"

Kate was leaning against one of the pillars, still looking down toward the river. It might have been the moonlight made her look so strange as she said, with a smile of the same quality as those shadows on the grass: "Why yes; in fact, Ann's fondness for the water was the first thing I ever noticed about her. I think I might even say it was the water drew us together."

"Oh, well then, that is great. We can take the boat and do all sorts of jolly things. Now I wonder—about a horse for her. She rides?"

"Perhaps you had better make no plans for Ann," she suddenly advised. "It really would not surprise me at all if she went away to-morrow. There is a great deal of uncertainty about the whole thing. In fact, Ann has had a great deal of trouble."

"I'm sorry," he said with a simplicity she liked in him.

"Yes, a great deal of trouble. Last year both her father and mother died, which was a great blow to her."

"Well, rather!"

"And now there are all sorts of business things to straighten out. It's really very hard for Ann."

"Perhaps we can help her," he suggested.

"Perhaps we can," agreed Kate. Her eyes left him to wander across the shadows down to the river again. But she came back to him to say, and this with the oddest smile of all, "Wouldn't it be a queer sensation for us? That thing of really 'helping' some one?"

She could not go to sleep that night. For a long time she sat in her room in the same big chair in which Ann had sat that afternoon. Poor Ann, who had sat there before she knew she was Ann, who was sleeping now without knowing she was Ann. For Ann was indeed sleeping. From her door as Kate carefully opened it had come the deep breathing as of an exhausted child.

Who was Ann? Where had she come from? How did she get there? What had happened? Why had she wanted to kill herself?

She wanted to know. In truth, she was madly curious to know. And probably she never would know.

And what would happen now? It suddenly occurred to her that Wayne might be rather annoyed at having Ann commit suicide. But there was a little catch in her laugh at the thought of Wayne's consternation.

A long time she sat there wondering. Where *had* Ann come from? She had just seemed whirled out of the nowhere into the there, as an unannounced comet in well-ordered heavens Ann had come. From what other world?—and why? Did she belong to anybody? Another pleasant prospect for poor Wayne! Was some one looking for Ann? Would there be things in the paper about her?

Surely a girl could not step out of her life and leave no trail behind. Things could not close up like that, even about Ann. Every one had a place. Then how could one step from that place without leaving a conspicuous looking vacancy?

Why had Ann been dressed that way? It seemed a strange costume in which to kill one's self. It seemed to Katie that one would prefer to meet the unknown in a smaller hat.

She went to the closet and took out the organdie dress and satin slippers. From whence? and why thither? They opened long paths of wondering. The dress was bedraggled about the bottom, as though trailed through fields and over roads. And so strangely crumpled, and so strange the scent—a scent hauntingly familiar, yet baffling in its relation to gowns. A poorly made gown, Katie noted, but effective. She tried to read the story, but could not read beyond the fact that there was a story. The pink satin slippers had broken heels and were stained and soaked. They had traveled ground never meant for them. Something about Ann made one feel she was not the girl to be walking about in satin slippers. Something had happened. She had been dressed for one thing and then had done another thing. Could it be that ever since the night before she had been out of her place in the scheme of things?—loosened from the great human unit?—seeking destruction, perhaps, because she could not regain her place therein? "Where have you been?" Katie murmured to the ruined slippers. "What did it? What do you know? What did you want?"

Many a pair of just such slippers she had danced to the verge of shabbiness. To her they were associated with hops, the gayest of music and lightest of laughter, brilliant crowds in flower-scented rooms, dancing and flirtation—the froth and bubble of life. But something sterner than waxed floors had wrought the havoc here. How much of life's ground all unknown to her had these poor little slippers trodden? Was it often like that?—that the things created for the fun and the joy found the paths of tragedy?

She had put them away and was at last going to bed when she idly picked up the evening paper. What she saw was that the Daisey-Maisey Opera Company was playing at the city across the river. Something made her stand there very still. Could it be—? Might it not be—?

She did not know. Would she ever know?

It drew her back to the girl's room. She was sleeping serenely. With shaded candle Katie stood at the door watching her. Surely the hour was past! Sleep such as that must draw one back to life.

Lying there in the sweet dignity of her braided hair, in that simple lovely gown, she might have been Ann indeed.

There was tenderness just then in the heart of Katherine Wayneworth Jones. She was glad that this girl who was sleeping as though sleep had been a treasure long withheld, was knowing to-night the balm of a good bed, glad that she could sink so unquestioningly into the lap of protection. Protection!—it was that which one had in a place like this. Why was it given the Anns—and not the Vernas? The sleeping girl seemed to feel that all was well in the house which sheltered her that night. Suddenly Katie knew what it was had gone. Fear. It was terror had slipped back, leaving the weariness which can give itself over to sleep. Katie was thinking, striking deeper things than were wont to invade Katie's meditations. The protection of a Wayne, the chivalrous comradeship of a Captain Prescott—how different the life of an Ann from the life this girl might have had! She stood at the door for a long moment, looking at her with a searching tenderness. What had she been through? What was there left for her?

Once, as a child, she had taken a turtle from its native mud and brought it home. Soon after that they moved into an apartment and her father said that she must give the turtle up. "But, father," she had cried, "you don't understand! I took it! Now how can I throw it away?"

"You are right, Katherine," he had replied gravely—her dear, honorable, understanding father; "it is rather inconvenient to have a turtle in an apartment, but, as you say, responsibilities are greater than conveniences."

She was thinking of that story as she finally went to bed.

CHAPTER V

"Nora," said Katie next morning, "Miss Forrest has had a great misfortune."

Nora paused in her dusting, all ready with the emotion which Katie's tone invited.

"She has lost all of her luggage!"

"The poor young lady!" cried good Nora.

"Yes, it is really terrible, isn't it? Everything lost; through the carelessness of the railroads, you know. And such beautiful gowns as they were. So—so unusual. Poor Miss Ann was forced to arrive in a dress most unsuited to traveling, and is now quite—oh quite—destitute."

Nora held her head with both hands, speechless.

"Didn't you tell me, Nora, that your cousin's wife was very clever at sewing—at fixing things over?"

"Yes, yes, Miss Kate—yes'm."

"I wonder, Nora, would she come and help us?"

"She would be that glad, Miss Kate. She—"

"You see, Miss Ann is not very well. She—poor Miss Ann, I hope you will be very kind to her. She is an orphan, like you, Nora."

Nora wiped both eyes.

"And just now it would be too dreadful for her to have to see about a lot of things. So I think, temporarily, we could arrange some of my things; let them down a little, and perhaps take them in—Miss Ann is a little taller and a little slimmer than I. Could you send for your cousin's wife to help us, Nora?"

Profusely, o'erflowingly, Nora affirmed that this would be possible.

When Captain Jones came in from the shops for luncheon it was to find his sister installed in the hall, one of those roomy halls adapted to all purposes of living, some white and pink and blue things strewn around her, doing something with a scissors. Just what she was doing seemed to concern him very little, for he sat down at a table near her, pulled out some blue prints, and began studying them. "Thank heaven for the saving qualities of firearms," mused Katherine, industriously letting out a tuck.

But luncheon seemed to suggest the social side of life, for after they were seated he asked: "Oh yes, by the way, where's Miss—"

"Ann is still sleeping," replied Kate easily.

"She must be a good sleeper," ventured Wayne.

"Ann is tired, Wayne," she said with reproving dignity, "and as I have already told you several times without seeming to reach through the bullets on your brain, not well. She is here for a rest. She may not come down for several days."

"Not what one would call a hilarious guest," he commented.

"No, less hilarious than Zelda Fraser." Katie spitefully mentioned a former guest whom Wayne had particularly detested.

He laughed. "Well, who is she? What did you say her name was?"

"Oh Wayne," she sighed long-sufferingly, "again—once again—let me tell you that her name is Forrest."

"What Forrest?"

"'Um, I don't believe you know Ann's people."

"Not the Major Forrest family?"

"No, not that family; not army people at all."

"Well, what people? I can't seem to place her."

"Ann is of—artistic people. Her father was a great artist. That is, he would have been a great artist had he not died when he was very young."

"Rather an assumption, isn't it, that a man would have—"

"Why not at all, if he has done enough during his brief lifetime to warrant the assumption."

"Is her mother living?"

"Oh no," said Katie irritably, "certainly not. Her mother has been dead—five years." Then, looking into the dreamy distance and drawing it out as though she loved it: "Her mother was a great musician."

"I shan't like her," announced Wayne decisively; "she is probably exotic and self-conscious and supercilious, and not at all a comfortable person to have about. It's bad enough for her father to have been a great artist— without her mother needs having been a great musician."

"She is simple and sweet and very shy," reproved Kate. "So shy that she will doubtless be painfully embarrassed at meeting you, and seem—well, really ill at ease."

"That will be an odd spectacle—a young woman of to-day 'painfully embarrassed' at meeting a man. I never saw any of them very ill at ease, save when there were no men about."

"Ann's experiences have not all been happy ones, Wayne," said Katie in the manner of the deeply understanding to one of lesser comprehension.

"I hope she'll go on sleeping. A young woman of artistic people—painfully embarrassed—unhappy experiences—it doesn't sound at all comfortable to me."

But a little later he said: "Prescott seems to think that Daisey-Maisey company not bad. If you girls would like to go we'll telephone for seats."

Katie paused in the eating of a peach. "Thank you, Wayne, but I have an idea—just a vague sort of idea—that Ann would not care especially for that."

"She's probably right," said Wayne, returning with relief to the blue prints.

Katie's sporting blood was up. Ann was to be Ann. Never in her life had she been so fascinated with anything as with this creation of an Ann.

"I have prepared a place for her," she mused, over the untucking of the softest of rose pink muslins. "I have prepared for her a family and a temperament and a sorrow and all that a young woman could most desire. From out the nothing a conscious something I have evoked. It would be most ungracious—ungrateful—of Ann to refuse to be what I made her. I invented her. By all laws of decency, she must be Ann. Indeed, she *is* Ann."

And Katie was truly beginning to think so. Katie's imagination coquetted successfully with conviction.

Ann, or more accurately the idea of Ann, fascinated her. Never before had she known any one all unencumbered, unbound, by facts. Most people were rendered commonplace by the commonplace things one knew about them. But Ann was as interesting as one's brain could make her. Anything one choose to think—or say—about Ann could just as well as not be true. It swept one all unchained out into a virgin land of fancy.

There was but one question. Could Ann keep within hailing distance of one's imagination? Did Ann have it in her to live up to the things one wished to believe about her? Was she capable of taking unto herself the past and temperament with which one would graciously endow her?

Katie's sense of justice forced from her the admission that it was expecting a good deal of Ann. She could see that nothing would be more bootless than thrusting traditions upon people who would not know what to do with them. But something about Ann encouraged one to believe she could fit into a background prepared for her. And if she could—would—! The prospect lured—excited. It was as inexplicably intoxicating as a grimace at the preacher—a wink at the professor. It seemed to be saucily tweaking the ear of that insufferably solemn Things-as-They-Are goddess.

There was in her eyes the light of battle when Nora finally came to tell her that Miss Forrest was awake.

But it changed to another light at sight of the girl sitting up in bed so bewilderedly, turning upon her eyes which seemed to say—"And what are you going to do with me now?"

Fighting down the lump in her throat Katie seized briskly upon that look of inquiry. "What she needs now," she decided, "is not tears, but a high hand."

"Next thing on the program," she began, buoyantly raising the shades and throwing the windows wide, "is air. You're a good patient, for you do as you're told. It's been a fine sleep, hasn't it? And now I mean to get you into some clothes and take you out for a drive."

The girl shrank down in the pillows, pulling the covers clear to her chin, as if to shut herself in. She did not speak, but shook her head.

But Katie rode right over that look of pain and fear in her eyes, refusing to emphasize it by recognition.

She left the room and returned after a moment with a white flannel suit which she spread out on the bed. "This is not a bad looking suit, is it? Your dress is scarcely warm enough for driving, so I want you to wear this. I told Nora that your luggage was lost. It may be just as well for you to know, from time to time, what I'm telling about you. I have an idea this suit will be very becoming to you. It came from Paris. I presume I'm rather foolish about things from Paris, but they always seem to me to have brought a little life and gayety along. There's a dear little white hat and stunning automobile veil goes with this suit. I can scarcely wait to see how pretty you're going to look in it all."

For answer the girl turned to the wall, hid her face in the pillows, and sobbed.

Kate laid a hand upon her hair—soft, fine brown hair with tempting little waves and gleams in it. There came to her a hideous vision of how that hair might have looked by this time had she not—by the merest chance—

It gave her a feeling of proprietary tenderness for the girl. It seemed indeed that this life was in her hands—for was it not her hands had kept it a life?

"Please," she murmured gently, persuasively, as the sobs grew wilder.

Suddenly the girl raised her head and turned upon Katie passionately. "What do you mean? What is this all about? I know well enough that people are not like this! This is not the way the world is!"

"Not like what?" Kate asked quietly.

"Doing things for people they don't have to do things for! Taking people into their houses and giving them things—their best things!—treating them as if there was some reason for treating them like that! I never heard of such a thing. What are you doing it for?"

Katie sat there smiling at her calmly. "Do you want to know the honest truth?"

The girl nodded, looking at her with anticipatory defiance, but that defiance which could so easily crumble to despair.

"Very well then," she began lightly, "here goes. I don't know that it will sound very well, but it has the doubtful virtue of being true. The first reason is that it interests me; perhaps I should even say—amuses me. I always did like new things—queer things—surprises—things different. And the other reason is that I've taken a sure enough liking to you."

She had drawn back at the first reason; but the bluntness of the first must have conveyed a sense of honesty in the second, for like the child who has been told something nice, a smile was faintly suggested beneath the tears.

"Would you like to hear my favorite quotation from Scripture?" Kate wanted to know.

At thought of Katie's having a favorite quotation the smile grew a little more defined.

"My favorite quotation is this: 'Take no thought for the morrow.' Perhaps it ends in a way that spoils it; I would never read the rest of it, fearing it would ruin itself, but taking just so much and no more—and it certainly is your privilege to do that if you wish—if all of a thing is good for you, part of it must be somewhat good—it does make the most comfortable philosophy of life I know of. It's a great solace to me. Now when I am seventy, I don't doubt I will have lost my teeth. Losing one's teeth is such a distressing thing that I could sit here and weep bitterly for mine were it not for the sustaining power of my favorite quotation. Why don't you adopt it for your favorite, too? And, taking no thought for the morrow, is there any reason in the world why you shouldn't go out now and have a beautiful drive? Going for a drive doesn't commit one to any philosophy of life, or line of action, does it? And whatever you do, don't ever refuse nice things because you can't see the reason for people's doing them. I shudder to think how much—or better, how little fun I would have had in life had I first been compelled to satisfy myself I was entitled to it. We're entitled to nothing— most of us; that's all the more reason for taking all we can get. But come now! Here are some fresh things—yours seem a bit dusty."

In such wise she rambled on as a bewildered but unresisting girl surrendered herself to her wiles and hands.

When Katie returned from a call to the telephone it was to find Ann rubbing her hand over a pretty ankle adorned with the most silky of silken hose. "Likes them," Katie made of it, at sight of the down-turned face; "always wanted them—maybe never had them. Moral—If you want people to believe in you, give them something they don't need, but would like to have."

She did her hair for her, chatting all the while about ways of doing hair, exclaiming about the beauty of Ann's and planning things she was going to do with it. "Were I as proud of all my works as I am of this, I might be a more self-respecting person," she said, finally passing Ann the hand mirror as if the girl's one concern in life was to see whether she approved of the plaiting of those soft glossy braids.

And unmistakably she did approve. "It does look nice this way, doesn't it?" she agreed, looking up at Katie with a shy eagerness.

When at last Ann had been made ready, when Katie had slipped on the long loosely fitted white coat, had adjusted the big veil with just the right touch of sophisticated carelessness, as she surveyed the work of her hands her excitement could with difficulty contain itself. "She is Ann,"she gloated. "Her father *was* a great artist. Her mother simply couldn't *be* anything but a great musician. And she's lived all her life in—Italy, I think it is. Oh—I know! She's from Florence. Why she couldn't be any place but from Florence—and she doesn't know anything about bridge and scandal and pay and promotion—but she knows all about dreaming dreams and seeing visions. She's lived a life apart—aloof—looking at great pictures and hearing great music. Of course, she's a little shy with us—she doesn't understand our roistering ways—that's part of her being Ann."

But when she came back after getting her own things, Ann had gone. The girl in white was still sitting there in the chair, but she was not at all Ann. Things not from Florence, other things than dreams and visions and great pictures and music had taken hold of her. Frightened and disorganized again, she was huddled in the chair, and as Katie stood in the doorway she said not a word, but shook her head, and the eyes told all.

Katie bent over the chair. "It's all 'up to me,'" she said quietly. "Don't you see that it is? You haven't a thing in the world to do but follow my lead. Won't you trust me enough to know that you will not be asked to do anything that would be too hard? Believe in me enough to feel I will put through anything I begin? Isn't it rather—oh, unthrifty, to let pasts and futures spoil presents? Some time soon we may want to talk of the future, but just now there's only the present. And not a very terrifying present. Nothing more fearful than winding in and out of the wooded roads of this beautiful place—listening to birds and—but come—" changing briskly to the practical and helping her rise as though dismissing the question—"I hear our horse."

"I see Miss Jones has got some of her swell friends visitin' her," a soldier who was cutting grass remarked to a comrade newer to the service. "Great swell—they tell me Miss Jones is. They say she's it in Washington all right—way ahead of some that outranks her. Got outside money—their own money. Handy, ain't it?" he laughed. "Though it ain't just the money, either. Her mother was—well, somebody big—don't just recollect the name. Friendly, Miss Jones is. Not like some, afraid you're going to forget your place the minute she has a civil word with you. That one with her is some swell from Washington or New York. You can tell that by the looks of her, all right. Lord, don't they have it easy though?"

CHAPTER VI

It would indeed seem so. Men looking from the windows of the big shops—those great shops where army supplies were manufactured—noticed them with much the same thought, some of them admiringly, some resentfully, as they chanced to feel about things. They drove past building after building, buildings in which hundreds of men toiled on preparations for a possible war. The throb of those engines, sight of the perspiring faces, might suggest that rather large, a trifle extravagant, a bit cumbersome, was the price for peace. But these girls did not seem to be thinking of the possible war, or of the men who earned their bread thwarting it by preparation. One would suppose them to be just two beautifully cared for, careless-of-life girls, thinking of what some man had said at the dance the night before, or of the texture of the plume on some one's hat, or, to get down to the really serious issues of life, whether or not they could afford that love of a dinner gown.

They left the main avenue and were winding in and out of the by-roads, roads which had all the care of a great park and all the charm of the deep woods. Here and there were soldiers doing nothing more warlike than raking grass or repairing roads. It seemed far removed from the stress and the struggle, place where the sense of protection but contributed to the sense of freedom. There would come occasional glimpses of the river, the beautiful homes and great factories of the busy, prosperous, middle-western city opposite. To the other side was a town, too, a little city of large enterprises; to either side seethed the questions of steel, and all those attendant questions of mind and heart whose pressure grew ever bigger and whose safety valves seemed tested to their uttermost. To either side the savage battles of peace, and there in between—an island—the peaceful preparations for war.

And in such places, sheltered, detached, yet offered all she would have from without, had always lived Katie Jones, a favorite child of the favored men whom precautions against war offered so serene a life; surrounded by friends who were likewise removed from the battles of peace to the peace of possible war, knowing the social struggle only as it touched their own detached questions of pay and rank, pleasant and stupid posts, hospitable and inhospitable commandants.

And into this had rushed a victim of the battles of peace! From the stony paths of peace there to the well-kept roads of war!

The irony of it struck Katie anew: the incongruity of choosing so well-regulated a place for the performance of so disorderly an act as the taking of one's life. Choosing army headquarters as the place in which to desert from the army of life! Such an infringement of discipline as seeking self-destruction in that well-ordered spot where the machinery of destruction was so peacefully accumulated!

She looked covertly at Ann; she could do it, for the girl seemed for the most part unconscious of her. She was leaning back in the comfortably rounded corner of the stanhope, her hands lax in her lap, her eyes often closed—a tired child of peace drinking in the peace furnished by the military, was Ann. It was plain that Ann was one who could drink things in, could draw beauty to her as something which was of her, something, too, it seemed, of which she had been long in need. Could it be that in the big outside world into which these new wonderings were sent, world which they seemed to penetrate but such a little way, there were many who did not find their own? Might it not be that some of the most genuine Florentines had never been to Florence?

And because all this was *of* Ann, it was banishing the things it could not assimilate. Those hurt looks, fretted looks, that hard look, already Kate had come to know them, would come, but always to go as Ann would swiftly raise her head to get the song of a bird, or yield her face to the caress of a soft spring breeze. Katie was grateful to the benign breezes, rich with the messages of opening buds, full, tender, restoring, which could blow away hard memories and bitter visions. Yet those same breezes had blown yesterday. Why could they not reach then? What was it had closed the door and shut in those things that were killing Ann? What were those things that had filled up and choked Ann's poor soul?

From a hundred different paths she kept approaching it, could not keep away from it. One read of those things in the papers; they had always seemed to concern a people apart, to be pitied, but not understood, much less reached. Overwhelming that one who had wished to kill one's self should be enjoying anything! That a door so tragically shut should open to so simple a knock! Mere human voice reach that incomprehensible outermost brink! Were they not people different, but just people like one's self, who had simply fallen down in the struggle, and only needed some one to help them up, give them a cool drink and chance for a moment's rest?

Were the big and the little things so close? One's own kind and the other kind just one kind, after all?

"I love winding roads," Katie was saying, after a long silence. "I suppose the thing so alluring about them is that one can never be sure just what is around the bend. When I was a little girl I used to pretend it was fairies waiting around the next curve, and I have never—"

But she drew in her horse sharply, for the moment at a loss; for it was not fairies, but Captain Prescott, riding smilingly toward them, very handsome on his fine mount.

"It's—one of our officers," she said sharply. "I—I'll have to present him."

"Oh please—*please!*" was the girl's panic-stricken whisper. "Let me get out! I must! I can't!"

"You *can*. You must!" commanded Katie. And then she had just time for just an imploring little: "For my sake."

He had halted beside them and Katie was saying, with her usual cool gaiety: "You care for this day, too, do you? We're fairly steeped in it. Ann,"—not with the courage to look squarely at her—"at this moment I present your next-door neighbor. And a very good neighbor he is. We use his telephone when our telephone is discouraged. We borrow his books and bridles; we eat his bread and salt, drink his water and wine—especially his wine—we impose on him in every way known to good neighboring. Yes, to be sure, this is Miss Forrest of whom I told you last night."

As the Captain was looking at Ann and not seeming overpowered with amazement, looking, on the other hand, as though seeing something rarely good to look at, Katie had the courage to look too. And at what she saw her heart swelled quite as the heart of the mother swells when the child speaks his piece unstutteringly. Ann was *doing* it!—rising to the occasion—meeting the situation. Then she had other qualities no less valuable than looking Florentine. That thing of *doing* it was a thing that had always commanded the affectionate admiration of Katie Jones.

It was not what Ann did so much as her effective manner of doing nothing. One would not say she lacked assurance; one would put it the other way—that she seemed shy. It seemed to Katie she looked for all the world like a startled bird, and it also seemed that Captain Prescott particularly admired startled birds.

He turned and rode a little way beside them, he and Katie assuming conversational responsibilities. But Ann's smile warmed her aloofness, and her very shyness seemed well adjusted to her fragility. "And just fits in with what I told him!" gloated Kate. And though she said so little, for some reason, perhaps because she looked so different, one got the impression of her having said something unusual. She had a way of listening which conveyed the impression she could say things worth listening to—if she chose. One took her on faith.

He said to her at the last, with that direct boyish smile it seemed could not frighten even a startled bird: "You think you are going to like it here?" And Ann replied, slowly, a tremor in her voice, and a child's earnestness and sweetness in it too: "I think it the most beautiful place I ever saw in all my life."

At the simple enough words his face softened strangely. It was with an odd gentleness he said he hoped they could all have some good times together.

But, the moment conquered, things which it had called up swept in. The whole of it seemed to rush in upon her.

She turned harshly upon Katie. "This is—ridiculous! I'm going away to-night!"

"We will talk it over this evening," replied Kate quietly. "You will wait for that, won't you? I have something to suggest. And in the end you will be at liberty to do exactly as you think best. Certainly there can be no question as to that."

On their way home they encountered the throng of men from the shops—dirty, greasy, alien. It was not pleasant—meeting the men when one was driving. And yet, though certainly distasteful, they interested Katie, perhaps just because they were so different. She wondered how they lived and what they talked about.

Chancing to look at Ann, she saw that stranger than the men was the look with which Ann regarded them. She could not make it out. But one thing she did see—the soft spring breezes had much yet to do.

CHAPTER VII

Wayne had gone over to Colonel Leonard's for bridge. Kate was to have gone too, but had pleaded fatigue. The plea was not wholly hollow. The last thirty hours had not been restful ones.

And now she was to go upstairs and do something which she did not know how to do, or why she was doing. Sitting there alone in the library she grew serious in the thought that a game was something more than a game when played with human beings.

Not that seriousness robbed her of the charm that was her own. The distinctive thing about Katie was that there always seemed a certain light about her, upon her, coming from her. Usually it was as iridescent lights dancing upon the water; but to-night it was more as one light, a more steady, deeper light. It made her gray eyes almost black; made her clear-cut nose and chin seem more finely chiseled than they actually were, and brought out both the strength and the tenderness of her not very small mouth. Katie's friends, when pinned down to it, always admitted with some little surprise that she was not pretty; they made amends for that, however, in saying that she just missed being beautiful. "But that's not what you think of when you see her," they would tell you. "You think, 'What a good sort! She must be great fun!'" And there were some few who would add: "Katie is the kind you would expect to find doing splendid service in that last ditch."

Yet even those few were not familiar with the Katie Jones of that moment, for it was a new Katie, less new when leaning forward, tense, puzzled, hand clenched, brow knitted, her whole well-knit, athletic body at attention than when leaning back—lax, open to new and awesome things. And as though she must come back where she felt acquainted with herself, she suddenly began to whistle. Katie found whistling a convenient and pleasant recepticle for excess emotion. She had enjoyed it when a little girl because she had been told it was unladylike; kept it up to find out if it were really true that it would spoil her mouth, and now liked doing it because she could do it so successfully.

She was still whistling herself back to familiar things as she ran lightly up the stairs; had warmed to a long final trill as she stood in the doorway. The girl looked up in amazement. She had been sitting there, elbows on her knees, face in her hands. It was hard to see what might have been seen in her face because at that moment the chief thing seen was astonishment. Katie slipped down among the pillows of the couch, an arm curled about her head. "Didn't know I could do that, did you?" she laughed. "Oh yes, I have several accomplishments. Whistling is perhaps the chiefest thereof. Then next I think would come golf. My game's not bad. Then there are a few wizardy things I do with a chafing dish, and lastly, and after all lastly should be firstly, is my genius for getting everything and everybody into a most hopeless mess."

The girl moved impatiently at first, as if determined not to be evaded by that light mood, but sight of Katie, lying there so much as a child would lie, seemed to suggest how truly Katie might have spoken and she was betrayed into the shadow of a smile.

"I suppose there has never been a human being as gifted in balling things up as I am," meditatively boasted Kate.

"Now here you are," she continued plaintively. "You want to go away. Well, of course, that's your affair. Why should you have to stay here—if you don't want to? But in the twenty-four hours you've been here I presume I've told twenty-four unnecessary lies to my brother. And if you do go away—as I admit you have a perfect right to do—it will put me in such a compromising position, because of those deathless lies that will trail me round through life that—oh, well," she concluded petulantly, "I suppose I'll just have to go away too."

But the girl put it resolutely from her. A wave of sternness swept her face as she said, with a certain dignity that made Katie draw herself to a position more adapted to the contemplation of serious things: "That's all very well. Your pretending—trying to pretend—that I would be doing you a favor in staying. It is so—so clever. I mean so cleverly kind. But I can't help seeing through it, and I'm not going to accept hospitality I've no right to— stay here under false pretenses—pretend to be what I'm not—why what I couldn't even pretend to be!" she concluded with bitterness.

Katie was leaning forward, all keen interest. "But do you know, I think you could. I honestly believe we could put it through! And don't you see that it would be the most fascinating—altogether jolliest sort of thing for us to try? It would be a game—a lark—the very best kind of sport!"

She saw in an instant that she had wounded her. "I'm sorry; I would like very much to do something for you after all this. But I am afraid this is sport I cannot furnish you. I am not—I'm not feeling just like—a lark."

"Now do you *see*?" Kate demanded with turbulent gesture. "Talk about balling things *up*! I like you; I want you to stay; and when I come in here and try and induce you to stay what do I do but muddle things so that you'll probably walk right out of the house! Why was I born like that?" she demanded in righteous resentment.

"'Katherine,' a worldly-wise aunt of mine said to me once, 'you have two grave faults. One is telling the truth. The other is telling lies. I have never known you to fail in telling the one when it was a time to tell the other.' Can't you see what a curse it is to mix times that way?"

As one too tired to resist the tide, not accepting, but going with it for the minute because the tide was kindly and the force to withstand it small, the girl, her arm upon the table, her head leaning wearily upon her hand, sat there looking at Katie, that combination of the non-accepting and the unresisting which weariness can breed.

Kate seemed in profound thought. "Of course, you would naturally be suspicious of me," she broke in as if merely continuing the thinking aloud; Katie's fashion of doing that often made commonplace things seem very intimate—a statement to which considerable masculine testimony could be affixed. "I don't blame you in the least. I'd be suspicious, too, in your place. It's not unnatural that, not knowing me well, you should think I had some designs about 'doing good,' or helping you, and of course nothing makes self-respecting persons so furious as the thought that some one may be trying to do them good. Now if I could only prove to you, as could be proved, that I never did any good in my life, then perhaps you'd have more belief in me, or less suspicion of me. I wonder if you would do this? Could you bring yourself to stay just long enough to see that I am not trying to do you good? Fancy how I should feel to have you go away looking upon me as an officious philanthropist! Isn't it only square to give me a chance to demonstrate the honor of my worthlessness?"

Still the girl just drifted, her eyes now revealing a certain half-amused, half-affectionate tenderness for the tide which would bear her so craftily.

"And speaking of honor, moves me to my usual truth-telling blunder, and I can't resist telling you that in one respect I really have designs on you. But be at peace—it has nothing to do with your soul. Never having so much as discovered my own soul, I should scarcely presume to undertake the management of yours, but what I do want to do is to feed you eggs!

"No—now don't take it that way. You're thinking of eggs one orders at a hotel, or—or a boarding-house, maybe. But did you ever eat the eggs that were triumphantly announced by the darlingest bantam—?"

She paused—beaten back by the things gathering in the girl's face.

"Tell me the truth!" it broke. "What are you doing this for? What have you to *gain* by it?"

"I hadn't thought just what I had to—gain by it," Katie stammered, at a loss before so fierce an intensity. "Does—must one always 'gain' something?"

"If you knew the world," the girl threw out at her, "you'd know well enough one always expects to gain something! But you don't know the world—that's plain."

Katie was humbly silent. She had thought she knew the world. She had lived in the Philippines and Japan and all over Europe and America. She would have said that the difference between her and this other girl was in just that thing of her knowing the world—being of it. But there seemed nothing to say when Ann told her so emphatically that she did not know the world.

The girl seemed on fire. "No, of course not; you don't know the world— you don't know life—that's why you don't know what an unheard-of thing you're doing! What do you know about *me*?" she thrust at her fiercely. "What do you *think* about me?"

"I think you have had a hard time," Katie murmured, thinking to herself that one must have had hard time—

"And what's that to you? Why's that your affair?"

"It's not exactly my affair, to be sure," Katie admitted; "except that we seem to have been—thrown together, and, as I said, there's something about you that I've—taken a fancy to."

It drew her, but she beat it back. Resistance made her face the more stern as she went on: "Do you think I'm going to impose on you—just because you know so little? Why with all your cleverness, you're just a baby—when it comes to life! Shall I tell you what life is like?" Her gaze narrowed and grew hard. "Life is everybody fighting for something—and knocking down everybody in their way. Life is people who are strong kicking people who are weak out of their road—then going on with a laugh—a laugh loud enough to drown the groans. Life is lying and scheming to get what you want. Life is not caring—giving up—getting hardened—I know it. I *loathe* it."

Katie sat there quite still. She was frightened.

"And you! Here in a place like this—what do you know about it? Why you're nothing but an—outsider!"

An outsider, was she?—and she had thought that Ann—

The girl's passion seemed suddenly to flow into one long, cunning look. "What are you doing it for?" she asked quietly with a sort of insolently indifferent suspicion.

"I don't know," Katie replied simply. "At least until a minute ago I didn't know, and now I wonder if perhaps, without knowing it, I was not trying to make up for some of those people—for I fear some of them were friends of mine—who have gone ahead by kicking other people out of their way. Perhaps their kicks provided my laughs. Perhaps, unconsciously, it— bothered me."

Passion had burned to helplessness, the appealing helplessness of the weary child. She sat there, hands loosely clasped in her lap, looking at Katie with great solemn eyes, tired wistful mouth. And it seemed to Kate that she was looking, not at her, but at life, that life which had cast her out, looking, not with rage now, but with a hurt reproachfulness in which there was a heartbreaking longing.

It drew Katie over to the table. She stretched her hand out across it, as if seeking to bridge something, and spoke with an earnest dignity. "You say I'm an outsider. Then won't you take me in? I don't want to be an outsider. You mustn't think too badly of me for it because you see I have just stayed where I was put. But I want to know life. I love it now, and yet, easy and pleasant though it is, I can't say that I find it very satisfying. I have more than once felt it was cheating me. I'm not getting enough—just because I don't know. Loving a thing because you don't know it isn't a very high way of loving it, is it? I believe I could know it and still love it—love it, indeed, the more truly. No, you don't think so; but I want to try." She paused, thinking; then saw it and spoke it strongly. "I've never done anything real. I've never done anything that counted. That's why I'm an outsider. If making a place for you here is going to make one for me there—on the inside, I mean— you're not going to refuse to take me in, are you?"

Something seemed to leap up in the girl's eyes, but to crouch back, afraid. "What do you know about me?" she whispered.

"Not much. Only that you've met things I never had to meet, met them much better, doubtless, than I should have met them. Only that you've fought in the real, while I've flitted around here on the playground." Katie's eyes contracted to keenness. "And I wonder if there isn't more dignity in fighting—yes, and losing—in the real, than just sitting around where you get nothing more unpleasant than the faint roar of the guns. To lose fighting—or not to fight! Why certainly there can be no question about it. What do I know about you?" she came back to it.

"Only that you seemed just shot into my life, strangely disturbing it, ruffling it so queerly. It's too ruffled now to settle down without—more ruffling. So you're not going away leaving it in any such distressing state, are you?" she concluded with a smile which lighted her face with a fine seriousness.

She made a last stand. "But you don't know. You don't understand."

"No, I don't know. And don't think I ever need know, as a matter of obligation. But should there ever come a time when you feel I would understand, understand enough to help, then I should be glad and proud to know, for it would make me feel I was no longer an outsider. And let me tell you something. In whatever school you learned about life, there's one thing they taught you wrong. They've developed you too much in suspicion. They didn't give you a big enough course in trust. All the people in this world aren't designing and cruel. Why the old globe is just covered with beautiful people who are made happy in doing things for the people about them."

"I haven't met them," were the words which came from the sob.

"I see you haven't; that's why I want you to. Your education has been one-sided. So has mine. Perhaps we can strike a balance. What would you think of our trying to do that?"

The wonder of it seemed stealing up upon the girl, growing upon her. "You mean," she asked, in slow, hushed voice, "that I should stay here—here?—as a friend of yours?"

"Stay here as a friend—and become a friend," came the answer, quick and true.

So true that it went straight to the girl's heart. Tears came, different tears, tears which were melting something. And yet, once again she whispered: "But I don't understand."

"Try to understand. Stay here with me and learn to laugh and be foolish, that'll help you understand. And if you're ever in the least oppressed with a sense of obligation—horrid thing, isn't it?—just put it down with, 'But she likes it. It's fun for her.' For really now, Ann, I hope this is not going to hurt you, but I simply can't help getting fun out of things. I get fun out of everything. It's my great failing. Not a particularly unkind sort of fun, though. I don't believe you'll mind it as you get used to it. My friends all seem to accept the fact that I—enjoy them. And then my curiosity. Well, like the eggs. It's not entirely to make you stronger. It's to see whether the things I've always heard about milk and eggs are really so. See how it works—not altogether for the good of the works, you see? Oh, I don't know. Motives are slippery things, don't you think so? Mine seem particularly athletic. They hop from their pigeon holes and turn hand-springs and do all sorts of stunts the minute I turn my back. So I never know for sure why I want to do a thing. For that matter, I don't know why I named you Ann. I had to give you a name—I thought you might prefer my not using yours—so all in a flash I had to make one up—and Ann was what came. I love that name. It never would have come if something in you hadn't called it. The Ann in you has had a hard time." She was speaking uncertainly, timidly, as if on ground where words had broken no paths. "Oh, I'm not so much the outsider I can't see that. But the Ann in you has never died. That I see, too. Maybe it was to save Ann you were going to—give up Verna. And because I see Ann—like her—because I called her back, won't you let her stay here and—" Katie's voice broke, so to offset that she cocked her head and made a wry little face as she concluded, not succeeding in concealing the deep tenderness in her eyes, "just try—the eggs?"

CHAPTER VIII

Katie was writing to her uncle the Bishop. At least that was what she would have said she was doing. To be literal, she was nibbling at the end of her pen.

Writing to her uncle had never been a solemn affair with Kate. She gossiped and jested with him quite as she would with a playfellow; it was playfellow, rather than spiritual adviser, he had always been to her, Kate's need seeming rather more for playfellows than for spiritual advisers. But the trouble that morning was that the things of which she was wont to gossip and jest seemed remote and uninteresting things.

Finally she wrote: "My friend Ann Forrest is with us now. I am hoping to be able to keep her for some time. Poor dear, she has not been well and has had much sorrow—such a story!—and I think the peace of things here—peace you know, uncle, being poetic rendition of stupidity—is just what Ann needs."

A robin on a lilac bush entered passionate protest against the word stupidity. "What will you have? What will you *have?*" trilled the robin in joyous frenzy.

Wise robin! After all, what would one have? And when within the world of May that robins love one was finding a whole undiscovered country to explore?

"No, I don't mean that about stupidity," she wrote after a wide look and a deep breath. "It does seem peace. Peace that makes some other things seem stupidity. I must be tired, for you will be saying, dear uncle, that a yearning for peace has never been one of the most conspicuous of my attributes."

There she fell to nibbling again, looking over at the girl in the deep garden chair in the choice corner of the big porch. "My friend Ann Forrest!" Katie murmured, smiling strangely.

Her friend Ann Forrest was turning the leaves of a book, "Days in Florence," which Kate had left carelessly upon the arm of the chair she commended to Ann. It was after watching her covertly for sometime that

Katie set down, a little elf dancing in her eye, yet something of the seer in that very eye in which the elf danced:

"Of course you have heard me tell of Ann, the girl to whom I was so devoted in Italy. I should think, uncle, that you of the cloth would find Ann a most interesting subject. Not that she's of your flock. Her mother was a passionate Catholic. Her father a relentless atheist. He wrote a famous attack on the church which Ann tells me hastened her mother's death. The conflict shows curiously in Ann. When we were together in Florence a restlessness would many times come upon her. She would say, 'You go on home, Katie, without me. I have things to attend to.' I came to know what it meant. Once I followed her and saw her go to the church and literally fling herself into its arms in a passion of surrender. And that night she sat up until daybreak reading her father's books. You see what I mean? A wealth of feeling—but always pulled two ways. It has left its mark upon her."

She read it over, gloated over it, and destroyed it. "Uncle would be coming on the next train," she saw. "He'd hold Ann up for a copy of the attack! And why this mad passion of mine for destruction? Should a man walking on a tight-rope yield to every playful little desire to chase butterflies?"

But as she looked again—Ann was deep in the illustrations of "Days in Florence" and could be surveyed with impunity—she wondered if she might not have written better than she knew. Her choice of facts doubtless was preposterous enough; what had been the conflicting elements—her fancy might wander far afield in finding that. But she was sure she saw truly in seeing marks of conflict. Life had pulled her now this way, now that, as if playing some sort of cruel game with her. And that game had left her very tired. Tired as some lovely creature of the woods is tired after pursuit, and fearful with that fear of the hunted from which safety cannot rescue. It was in Ann's eyes—that looking out from shadowy retreat, that pain of pain remembered, that fear which fear has left. Katie had seen it once in the eyes of an exhausted fawn, who, fleeing from the searchers for the stag, had come full upon the waiting hunt—in face of the frantic hounds in leash. The terror in those eyes that should have been so soft and gentle, the sick certitude of doom where there should have been the glad joy of life struck the death blow to Katie's ambitions to become the mighty huntress. She had never joined another hunt or wished to hear another story of the hunt, saying she flattered herself she could be resourceful enough to gain her pleasures in some other way than crazing gentle creatures with terror. Ann made her think of that quivering fawn, suggesting, as the fawn had suggested, what life might have been in a woods uninvaded. She had a vision of Ann as the creature of pure delight she had been fashioned to be, loving life and not knowing fear.

From which musings she broke off with a hearty: "Good drive!" and Ann looked up inquiringly.

She pointed to the teeing ground some men were just leaving—caddies straggling on behind, two girls driving in a runabout along the river road calling gaily over to the men. It all seemed sunny and unfettered as the morning.

"I'll wager he feels good," she laughed. "I know no more exhilarating feeling than that thing of having just made a good drive. It makes life seem at your feet. You must play, Ann. I'm going to teach you."

"Do all those people belong here?" Ann asked, still looking at the girls who were calling laughingly back and forth to the men.

"On the Island? Oh, no; they belong over there." She nodded to the city which rose upon the hills across the river. "But they use these links."

"Don't they—don't they have to—work?" Ann asked timidly.

"Oh, yes," laughed Katie; "I fancy most of them work some. Though what's the good working a morning like this? I think they're very wise. But look now at the Hope of the Future! He's certainly working."

The Hope of the Future was ascending the steps, heavily burdened. So heavily was he burdened that for the moment ascent looked impossible. Each arm was filled with a shapeless bundle of white and yellow fur which closer inspection revealed as the collie pups.

With each step the hind legs of a wriggling puppy slipped a little farther through Worth's arms. When finally he stood before them only a big puppy head was visible underneath each shoulder. Approaching Ann, then backing around, he let one squirming pair of legs rest on her lap, freed his arm, and Ann had the puppy. "You can play with him a little while," he remarked graciously.

"Worth," said Katie, "it is unto my friend Miss Forrest, known in the intimacies of the household as Miss Ann, that you have just made this tender offering."

Worth took firm hold on his remaining puppy and stood there surveying Ann. "I came last night," he volunteered, after what seemed satisfactory inspection.

Ann just smiled at him, rumpling the puppy's soft woolly coat.

"How long you been here?" he asked cordially.

"Just two days," she told him.

"I'm going to stay all summer," he announced, hoisting his puppy a little higher.

"That's nice," said Ann; her puppy was climbing too.

"How long you goin' to stay?" he wanted to know.

"Miss Ann is going to stay just as long as we are real nice to her, Worthie," said Katie, looking up from the magazine she was cutting.

"She can play with the puppies every morning, Aunt Kate," he cried in a fervent burst of hospitality.

"You got a dog at home?" he asked of Ann.

At the silence, Katie looked up. The puppy was now cuddled upon Ann's breast, her two arms about it. As she shook her head her chin brushed the soft puppy fur—then buried itself in it. Her eyes deepened.

"It must be just the dreadfulest thing there is not to have a dog," Worth condoled.

There was no response. The puppy's head was on Ann's shoulder. He was ambitious to mount to her face.

"Didn't you *never* have a dog?" Worth asked, drawling it out tragically.

The head nodded yes, but the eyes did not grow any more glad at thought of once having had a dog.

Worth took a step nearer and lay an awed hand upon her arm. "Did he—*die?*"

She nodded. Her face had grown less sorrowful than hard. It was the look of that first day.

Worth shook his head slowly to express deep melancholy. "It's awful— to have 'em die. Mine died once. I cried and cried and cried. Then papa got me a bigger one."

He waited for confidences which did not come. Ann was holding the puppy tight.

"Didn't your papa get you 'nother one?" he asked, as one searching for the best.

"Worth dear," called Katie, "let's talk about the live puppies. There are so many live puppies in the world. And just see how the puppy loves Miss Ann."

"And Miss Ann loves the puppy. Mustn't squeeze him too tight," he admonished. "Watts says it's bad for 'em to squeeze 'em. Watts knows just everything 'bout puppies. He knows when they have got to eat and when they have got to sleep, and when they ought to have a bath. Do you suppose, Aunt Kate, we'll ever know as much as Watts?"

"Probably not. Don't hitch your wagon to too far a star, Worthie. No use smashing the wagon."

Suddenly Ann had squeezed her puppy very tight. "O—h," cried Worth, "*you mustn't*! I like to do it, too, but Watts says it squeezes the grows out of 'em. It's hard not to squeeze 'em though, ain't it?" he concluded with tolerance.

Again Katie looked up. The girl, holding the puppy close, was looking at the little boy. Something long beaten back seemed rushing on; and in her eyes was the consciousness of its having been long beaten back.

Something of which did not escape the astute Wayne the Worthy. "Aunt Kate," he called excitedly, "Aunt Kate—Miss Ann's eyes go such a long way down!"

"Worth, I'm not at all sure that it is the best of form for a grown-up young gentleman of six summers to be audibly estimating the fathomless depths of a young woman's eyes. Note well the word audibly, Worthie."

"They go farther down than yours, Aunt Kate."

"'Um—yes; another remark better left with the inaudible."

"It looks—it looks as if there was such a lot of cries in them! o—h—one's coming now!"

"Worth," she called sharply, "come here. You mustn't talk to Miss Ann about cries, dear. When you talk about cries it brings the cries, and when you talk about laughs the laughs come, and Miss Ann is so pretty when she laughs."

"Miss Ann is pretty all the time," announced gallant Worth. "She has a mouth like—a mouth like—She has a mouth like—"

"Yes dear, I understand. When they say 'She has a mouth like—a mouth like—' I know just what kind of mouth they mean."

"But how do you know, Aunt Kate? I didn't say what kind, did I?"

"No; but as years and wisdom and guile descend upon you, you will learn that sometimes the surest way of making one's self clear is not to say what one means."

"But I don't see—"

"No, one doesn't—at six. Wait till you've added twenty thereto."

"Aunt Kate?"

"Yes?"

"How old is Miss Ann?"

"Worth, when this twenty I'm talking about has been added on, you will know that never, never, *never* must one speak or think or dream of a lady's age."

"Why not?"

"Oh, because it brings the cries—lots of times."

He had seated himself on the floor. The puppy was in spasms of excitement over the discovery of a considerable expanse of bare legs.

"Are they sorry they're not as old as somebody else?" he asked, trying to get his legs out of the puppy's lurching reach.

"No, they're usually able to endure the grief brought them by that thought."

"Aunt Kate?"

"Oh—*yes*?" It was a good story.

"Would Miss Ann be sorry she's not as old as you?"

"Hateful, ungrateful little wretch!"

"Aunt Kate?"

"I am all attention, Wayneworth," she said, with inflection which should not have been wasted on ears too young.

"Do you know, Aunt Kate, sometimes I don't know just what you're talking about."

"No? Really? And this from your sex to mine!"

"Do you always say what you mean, Aunt Kate?"

"Very seldom."

"Why not?"

"Somebody might find out what I thought."

"Don't you want them to know what you think, Aunt Kate?" he pursued, making a complete revolution and for the instant evading the frisking puppy.

"Certainly not."

"But why not, Aunt Kate?"—squirming as the puppy placed a long warm lick right below the knee.

"Oh, I don't know." The story was getting better. Then, looking up with Kate's queer smile: "It might hurt their feelings."

"Why would it—?"

"Oh, Wayneworth Jones! Why were you born with your brain cells screwed into question marks?—and *why* do I have to go through life getting them unscrewed?"

She actually read a paragraph; and as there she had to turn a page she looked over at Ann. Ann's puppy had joined Worth's on the floor and together they were indulging in bites of puppyish delight at the little boy's legs, at each other's tails, at so much of the earth's atmosphere as came within range of their newly created jaws craving the exercise of their function. Mad with the joy of living were those two collie pups on that essentially live and joyous morning.

And Ann, if not mad with the joy of living, seemed sensible of the wonder of it. "Days in Florence" open on her lap, hands loose upon it, she was looking off at the river. From hard thoughts of other days Kate could see her drawn to that day—its softness and sunshine, its breath of the river and breath of the trees. Folded in the arms of that day was Ann just then. The breeze stirred a little wisp of hair on her temple—gently swayed the knot of ribbon at her throat. The spring was wooing Ann; her face softened as she listened. Was it something of that same force which bounded boisterously up in boy and dogs which was stealing over Ann—softening, healing, claiming?

The next paragraph of the story on the printed page was less interesting.

"Aunt Kate," said Worth, gathering both puppies into his arms as they were succeeding all too well in demonstrating that they were going to grow up and be real dogs, "Watts says it is the ungodliest thing he knows of that these puppies haven't got any names."

"I am glad to learn," murmured Kate, "that Watts is a true son of the church. He yearns for a christening?"

"He says that being as nobody else has thought up names for them, he calls the one that is most yellow, Mike; and the one that is most white, Pat. Do you think Mike and Pat are pretty names, Aunt Kate?"

"Well, I can't say that my esthetic sense fairly swoons with delight at sound of Mike and Pat," she laughed.

"I'll tell you, Worthie," she suggested, looking up with twinkling eye after her young nephew had been experimenting with various intonations of Mike—Pat, Pat—Mike, "why don't you call one of them *Pourquoi*?"

He walked right into it with the never-failing "Why?"

"Just so. Call one *Pourquoi* and the other *N'est-ce-pas*. They do good team work in both the spirit and the letter. *Pourquoi*, Worth, is your favorite word in French. Need I add that it means 'why'? And *N'est-ce-pas*—well, Watts would say *N'est-ce-pas* meant 'ain't it'? and more flexible translators find it to mean anything they are seeking to persuade you is true. Pourquoi is the inquirer and N'est-ce-pas the universalist. I trust Watts will give this his endorsement."

"I'll ask him," gravely replied Worth, and sought to accustom the puppies to their new names with chanting—Poor Qua—Nessa Pa. The chant grew so melancholy that the puppies subsided; oppressed, overpowered, perhaps, with the sense of being anything as large and terrible as inquirer and universalist.

But Worth was too true a son of the army to leave a brooding damsel long alone in the corner. "You seen the new cow?" was his friendly approach.

"Why, I don't believe I have," she confessed.

"I s'pose you've seen the chickens?" he asked, a trifle condescendingly.

Ann shamefacedly confessed that she had not as yet seen the chickens.

He took a step backward for the weighty, crushing: "Well, you've seen the *horses*, haven't you?"

"Aunt Kate—Aunt Kate!" he called peremptorily, as Ann humbly shook her head, "Miss Ann's not seen the cow—or the, chickens—nor the horses!"

"Isn't it scandalous?" agreed Kate. "It shows what sort of hostess I am, doesn't it? But you see, Worth, I thought as long as you were coming so soon you could do the honors of the stables. I think it's always a little more satisfactory to have a man do those things."

"I'll take you now," announced Worth, in manner which brooked neither delay nor gratitude.

And so the girl and the little boy and the two puppies, the joy of motion freeing them from the sad weight of inquirer and universalist, started across the lawn for the stables. Pourquoi caught at Ann's dress and she had to be manfully rescued by Worth. And no sooner had the inquirer been loosened from one side than the universalist was firmly fastened to the other and the rescue must be enacted all over again, amid considerable confusion and laughter. Ann's laugh was borne to Katie on a wave of the spring—just the laugh of a girl playing with a boy and his dogs.

It was a whole hour later, and as Kate was starting out for golf she saw Ann and Worth sitting on the sandpile, a tired inquirer and very weary universalist asleep at their feet. Ann was picking sand up in her hands and letting it sift through. Worth was digging with masculine vigor. Kate passed close enough to hear Ann's, "Well, once upon a time—"

Ann!—opening to a little child the door of that wondrous country of Once upon a Time! No mother had ever done it more sweetly, with more tender zeal, more loving understanding of the joys and necessities of Once upon a Time. Some once upon a time notions of Kate's were quite overturned by that "once upon a time" voice of Ann's. Then the once upon a time of the sandpile did not shut them out—they who had known another once upon a time? Did it perhaps love to take them in, knowing that upon the sands of this once upon a time the other could keep no foothold?

"Once upon a Time—Once upon a Time"—it kept singing itself in her ears. For her, too, it opened a door.

CHAPTER IX

Having conquered the son, Katie that evening set vigorously about for the conquest of the father.

"The trouble is," she turned it over in giving a few minutes to her own toilet for dinner, after having given many minutes to Ann's, "that there's simply no telling about Wayne. He is just the most provokingly uncertain man now living."

And yet it was not a formidable looking man she found in the library a few minutes before the dinner hour. He was poring over some pictures of Panama in one of the weeklies, sufficiently deep in them to permit Katie to sit there for the moment pondering methods of attack. But instead of outlining her campaign she found herself concluding, what she had concluded many times before, that Wayne was very good-looking. "Not handsome, like Harry Prescott," she granted, "but Wayne seems the product of something—the result of things to be desired. He hasn't a new look."

"Katherine is going to give us more trouble than Wayne ever will," their mother had sighed after one of those escapades which made life more colorful than restful during Katie's childhood. To which Major Jones replied that while Kate might give them more trouble, he thought it probable Wayne would give himself the more. Certain it had been from the first that if Wayne could help it no one would know what trouble he might be giving himself.

Old-fashioned folk who expected brothers and sisters to be alike had, on the surface at least, a sorry time with Wayneworth and Katherine Jones. Katie was sunny. Katie had a genius for play. She laughed and danced up and down the highways and the byways of life and she had such a joyous time about it that it had not yet occurred to any one to expect her to help pay the fiddler. Just watching Katie dance would seem pay enough for any reasonable fiddler. Katie laughed a great deal, and was smiling most of the time; she seemed always to have things in her thoughts to make smiles. Wayne laughed little and some of his smiles made one understand how the cat felt about having its fur rubbed the wrong way. Their friend Major Darrett once said: "When I meet Katie I have a fancy she has just come from a jolly dip in the ocean; that she lay on the sands in the sun and kicked up her heels longer than she had any business to, and now she's flying along to keep the most enchanting engagement she ever had in all her life. She's smiling to herself to think how bad she was to lie in the sand so long, and she's not at all concerned, because she knows her friends will be so happy to see her that they'll forget to scold her for being late. Katie's spoiled," the Major concluded, "but we like her that way."

Of Wayne this same friend remarked: "Wayne's a hard nut to crack."

Many army people felt that way. In fact, Wayne was a nut the army itself had not quite cracked. Some army people maintained that Wayne was disagreeable. But that may have been because he was not just like all other army people. He did not seem to have grasped the idea that being "army" set him apart. Sometimes he made the mistake of judging army affairs by ordinary standards. That was when they got some idea of how the cat felt. And of all cats an army cat would most resent having its fur rubbed in any but the prescribed direction.

Katie, continuing her ruminations about Wayne as the product of things, had come to see that with it all he was detached from those desirable things which had produced him. One knew that Wayne had traditions, yet he was not tradition fettered; he suggested ancestors without being ancestor conscious. Was it the gun—as Wayne the Worthy persisted in calling it— and the gun's predecessors—for Wayne always had something—made him so distinctly more than the mere result of things which had formed him? "It is the gun," Katie decided, taking him in with half shut eyes as a portrait painter might. "Had the same ancestors myself, and yet I'm both less and more of them than he is. What I need's a gun! Then I'd stand out of the background better, too." Then with one of Katie's queer twists of fancy— Ann! Might not Ann be her gun? Perhaps she had been wanting a gun for a long time without knowing what it was she was wanting when surely wanting something. Perhaps every one felt the gun need to make them less the product and more the person.

Then there was another thing. The thing that had traced those lines about Wayne's mouth, and had whitened, a little, the brown hair of his temples. Wayne had cared for Clara. Heaven only knew how he could—Katie's thoughts ran on. Perhaps heaven did understand those things—certainly it was too much for mere earth. Why Wayne, about whom there had always seemed a certain brooding bigness, certainly a certain rare indifference, should have fallen so absurdly in love with the most vain and selfish and vapid girl that ever wrecked a post was more than Katie could make out. And it had been her painful experience to watch Wayne's disappointment develop, watch that happiness which had so mellowed him recede as day by day Clara fretted and pouted and showed plainly enough that to her love was just a convenient thing which might impel one's husband to get one a new set of furs. She remembered so well one evening she had been in Clara's room when Wayne came in after having been away since early morning. So eager and tender was Wayne's face as he approached Clara, who was looking over an advertising circular. There was a light in his eyes which it would seem would have made Clara forget all about advertising circulars. But before he had said a word, but stood there, loving her with that look—and it would have to be admitted Clara did look lovely, in one of the *neglige* affairs she affected so much—she said, with a babyish little whine she evidently thought alluring: "I just don't see, Wayne, why we can't have a new rug for the reception room. We can certainly afford things as well as the Mitchells."And Wayne had just stood there, with a smile which closed the gates and said, with an irony not lost upon Katie, at least: "Why I fancy we can have a new rug, if that is the thing most essential to our happiness." Clara had cried: "Oh Wayne—you *dear!*" and twittered and fluttered around, but the twittering and fluttering did not bring that light back to Wayne's face. He went over to the far side of the room and began reading the paper, and that grim little understanding smile—a smile at himself—made Katie yearn to go over and wind her arms about his neck— dear strange Wayne who had believed there was so much, and found so little, and who was so alive to the bitter humor of being drawn to the heart of things only to be pushed back to the outer rim. But Katie knew it was not her arms could do any good, and so she had left the room, not clear-eyed, Clara still twittering about the kind of rug she would have. And day by day she had watched Wayne go back to the outer circle, that grim little smile as mile-stones in his progress.

But he was folding his paper; it was growing too near the hour to speculate longer on Wayne and his past.

"Wayne?" she began.

He looked up, smiling at the beseeching tone. "Yes? What is it, Katie? Just what brand of boredom are you planning to inflict?"

"You can be *so* nice, Wayne—when you want to be."

"'Um—hum. A none too subtle way of calling a man a brute."

"I presume there are times when you can't help being a brute, Wayne; but I do hope to-night will not be one of them."

"Why it must be something very horrible indeed, that you must approach with all this flaunting of diplomacy."

"It is something a long way from horrible, I assure you," she replied with dignity. "Ann will be down for dinner to-night, Wayne."

He leaned back and devoted himself to his cigarette with maddening deliberation. Then he smiled. "Through sleeping?"

"Wayne—I'm in earnest. Please don't get yourself into a hateful mood!"

He laughed in real amusement at sight of Katie's puckered face. "I am conscious that feminine wiles are being exercised upon me. I wonder—why?"

"Because I am so anxious you should like Ann, Wayne, and—be nice to her."

"Why?" Again it was that probing, provoking why.

"Because of what she means to me, I suppose."

Something in her voice made him look at her differently. "And what does she mean to you, Katie?"

"Ann is different from all the other girls I've known. She means—something different."

"Strange I've never heard you speak of her."

"I think you have, and have forgotten. Though possibly not—just because of the way I feel about her." She paused, seeking to express how she felt about her. Unable to do so, she concluded simply: "I have a very tender feeling for Ann."

"I see you have," he replied quietly. He looked at her meditatively, and then asked, humorously but gently: "Well Katie, what were you expecting me to do? Order her out of the house?"

"But I want you to be more than civil, Wayne; I want you to be sympathetic."

"I'll be civil and you can bring Prescott on for the sympathetic," he laughed. "You know I haven't great founts of sympathy gushing up in my heart for the *jeune fille*."

"Ann's not the *jeune fille*, Wayne. She's something far more interesting and worth while than that." She paused, again trying to get it, but could do no better than: "I sometimes think of Ann as sitting a little apart, listening to beautiful music."

He smiled. "I can only reply to that, Katie, that I trust she is more inviting than your pictures of her. A young woman who looked as though sitting apart listening to beautiful music should certainly be left sitting apart."

"I'll bring her down," laughed Kate, rising; "then you can get your own picture."

"I'll be decent, Katie," he called after her in laughing but reassuring voice.

The meeting had been accomplished. Dinner had reached the salad, and all was well. Yes, and a little more than well.

From the moment she stood in the doorway of Ann's room and the girl rose at her suggestion of dinner, Katie's courage had gone up. Ann's whole bearing told that she was on her mettle. And what Katie found most reassuring was less the results of the effort Ann was making than her unmistakable sense of the necessity for making it. There was hope in that.

Not that she suggested anything so hopeless as effort. She suggested reserve feeling, and she was so beautiful—so rare—that the suggestion was of feeling more beautiful and rare than a determination to live up to the way she was gowned. Her timidity was of a quality which seemed related to things of the spirit rather than to social embarrassment. Jubilantly Kate saw that Ann meant to "put it over," and her depth of feeling on the subject suggested a depth which in itself dismissed the subject.

She saw at a glance that Wayne related Ann to the things her appearance suggested rather than to the suggestions causing that appearance. As Katie said, "Ann, I am so glad that at last my brother is to know you," she was thinking that it seemed a friend to whom one might indeed be proud to present one's brother. She never lost the picture of the Ann whom Wayne advanced to meet. She loved her in that rose pink muslin, the skirt cascaded in old-fashioned way, an old-fashioned looking surplice about the shoulders, and on her long slim throat a lovely Florentine cameo swinging on the thinnest of old silver chains. She might have been a cameo herself.

And she never forgot the way Ann said her first words to Wayne. They were two most commonplace words, merely the "Thank you" with which she responded to his hospitable greeting, but that "Thank you" seemed let out of a whole under sea of feeling for which it would try to speak.

Before Wayne could carry out his unmistakable intention of saying more, Katie was airily off into a story about the cook, dragging it in with a thin hook about the late dinner, and the cook in the present case suggested a former cook in Washington whom Katie held, and sought to prove, nature had ordained for a great humorist. The ever faithful subject of cooks served stanchly until they had reached the safety of soup.

Katie was in story-telling mood. She seemed to have an inexhaustible fund of them in reserve which she could deftly strap on as life-preserver at the first far sign of danger. And she would flash into her stories an "As you said, Ann," or "As you would put it, Ann," whenever she found anything to fit the Ann she would create.

Several times, however, the rescuing party had to knock down good form and trample gentle breeding under foot to reach the spot in time. Wayne spoke of a friend in Vienna from whom he had heard that day and turned to Ann with an interrogation about the Viennese. Katie, contemplating the suppleness of Ann's neck, momentarily asleep at her post, missed the "Come over and help us" look, and Ann had begun upon a fatal, "I have never been in—" when Katie, with ringing laugh broke in: "Isn't it odd, Ann, that you should never have been in Vienna, when you lived all those years right there in Florence? I *do* think it the oddest thing!"

Ann agreed that it *was* odd—Wayne concurring.

But driven from Vienna, he sought Florence. "And Italy? I presume I go on record as the worst sort of bounder in asking if you really care greatly about living there?"

Katie thought it time Ann try a stroke for herself. One would never develop strength on a life-preserver.

Seeing that she had it to make, she paused before it an instant. Fear seemed to be feeling, and a possible sense of the absurdity of her situation made for a slightly tremulous dignity as she said: "I do love it. Love it so much it is hard to tell just how much—or why." And then it was as if she shrank back, having uncovered too much. She looked as though she might be dreaming of the Court of the Uffizi, or Santa Maria Novella, but Katie surmised that that dreamy look was not failing to find out what Wayne was going to do with his lettuce. But one who suggested dreams of Tuscany when taking observations on the use of the salad fork—was there not hope unbounded for such a one?

Wayne was silent for the moment, as though getting the fact that the love of Italy, or perhaps its associations, was to this girl not a thing to be compressed within the thin vein of dinner talk. "Well," he laughed understanding, "to be sure I don't know it from the inside. I never was of it; I merely looked at it. And I thought the plumbing was abominable."

"Wayne," scoffed Kate, "plumbing indeed! Have you no soul?"

"Yes, I have; and bad plumbing is bad for it."

Ann laughed quite blithely at that, and as though finding confidence in the sound of her own laugh, she boldly volunteered a stroke. "I don't know much about plumbing," Katie heard Ann saying. "I suppose perhaps it is bad. But do you care much about plumbing when looking at"—her pause before it might have been one of reverence—"The Madonna of the Chair?"

Katie treated herself to a particularly tender bit of lettuce and secretly hugged herself, Ann, and "Days in Florence." The Madonna of the Chair furnished the frontispiece for that valuable work.

Ann had receded, flushed, her lip trembling a little; Wayne was looking at her thoughtfully—and a little as one might look at the Madonna of the Chair. Katie heard the trump of duty call her to another story.

CHAPTER X

Feeling that first efforts, even on life-preservers, should not be long ones, it was soon after they returned to the library that Katie threw out: "Well, Ann, if that letter must be written—"

Ann rose. "Yes, and it must."

"But morning is the time for letter writing," urged Wayne.

"Morning in this instance is the time for shopping," said Kate.

She had left Ann at the foot of the stairs, murmuring something about having to see Nora. It was a half hour later that she looked in upon her.

What she saw was too much for Katie. Had the whole of creation been wrecked by her laughing, Katie must needs have laughed just then.

For Ann's two hands gripped "Days in Florence" with fierce resolution. Ann's head was bent over the book in a sort of stern frenzy. Ann, not even having waited to disrobe, was attacking Florence as the good old city had never been attacked before.

She seemed to get the significance of Katie's laugh, however, for it was as to a confederate she whispered: "I'll get caught!"

"Trust me," said Kate, and laughed from a new angle.

Ann could laugh, too, and when Katie sat down to "talk it over" they were that most intimate of all things in the world, two girls with a secret, two girls set apart from all the world by that secret they held from all the world, hugging between them a beautiful, brilliant secret and laughing at the rest of the world because it couldn't get in. That secret, shared and recognized and laughed over and loved, did what no amount of sympathy or gratitude could have done. It was as if the whole situation heaved a sigh of relief and settled itself in more comfortable position.

"Why no," sparkled Kate, in response to Ann's protestation, "the only thing you have to do is not to try. Lovers of Italy must take their Italy with a superior calm. And when you don't know what to say—just seem too full for utterance. That being too full for utterance throws such a safe and lovely cover over the lack of utterance. And if you fear you're mixed up just look as though you were going to cry. Wayne will be so terrified at that prospect that he'll turn the conversation to air-ships, and you'll always be safe with Wayne in an air-ship because he'll do all the talking himself."

Ann grew thoughtful. She seemed to have turned back to something. Katie would have given much to know what it was Ann's deep brown eyes were surveying so somberly.

"The strange part of it is," she said, "I used to dream of some such place."

"Of course you did. That's why you belong there. A great deal more than some of us who've tramped miles through galleries." Then swiftly Katie changed her position, her expression and the conversation. "Elizabeth Barrett Browning is your favorite poet, isn't she, Ann?"

"Why—why no," stammered Ann. "I'm afraid I haven't any favorite. You see—"

"So much the better. Then you can take Elizabeth without being untrue to any one else. She loved Florence. You know she's buried there. I think you used to make pilgrimages to her tomb."

Again Ann turned back, and at what she saw smiled a little, half bitterly, half wistfully. "I'd like to have made pilgrimages somewhere."

"To be sure you would. That's why you did. The things we would like to have done, and would have done if we could, are lots more part of us than just the things we did do because we had to do them. Just consider that all those things you'd like to have done are things you did. It will make you feel at home with yourself. And to-morrow we'll go over the river and order Elizabeth Barrett Browning and a tailored suit."

But with that the girl who would like to have done things receded, leaving baldly exposed the girl who had done the things she had had to do. "No," said Ann stubbornly and sullenly.

"But blue gingham morning dress and rose-colored evening dress are scarcely sufficient unto one's needs," murmured Kate.

Ann turned away her head. "I can't take things—not things like that."

"But why not?" pursued Kate. "Why can't you take as well as I can take?"

She turned upon her hotly, as if resentful of being toyed with. "How silly! It is yours."

Katie had said it at random, but once expressed it interested her.

"Why I don't know whether it is or not," she said, suddenly more interested in the idea itself than in its effect upon Ann. "Why is it? I didn't earn it."

"There's no use talking *that* way. It's yours because you've got it." That not seeming to bring ethical satisfaction she added: "It's yours because your family earned it."

Katie was unfastening the muslin gown. "But as a matter of fact," — getting more and more interested—"they didn't. They didn't earn it. They just got it. What they earned they had to use to live on. This that is left over is just something my grandfather fell upon through luck. Then why should it be mine now—any more than yours?"

Ann deemed her intelligence insulted. "That's ridiculous."

"Well now I don't know whether it is or not." She was silent for a moment, considering it. "But anyhow," she came back to the issue, "we have our hands on this money, so we'll get the suit. You're in the army now, Ann. You're enlisted under me, and I'll have no insubordination. You know—into the jaws of death!—Even so into the jaws of Elizabeth Barrett Browning—and a tailor-made suit!"

So Katie laughed herself out of the room.

And softly she whistled herself back into the library. The whistling did not seem to break through the smoke which surrounded Wayne. After several moments of ostentatious indifference, she threw out at him, with a conspicuous yawn: "Well, Wayne, what did you think of the terrifying jeune fille?"

Wayne's reply was long in coming, simple, quiet, and queer: "She's a lady."

Startled, peculiarly gratified, impishly delighted, she yet replied lightly: "A lady, is she? Um. Once at school one of the girls said she had a 'trade-last' for me, and after I had searched the closets of memory and dragged out that some one had said she had pretty eyes, dressed it up until this some one had called her ravishingly beautiful—after all that conscientious dishonesty what does she tell me but that some one had said I was so 'clean-looking.' One rather takes 'clean-looking' for granted! Even so with our friends being ladies. Quaint old word for you to resurrect, Wayne."

"Yes," he laughed, "quite quaint. But she seems to me just that old-fashioned thing our forefathers called a lady. Now we have good fellows, and thoroughbreds, and belongers. Not many of this girl's type."

Katie wanted to chuckle. But suddenly the unborn chuckle dissolved into a sea of awe.

Thoughts and smoke seemed circling around Wayne together; and perhaps the blue rim of it all was dreams. His face was not what one would expect the face of a man engaged in making warfare more deadly to be as he murmured, not to Katie but to the thin outer rim, softly, as to rims barely material: "And more than that—a woman."

He puzzled her. "Well, Wayne," she laughed, "aren't you getting a little—cryptic? I certainly told you—by implication—that she was both a lady and a woman. Then why this air of discovery?"

But it did not get Katie into the smoke. He made no effort to get her in, but after a moment came back to her with a kindly: "I am glad you have such a friend, Katie. It will do you good."

That inward chuckle showed no disposition to dissolve into anything; it fought hard to be just a live, healthy chuckle.

Moved by an impulse half serious, half mischievous she asked: "You would say then, Wayne, that Ann seems to you more of a lady than Zelda Fraser?"

Wayne's real answer lay in his look of disgust. He did condescend to put into words: "Oh, don't be absurd, Katie."

"But Zelda has a splendid ancestry," she pressed.

"And suggests a chorus girl."

That stilled her. It left her things to think about.

At last she asked: "And Wayne, which would you say I was?"

He came back from a considerable distance. "Which of what?"

"Lady or chorus girl?"

He looked at her and smiled. Katie was all aglow with the daring of her adventure. "I should say, Katie dear, that you were a half-breed."

"What a sounding thing to be! But Major Darrett in his last letter tells me I am his idea of a thoroughbred. How can I be a half-breed if I'm a thoroughbred?"

"True, it makes you a biological freak. But you should be too original to complain of that."

"But I do complain. It sounds like something with three legs. Not but what I'd rather be a biological freak than a grind—or a prude."

"Be at peace," drily advised Wayne.

"Ann was quiet to-night," mused Katie, feeling an irresistible desire to get back to her post of duty, not because there was any need for her being there, but merely because she liked the post. "She felt a little strange, I think. She has been much alone and with people of a different sort."

"And I presume it never occurred to you, Katie, that neither Ann nor I was fairly surfeited with opportunities for conversational initiative? Just drop me a hint sometime when you are not going to be at home, will you? I should like a chance to get acquainted with your friend."

Katie was straightway the hen with feathers ruffled over her brood. "You must be careful, Wayne," she clucked at him. "When you are alone with Ann please try to avoid all unpleasant subjects, or anything you see she would rather not talk about."

"Thanks awfully for the hint," returned Wayne quietly. "I had been meaning to speak first of her father's funeral. I thought I would follow that with a searching inquiry into her mother's last illness. But of course if you think this not wise I am glad to be guided by your judgment, Katie."

"Wayne!" she reproached laughingly. "Now you know well enough! I simply meant if you saw Ann wished to avoid a subject, not to pursue it."

"Thanks again, dear Sister Kate, for these easy lessons in behavior. Rule 1—"

But she waved it laughingly aside, rising to leave him. "Just the same," she maintained, from the doorway, "experience may make the familiar things—and dear things—the very things of which one wishes least to speak. Talk to Ann about the army, Wayne; talk about—"

But as he was holding out note-book and pencil she beat grimacing retreat.

That night Miss Jones dreamed. The world had been all shaken up and everything was confused and no one could put it to rights. All those dames whose ancestors had sailed unknown waters were in the front row of the chorus, and all the chorus girls were dancing a stately minuet at Old Point Comfort. Elizabeth Barrett Browning was trying to commit suicide by becoming a biological freak, and the Madonna of the Chair was wearing a smartly tailored brown rajah suit.

CHAPTER XI

Peacefully and pleasantly one day slipped after another. Some thirty of them had joined their unnumbered fellows and to-morrow bade fair to pass serenely as yesterday. "This, dear Queen," Katie confided to the dog stretched at her feet, "is what in vulgar parlance is known as 'nothing doing,' and in poetic language is termed the 'simple life.'"

Thirty days of "nothing doing"—and yet there had been more "doing" in those days than in all the thousands of their predecessors gaily crowded to the brim. Those crowded days seemed days of a long sleep; these quiet ones, days of waking.

Ann was out on the links that afternoon with Captain Prescott. From her place on the porch Katie had a glimpse of them at that moment. Ann's white dress with its big knot of red ribbon was a vivid and a pleasing spot. The olive of the Captain's uniform seemed part of the background of turf and trees—all of it for Ann, so live and so pretty in white and red.

He was seeking to correct her stroke. Both were much in earnest about it. It would seem that the whole of Ann's life hung upon that thing of better form in her golf. Finally she made a fair drive and turned to him jubilantly. He was commending enthusiastically and Ann quite pranced under his enthusiasm. Seeing Katie, she waved her hand and pointed off to her ball that Katie, too, might mark the triumph. Then they came along, laughing and chatting. When the ball was reached they were in about the spot where Katie had first seen Ann, thirty days before.

She knew how Ann felt. There was joy in the good stroke. In this other game she had been playing in the last thirty days—this more difficult and more alluring game—she had come to know anew the exhilaration of bunker cleared, the satisfaction of the long drive and the sure putt.

And Katie had played a good game. It was not strange she should have convinced others, for there were times when her game was so good as to convince even herself. Though it had ever been so with Kate. The things in the world of "Let's play like" had always been persuasive things. Curious she was to know how often or how completely Ann was able to forget they were playing a game.

She had come to think of Ann, not as a hard-and-fast, all-finished product, but as something fluid, certainly plastic. It was as if anything could be poured into Ann, making her. A dream could be woven round her, and Ann could grow into that dream. That was a new fancy to Kate; she had always thought of people more as made than as constantly in the making. It opened up long paths of wondering. To all sides those paths were opening in those days—it was that that made them such eventful days. Down this path strayed the fancy how much people were made by the things which surrounded them—the things expected of them. That path led to the vista that amazing responsibility might lie with the things surrounding—the things expected. It even made her wonder in what measure she would have been Katie Jones, differently surrounded, differently called upon. Her little trip down that path jostled both her approval of herself and her disapproval of others.

It was only once or twice that the real girl had stirred in the dream. For the most part she had remained in the shadow of Katie's fancyings. She was as an actor on the stage, inarticulate save as regards her part. Katie had grown so absorbed in that part that there were times of forgetting there was a real girl behind it. Often she believed in her friend Ann Forrest, the dear girl she had known in Florence, the poor child who had gone through so many hard things and was so different from the Zelda Frasers of the world. She rejoiced with Wayne and Captain Prescott in seeing dear Ann grow a little more plump, a little rosier, a little more smiling. She could understand perfectly, as she had made them understand, why Ann did not talk more of Italy and the things of her own life. Life had crowded in too hard upon her, that setting of the other days made other days live again too acutely. Ann was taking a vacation from her life, she had laughingly put it to Wayne. That was why she played so much with Worth and the dogs and talked so little of grown-up things. Though one could never completely take a vacation from one's life; that was why Ann looked that way when she was sometimes sitting very still and did not know that any one was looking at her.

Persuasion was the easier as fabrication was but a fanciful dress for truth. Imagination did not have it all to do; it only followed where Ann called—blazing its own trail.

Yet there were times when the country of make-believe was swept down by a whirlwind, a whirlwind of realization which crashed through Katie's consciousness and knocked over the fancyings. Those whirlwinds would come all unannounced; when Ann seemed most Ann, playing with Worth, perhaps wearing one of the prettiest dresses and smilingly listening to something Wayne was telling her had happened over at the shops. And on the heels of the whirlwind knocking down the country of make-believe would come the girl from a vast unknown rushing wildly from—what? What had become of that girl? Would she hear from *her* again? It was almost as if the girl made by reality had indeed gone down under the waters that day, and the things the years had made her had abdicated in favor of the things Katie would make her. And yet did the things the years had made one ever really abdicate? Was it because the girl of the years was too worn for assertiveness that the girl of fancy could seem the all? Was it only that she slumbered—and sometimes stirred a little in her sleep?—And when *she* awoke?

Even to each other they did not speak of that other girl, as if fearing a word might wake her. Sometimes they heard her stir; as one day soon after Ann's coming Katie had said: "Ann, just what is it is the matter with your vocal chords?"

"Why I didn't know anything was," stammered Ann.

"But you seem unable to pronounce my name."

Ann colored.

"It is spelled K-a-t-i-e," Kate went on, "and is pronounced K—T. Try it, Ann. See if you can say it."

Ann looked at her. The look itself crossed the border country. "Katie—" she choked—and the country of make-believe fell palely away.

But they did not speak of the things they had stirred.

That thing of not saying it had been established the day Ann's bank account was opened. Katie had been "over the river," as she called going over to the city. Upon returning she found Ann up in her room. She stood there unpinning her hat, telling of an automobile accident on the bridge—Katie seldom came in without some stirring tale. As she was leaving she rummaged in her bag. "And oh yes, Ann," she said, carelessly, "here's your bank book. I presumed to draw twenty dollars for you, thinking you might need it before you could get over. Oh dear—that telephone! And I know it's Wayne for me."

But she did not escape. Ann was waiting for her when she came back up stairs.

She held out the book, shaking her head. Her face told that she had been pulled back.

"Not money," she said unsteadily. "All the rest of it is bad enough—but not money. I'd have no—self-respect."

"Self-respect!" jeered Kate. "I'd have no self-respect if I didn't take money. Nobody can be self-respecting when broke. None of the rest of us seem to be inquiring into our sources of revenue, so why should you?"

As had happened that other time, in relation to the suit, the thing shot out at Ann turned back to her. It had more than once occurred that the thing thrown out sparingly persisted as thing to be considered genuinely. Her browbeating of Ann—for it was a sort of tender, protective browbeating—led her to reach out blindly for weapons, and once in her hand many of those weapons proved ideas.

"We take everything we can get," she followed it up, forcing herself from interest in the weapon to the use of it, "from everybody we can get it from. We take this house from the government—and heaven only knows how many sons of toil the government takes it from. I take this money we're so stupidly quibbling about now from a company the papers say takes it from everybody in reach. Take or you will be taken from is the basis of modern finance. Please don't be fanatical, Ann."

"I can't take it," repeated Ann.

Katie looked worried. Then she took new ground. "Well, Ann, if you won't take the sane financial outlook, at least be a good sport. We're in this game; the money has got to be part of making it go. We'll never get anywhere at all if we're going to balk and fuss at every turn. There now, honey,"—as if to Worth—"put your book away. Don't lose it; it makes them cross to have you lose them. And another principle of modern finance with which I am heartily in sympathy is that money should be kept in circulation. It encourages embezzlement to leave it in banks too long." Then, seeing what was gathering, she said quietly but authoritatively: "Leave it unsaid, Ann. Can't we always just leave it unsaid? Nothing makes me so uncomfortable as to feel I'm constantly in danger of having something nice said to me."

Perhaps Katie knew that countries of make-believe are sensitive things, that it does not do to admit you know them for that.

There had been that one time when the hand of reality reached savagely into the dream, as if the things the girl had run away from had come to claim her. It seemed through that long night that they had claimed her, that Ann's "vacation" was over.

Captain Prescott had been dining with them that night and after dinner they were sitting out on the porch. He was humming a snatch of something. Katie heard a chair scrape and saw that Ann had moved farther into the shadow. She was all in shadow save her hand; that Katie could see was gripping the arm of her chair.

He turned to Ann. "Did you see 'Daisey-Maisey'?"

"Ann wasn't here then," said Kate.

"Did you see it, Katie?"

"No."

"It was a jolly, joyous sort of thing," he laughed. "Sort of thing to make you feel nothing matters. That was the name of that thing I was humming. No, not 'Nothing Matters,' but 'Don't You Care.' And there were the 'Don't You Care' girls—pink dresses and big black hats. They seemed to mean what they sang. They didn't care, certainly."

It was Wayne who spoke. "Think not?"

Ann came a little way out of the shadow. She had leaned toward Wayne.

"Well you'd never know it if they did," laughed Prescott.
He turned to
Wayne. "What's your theory?"

"Oh I have no theory. Just a wondering. Can't see how girls who have their living to earn could sing 'Don't You Care' with complete abandon."

Ann leaned forward, looking at him tensely. Then, as if afraid, she sank back into shadow. Katie could still see her hand gripping the arm of her chair.

"But they're not the caring sort," Prescott was holding.

"Think not?" said Wayne again, in Wayne's queer way.

There was a silence, and then Ann had murmured something and slipped away.

Katie followed her; for hours she sat by her bed, holding her hand, trying to soothe her. It was almost morning before that other girl, that girl they were trying to get away from, would let Ann go to sleep.

Sitting beside the tortured girl that night, hearing the heart-breaking little moans which as sleep finally drew near replaced the sobs, Katie Jones wondered whether many of the things people so serenely took for granted were as absurd—and perhaps as tragically absurd—as Captain Prescott's complacent conclusion that the "Don't You Care" girls were girls who didn't care.

How she would love—turning it all over in her mind that afternoon—to talk some of those things over with "the man who mends the boats"!

CHAPTER XII

She had only known him for about twenty days—"The man who mends the boats"—but she had fallen into the way of referring all interesting questions to him. That was perhaps the more remarkable as her eyes had never rested upon him.

One morning Worth had looked up from some comparative measurements of the tails of Pourquoi and N'est-ce-pas to demand: "Why, Aunt Kate, what do you think?"

"There are times," replied Aunt Kate, looking over at the girl swaying in the hammock, humming gently to herself, "when I don't know just what to think."

"Well sir, what do you think? The man that mends the boats knows more 'an Watts!"

"Worthie," she admonished, "it's bad business for an army man to turn traitor."

"But yes, he does. 'Cause I asked Watts why Pourquoi had more yellow than white, and why N'est-ce-pas was more white 'an yellow, and he said I sure had him there. He'd be blowed if he knew, and he guessed nobody did, 'less maybe the Almighty had some ideas about it; but yesterday I asked the man that mends the boats, and he explained it—oh a whole lot of long words, Aunt Kate. More long words 'an I ever heard before."

"And the explanation? I trust it was satisfactory?"

"I guess it was," replied Worth uncertainly. "'Twas an awful lot of long words."

"My experience, too," laughed Aunt Kate.

"With the man that mends the boats?"

"No, with other sages. You see when they're afraid to stay down here on the ground with us any longer, afraid they'll be hit with a question that will knock them over, they get into little air-ships they have and hurl the long words down at our heads until we're too stunned to ask any more questions, and in such wise is learning disseminated."

"I'll ask the man that mends the boats if he's got any air-ships. He's got most everything up there."

"Up where?"

"Oh, up there," —with vague nod toward the head of the Island.

"He says he'd like to get acquainted with you, Aunt Kate. He says he really believes you might be worth knowing."

Thereupon Aunt Kate's book fell to the floor with a thud of amazement that reverberated indignation. "Well upon my word!" gasped she. Then, recovering her book—and more—"Why what a kindly gentleman he must be," she drawled.

"Oh yes, he's kind. He's awful kind, I guess. He'll talk to you any time you want him to, Aunt Kate. He'll tell you just anything you want to know. He said you must be a—I forgot the word."

"Oh no, you haven't," wheedled Aunt Kate. "Try to think of it, dearie."

"Can't think of it now. Shall I ask him again?"

"Certainly not! How preposterous! As if it made the slightest difference in the world!"

But it made difference enough for Aunt Kate to ask a moment later: "And how did it happen, Worthie, that this kindly philosopher should have deemed me worth knowing?"

"Oh, I don't know. 'Cause he liked the puppies' names, I guess. I told him how their mother was just Queen, but how they was Pourquoi and N'est-ce-pas—a 'quirer and 'versalist and so then he said: 'And which is Aunt Kate?'"

"Which is Aunt *Kate*? *What* did he mean?"

"'Is she content to be just Queen,' he said, 'or is she' —there was a lot of long words, you wouldn't understand them, Aunt Kate—I didn't either— 'does she show a puppyish tendon'—tendon something—'to butt into the universe?'"

Suddenly Aunt Kate's face grew pink and she sat straight. "Worth, was this one of the men?"

"Oh no, Aunt Kate. He's not one of the men. He's just a man. He's the man that mends the boats."

"'The man that mends the boats!' He sounds like a creature in flowing robes out of a mythology book, or the being expressing the high and noble sentiments calling everybody down in a new-thoughtish play."

From time to time Worth would bring word of him. What boats does he mend, Aunt Kate wanted to know, and what business has he landing them on our Island? To which came the answer that he mended boats sick unto death with speed mania and other social disease, and that he didn't land them on the Island, but on an island off the tip of the Island, a tiny island which the Lord had thoughtlessly left lying disrespectfully close to the Isle of Dignity. Katie was too true a romancer to inquire closely about the man who mended the boats, for she liked to think of him as an unreal being who only touched the earth off the tip of the Island, and only touched humanity through Worth. That wove something alluringly mysterious—and mysteriously alluring—about the man who made sick boats well, whereas had she given rein to the possibility of his belonging to the motorboat factory across the river, and scientifically testing gasoline engines it would be neither proper nor interesting that her young nephew should run back and forth with pearls of wit and wisdom. It developed that Worth visited this tip of the Island with the ever faithful Watts, and that one day the boat mender and Watts had—oh just the awfulest fight with words Worth had ever heard. It was about the Government, which the man who mended the boats said was running on one cylinder, drawing from patriotic Watts the profane defense that it had all the power it needed for blowing up just such fools as that! He further held that soldiers were first-class dishwashers and should be brave enough to demand first-class dishwashing pay. Katie had chuckled over that. But she had puzzled rather than chuckled over the statement that the first war the saddles manufactured on that Island would see would be the war over the manufacturing of them. Now what in the world had he meant by that? She had asked Wayne, but Wayne had seemed so seriously interested in the remark, and asked such direct questions as to who made it, that she had tried to cover her tracks, thinking perhaps the man who mended the boats could be thrown into the guard-house for saying such dark things about army saddles.

On the way home from that talk Watts had branded the man who mended the boats as one of them low-down anarchists that ought to be shot at sunrise. Things was as they *was*, held Watts, and how could anybody but a fool expect them to be any way but the way they *was*? It showed what *he* was—and after that Worth had had no more fireworks of thought for a week, Watts standing guard over the world as it was.

But he slipped into an odd place in Katie's life of wonderings and fancyings, and that life of musing and questioning was so big and so real a life in those days. He was something to shoot things out at, to hang things to. She held imaginary conversations with him, demolished him in imaginary arguments only to stand him up and demolish him again. Sometimes she quite winked with him at the world as it was, and at other times she withdrew to lofty heights and said cutting things. In more friendly mood she asked him questions, sometimes questions he could not answer, and she could not answer them either, and then their thoughts would hover around together, brooding over a world of unanswerable things. All her life she had held those imaginary conversations, but heretofore it had been with her horse, her dog, the trees, a white cloud against the blue, something somewhere. None of the hundreds of nice people she knew had ever moved her to imaginary conversations. And so now it was stimulating—energizing—not to have to diffuse her thought into the unknown, but to direct it at, and through, the man who mended the boats and said strange things to Worth up at the tip of the Island.

And he came at a time when she had great need of him. Never before had there been so many things to start one on imaginary conversations, conversations which ended usually in a limitless wondering. Since Ann had come the simplest thought had a way of opening a door into a vast country.

Too many doors were opening that afternoon. She was making no headway with the letters she had told herself she would dispose of while Ann and Captain Prescott were out on the links.

The letter from Harry Prescott's mother was the most imperative. She was returning from California and sent some inquiries as to the habitability of her son's house.

Katie was thinking, as she re-read it, that it was a letter with a background. It expressed one whom dead days loved well. The writer of the letter seemed to be holding in life all those gentlewomen who had formed her.

In a short time Mrs. Prescott would be at the Arsenal. That meant a more difficult game. Did it also mean an impossible one?

Yet Katie would prefer showing her Ann to Mrs. Prescott than to Zelda Fraser. Zelda, the fashionable young woman, would pounce upon the absence of certain little tricks and get no glimmer of what Katie vaguely called the essence. Might not Mrs. Prescott find the reality in the possibilities? "It comes to this," Katie suddenly saw, "I'm not shamming, I'm revealing. I'm not vulgarly imitating; I'm restoring. The connoisseur should be the first to appreciate that."

It turned her off into one of those long paths of wondering, paths which sometimes seemed to circle the whole of the globe. It was on those paths she frequently found the man who mended the boats waiting for her. Sometimes he was irritating, turning off into little by-paths, by-paths leading off to the dim source of things. Katie could not follow him there; she did not know her way; and often, as to-day, he turned off there just when she was most eager to ask him something. She would ask him what he thought about backgrounds. How much there was in that thing of having the background all prepared for one, in simply fitting into the place one was expected to fit into. How many people would create for themselves the background it was assumed they belonged in just because they had been put in it? Suddenly she laughed. She had a most absurd vision of Jove—Katie believed it would be Jove—standing over humanity with some kind of heroic feather duster and mightily calling "Shoo!—Shoo!—Move on!—Every fellow find his place for himself!"

Such a scampering as there would be! And how many would be let stay in the places where they had been put? Who would get the nice corners it had been taken for granted certain people should have just because they had been fixed up for them in advance? How about the case of Miss Katherine Wayneworth Jones? Would she be ranked out of quarters?

Certain it was that a very choice corner had been fitted up for said Katherine Wayneworth Jones. People said that she belonged in her corner; that no one else could fit it, that she could not as well fit anywhere else. But she was not at all sure that under the feather duster act that would give her the right of possession. People were so stupid. Just because they saw a person sitting in a place they held that was the place for that person to be sitting. Katie almost wished that mighty "Shoo!" would indeed reverberate 'round the world. It would be such fun to see them scamper and squirm. And would there not be the keenest of satisfaction in finding out what sort of place one would fit up for one's self if none had been fitted up for one in advance?

Few people were called upon to prove themselves. Most people judged people as they judged pictures at an exhibition. They went around with a catalogue and when they saw a good name they held that they saw a good picture. And when they did not know the name, even though the picture pleased them, they waited around until they heard someone else saying good things, then they stood before it murmuring, "How lovely."

She had put Ann in the catalogue; she had seen to it that she was properly hung, and she herself had stood before her proclaiming something rare and fine. That meant that Ann was taken for granted. And being taken for granted meant nine-tenths the battle.

It would be fun to fool the catalogue folks. And she need have no compunctions about lowering the standard of art because the picture she had found out in the back room and surreptitiously hung in the night belonged in the gallery a great deal more than some of the pictures which had been solemnly carried in the front way. It was the catalogue folks, rather than the lovers of art, were being imposed upon.

And Mrs. Prescott, though to be sure a maker of catalogues, was also a lover of art. There lay Katie's hope for her, and apology to her.

Though she was apprehensive, a stronger light was to be turned on— that was indisputable. "You and I know, dear Queen," Katie confided to the member of her sex lying at her feet, "that men are not at all difficult. You can get them to swallow most anything—if the girl in the case is beautiful enough. And feminine enough! Masculine dotes on discovering feminine— but have you ever noticed what the rest of the feminine dote on doing to that discovery? Women can even look at wondrous soft brown eyes and lovely tender mouths through those 'Who was your father?' 'specs' they keep so well dusted. The manner of holding a teacup is more important than the heart's deep dreams. When it comes to passing inspection, the soul's not in it with the fork. We know 'em—don't we, old Queen?"

Queen wagged concurrence, and Katie pulled herself sternly back to her letters.

Mrs. Prescott spoke of the chance of her son's being ordered away. "I hope not," she wrote, "for I want the quiet summer for him. And for myself, too. The great trees and the river, and you there, dear Katie, it seems the thing I most desire. But we of the army learn often to relinquish the things we most desire. We, the homeless, for in the abiding sense we are homeless, make homes possible. Think of it with pride sometimes, Katie. Our girls think of it all too little now. I sometimes wonder how they can forego that just pride in their traditions. During this spring in the West my thoughts have many times turned to those other days, days when men like your father and my husband performed the frontier service which made the West of to-day possible. Recently at a dinner I heard a young woman, one of the 'advanced' type, and I am sorry to say of army people, speak laughingly to one of our men of the uselessness of the army. She was worthy nothing but scorn, or I might have spoken of some of the things your mother and I endured in those days of frontier posts. And now we have a California— serene—fruitful—and can speak of the uselessness of the army! Does the absurdity of it never strike them?"

Katie pondered that; wondered if Mrs. Prescott's attitude and spirit were not passing with the frontier. Few of the army girls she knew thought of themselves as homeless, or gave much consideration to that thing of making other homes possible, save, to be sure, the homes they were hoping—and plotting—to make for themselves. And she could not see that the "young woman" was answered. The young woman had not been talking about traditions. Probably the young woman would say that yesterday having made to-day possible it was quite time to be quit of yesterday. "Though to be sure," Katie now answered her, "while we may not seem to be doing anything, we're keeping something from being done, and that perhaps is the greatest service of all. Were it not for us and our dear navy we should be sailed on from East and West, marched on from North and South. At least that's what we're told by our superiors, and are you the kind of young woman to question what you're told by your superiors? Because if you are!—I'd like to meet you."

Her letter continued: "Harry writes glowingly of your charming friend. Strange that I am not able to recall her, though to be sure I knew little of you in those years abroad. Was she a school friend? I presume so. Harry speaks of her as 'the dear sort of girl,' not leaving a clear image in my mind. But soon my vision will be cleared."

"Oh, will it?" mumbled Kate. "I don't know whether it will or not. 'The dear sort of girl!' And I presume the young goose thought he had given a vivid picture."

She turned to Major Darrett's note: a charming note it was to turn to. He had the gift of making himself very real—and correspondingly attractive—in those notes.

A few days before she had been telling Ann about Major Darrett. "He's a bachelor," she had said, "and a joy." Ann had looked vague, and Katie laughed now in seeing that her characterization was broad as "the dear sort of girl."

It was probable Major Darrett would relieve one of the officers at the Arsenal. He touched it lightly. "Should fate—that part of it dwelling in Washington—waft me to your Island, Katie Jones, I foresee a summer to compensate me for all the hard, cruel, lonely years."

Kate smiled knowingly; not that she actually knew much to be knowing about.

She wondered why she did not disapprove of Major Darrett. Certain she was that some of the things which had kept his years from being hard, cruel, and lonely were in the category for disapproval. But he managed them so well; one could not but admire his deftness, and admiration was weakening to disapproval. One disapproved of things which offended one, and in this instance the results of the things one knew one should disapprove were so far from offensive that one let it go at smiling knowingly, mildly disapproving of one's self for not disapproving.

Ann had not responded enthusiastically to Katie's drawing of Major Darrett. She had not seemed to grasp the idea that much was forgiven the very charming; that ordinary standards were not rigidly applied to the extraordinarily fascinating. When Katie was laughingly telling of one of the Major's most interesting flirtations Ann's eyes had seemed to crouch back in that queer way they had. Katie had had an odd sense of Ann's disapproving of her—disapproving of her for her not disapproving of him. More than once Ann had given her that sense of being disapproved of.

As with all things in the universe just then, he was a new angle back to Ann. If he were to come there—? For Major Darrett would not at all disapprove of those eyes of Ann's. And yet his own eyes would see more than Wayne and Harry Prescott had seen. Major Darrett had been little on the frontier, but much in the drawing-room; he had never led up San Juan hill, but he had led many a cotillion. He had had that form of military training which makes society favorites. As to Ann, he would have the feminine "specs" and the masculine delight at one and the same time. What of that union?

Katie's eyes began to dance. She hoped he would come. He would be a foe worthy her steel. She would have to fix up all her fortifications—look well to her ammunition. Whatever might be held against Major Darrett it could not be said he was not worthy one's cleverest fabrications. But the triumph of holding one's own with a veteran!

Then of a sudden she wondered what the man who mended the boats would think of the Major.

CHAPTER XIII

Before she had finished her writing Wayne and Worth
came up on the porch. The little boy had been over at the
shops with his father.

"Father," he was saying, imagination under the stimulus of things he
had been seeing, "I suppose our gun will kill 'bout forty thousand million
folks—won't it, father?"

"Why no, son, I hope it's not going to be such a beastly gun as that,"
laughed Captain Jones.

"Yes, but, father, isn't a good gun a gun that kills folks? What's the use
making a gun at all if it isn't going to kill folks?"

His father looked at him strangely. "Sonny," he said, "you're hitting
home rather hard."

"Your reasoning is poor, Worth," said Katie; "fact is we make guns to
keep folks from getting killed. If we didn't have the guns everybody would
get killed. Now don't say 'why.'"

"'Cause you don't know why," calmly remarked Worth,
adding: "I'll ask Watts, and if he don't know I'll ask the
man that mends the boats."

"Do," said Katie.

Having, to his own satisfaction, exterminated some forty thousand
million members of the human family, Worth opened attack on the puppies.
He was an Indian and they were poor white settlers and he was going to kill
them. No poor white settlers had ever received an Indian so joyously.

But he seemed to have left those forty thousand million souls on his
father's hands. Wayne was looking very serious. He did not respond to—
did not appear to have heard—Katie's remark about Worth needing some
new clothes.

Katie wondered what he was thinking about; she supposed some new
kind of barrel steel. She took it for granted that nothing short of steel could
produce *that* look.

She was proud of the things that look had done, proud of the distinction her brother had already won in the army, proud, in advance, of the things she was confident he would do.

Captain Jones was at the Arsenal on special detail. An invention of his pertaining to the rifle was being manufactured for tests. There was keen interest in it and its final adoption seemed assured. It was of sufficient importance to make his name one of those conspicuous in army affairs. He had already several lesser things—devices pertaining to equipment—to his credit and was looked upon as one of the most promising of the army's men of invention.

And aside from her pride in him, Katie's affection for her brother was deep, intensified because of their being alone. Their father had died when Katie was sixteen, died as a result of wounds received long before in frontier skirmishes, where he had been one of those many brave men to serve fearlessly and faithfully, men who gave more to their country than their country perhaps understood. Their mother survived him only two years. Katie sometimes said that her mother, too, gave her life to her country. Her health had been undermined by hard living on the frontier—she who had been so tenderly reared in her southern home—and in the end she also died from a wound, that wound dealt the heart in the death of her husband. Katie revered her father's memory and adored her mother's, and while youth and Katie's indomitable spirit made it hard for one to think of her as sad, the memory of those two was the deepest, biggest thing in the girl's life.

"Oh Katie," Wayne suddenly roused himself to say, "your cousin Fred Wayneworth is in town. I had luncheon with him over the river. He sent all sorts of messages to you."

"Well—really! Messages! Why this haughty aloofness? Doesn't he mean to come over?"

"Oh yes, of course; to-morrow—perhaps to-night. He's fearfully busy—stopped off on his way East. There's a row on in the forest service about some of Osborne's timber claims—mining claims, too, I believe—in Colorado. Those years in the West have developed Fred splendidly. He's gone from boy to man, and a fine specimen of man, at that."

"He likes his work?"

"Full of it." Wayne was silent for a moment, then added: "I envied him."

It startled Katie. "Envied him? Why—why, Wayne? Surely you're lucky."

He laughed: not the laugh of a man too pleased with his luck. "Oh, am I? Perhaps I am, but just the same I envy a fellow who can look that way when talking about his work."

"But you have a work, Wayne."

"No, I have a place."

She grew more and more puzzled. "Why, Wayne, you've been all wrapped up in this thing you were doing."

He threw his cigarette away impatiently. "Oh yes, just for the sake of doing it. I get a certain satisfaction in scheming things out. I must say, however, I'd like to scheme out something I'd get some satisfaction in having schemed out. A morsel of truth dropped from the mouth of a babe a minute ago. You may have observed, Katie, that his inquiry was more direct and reasonable than your reply. An improvement on a rifle. Not such a satisfying thing to leave to a rifle eliminating future."

"But I didn't know the army admitted it was to be a rifle eliminating future."

"I'm not saying that the army does," he laughed.

He passed again to that look of almost passionate concentration which Katie had always supposed meant metallic fouling or some—to her—equally incomprehensible thing. He emerged from it to exclaim tensely: "Oh I get so sick of the spirit of the army!"

Instinctively Katie looked around. He saw it, and laughed.

"There you go! We've made a perfect fetich of loyalty. It's a different sort of loyalty those forestry fellows have—a more live, more constructive loyalty. The loyalty that comes, not through form, but through devotion to the work—a common interest in a common cause. Ours is built on dead things. Custom, and the caste—I know no other word—just the bull-headed, asinine, undemocratic caste that custom has built up."

"And yet—there must be discipline," Katie murmured: it seemed dreadful Wayne should be tearing down their house in that rude fashion, house in which they had dwelt so long, and so comfortably.

"Discipline is one thing. Bullying's another. I've never been satisfied discipline couldn't be enforced without snobbery. To-day Solesby—one year out of West Point!—walked through a shop I was in. He passed men working at their machines—skilled mechanics, many of them men of intelligence, ideas, character—as though he were passing so much cattle. I wanted to take him by the neck and throw him out!"

"Oh well," protested Katie, "one year out of the Point! He's yet to learn men are not cattle."

"Well, Leonard never learned it. His back gets some black looks, let me tell you."

"Wayne dear," she laughed, "I'm afraid you're not talking like an officer and a gentleman."

"I get tired talking like an officer and a gentleman. Sometimes I feel like talking like a man."

"But couldn't you be court-martialed for doing that?" she laughed.

"I think Leonard thinks I should be."

"Why—why, Wayne?"

"Because I talk to the men. There's a young mechanic who has been detailed to me, and he and I get on famously. All too famously, I take it Leonard thinks. He came in to-day when this young Ferguson was telling me some things about his union. He treated Ferguson like a dog and me like a suspicious character."

"Dear me, Wayne," she murmured, "don't get in trouble."

"Trouble!" he scoffed. "Well if I can get in trouble for talking with an intelligent man I'm working with about the things that man knows—then let me get in trouble! I'd rather talk to Ferguson than Solesby—we've more in common. Oh I'll get in no trouble," he added grimly. "Leonard knows it wouldn't sound well to say it. But he feels it, just the same. Right there's the difference between our service and this forest service. That's where they're democrats and we're fossils. Look at the difference in the spirit of the ranger and the spirit of the soldier! And it's not because they're whipped into line and bullied and snarled at. It's because they're treated like men—and made to feel they're a needed part of a big whole. You should hear Fred tell of the way men meet in this forest service—superintendent meeting ranger on a common ground. And why? Because they're doing something constructive. Because the work's the thing that counts. You'll see what it's done for Fred. The boy has a real dignity; not the stiff-necked kind he'd acquire around an army post, but the dignity that comes with the consciousness of being, not in the service, but of service."

He fell silent there, and Katie watched him. He had never spoken to her that way before—she had not dreamed he felt like that; heretofore it had been only through laughing little jibes at the army she had had any inkling of his feeling toward it. That she had not taken seriously; half the people she knew in the service jibed at it to others in the service. This depth of feeling disturbed her, moved her to defense. After a moment's consideration she emerged triumphant with the Panama canal.

He shook his head. "When you consider the percentage of the army so engaged, you can't feel as happy about it as you'd like to. We ought all to be digging Panama canals!"

"Heavens, Wayne—we don't need them."

"Plenty of things we do need."

"Well I don't think you're fair to the army, Wayne. You're not looking into it—deeply enough. You're doing just as much as Fred, for in safeguarding the country you permit this constructive work to go on. As to our formalities—they have run off into absurdity at some points, but it was a real spirit created those very forms."

"True. And now the spirit's dead and the form's left—and what's so absurd as a form that rattles dead bones?"

"Father didn't feel as you do, Wayne."

"He had no cause to. He was needed. But we don't need the army on the frontier now. That's *done*. And we do need the forest service—the thing to build up. There's no use harking back to traditions. The world moves on too fast for that. Question is—not what did you do yesterday—but what good are you to-day—what are you worth to-morrow? Oh, I'm not condemning the army half so much as I'm sympathizing with it," he laughed. "It's full of live men who want to be doing something—instead of being compelled to argue that they're some good. They get very tired saying they're useful. They'd like to make it self-evident."

"Well, perhaps we'll have a war with Japan," said Katie consolingly.

"Perhaps we will. Having an army that's spoiling for it, I don't see how we can very well miss it."

"But if we had no army we certainly should have a war."

His silence led Katie to gasp: "Wayne, are you becoming—anti-militarist?"

He laughed. "Oh, I don't know what I'm becoming. But as to myself—I do know this. There would be more satisfaction in constructive work than in work that constructs only that it may be ready to destroy. I would find it more satisfying to help give my country itself—through natural and legitimate means—than stand ready to give it some corner of some other country."

"But to keep the other country from getting a corner of it?"

"Doesn't it occur to you, Katie, that as a matter of fact the other country might like a chance to develop its resources? We're like a crowd of boys with rocks in their hands and all afraid to throw down the rocks. If one did, the others might be immensely relieved. It seems rather absurd, standing there with rocks nobody wants to throw—especially when there are so many other things to be doing—and everybody saying, 'I've got to keep mine because he's got his.' Would you call that a very intelligent gang of kids? Ferguson says it's the workingmen of the world will bring about disarmament. That they're coming to feel their common cause as workers too keenly to be forced into war with each other."

"That's what the man that mends the boats says," piped up Worth. "He says that when they're all socialists there won't be any wars—'cause nobody'll go. But Watts says that day'll never come, thank God."

"Are you thanking God for yourself or for Watts, sonny?" laughed his father. "And who, pray, is the man that mends the boats?"

"The man that mends the boats, father, is a man that's 'most as smart as you are."

"It has been a long time," gravely remarked Wayne, "since any man has been brought to my attention so highly commended as that."

But their talk had been sobering to them both, for they spoke seriously then of various things. It was probable that before long Wayne would be ordered to Washington. He wanted to know what Katie would do then. Why not spend next season in Washington with him? Just what were her plans?

But Katie had no plans. And suddenly she realized how completely all things had been changed by the coming of Ann.

She had spent much of her life in Washington. She loved it; loved its official life, in particular its army and diplomatic life; and loved, too, that rigidly guarded old Washington to which, as her mother's daughter, the door stood open to her. Her uncle, the Bishop, lived in a city close by. His home was the fixed spot which Katie called home. In Washington—and near it—she would find friends on all sides. Just thirty days before she would have gloated over that prospect of next season there.

But she was not prepared to bombard Washington with Ann. The mere suggestion carried realization of how propitious things had been, how simple she had found it.

The little game they were playing seemed to cut Katie off from her life, too, and without leaving the luxury of feeling sorry for herself. With it all, Washington did not greatly allure. Washington, as she knew it, was distinctly things as they were; just now nothing allured half so much as those long dim paths of wondering leading off into the unknown.

Suddenly she had an odd sense of Washington—all that it represented to her—being the play, the game, the thing made to order and seeming very tame to her because she was dwelling with real things. It was as if her craft of make-believe was the thing which had been able to carry her toward the shore of reality.

And so she told Wayne that she had no plans. Perhaps she would go back to Europe with Ann.

He turned quickly at that. "She goes back?"

"Oh yes—I suppose so."

"But why? Where? To whom?"

"Why? Why, why not? Why does one go anywhere? Florence is to Ann what Washington is to me—a sort of center."

"Katie," he asked abruptly, "has she no people? No ties? Isn't she—moored any place?"

"Am I 'moored' any place?" returned Kate.

"Why, yes; to the things that have made you—to the things you're part of. By moored I don't mean necessarily a fixed spot. But I have a feeling—"

He seemed either unable or unwilling to express it, and instead laughed: "I'd like to know how much her father made a month, and whether her mother was a good cook—a few little things like that to make her less a shadow. Do you really get *at* her, Katie?"

"Why—why, yes," stammered Katie; "though I told you, Wayne, that Ann was different. Quiet—and just now, sad."

"I don't think of her as particularly quiet," he replied; "and sad isn't it, either. I think of her"—he paused and concluded uncertainly—"as a girl in a dream."

"Her dream or your dream, Wayne?" laughed Katie, just to turn it.

She was throwing sticks for the puppies and missed his startled look.

But it was Katie who was startled when he said, still uncertainly, and more to himself than to Katie: "Though she's so real."

Ann and Captain Prescott were coming toward them. She had never looked less like a girl in a dream. Laughing and jesting with her companion, she looked simply like an exceedingly pretty girl having a very good time.

"But you like Ann, don't you, Wayne?" Katie asked anxiously.

"Yes," said Wayne, "I like her."

She came running up the steps to them, flushed, happy, as free from self-consciousness as Worth would have been. "Katie," she cried, "I played the last one in four. Didn't I?" turning proudly to the Captain for endorsement.

Both men were looking at her with pleasure: cheeks flushed, eyes glowing, hair a little disheveled and a little damp about the forehead, panting a little, her lithe, beautiful body swaying gently, hands outstretched to show Wayne how she had hardened her palms, Ann had never seemed so lovely and so live. In that moment it mattered not whether one knew anything about the earning capacity of her father or the culinary abilities of her mother. *She* was real. Real as sunshine and breezes and birds are real, as Worth and the puppies tumbling over each other on the grass were real, as all that is life-loving is real. And not detached, not mistily floating, but moored to that very love of life, capacity for life, to that look she had awakened in the faces of the men to whom she was talking. It seemed a paltry thing just then to wonder whether Ann was child of farmer, or clothing merchant, or great artist. She was Life's child. Love's child. Love's child—only she had not dwelt all her days in her father's house. But it was her father's house; that was why, once warmed and comforted, she could radiantly take her place. Watching her as she was going over her game for Wayne, demonstrating some of her strokes, and her slim, beautiful body made even the poor strokes wonderful things, Katie was not speculating on whether Ann had come from Chicago, or Florence, or Big Creek. She was thinking that Ann was product, expression, of the love of the world, that love which had brought the laughter and the tears, brought the hope and the radiance and the tragedy of life.

And then, suddenly and inexplicably, Katie was afraid. Of just what, she did not know; of things—big, tempestuous things—which Katie did not very well understand, and which Ann—perhaps not understanding either—seemed to embody. "Come, Ann," she said, "we must make ready for dinner."

Captain Prescott called after them that next he was going to teach Ann to ride. "Oh, we'll make an army girl of her yet," he laughed.

Ann turned back. "Do you know," she said, "I don't understand the army very well. Just what is it the army does?"

They laughed. "Ask the peace society in Boston," suggested Prescott.

But Wayne said: "Some day soon you and I'll take a ride on the river and I'll deliver a little lecture on the army."

"Oh, that will be nice," said Ann radiantly.

CHAPTER XIV

It was astonishing how Ann seemed to find herself in just that thing of being able to learn to play golf.

They were gay at dinner that night, and Ann was as gay as any one. She continued to talk about her game, which they jestingly permitted her to do, and the men told some good golf stories which she entered into merrily. It was Katie who was rather quiet. While they still lingered around the table Fred Wayneworth joined them, and Katie, eager to talk with him of his people and his work, left Ann alone with Wayne and Captain Prescott, something which up to that time she had been reluctant to do. But to-night she did not feel Ann clinging to her, calling out to her, as she had felt her before. She seemed on surer ground; it was as if golf had given her a passport. From her place in the garden with her cousin, Ann's laugh came down to them from time to time—just a girl's happy laugh.

"Who is your stunning friend, Katie?" Fred asked. "No, stunning doesn't fit her, but lovely. She is lovely, isn't she?"

"Ann's very pretty," said Kate shortly.

"Oh—pretty," he laughed, "that won't do at all. So many girls are pretty, and I never saw any girl just like her."

Again she was vaguely uneasy, and the uneasiness irritated her, and then she was ashamed of the irritation. Didn't she want poor Ann to have a good time—and feel at home—and be admired? Did she care for her when she was somber and shy, and resent her when happy and confident? She told herself she was glad to hear Ann laughing; and yet each time the happy little laugh stirred that elusive foreboding in the not usually apprehensive soul of Katie Jones.

"I want to tell you about my girl, Katie," her cousin was saying. "I've got the *only* girl."

He was off into the story of Helen: Helen, who was a clerk in the forest service and "put it all over" any girl he had ever known before, who was worth the whole bunch of girls he had known in the East—girls who had been brought up like doll-babies and had doll-baby brains. Didn't Katie agree that a girl who could make her own way distanced the girls who could do nothing but spend their fathers' money?

In her heart, Katie did; had she been defending Fred to his father, the Bishop, or to his Bostonian mother, she would have grown eloquent for Helen. But listening to Fred, it seemed something was being attacked, and she, unreasonably enough, instead of throwing herself with the aggressor was in the stormed citadel with her aunt and uncle and the girls with the doll-baby brains.

And she had been within the citadel that afternoon when Wayne was attacking the army. She gloried in attacks of her own, but let some one else begin one and she found herself running for cover—and to defense. She wondered if that were anything more meaningful than just natural perversity.

The Bishop had wanted his son for the church; but Fred not taking amicably to the cloth, he had urged the navy. Fred had settled that by failing to pass the examinations for Annapolis. Failing purposely, his father stormily held; a theory supported by the good work he did subsequently at Yale. There he became interested in forestry, again to the disapproval of his parents, who looked upon forestry as an upstart institution, not hallowed by the mellowing traditions of church or navy. Now they would hold that Helen proved it.

And Helen did prove something. Certain it was that from neither church nor navy would Fred have seen his Helen in just this way.

Perhaps it was that democracy Wayne had been talking about. Perhaps this democracy was a thing not contented with any one section of a man's life. Perhaps once it *had* him—it had its way with him. Katie thought of the last thirty days—of paths leading out from other paths. Once one started—

Fred's father had never started. Bishop Wayneworth was only democratic when delivering addresses on the signers of the Declaration of Independence. The democracy of the past was sanctified; the democracy of the present, pernicious and uncouth. Thought of her uncle put Katie on the outside, eyes dancing with the fun of the attack.

"Who are her people, Fred?"

"Oh, Western people—ranchers; best sort of people. They raised the best crop of potatoes in the valley this year."

Katie yearned to commend the family of her daughter-in-law to her Aunt Elizabeth with the boast that they raised the best crop of potatoes in the valley!

"They had hard sledding for a long time; but they're making a go of it now. They've worked—let me tell you. Helen wouldn't have to work now—but don't you say that to Helen! What do you think, Katie? She even wants to keep on working after we're married!"

That planted Katie firmly within. "Oh, she can't do that, Fred."

"Well, I wish you'd tell her she can't. That's where we are now. We stick on that point. I try to assert my manly authority, but manly authority doesn't faze Helen much. She has some kind of theory about the economic independence of woman. You know anything about it, Katie?"

"You forget that I'm one of the doll-baby girls," she replied in a light voice which trailed a little bitterness on behind.

"Not you! Just before I left I said to Helen: 'Well there's at least one relative of mine who will have sense enough to appreciate you, and that's my corking cousin Katie Jones!'"

That lured feminine Kate outside again. "Fred," she asked, moved by her never slumbering impulse to find out about things, "just what is it you care for in Helen? Is she pretty? Funny? Sympathetic? Clever? What?"

She watched his face as he tried to frame it. And watching, she decided that whatever kind of girl Helen was, she was a girl to be envied. Yes, and to be admired.

"Well I fear it doesn't sound sufficiently romantic," he laughed, "but Helen's such a *sturdy* little wretch. The first things I ever noticed about her was her horse sense. She's good on her job, too. She seems to me like the West. Though that's rather amusing, for she's such a little bit of a thing. She's afraid she'll get fat. But she won't. She's not that kind."

"Why of course not," said Katie stoutly, and they laughed and seemed very near to Helen in thus scorning her fear of getting fat.

He continued his confidences, laughter from the porch coming down to them all the while. Helen was so real—she was so square—so independent—so dauntless—and yet she had such dear little ways. He couldn't make her sound as nice as she was; Katie would have to come and see her. In fact they were counting on Katie's coming. She was to come and stay a long time with them and really get acquainted with the West. "I'll tell you what Helen's like," he summed it up. "She's very much what you would have been if you'd lived out there and had the advantages she has."

Katie stared. No, he was not trying to be funny.

They started toward the house. "Katie," he broke out, "if you have any cousinly love in your heart, and know anything about Walt Whitman, tell me something, so I can go back and spring it on Helen. She's mad over him."

"He was one of the 'advantages' I didn't have," said Katie. "He didn't play a heavy part in the thing I had that passed for an education."

"Isn't it the limit the way they 'do you' at those girls' schools?" agreed Fred sympathetically. "Helen says that in religion and education the more you pay the less you get."

"I should like her," laughed Katie.

But what would her Aunt Elizabeth think of a "sturdy little wretch," believing in the economic independence of woman—whatever that might be—with lots of horse sense, and good on her job!

Katie was on the outside now, and for good. If nothing else, the fun was out there. And there was something else. That light on Fred's face when he was trying to tell about Helen.

Captain Prescott had come down the steps to meet them. "I was just coming for you. Don't you think, Katie, it would be fun to look in on the dance up here at the club house?"

On the alert for shielding Ann, Katie demurred. It was late, and Ann was tired from her golf.

There was an eager little flutter, and Ann had stepped forward. "Oh, I'm not at all tired, Katie," she said.

"Does she *look* tired?" scoffed Wayne. "She's only tired of being made to play the invalid. Hurry along, Katie. If you girls aren't sufficiently befrocked, frock up at once."

Katie hesitated, annoyed. She felt shorn of the function of her office. And she was dubious. The party was one which the younger set over the river were giving—at the golf club-house on the Island—for the returned college boys. She did not know who might be there—she was always meeting friends of her friends. She felt a trifle injured in thinking that just for the sake of Ann she had avoided the social life those people offered her, and now—

Ann was speaking again, her voice stripped of the happy eagerness. "Just as you say, Katie. It is late, and perhaps I am—too tired."

That moved Katie. That a girl should not be privileged to be insistent about going to a dance—it seemed depriving her of her birthright. And more cruel than taking away a birthright was bringing the consciousness of having no birthright.

Katie entered gayly into the plans. They decided that Ann was to wear the rose-colored muslin—the same gown she had worn that first night. As she was fastening it for her Katie saw that Ann was smiling at herself in the mirror, giving herself little pats of approval here and there.

She had not done that the first time Katie helped her into that dress.

But it was the Ann of the first days who turned strained face to her in the dressing-room at the club-house. All the girlish radiance—girlish vanity—was gone. "Katie," she whispered, "I think I'd better go home. I—I didn't know it would be like this. So many people—so many lights—and things."

Gently Katie reassured her. Ann needing her was the Ann she knew how to care for, and would care for in the face of all the people—all the "lights—and things." "You needn't dance if you don't want to," she told her. "I'll tell Wayne to look out for you, that you're really not able to meet people. If I put him on guard he'll go through fire and water for you."

"Yes—I know that," said Ann, and seemed to take heart.

And for some time she did not dance. From the floor Katie Would get glimpses of Ann and Wayne sauntering on the veranda on which the ball-room opened. More than once she found Ann's eyes following her—Ann out in the shadow, looking in at the gay people in the light.

But with the opening of a lively two-step Captain Prescott insisted Ann dance with him. "Oh come now," he urged. "Life's too short to sit on the side lines. This is a ripping two-step."

The music, too, was urgent—and persuasive. As if without volition she fell into gliding little steps, moving toward the dancing floor.

It was Katie who watched that time. She wanted to see Ann dancing. At first it puzzled her; she was too graceful not to dance well, but she danced as if differently trained, as if unaccustomed to their way of dancing. But as the two-step progressed she fell into the swing of it and seemed no different from the rest of the pretty, happy girls all about her.

She was radiant when she came back to them. Like the golf, the dancing seemed to have given her confidence—and confidence, happiness.

Though she still shrank from meeting people. Katie fell in with a whole troop of college boys who hovered around her, as both college boys and their elders were wont to hover around Katie. She wanted to bring some of them to Ann, but Ann demurred. "Oh no, Katie. I don't want to dance with any strange men, please. Just our own."

Why, Katie wondered, should one not wish to dance with "strange men." It seemed so curious a thing to shrink from. Katie herself had never felt at all strange with "strange men." Nice fellows were nice fellows the world over, and she never felt farther from strange than when dancing with a nice man—strange or otherwise. Even in the swing of her gayety Katie wondered what it was could make one feel like that. And she wondered what Wayne must think of that plaintive little "Just our own" which she was sure he had overheard.

Katie had come out at last to say she thought they should go. Ann must not get too tired.

But just then the orchestra began dreaming out a waltz, one of those waltzes lovers love to remember having danced together. "Now there," said Wayne, "is a nice peaceful waltz. You'll have to wait, Katie," and his arm was about Ann and they had glided away together.

Katie told her cousin she would rather not dance. "Let's stand here and watch," she said.

Couple after couple passed by, not the crowd of the gay two-step of a few moments before. Few were talking; some were gently humming, many dreaming—with a veiled smile for the dream. It was one of those waltzes to find its way back to cherished moments, flood with lovely color the dear things held apart. Fred was saying he wished Helen were there. Katie turned from the vivid picture out to the subtle night—warm summer's night. The dreaming music carried her back to vanished things—other waltzes, other warm summer's nights, to the times when she had been, in her light-hearted fashion, in love, to those various flirtations for which she had more tenderness than regret just for the glimpses they brought. And suddenly the heart of things gone seemed to flow into a great longing for that never known tenderness and wildness of feeling that sobbed in the music. She was being borne out to the heart of the night, and at the heart of the night some one waited for her with arms held out. But as she was swept nearer the some one was the man who mended the boats! With a little catch of her breath for that sorry twist of her consciousness that must make lovely moments ludicrous ones, she turned back to the bright room—crowded, colorful, moving room which seemed set in the vast, soft night.

Her brother was just passing—her brother and her friend Ann Forrest. They did not look out at her. They did not seem to know that Katie was near. She had never seen Ann's face so beautiful. It had that beauty she had all the while seen as possible for it, only more intense, more exalted than she had been able to foresee it. The music stopped on a sob. Every one was still for an instant—then they were applauding for more. Ann was not clapping. Katie had never seen anything as beautiful as that look of rapt loveliness on Ann's face as she stood there waiting. She might have been the very spirit of love waiting in the mists at the heart of the night. As softly the music began again and Wayne once more guided her in and out among those boys and girls—boys and girls for whom life had meant little more than laughing and dancing—Katie had a piercing vision of the girl with her hands over her face stumbling on toward the river.

They were all very quiet on the way home.

That night just as she was falling asleep Katie was startled. It seemed at first she was being awakened by a sharp dart, one of those darts of apprehension seemed shot into her approaching slumber. But it was nothing more than Wayne whistling out on the porch, whistling the dreaming waltz which would bear one to the love waiting at the heart of the night.

But Katie was sleepy now. How did Wayne expect any one to go to sleep, she thought crossly, whistling at that time of night.

But across the hall was another girl who listened. She had not been asleep. She had been lying there looking out into the night, very wide awake. And when she heard the whistling she too sat up in bed, swaying ever so gently to the rhythm of it, inarticulately following it under her breath and smiling a hushed, tender little smile. Something lovely seemed stealing over her. But in the wake of it was something else—something cold, blighting. Before he had finished she had covered her ears with her hands, and was sobbing.

CHAPTER XV

As she looked back afterward upon that span of days, searching them, translating, Katie saw that the day of the golf and the dancing marked the farthest advance.

After that it was as if Ann, frightened at finding herself so far out in the open, shrank back into the shadows. But having gone a little way into the open she was not again the same girl of the shadows. Her response to life seeming thwarted, there came an incipient sullenness in her view of that life which she had reached over the bridge of make-believe.

It did not show itself at once, but afterward it seemed to Katie that the next day marked the beginning of Ann's retreat on the bridge of make-believe.

And she wondered whether the stray dog or the dangerous literature had most to do with that retreat.

Ann was pale and quiet the day after the dance, and it was not merely the languor of the girl who has fatigued herself in having a good time.

At luncheon Katie suddenly demanded: "Wayne, where do you get dangerous literature?"

"I don't know what form of danger you're courting, Katie. I have a valuable work on high explosives, and I have a couple of volumes of De Maupassant."

"Oh I weathered all that kind of danger long ago," said she airily. "I want the kind that is distressing editors of church papers. The man who edits this religious paper uncle sends me is a most unchristian gentleman. He devoted a whole page to talking about dangerous literature and then didn't tell you where to get it. Well, I'll try Walt Whitman. He's very popular in the West, I'm told, and as the West likes danger perhaps he's dangerous enough to begin on."

"And you feel, do you, Katie, that the need of your life just now is for danger?"

"Yes, dear brother. Danger I must have at any cost. What's the good living in a dangerous age if you don't get hold of any of the danger? This unchristian editor says that little do we realize what a dangerous age it is. And he says it's the literature that's making it so. Then find the literature. Only he—beast!—doesn't tell you where to."

Worth there requested the privilege of whispering in his Aunt Kate's ear. The ear being proffered, he poured into it: "I guess the man that mends the boats has got some dangerous literature, Aunt Kate."

"Tell him to endanger Aunt Kate," she whispered back.

"Do you suppose there is any way, Wayne," she began, after a moment of seeming to have a very good time all to herself, "of getting back the money we spent for my so-called education?"

"It would considerably enrich us," grimly observed Wayne.

"When doctors or lawyers don't do things right can't you sue them and get your money back? Why can't you do the same thing with educators? I'm going to enter suit against Miss Sisson. This unchristian editor says modern education is dangerous; but there was no danger in the course at Miss Sisson's. I want my money back."

"That you may invest it in dangerous literature?" laughed Wayne.

After he had gone Ann was standing at the window, looking down toward the river. Suddenly she turned passionately upon Katie. "If you had ever had anything to *do* with danger—you might not be so anxious to find it."

She was trembling, and seemed close to tears. Katie felt it no time to explain herself.

And when she spoke again the tears were in her voice. "I can't tell you—when I begin to talk about it—" The tears were in her eyes, too, then, and upon her cheeks. "You see—I can't—But, Katie—I want *you* to be safe. I want you to be *safe*. You don't know what it means—to be safe."

With that she passed swiftly from her room.

Katie sat brooding over it for some time. "If you've been in danger," she concluded, "you think it beautiful to be 'safe.' But if you've never been anything but 'safe'—" Her smile finished that.

But Katie was more in earnest than her manner of treating herself might indicate. To be safe seemed to mean being shielded from life. She had always been shielded from life. And now she was beginning to feel that that same shielding had kept her from knowledge of life, understanding of it. Katie was disturbingly conscious of a great deal going on around her that she knew nothing about. Ann wished her to be 'safe'; yet it was Ann who had brought a dissatisfaction with that very safety. It was Ann had stirred the vague feeling that perhaps the greatest danger of all was in being too safe.

Katie felt an acute humiliation in the idea that she might be living in a dangerous age and knowing nothing of the danger. She would rather brave it than be ignorant of it. Indeed braving it was just what she was keen for. But she could not brave it until she found it.

She would find it.

But the next afternoon she went over to the city with Ann and found nothing more dangerous than a forlorn little stray dog.

It was evident that he had never belonged to anybody. It was written all over his thin, squirming little yellow body that he was Nobody's dog — written just as plainly as the name of Somebody's dog would be written on a name-plate on a collar.

And it was written in his wistful little watery eyes, told by his unconquerable tail, that with all his dog's heart he yearned to be Somebody's dog.

So he thought he would try Miss Katherine Wayneworth Jones.

She had a number of errands to do, and he followed her from place to place.

She saw him first when she came out from the hair-dresser's. He seemed to have been waiting for her. His heart was too experienced in being broken for him to dance around her with barks of joy, but he stood a little way off and wigglingly tried to ingratiate himself, his eyes looking love, and the longing for love.

Impulsively Katie stooped down to him. "Poor little doggie, does he want a pat?"

He fairly crouched to the sidewalk in his thankfulness for the pat, his tail and eyes saying all they could.

Then she saw that he was following her. "Don't come with me, doggie," she said; "please don't. You must go home. You'll get lost."

But in her heart Katie knew he would not get lost, for to be so unfortunate as to be lost presupposed being so fortunate as to have a home. And she knew that he was of the homeless. But because that was so terrible a thing to face, between him and her she kept up that pretense of a home.

When she came out from the confectioner's he was waiting for her again, a little braver this time, until Katie mildly stamped her foot and told him to "Go back!"

At the third place she expostulated with him. "Please, doggie, you're making me feel so badly. Won't you run along and play?"

The hypocrisy of that left a lump in her throat as she turned from him.

When she found him waiting again she said nothing at all, but began talking to Ann about some flowers in a window across the street.

Ann had seemed to dislike the dog. She would step away when Katie stopped to speak to him and be looking intently at something else, as if trying not to know that there were such things as homeless dogs.

Watts was waiting for them with the station wagon when they had finished their shopping. After they had gone a little way Katie, in the manner of one doing what she was forced to do, turned around.

He was coming after them. He had not yet fallen to the ranks of those human and other living creatures too drugged in wretchedness to make a fight for happiness. Nor was he finding it a sympathetic world in which to fight for happiness. At that very moment a man crossing the street was giving him a kick. He yelped and crouched away for an instant, but his eyes told that the real hurt was in the thought of losing sight of the carriage that held Katie Jones. As he dodged in and out, crouching always before the possible kick, she could read all too clearly how harassed he was with that fear.

They were approaching the bridge. The guard on the bridge would foil that quest. He would not permit a forlorn little yellow dog to seek happiness by following members of an officer's family across the Government bridge. Probably in the name of law and order he would kick him, as the other man had done; the dog's bleared little eyes, eyes through which the love longing must look, would cast one last look after the unattainable, and then, another hope gone, another promise unrealized, he would return miserably back to his loveless world, but always—

"Watts," said Katie sharply, "stop a moment, please. I want to get something."

Ann was sitting very straight, looking with great absorption up the river when Katie got back in the carriage with her dog. Her face was pale, and, it seemed to Katie, hard. She moved as far away from the dog as she could—her mouth set.

He sat just where Katie put him on the floor, trembling, and looking up at her with those asking eyes.

When they were almost home Ann spoke. "You can't take in all the homeless dogs of the world, Katie."

"I don't know that that's any reason for not taking in this one," replied Katie shortly.

"I hate to have you make yourself feel badly," Ann said tremulously.

"Why shouldn't I let myself feel badly?" demanded Katie roughly. "In a world of homeless dogs, why shouldn't I feel badly?"

They made a great deal of fun of Katie's dog. They named him "Pet." Captain Prescott wanted to know if she meant to exhibit him at a bench show and mention various points he was sure would excite attention.

"What I hate, Katie," said Wayne, "is the way he cringes. None of that cringing about Queen."

"And why not?" she demanded hotly. "Because Queen was never kicked. Because Queen was never chased down alleys by boys with rocks and tin cans. Because Queen never asked for a pat and got a cuff. Nor did Queen's mother. Queen hasn't a drop of kicked blood in her. This sorry little dog comes from a long line of the kicked and the cuffed. And then you blame *him* for cringing. I'm ashamed of you, Wayne!"

He was about to make laughing retort, but Katie's cheeks were so red, her eyes so bright, that he refrained and turned to Ann with: "Katie was always great for taking in all kinds of superfluous things."

"Yes," said Ann, "I know."

"And she always takes her outcasts so very seriously."

"Yes," agreed Ann.

"The trouble is, she can't hope to make them over."

"No," admitted Ann, "she can't do that."

"And then she breaks her heart over their forlorn condition."

"Yes," said Ann.

"These wretched things exist in the world, but Katie only makes her own life wretched in trying to do anything about them. She can't reach far enough to count, so why make herself unhappy?"

"Katie doesn't look at it that way," replied Ann, and turned away.

After the others had gone Katie committed her new dog to Worth. "Honey, will you play with him sometimes? I know he's not as nice to play with as the puppies, but maybe that's because nobody ever did play with him. The things that aren't nice about him aren't his fault, Worthie, so we mustn't be hard on him for them, must we? The reason he's so queer acting is just because he never had anybody to love him."

Worth was so impressed that he not only accepted the dog himself but volunteered to say a good word for him to Watts.

But a little later he brought back word that Watts said the newcomer was an ornery cur—that he was born an ornery cur—that he was meant to be an ornery cur, and never would be anything but an ornery cur.

"Watts is what you might call a conservative," said Katie.

And not being sure how a conservative member of the United States Army would treat a canine child of the alley, Katie went herself to the stable that night to see that the newcomer was fed and made to feel at home.

He did not appear to be feeling at all at home. He was crouching in his comfortable corner just as dejectedly as he would crouch in the most miserable alley his native city afforded.

He came, thankfully but cringingly, out to see Katie. "Doggie," said she, "don't be so apologetic. I don't like the apologetic temperament. You were born into this world. You have a right to live in it. Why don't you assert your right?"

His answer was to look around for the possible tin can.

Watts had approached. "Begging your pardon, Miss Jones, but he's the ungrateful kind. There's no use trying to do anything for that kind. He's deservin' no better than he gets. He snapped at one of our own pups to-night."

"I suppose so," said Kate. "I suppose when you spend your life asking for pats and getting kicks you do get suspicious and learn to snap. It seems too bad that little dogs that want to be loved should have to learn to snarl. You see, Watts, he's had a hard life. He's wandered up and down a world where nobody wanted him. He's spent his days trying now this one, now that. 'Maybe they'll take me,' he thinks; his poor little heart warms at the thought that maybe they will. He opens it up anew every day—opens it for a new wound. And now that he's found somebody to say the kind word he's still expecting the surly one. His life's shut him out from life—even though he wants it. It seems to me rather sad, Watts."

Watts was surveying him dubiously. "That kind is deserving what they get. They couldn't have been no other way. And beggin' your pardon, Miss Jones, but it's not us that's responsible for his life."

"Isn't it?" said Katie. "I wonder."

Watts not responding to the suggestion of the complexity of responsibility, she sought the personal. "As a favor to me, Watts, will you be good to the little dog?"

"As a favor to *you*, Miss Jones," said Watts, making it clear that for his part—

"Watts," she asked, "how long have you been in the service?"

"'Twill be five years in December, Miss Jones."

"Re-enlistment must mean that you like it."

"I've no complaint to offer, Miss Jones. Of course there are sometimes a few little things—"

"Why did you enter the army, Watts?"

"A man has to make a living some way, Miss Jones."

Katie was thinking that she had not asked for an apology.

"And yet I presume you could make more in some other way. Working in these shops, for instance."

"There's nothin' sure about them," said Watts.

"The army's certain. And I like things to move on decent and orderly like. For one that's willing to recognize his betters, the service is a good place, Miss Jones."

"But I suppose there are some not willing to recognize their betters," ventured Kate.

"There's all too many such," said Watts. "All too many nowadays thinks they're just as good as them that's above them."

"But you never feel that way, so you are contented and like the service, Watts?"

"Yes, Miss. It suits me well enough, Miss Jones. I'm not one to think I can make over the world. There's a fellow workin' up here at the point I sometimes have some conversation with. I was up there to-night at sundown—me and the little boy. Now there's a man, Miss, that don't know his place. He's a trouble-maker. He said to me tonight—"

But as Watts was there joined by a fellow-soldier Katie said: "Thank you for looking out for the poor little dog, Watts," and turned reluctantly to the house.

She would like to have remained; she would like to have talked with the other soldier and found out why he entered the service and what he thought of it. She was possessed of a great desire to ask people questions, find out why they had done what they did and what they thought about things other people were doing. Her mind was sending out little shoots in all directions and those little shoots were begging for food and drink.

She wished she might have a long talk with the "trouble-maker." She would like to talk about dogs who had lived in alleys and dogs that had been reared in kennels, about soldiers who were willing to recognize their betters and soldiers who thought they were as good as some above them. She would like to talk about Watts. Watts was the son of an old English servant. It was in Watts' blood to "recognize his betters." Was that why he could be moved to no sense of responsibility about stray dogs? Was that why he was a good man for the service and had no ambitions as civilian?

And Ann—she would like to talk to the boat-mending trouble-maker about Ann: Why Ann, whom one would expect to find sympathetic with the homeless, should be so hard and so queer about forlorn little stray dogs. Oh the world was just full of things that Katie Jones wanted to talk about that night!

When she reached the house she found that she had just received a package by special messenger. She tore off the outer wrapper and on the inner was written in red ink: "Danger." Murmuring some inane thing about its being her shoes, she ran with the package to her room. For a young woman who had all her life received packages of all kinds she was inordinately excited.

It held three books. One of them was about women who worked. There were pictures of girls working in factories and in different places. One was something about evolution, and one was on socialism. And there was a pamphlet about the United States Army, and another pamphlet about religion.

She looked for a name in the books, but found none. The fly-leaves had been torn out.

She was not sorry; she was just as glad to go on thinking of her trouble-maker as the man who mended the boats. There was something freeing about keeping him impersonal.

But in the book about women she found an envelope addressed: "To one looking for trouble."

This was what was type-written on the single sheet it contained:

"Here are a couple of books warranted to disturb one's peace of mind. They are marked danger as both warning and commendation. It is absolutely guaranteed that one will not be so pleased with the world—and with one's self—after reading them. There is more—both books and danger—where they came from."

It was signed: "One who loves to lead adventurous souls into dangerous paths."

It was two o'clock when Katie turned off her light that night.

CHAPTER XVI

Perhaps after all it was neither the dog nor the literature, but the heat. For the heat of that next day was the kind to prey through countries of make-believe. It oppressed every one, but Ann it seemed to excite, as if it stirred memories in their sleep. "Don't fight heat, Ann," Katie finally admonished, puzzled and disturbed by the way Ann kept moving about. "The only way to get ahead of the heat is to give up to it."

"Can you always do what you want to do?" Ann demanded with a touch of petulance. "Isn't there ever something makes you do things you know aren't the things to do?"

"Oh, dear me, yes," laughed Kate. "But you're simply your own worst enemy when you try to get ahead of the heat."

"I don't know how you're going to help being your own worst enemy," Ann murmured.

She picked some leaves from the vines and threw them away, purposelessly; she made the cat get out of a chair and sat down in it herself, only to get up again and pile all the magazines in a different way, not facilitating anything by the change. Then, after walking the length of the veranda, she stood there looking at Katie: Katie in the coolest and coolest-looking of summer dresses, leaning back in a cool-looking chair—adjusting herself to things as they were, poised, victorious in her submission.

Then Ann said a strange thing. "A hot day's just nothing but a hot day to you, is it?"

The words themselves said less than the laugh which followed them—a laugh which carried both envy and resentment, which at once admired and accused, a laugh straight from the girl they were trying to ignore.

And pray what was a hot day to her, Katie wondered. What *was* a hot day—save a hot day? But as she watched Ann in the next few moments she seemed to be surveying a figure oppressed less by heat than by that to which the heat laid her open. It seemed that the hot day might stand for the friction and the fretting of the world, for things which closed in upon one as heat closed in, bore down as heat bore down. As Ann pushed back the hair from her forehead it seemed she would push back the weight of the years.

It was at that moment that Caroline Osborne, richest and most prominent girl of the vicinity, stepped from her motor car.

Katie had met her a few nights before at the dance. And Wayne knew her father—a man of many interests. It was his quarrel with the forest service that had brought her cousin Fred Wayneworth there. Fred was not one of his admirers.

"Isn't this heat distressing?" was her greeting, though she had succeeded in keeping herself very fresh and sweet looking under the distress.

As Katie turned to introduce the two girls she saw that Ann was pulling at her handkerchief nervously. Was it irritating to have people for whom hot days were but hot days call heat distressing?

"Though one always has a breeze motoring," she took it up. "There are so many ways in which automobiles make life more bearable, don't you find it so, Miss Jones?"

Katie replied, inanely—Ann was still pulling at her handkerchief—that they were indispensable, of course, though personally she was so fond of horses—.

Yes, Miss Osborne loved horses too. Indeed it was army people had taught her to ride; once when she visited at Fort Riley—she had spent a month there with Mrs. Baxter. Katie knew her?

Oh, yes, Katie knew her, and almost all the rest of the army people whom Miss Osborne told of adoring. Of a common world, they were not long strangers. They came together through a whole network of associations. Finally they reached South Carolina and concluded they must be related— something about Katie's grandmother and Miss Osborne's great-aunt—.

Katie, in the midst of her interest turning instinctively to include Ann, was curiously arrested. Ann was sitting a little apart. And there seemed so poignant a significance in her sitting apart. It was an order of things from which she sat apart. The network went too far back, too deep down; it was too intricate for either sympathy or ingenuity to shape it at will.

Though Katie tried. For Katie, enough that she was sitting apart, and consciously. Leaving grandmothers and great-aunts in a sadly unfinished state she was lightly off into a story of something which had once happened to her and Ann in Rome.

But Ann was as an actor refusing to play her part. Perhaps she was too resentfully conscious of its being but a part—of her having no approach save through a part. For the first time she failed in that adaptability which had always made the stories plausible. In the midst of her tale Katie met Ann's eyes, and faltered. They were mocking eyes.

As best she could she turned the conversation to local affairs, for Miss Osborne was looking curiously at Miss Jones' unresponsive friend.

And as Ann for the first time seemed deliberately—yes, maliciously to fail—Katie for the first time felt out of patience, and injured. Perhaps the heat was enervating, but was that sufficient reason for embarrassing one's hostess? Perhaps it did make her think of hard things, but was that any reason for failing in the things that made all this possible? It was not appreciative, it was not kind, it did not show the right spirit, Katie told herself as she listened, with what she was pleased to consider both atoning and rebuking graciousness, to the plans for Miss Osborne's garden party.

"It is for the working girls, especially the lower class of working girls, who are in the factories. For instance, the candy factory girls. I am especially interested in that as father owns the candy factory—it is a pet side issue of his. You can see it from here, across the river there on the little neck of land. You see? The girls are just beginning to come from work now."

The three girls looked across the river, where groups of other girls were quitting a large building. They could be seen but dimly, but even at that distance something in the prevalent droop suggested that they, too, had found the day "distressingly warm."

"I hadn't realized," said Katie, "that making candy was such serious business."

"It couldn't have been very pleasant today," their guest granted, "but I believe it is regarded a very good place to work."

The book Katie had been reading the night before had shown her the value of facts when it came to judging places where women worked, and she was moved to the blunt inquiry: "How much do those girls make?"

"About six dollars a week, I believe," Miss Osborne replied.

Katie watched them: the long dim line of girls engaged in preparation of the sweets of life. She was wondering what she would have thought it worth to go over there and work all day. "Then each of those girls made a dollar today?" she asked, and her inflection was curious.

"Well—no," Miss Osborne confessed. "The experienced and the skillful made a dollar."

"And how much," pressed Katie, "did the least experienced and skillful make?"

"Fifty cents, I believe," replied Miss Osborne, seeming to have less enthusiasm when the scientific method was employed.

There was a jarring sound. The girl "sitting apart" had pushed her chair still farther back. "You call that a good place to work?" She addressed it to Miss Osborne in voice that scraped as the chair had scraped.

"Why yes, as places go, I believe so. Though that is why I am giving the garden party. They do need more pleasure in their lives. It is one of the under-lying principles of life—is it not?—that all must have their pleasures."

Ann laughed recklessly. Miss Osborne looked puzzled; Katie worried.

"And we are organizing this working girl's club. We think we can do a great deal through that."

"Oh yes, help them get higher wages, I suppose?" Katie asked innocently.

"N—o; that would scarcely be possible. But help them to get on better with what they have. Help them learn to manage better."

Again Ann laughed, not only recklessly but rudely. "That is surely a splendid thing," she said, and the voice which said it was high-pitched and unsteady, "helping a girl to 'manage better' on fifty cents a day!"

"You do not approve of these things?" Miss Osborne asked coldly.

And with all the heat Katie felt herself growing suddenly cold as she heard Ann replying: "Oh, if they help you—pass the time, I don't suppose they do any harm."

"You see," Katie hastened, "Miss Forrest and I were once associated with one of those things which wasn't very well conducted. I fear it— prejudiced us."

"Evidently," was Miss Osborne's reply.

"Though to be sure," Kate further propitiated, resentment at having to do so growing with the propitiation, "that is very narrow of us. I am sure your club will be quite different. We may come to the garden party?"

Katie followed her guest to her car. "I am hoping it will be cooler soon," she said. "My friend is here to grow stronger, and this heat is quite unnerving her."

Miss Osborne accepted it with polite, "I trust she will soon be much better. Yes, the heat is trying."

Katie did not return to Ann, but sat at the head of the steps, looking across the river.

She was genuinely offended. She knew nothing more unpardonable than to embarrass one's hostess. She grew hard in contemplation of it. Nothing justified it;—nothing.

A few girls were still coming from the candy factory. Miss Osborne's car had crossed the bridge and was speeding toward her beautiful home up the river—just the home for a garden party. The last group of girls, going along very slowly, had to step back for the machine to rush by.

Katie forgot her own grievance in wondering about those girls who had waited for the Osborne car to pass.

She knew where Miss Osborne was going, where and how she lived; she was wondering where the girls not enjoying the breeze always to be found in motoring were going, what they would do when they got there, and what they thought of the efforts to help them "manage better" on their dollar or less a day.

It made her rise and return to Ann.

Ann, too, was looking across the river at the girls who had given Miss Osborne right of way. Two very red spots burned in Ann's cheeks and her eyes, also, were feverish.

"I suppose I shouldn't have spoken that way to your friend," she began, but less contritely than defiantly.

Katie flushed. She had been prepared to understand and be kind. But she was not equal to being scoffed at, she who had been so embarrassed— and betrayed.

"It was certainly not very good form," she said coolly.

"And of course that's all that matters," said Ann shrilly. "It's just good form that matters—not the truth."

"Oh I don't see that you achieved any great thing for the truth, Ann. Anyhow, rudeness is no less rude when called truth."

"Garden parties!" choked Ann.

"I am not giving the garden party, Ann," said Katie long-sufferingly. "I was doing nothing more than being civil to a guest—against rather heavy odds."

"You were pretending to think it was lovely. But of course that's good form!"

Her perilously bright eyes had so much the look of an animal pushed into a corner that Katie changed. "Come, Ann dear, let's not quarrel with each other just because it has been a disagreeable day, or because Caroline Osborne may have a mistaken idea of doing good—and I a mistaken idea of being pleasant. I promised Worth a little spin on the river before dinner. You'll come? It will be cooling."

"My head aches," said Ann, but the tension of her voice broke on a sob. "If you don't mind—I'll stay here." She looked up at her in a way which remotely suggested the look of that little dog the day before, "Katie, I don't mean you. When I say things like that—I don't mean *you*. I mean—I suppose I mean—the things back of you. All those things—"

She stopped, but Katie did not speak. "You see," said Ann, "there are two worlds, and you and I are in different ones."

"I don't believe in two worlds," said Katie promptly. "It's not a democratic view of things. It's all one world."

"Your Miss Osborne and the fifty cents a day girls—all one world? I am afraid," laughed Ann tremulously, "that even the 'underlying principles of life' would have a hard time making *them* one."

CHAPTER XVII

Even on the river it was not yet cool. Day had burned itself too deeply upon the earth for approaching night to hold messages for even its favorite messenger. Katie was herself at the steering wheel, and alone with Worth and Queen. She had learned to manage the boat, and much to the disappointment of Watts and the disapproval of Wayne sometimes went about on the river unattended. Katie contended that as a good swimmer and not a bad mechanic she was entitled to freedom in the matter. She held that to be taken about in a boat had no relation to taking a boat and going about in it; that when Watts went her soul stayed home.

Tonight, especially, she would have the boat for what it meant to self; for to Katie, too, the sultry day had become more than sultry day. The thing which pressed upon her seemed less humidity than the consciousness of a world she did not know. It was not the heat which was fretting her so much as that growing sense of limitations in her thought and experience.

She wondered what the man who mended the boats would say about Ann's two worlds.

She suspected that he would agree with Ann, and then proceeded to work herself into a fine passion at his agreeing with Ann against her. "That silly thing of two worlds is fixed up by people who can't get along in the one world," said she. "And that childish idea of one world is clung to by people who don't know the real world," retorted the trouble-maker.

To either side of the river were factories. Katie had never given much thought to factories beyond the thought that they disfigured the landscape. Now she wondered what the people who had spent that hot day in the unsightly buildings thought about the world in general—be it one world or two.

Worth had come up to the front of the boat. The day had weighed upon him too, for he seemed a wistful little boy just then.

She smiled at him lovingly. "What thinking about, Worthie dear?"

"Oh, I wasn't thinking, Aunt Kate," he replied soberly. "I was just wondering."

"You too?" she laughed.

"And what would you say, Worthie," she asked after they had gone a little way in silence, "was the difference between thinking and wondering?"

Worth maturely crossed his knees as a sign of the maturity of the subject. "Well, I don't know, 'cept when you think you know what you're thinking about, and when you wonder you just don't know anything."

"Maybe you wonder when you don't know what to think," Katie suggested.

"Yes, maybe so. There's more to wonder about than there is to think about, don't you think so, Aunt Kate?"

"I wonder," she laughed.

"You do wonder, don't you, Aunt Kate? You wonder more than you think."

She flashed him a keen, queer look.

"Worth," she asked, after another pause in which the mind of twenty-five and the mind of six were wondering in their respective fashions, "do you know anything about the underlying principles of life?"

"The what, Aunt Kate?"

"Underlying principles of life," she repeated grimly.

"Why no," he acknowledged, "I guess I never heard of them."

"I never did either, till just lately. I want to find out something about them. Do you know, Worthie dear, I'd go a long way to find out something about them."

"Where would you have to go, Aunt Kate? Could you go in a boat?"

"No, I fear you couldn't go in a boat. Trouble is," she murmured, more to herself than to him, "I don't know where you *would* go."

"Don't Papa know 'bout them?"

"I sometimes think he would like to learn."

"Papa knows all there is to know 'bout guns and powders," defended Worth loyally.

"Yes, I know; but I don't believe guns and powders have any power to get you to these underlying principles of life."

"Well, what *does* get you there?" demanded her companion of the practical sex.

She laughed. "I don't know, dear. I honestly don't know. And I'd like to know. Perhaps some time I will meet some one who is very wise, and then I'll ask whether it is experience, or wisdom, or sympathy. Whether some people are born to get there and other people not, or just how it is."

"Watts says you have more sympathy than wisdom, Aunt Kate."

"You mustn't talk about me to Watts," she admonished spiritedly. Then in the distance she heard a mocking voice insinuatingly inquiring: "But why not, if it's all one world?"

"But he said," Worth added, "that it shouldn't be held against you, 'cause of course you never had half a chance. No, it wasn't Watts said that, either. It was the man that mends the boats. It was Watts said you was a yard wide."

Katie's head had gone up; she was looking straight ahead, cheeks red. "Indeed! So it's the man that mends the boats says these hateful things about me, is it?"

"Why no, Aunt Kate; not hateful things. He says he's sorry for you. Why, he says he don't know anybody more to be pitied than you are."

"Well—*really!* I must say that of all the insolent —impertinent— insufferable—"

"He says you would have amounted to something if you'd had half a chance. But he's afraid you never will, Aunt Kate."

"I do not wish to hear anything more about him," said Aunt Kate haughtily. "Now, or at any future time."

But it was not five minutes later she asked, with studied indifference: "Pray what does this absurd being look like?"

"What being, Aunt Kate?" innocently inquired the being who was very young.

"Why this sympathetic gentleman!"

"Oh, I don't know. He's just a man. Sometimes he wears boots. He's real nice, Aunt Kate."

"Oh I'm sure he must be charming!"

She turned toward home, more erect, attending to her duties with a dignified sense of responsibility.

The glare of day had gone, but without bringing the cool of night. It made the world seem very worn. Little by little resentment slipped away and she had joined the man who mended the boats in pitying herself. She was disposed to agree with him that she might have amounted to something had she had half a chance. No one else had ever thought of her amounting to anything—amounting, or not amounting. They had merely thought of her as Katie Jones. And certainly no one else had ever pitied her. It made the man who mended the boats seem a wise and tender being. As against the whole world she felt drawn to his large and kindly understanding.

Excitement had suddenly seized Worth. "Aunt Kate—Aunt Kate!" he cried peremptorily, pointing to a cove in one of the islands they were passing, "please land there!"

"Why no, Worth, we can't land. It's too hard. And why should we?"

"Oh Aunt Kate—please! Oh please!"

She was puzzled. "But why, Worthie?"

"Cause I want you to. Don't you love me 't all any more, Aunt Kate?"

That was too much. He was suddenly just a baby who had been made to suffer for her grown-up disturbances. "But, dearie, what will you do when we land?"

"I want to look for something. I've got to get something. I want to show you something. 'Twon't take but a minute."

"What do you want to show me, dear?"

"Why I can't tell you, Aunt Kate. It's a surprise. It's a beautifulest surprise. Something I want to show you just because I love you, Aunt Kate."

Katie's eyes brooded over him. "Dear little chappie, and Aunt Kate's a cross mean old thing, isn't she?"

"Not if she'll stop the boat," said crafty Worth.

She laughed and surveyed the shore. It looked feasible. "I'm very 'easy,' Worth. Just don't get it into your head all the world is as easy as I am."

The little boy and the dog were out before she had made her landing. They were running through the brush. "Worth," she called, "don't go far. Don't go out of sound."

"No," he called back excitedly, "'tain't far."

She was anxious, reproaching herself as absurd and rash, and was just attempting to ground the boat and follow when Queen came bounding back. Then came Worth's voice: "Here 'tis! Here's Aunt Kate—waiting for you!"

Next there emerged from the brush a flushed and triumphant little boy, and after him came a somewhat less flushed and less obviously triumphant man.

CHAPTER XVIII

Her first emotion was fury at herself. She must be losing her mind not to have suspected!

Then the fury overflowed on Worth and his companion. It reached high-water mark with the stranger's smile.

And there dissolved; or rather, flowed into a savage interest, for the smile enticed her to mark what manner of man he was. And as she looked, the interest shed the savagery.

His sleeves were rolled up; he had no hat, no coat. He had been working with something muddy. A young man, a large man, and strong. The first thing which she saw as distinctive was the way his smile lived on in his eyes after it had died on his lips, as if his thought was smiling at the smile.

Even in that first outraged, panic-stricken moment Katie Jones knew she had never known a man like that.

"Here he is, Aunt Kate!" cried her young nephew, dancing up and down. "This is him!"

It was not a presentation calculated to set Katie at ease. She sought refuge in a frigid: "I beg pardon?"

But that was quite lost on Worth. "Why, Aunt Kate, don't you know him? You said you'd rather see him than anybody now living! Don't you know, Aunt Kate—the man that mends the boats?"

It seemed that in proclaiming their name for him Worth was shamelessly proclaiming it all: her conversations, the intimacy to which she had admitted him, her delight in him—yes, *need* of him. "But I thought," she murmured, as if in justification, "that you had a long white beard!"

And so she had—at times; then there had been other times when he had no beard at all—but just such a chin.

"I am sorry to be disappointing," the stranger replied—with his voice. With his eyes—it became clear even in that early moment that his eyes were insurgents—he said: "I don't take any stock in that long white beard!" Then, as if fearing his eyes had overstepped: "Perhaps you have visions of the future. A long white beard is a gift the years may bring me."

"You can just ask him anything you want to, Aunt Kate," Worth was brightly assuring her. "I told him you wanted to know about the under life—the under what it is of life. You needn't be 'fraid of him, Aunt Kate; you know he's the man's so sorry for you. He knows all about everything, and will tell you just everything he knows."

"Quite a sweeping commendation," Katie found herself murmuring foolishly—and in the imaginary conversations she had talked so brilliantly! But when one could not be brilliant one could always find cover under dignity. "If you will get in the boat now, Worth," she said, "we will go home."

But Worth, serene in the consciousness of having accomplished his mission, was sending Queen out after sticks and did not appear to have heard.

And suddenly, perhaps because the hot day had come to mean so much more than mere hot day, the feeling of being in a ridiculous position, together with that bristling sense of the need of a protective dignity, fell away. It became one of those rare moments when real things matter more than things which supposedly should matter. She looked at him to find him looking intently at her. He was not at all slipshod as inspector. "Why are you sorry for me?" she asked. "What is there about me to pity?"

He smiled as he surveyed her, considering it. Even people for whom smiling was difficult must have smiled at the idea of pitying Katie Jones—Katie, who looked so much as if the world existed that she might have the world.

But he looked with a different premise and saw a deeper thing. The world might exist for her enjoyment, but it eluded her understanding. And that was beginning to encroach upon the enjoyment.

She seemed to follow, and her divination stirred a singular emotion, possibly a more turbulent emotion than Katie Jones had ever known.

"It's all very well to pity me, but it's not a genuine pity—it's a jeering one. If you're going to pity me, why don't you do it sincerely instead of scoffingly? Is it my fault that I don't know anything about life? What chance did I ever have to know anything real? I wasn't educated. I was 'accomplished.' Oh, of course, if I had been a big person, a person with a real mind—if I had had anything exceptional about me—I would have stepped out. But I'm nothing but the most ordinary sort of girl. I haven't any talents. Nobody—myself included—can see any reason for my being any different from the people I'm associated with. I was brought up in the army. Army life isn't real life. It's army life. To an army man a girl is a girl, and what they mean by a girl has nothing to do with being a thinking being. Then what business has a man like you—I don't know who you are or what you're doing, but I believe you have some ideas about the real things of life—tell me, please—what business have you jeering at me?"

"I have no business jeering at you," he said quickly, simply and strongly.

But Katie had changed. He had a fancy that she would always be changing; that she was not one to rest in outlived emotions, that one mood was always but the making and enriching of another mood, moment ever flowing into moment, taking with it the heart of the moment that had gone. "You are quite right to pity me," she said, and tears surged beneath both eyes and voice. "Whether scoffingly or genuinely—you were quite right. Feeling just enough to feel there *is* something—but not a big enough feeling to go to that something, knowing just enough to know I'm being cheated, but without either the courage or the knowledge to do anything about it— I'm surely a pitiable and laughable object. Come, Worth," she said sharply, "we're going home."

But Worth had begun upon the construction of a raft, and was not in a home-going mood. Thus encouraged by his young friend the man who mended the boats sat down on a log.

"When did you begin to want to know about the 'underlying principles of life'?" His smile quoted it, though less mockingly than tenderly.

Katie was silent.

"Was it the day *she* came?" he asked quietly.

She gasped. Was he—a wizard? But looking at him and seeing he looked very much more like a man than like anything else, she met him as man should be met. "The day who came? I don't know what you mean."

"The girl. Was it the day you took her in? Saved her by making her save you?"

She was too startled by that for pretense. She could only stare at him.

"I saw her before you did," he said.

She looked around apprehensively. The man who mended the boats knowing about Ann? Was the whole world losing its mind just because it had been such a hot day?

But the world looking natural enough, she turned back to him. "I don't understand. Tell me, please."

As he summoned it, he changed. She had an impression of all but the central thing falling away, leaving his spirit exposed. And a thought or a vision gripped that spirit, and he tightened under it as a muscle would tighten.

When he turned to her, taking her in, self-consciousness fell away. There was no place for it.

"You want to hear about it?" he asked.

She nodded.

"As a matter of fact, it's nothing, as facts go. Only an impression. Yet an impression that swore to facts. Perhaps you know that she came on the Island from the south bridge?"

Katie shook her head. "I know nothing, save that suddenly she was there."

That held him. "And knowing nothing, you took her in?"

She kept silence, and he looked at her, dwelling upon it. "And you," he said softly, "don't know anything about the 'underlying principles of life'? Perhaps you don't. But if we had more you we'd have no her."

She disclaimed it. "It wasn't that way—an understanding way. I didn't do it because I thought it should be done; because I wanted to—do good. I—oh, I don't know. I did it because I wanted to do it. I did it because I couldn't help doing it."

That called to him. He seemed one for whom ideas were as doors, ever opening into new places. And he did not shut those doors, or turn from them, until he had looked as far as he could see.

"Perhaps," he saw now, "that is the way it must come. Doing it because you can't help doing it. It seems wonderful enough to work the wonder."

"Work what wonder?" Katie asked timidly.

"The wonder of saving the world."

He spoke it quietly, but passion, the passion of the visioner, leaped to his eyes at sound of what he had said.

Katie looked about at so much of the world as her vision afforded: Prosperous factories—beautiful homes—hundreds of other homes less beautiful, but comfortable looking—some other very humble homes which yet looked habitable, the beautifully kept Government island in between the two cities, seeming to stand for something stable and unifying—far away hills and a distant sky line—a steamboat going through the splendid Government bridge, automobiles and carriages and farm wagons passing over that bridge—this man who mended the boats, this young man so live that thoughts of life could change him as a sculptor can change his clay—dear little Worth who was happily building a raft, the beautiful dog lying there drawing restoration from the breath of the water—"But it doesn't look as though it needed 'saving,'" said Katie.

He shook his head. "You're looking at the framework. Her eyes that day brought word from the inside. To one knowing—"

He broke off, looking at her as though seeing her from a new angle.

He thought it aloud. "You've walked sunny paths, haven't you? You never had your soul twisted. Life never tried to wring you out of shape. And yet—oh there's quite a yet," he finished more lightly.

"But you were telling me of Ann," Katie felt she must say.

"Yes, and when I've finished telling you, you'll go back to your sunny paths, won't you? Please don't hurry me. I can tell it better if I think I'm not being hurried."

She smiled openly. "I am in no hurry." There was a sunny rim trying all the while to pierce the somber thing which drew them together. Little rays from the sunny paths would dart daringly in to the dark place from which Ann rose.

It made him wonder how far she of the sunny paths could penetrate an unlighted country. He looked at her—peered at her, fairly—trying to decide. But he could not decide. Katie baffled him on that.

"I wonder," he voiced it, "where it's going to lead you? I wonder if you're prepared to go where it may lead you? Have you thought of that? Perhaps it's going to take you into a country too dark for you of the sunny paths. She may be called back. You know we are called back to countries where we have—established a residence. You might have to go with her to settle a claim, or break a tie, or pull some one else out that she might not be pulled back in. Then what? Perhaps you might feel you needed a guide. If so,"—he went boldly to the edge of it, then halted, and concluded with a boyishly bashful humor—"will you keep my application on file?"

Katie was not going to miss her chance of finding out something. "I should want a guide who knew the territory," she said.

"I qualify," he replied shortly, with a short, unmirthful laugh. "That is one advantage of not having spent one's days on sunny paths." His voice on that was neither bashful nor boyish.

"But you must have spent some of them on sunny paths," she urged, with more feeling than she would have been able to account for. "You don't look," Katie added almost shyly, "as if you had grown in the dark."

He did not reply. He looked so much older when sternness set his face, leaving no hint of that teasing gleam in his eyes, that pleasing little humorous twist of his mouth.

Gently her voice went into the dark country claiming him then. "But you were telling me of my friend."

It brought him out, wondering anew. "Your friend! There you go again! How can you expect me to stick to a subject when paths open out on all sides of you like that? But I'll try to quit straying. It happened that on that day, just at that time, I was going under the south bridge. I chanced to look up. A face was bending down. Her face. Our eyes met—square. I *got* it— flung to me in that one look. What the world had done to her—what she thought of it for doing it—what she meant to do about it.

"I wish," he went on, with a slow, heavy calm, "that the 'good' men and women of the world—those 'good' men and women who eat good dinners and sleep in good beds—some of the 'God's in heaven all's well with the world' people—could have that look wake them up in the middle of the night. I'd like to think of them turning to the wall and trying to shut it out— and the harder they tried the nearer and clearer it grew. I'd like to think of them sitting up in bed praying God—the God of 'good' folks—to please make it stop. I'd like to have it haunt them—dog them—finally pierce their brains or souls or whatever it is they have, and begin to burrow. I'd like to have it right there on the job every time they mentioned the goodness of God or the justice of man, till finally they threw up their hands in crazed despair with, 'For God's sake, what do you want *me* to do about it!'"

He had scarcely raised his voice. He was smiling at her. It was the smile led her to gasp: "Why I believe you hate us!"

"Why I really believe I do," he replied quietly, still smiling.

Suddenly she flared. "That's not the thing! You're not going to set the world right by hating the world. You're not going to make it right for some people by hating other people. What good thing can come of hate?"

"The greatest things have come of hate. Of a divine hate that transcends love."

"Why no they haven't! The greatest things have come of love. What the world needs is more love. You can't bring love by hating."

He seemed about to make heated reply, but smiled, or rather his smile became really a smile as he said: "What a lot of things you and I would find to talk about."

"We must—" Katie began impetuously, but halted and flushed. "We must go on with our story," was what it came to.

"I haven't any story, except just the story of that look. Though it holds the story of love and hate and a hundred other things you and I would disagree about. And I don't know that I can convey to you—you of the sunny paths—what the look conveyed to me. But imagine a crowd, a crazed crowd, all pushing to the center, and then in the center a face thrown back so you can see it for just an instant before it sinks to suffocation. If you can fancy that look—the last gasp for breath of one caught—squeezed— just going down—a hatred of the crowd that got her there, just to suffocate her—and perhaps one last wild look at the hills out beyond the crowd. If you can get *that*—that fear, suffocation, terror—and don't forget the hate— yet like the dog you've kicked that grieved—'How could you—when it was a pat I wanted!'—"

"I know it in the dog language," said Katie quiveringly.

"Then imagine the dog crazed with thirst tied just out of reach of a leaping, dancing brook—"

"Oh—please. That's too plain."

"It hurts when applied to dogs, does it?" he asked roughly.

"But they're so helpless—and they love us so!"

"And *they're* so helpless—and they hate because they weren't let love."

"But surely there aren't many—such looks. Not many who feel they're— going down. Why such things couldn't *be*—in this beautiful world."

"Such," he said smilingly, "has ever been the philosophy of sunny paths."

"You needn't talk to me like that!" she retorted angrily. "I guess I saw the look as well as you did—and did a little more to banish it than you did, too."

"True. I was just coming to that thing of my not having done anything. Perhaps it was a case of fools rushing in where angels feared to tread. You mustn't mind being called a fool in any sentence so preposterous as to call me an angel. You see one who had never been in the crowd would say— 'Why don't you get out?' It would be droll, wouldn't it, to have some one on a far hill call—'But why don't you come over here?' Don't you see how that must appeal to the sense of humor of the one about to go down?"

She made no reply. The thing that hurt her was that he seemed to enjoy hurting her.

"You see I've been in the crowd," he said more simply and less bitterly. "I don't suppose men who have been most burned to death ever say—'The fire can't hurt you.'"

"And do they never try to rescue others from fires?" asked Katie scornfully. "Do they let them burn—just because they know fire for a dangerous thing?"

"Rescue them for what? More fires? It's a question whether it's very sane, or so very humane, either, to rescue a man from one fire just to have him on hand for another."

"I don't think I ever in my life heard anything more farfetched," pronounced Katie. "How do you know there'll be another?"

"Because there are people for whom there's nothing else. If you can't offer a safe place, why rescue at all? Though it's true," he laughed, "that I hadn't the courage of my convictions in the matter. After that look—oh I haven't been able to make it live—burn—as it did—she passed on the Island, the guard evidently thinking she was with some people who had just got out of an automobile and gone on for a walk. And suddenly I was corrupted, driven by that impulse for saving life, that beautiful passion for keeping things alive to suffer which is so humorously grounded in the human race."

He stopped with a little laugh. Watching him, Katie was thinking one need have small fear of his not always being "corrupted." There was a light in his eyes spoke for "corruption."

"I saw her making straight across the Island," he went back to his story. "I *knew*. And I knew that on the other side she might find things very conveniently arranged for her purpose. I turned the boat and went at its best speed around the head of the Island. Hugged the shore on your side. Pulled into a little cove. Waited."

He looked at Katie, comparing her with an *a priori* idea of her. "I saw you sitting up there in the sun—on the bunker. Just having received the last will and testament, as it were, of this other human soul, can't you fancy how I hated you—sitting there so serenely in the sun?"

"But why hate me?" she demanded passionately. "That's where you're small and unjust! I don't make the crazed crowds, do I?"

"Yes; that's just what you do. There'd be no crowds if it weren't for you. You take up too much room."

"I don't see why you want to—hurt me like that," she said unevenly. "Don't you want me to enjoy my place any more? Will it do any good for me to get in the crowd? What can I do about it?"

Looking into her passionately earnest face it was perhaps the gulf between the girl and his *a priori* idea of her brought the smile—a smile no kin to that hard smile of his. And looking with a different slant across the gulf there was a sort of affectionate roguery in his eyes as he asked: "Do you want to know what I honestly think about you?"

She nodded.

"I think you're in for it!"

"In for what?"

"I don't think you've the ghost of a chance to escape!" he gloated.

"Escape—what?"

"Seeing. And when you do—!" He laughed—that laugh one thinks of as the exclusive possession of an affectionate understanding. And when it died to a smile, something tenderly teasing flickered in that smile.

She flushed under it. "You were telling me—we keep stopping."

"Yes, don't we? I wonder if we always would."

"We keep stopping to quarrel."

"Yes—to quarrel. I wonder if we always would."

"I haven't a doubt of it in the world," said Katie feelingly, and they laughed together as friends laugh together.

"Well, where did I leave myself? Oh yes—waiting. Sitting there busily engaged in hating you. Then she came across the grass—making straight for the river—running. I saw that you saw, and the thing that mattered to me then was what you would do about it. Saved or not saved, she was gone—I thought. The crowd had squeezed it all out of her. The live thing to me was what you—the You of the world that you became to me—would do about her."

He paused, smiling at that absurd and noble vision of Katie tumbling down the bunker. "And when you did what you did do—it was so treacherously disarming, the quick-witted humanity, the clever tenderness of it—I loved you so for it that I just couldn't go on hating. There's where you're a dangerous person. How dare you—standing for the You of the world—dampen the splendid ardor of my hate?"

Katie did not let pass her chance. "Perhaps if the Me of the world were known a little more intimately it would be less hated."

He shook his head. "They just happened to have you. They can't keep you."

There was another one of those pauses which drew them so much closer than the words. She knew what he was wondering, and he knew that she knew. At length she colored a little and called him back to the greater reserve of words.

"I saw how royally you put it through. I could see you standing there on the porch, looking back to the river. I've wanted several things rather badly in my life, but I doubt if I've ever wanted anything much worse than to know what you were saying. And then with my own two eyes I saw the miracle: Saw her—the girl who had just had all the concentrated passion of the Her of the world—turn and follow you into the house. It was a blow to me! Oh 'twas an awful blow."

"Why a blow?"

"In the first place that you should want to, and then that you should be able to. My philosophy gives you of the sunny paths no such desire nor power."

"Showing," she deduced quickly and firmly, "that your philosophy is all wrong."

"Oh no; showing that the much toasted Miss Katherine Jones is too big for mere sunny paths. Showing that she has a latent ambition to climb a mountain in a storm."

Fleetingly she wondered how he should know her for the much toasted Miss Katherine Jones, but in the center of her consciousness rose that alluring picture of climbing a mountain in a storm.

"Tell me how you did it."

"Why—I don't know. I had no method. I told her I needed her."

"*You*—needed *her*?"

"And afterwards, in a different way, I told her that again. And I did. I do."

"Why do you need her? How do you need her?" he urged gently.

She hesitated. Her mouth—her splendid mouth shaped by stern or tender thinking to lines of exquisite fineness or firmness—trembled slightly, and the eyes which turned seriously upon him were wistful. "Perhaps," said Katie, "that even on sunny paths one guesses that there are such things as storms in the mountains."

It was only his eyes which answered, but the fullness of the response ushered them into a silence in which they rested together understandingly.

"I sat there watching the house," he went back to it after the moment. "I was sure the girl would come out again. 'She'll bungle it,' I said to myself. 'She'll never be able to put it through.' But time passed—and she did not come out!"—inconsistently enough that came with a ring of triumph. "And then the next day—after the wonder had grown and grown—I saw her driving with you. I was just off the head of the Island. She was turned toward me, looking up the river. Again I saw her eyes, and in them that time I read *you*. And I don't believe," he concluded with a little laugh, "that my stock of hate can ever be quite so secure again."

They talked on, not conscious that it was growing late. Time and place, and the conventions of time and place, seemed outside. She let him in quite freely: to that edge of fun and excitement as well as to the strange and somber places. It was fun sharing fun with him; and something in his way of receiving it suggested that he had been in need of sharing some one's fun. He had a way of looking at her when she laughed that had vague suggestion of something not far from gratitude.

But the fun light, and that other light which seemed wanting to thank her for something, went from his eyes, leaving a glimmer of something deeper as he asked: "But you've never asked for her story? You've demanded nothing?"

"Why no," said Katie; "only that I should be proud if she ever felt I could help."

He turned his face a little away. One looking into it then would not have given much for his stock of hate.

Worth had approached. "Ain't you getting awful hungry, Aunt Kate?"

It recalled her, and to embarrassment. "We must go at once," she said, confused.

"Did you find out all you wanted to know from him, Aunt Kate?" he asked, getting in the boat.

She transcended her embarrassment. "No, Worth. Only that there is a very great deal I would like to know."

He was standing ready to push her boat away. She did not give the word. As she looked at him she had a fancy that she was leaving him in a lonely place—she who was going back to what he called the sunny paths. And not only did she feel that he was lonely, but she felt curiously lonely herself, sitting there waiting to tell him to push her away. She wanted to say, "Come and see me," but she was too bound by the things to which she was returning to put it in the language of those things. And so she said, and the new shyness brought its own sweetness:

"You tell me to come to you if I need a guide. Thank you for that. I shall remember. And perhaps sunshine is a thing that soaks in and can be stored up, and given out again. If it ever seems I can be of any use—in any way—will you come where you know you can find me?"

Her eyes fell before the things which had leaped to his.

CHAPTER XIX

Two hours later she found herself alone on the porch with Captain Prescott.

A good deal had happened in the meantime.

Mrs. Prescott had arrived during Katie's absence, a stop-over of two weeks having been shortened to two hours because of the illness of her friend. Her room at her son's quarters being uninhabitable because of fresh paint, Wayne had insisted she come to them, and she was even then resting up in Ann's room, or rather the room which had been put at her disposal, a bed having been arranged for Ann in Katie's room. Had Katie been at home she would have planned it some other way, for above all things she did not want it to occur to Ann that she was in the way. But Katie had been very busy talking to the man who mended the boats, and naturally it would not occur to Wayne that Ann would be at all sensitive about giving up her room for a few days to accommodate a dear old friend of theirs. And perhaps she was not sensitive about it, only this was no time, Katie felt, to make Ann feel she was crowding any one.

And in Katie's absence "Pet" had been shot. Pet had not seemed to realize that alley methods of defense were not in good repute in the army. He could not believe that Pourquoi and N'est-ce-pas had no guile in their hearts when they pawed at him. Furthermore, he seemed to have a prejudice against enlisted men and showed his teeth at several of them. Katie began to explain that that was because—but Wayne had curtly cut her short with saying that he didn't care why it was, the fact that it was had made it impossible to have the dog around. If one of the men had been bitten by the contemptible cur Katie couldn't cauterize the wound with the story of the dog's hard life.

The only bright spot she could find in it was that probably Watts had taken a great deal of pleasure in executing Wayne's orders—and Caroline Osborne said that all needed pleasure.

She saw that Ann's hands were clenched, and so had not pursued the discussion.

Katie was not in high favor with her brother that night. He said it was outrageous she should not have been there to receive Mrs. Prescott. When

Katie demurred that she would have been less outrageous had she had the slightest notion Mrs. Prescott would be there to be received, it developed that Wayne was further irritated because he had come to take Ann out for a boat ride—and Katie had gone in the boat—heaven only knew where! Then when Katie sought to demolish that irritation with the suggestion that just then was the most beautiful time of day for the river—and she knew it would do Ann good to go—Wayne clung manfully to his grievance, this time labeling it worry. He forbade Katie's going any more by herself. It was preposterous she should have stayed so long. He would have been out looking for her had it not been that Watts had been able to get a glimpse of the boat pulled in on the upper island.

Katie wondered what else Watts had been able to get a glimpse of.

Wayne was so bent on being abused (hot days affected people differently) that the only way she could get him to relinquish a grievance for a pleasure was to put it in the form of a duty. Ann needed a ride on the river, Katie affirmed, and so they had gone, Wayne doing his best to cover his pleasure.

"Men never really grow up," she mused to Wayne's back. "Every so often they have to act just like little boys. Only little boys aren't half so apt to do it."

Though perhaps Wayne had been downright disappointed at not having the boat for Ann when he came home. Was he meaning to deliver that lecture on the army? She hoped that whatever he talked about it would bring Ann home without that strained, harassed look.

And now Katie was talking to Captain Prescott and thinking of the man who mended the boats. Captain Prescott was a good one to be talking to when one wished to be thinking of some one else. He called one to no dim, receding distances.

She was thinking that in everything save the things which counted most he was not unlike this other man—name unknown. Both were well-built, young, vigorous, attractive. But life had dealt differently with them, and they were dealing differently with life. That made a difference big as life itself.

From the far country in which she was dreaming she heard Captain Prescott talking about girls. He was talking sentimentally, but even his sentiment opened no vistas.

And suddenly she remembered how she had at one time thought it possible she would marry him. The remembrance appalled her; less in the idea of marrying him than in the consciousness of how far she had gone from the place where marrying him suggested itself to her at all.

Life had become different. This showed her how vastly different.

But as he talked on she began to feel that it had not become as different to him as to her. He had not been making little excursions up and down unknown paths. He had remained right in his place. That place seemed to him the place for Katie Jones.

As he talked on—about what he called Life—sublimely unconscious of the fences all around him shutting out all view of what was really life—it became unmistakable that Captain Prescott was getting ready to propose to her. She had had too much experience with the symptoms not to recognize them.

Katie did not want to be proposed to. She was in no mood for dealing with a proposal. She had too many other things to be thinking of, wondering about.

But she reprimanded herself for selfishness. It meant something to him, whether it did to her or not. She must be kind—as kind as she could.

The kindest thing she could think of was to keep him from proposing. To that end she answered every sentimental remark with a flippant one.

It grieved, but did not restrain him. "I had thought you would understand better, Katie," he said.

Something in his voice made her question the kindness of her method. Better decline a love than laugh at it.

He talked on of how he had, at various times, cared—in a way, he said—for various girls, but had never found the thing he knew was fated to mean the real thing to him; Katie had heard it all before, and always told with that same freedom from suspicion of its ever having been said before. But perhaps it was the very fact that it was familiar made her listen with a certain tenderness. For she seemed to be listening, less to him than to the voice of by-gone days—all those merry, unthinking days which in truth had dealt very kindly and generously with her.

She had a sense of leaving them behind. That alone was enough to make her feel tenderly toward them. Even a place within a high-board fence, intolerable if one thought one were to remain in it, became a kindly and a pleasant spot from the top of the fence. Once free to turn one's face to the wide sweep without, one was quite ready to cast loving looks back at the enclosure.

And so she softened, prepared to deal tenderly with Captain Prescott, as he seemed then, less the individual than the incarnation of outlived days.

It was into that mellowed, sweetly melancholy mood he sent the following:

"And so, Katie, I wanted to talk to you about it. You're such a good pal—such a bully sort—I wanted to tell you that I care for Ann—and want to marry her."

She dropped from the high-board fence with a jolt that well-nigh knocked her senseless.

"I suppose," he said, "that you must have suspected."

"Well, not exactly suspected," said Katie, feeling her bumps, as it were.

Her first emotion was that it was pretty shabby treatment to accord one who was at such pains to be kind. It gave one a distinctly injured feeling—getting all sweet and mellow only to be dashed to the ground and let lie there in that foolish looking—certainly foolish feeling heap!

But as soon as she had picked herself up—and Katie was too gamey to be long in picking herself up—she wondered what under heaven she was going to do about things! What had she let herself in for now! The pains of an injured dignity—throb of a pricked self love—were forgotten in this real problem, confronting her. She even grew too grave to think about how funny it was.

For Katie saw this as genuinely serious.

"Harry," she asked, "have you said anything to your mother?"

"Well, not *said* anything,"he laughed.

"But she knows?"

"Mother's keen," he replied.

"I once thought I was," was Katie's unspoken comment.

"And have you—you are so good as to confide in me, so I presume to ask questions—have you said anything to Ann?"

"No, not *said* anything,"he laughed again.

"But *she* knows?"

"I don't know. I wondered if you did."

"No," said Katie, "I don't. Truth is I've been so wrapped up in my own affairs—some things I've had on my mind—that I haven't been thinking about people around me falling in love."

"People are always falling in love," he remarked sentimentally. "One should always be prepared for that."

"So it seems," replied Katie. "And yet one is not always—entirely prepared."

She had picked herself up from her fall, but she was not yet able to walk very well. Fortunately he was too absorbed in his own happy striding to mark her hobbling.

A young man talking of his love does not need a brilliant conversationalist for companion.

And he was a young man in love—that grew plain. Had Katie ever seen such eyes? And as for the mouth—though perhaps most remarkable of all was the voice. Just what did it make Katie think of? He enumerated various things it made him think of, only to express his dissatisfaction with them all as inadequate. Had Katie ever seen any one so beautiful? And with such an adorable shy little way? Had Katie ever heard her say anything about him? Did she think he had any chance? Was there any other fellow? Of course there must have been lots of other fellows in love with her—a girl like that— but had she cared for any of them? Would Katie tell him something about her? She had been reserved about herself—the kind of reserve a fellow wouldn't try to break through. Would Katie tell him of her life and her people? Not that it made any difference with him—oh, he wanted just her. But his mother would want to know—Katie knew how mothers were about things like that. And he did want his mother to like her. Surely she would. How could she help it?

She wondered if Ann knew him for a young man in love. Katie's heart hardened against Ann at the possibility. That would not be playing a fair game. Ann was not in position to let Katie's friends fall in love with her. Katie had not counted on that.

"Have you any reason," she asked, "to think Ann cares for you?"

He laughed happily. "N—o; only I don't think it displeases her to have me say nice things to her." And again he laughed.

Then Ann had encouraged him. A girl had no business to encourage a man to say nice things to her when she knew nothing could come of it.

But Katie's memory there nudged Katie's primness; memory of all the men who had been encouraged to say nice things to Katie Jones, even when it was not desirable—or perhaps even possible—that anything could "come of it."

But of course that was different. Ann was in no position to permit nice things being said to her.

"Katie," he was asking, "where did you first meet her? How did you come to know her? Can't you tell me all about it?"

There came a mad impulse to do so. To say: "I first met her right down there at the edge of the water. She was about to commit suicide. I don't know why. I think she was one of those 'Don't You Care' girls you admired in 'Daisey-Maisey.' But I'm not sure of even that. I didn't want her to kill herself, so I took her in and pretended she was a friend of mine. I made the whole thing up. I even made up her name. She said her name was Verna Woods, but I think that's a made-up name, too. I haven't the glimmering of an idea what her real name is, who her people are, where she came from, or why she wanted to kill herself."

Then what?

First, bitter reproaches for Katie. She would be painted as having violated all the canons.

For the first time, watching her friend's face softened by his dreams, seeing him as his mother's son, she questioned her right to violate them. She did not know why she had not thought more about it before. It had seemed such a *joke* on the people in the enclosure. But it was not going to be a joke to hurt them. Was that what came of violating the canons? Was the hurt to one's friends the punishment one got for it?

"You can't cauterize the wounds with the story of the dog's hard life," Wayne had said of poor little unpetted — and because unpetted, unpettable — Pet.

Was Watts the real philosopher when he said "things was as they was"?

She was bewildered. She was in a country where she could not find her way. She needed a guide. Her throat grew tight, her eyes hot, at thought of how badly she needed her guide.

Then, perhaps in self-defense, she saw her friend Captain Prescott, not as a victim of the violation of canons, but as a violator of them himself. She turned from Ann's past to his.

"Harry," she asked, in rather metallic voice, "how about that affair of yours down in Cuba?"

He flushed with surprise and resentment. "I must say, Katie," he said stiffly, "I don't see what it has to do with this."

"Why, I should think it might have something to do with it. Isn't there a popular notion that our pasts have something to do with our futures?"

"It's all over," he said shortly.

"Then you would say, Harry, that when things are over they're over. That they needn't tie up the future."

"Certainly not," said he, making it clear that he wanted that phase of the conversation "over."

"It's my own theory," said Katie. "But I didn't know whether or not it was yours. Now if I had had a past, and it was, as you say yours is, all over, I shouldn't think it was any man's business to go poking around in it."

"That," he said, "is a different matter."

"What's a different matter?" she asked aggressively.

"A woman's past. That would be a man's business."

"Though a man's past is not a woman's business?"

"Oh, we certainly needn't argue that old nonsense. You're too much the girl of the world to take any such absurd position, Katie."

"Of course, being what you call a 'girl of the world' it's absurd I should question the man's point of view, but I can't quite get the logic of it. You wouldn't marry a woman with a past, and yet the woman who marries you is marrying a man with one."

"I've lived a man's life," he said. And he said it with a certain pride.

"And perhaps she's lived a woman's life," Katie was thinking. Only the woman was not entitled to the pride. For her it led toward self-destruction rather than self-approval.

"It's this way, Katie," he explained to her. "This is the difference. A woman's past doesn't stay in the past. It marks her. Why I can tell a woman with a past every time," he concluded confidently.

Katie sat there smiling at him. The smile puzzled him.

"Now look here, Katie, surely you—a girl of the world—the good sort— aren't going to be so melodramatic as to dig up a 'past' for me, are you?"

"No," said Katie, "I don't want to be melodramatic. I'll try to dig up no pasts."

His talk ran on, and her thoughts. It seemed so cruel a thing that Ann's past—whatever it might be, and surely nothing short of a "past" could make a girl want to kill herself—should rise up and damn her now. To him she was a dear lovely girl—the sort of a girl a man would want to marry. Very well then, intrinsically, she *was* that. Why not let people *be* what they were? Why not let them be themselves, instead of what one thought they would be from what one knew of their lives? It was so easy to see marks when one knew of things which one's philosophy held would leave marks. It seemed a fairer and a saner thing to let human beings be what their experiences had actually made them rather than what one thought those experiences would make them.

Captain Prescott had blighted a Cuban woman's life—for his own pleasure and vanity. With Ann it may have been the press of necessity, or it may have been—the call of life. Either one, being driven by life, or drawn to it, seemed less ignominious than trifling with life.

Why would it be so much worse for Captain Prescott to marry Ann than it would be for Ann to marry Captain Prescott?

The man who mended the boats would back her up in that!

Through her somber perplexity there suddenly darted the sportive idea of getting Ann in the army! The audacious little imp of an idea peeped around corners in Katie's consciousness and tried to coquet with her. Banished, it came scampering back to whisper that Ann would not bring the army its first "past"—either masculine or feminine. Only in the army they managed things in such wise that there was no need of committing suicide. Ann had been a bad manager.

But at that moment they were joined by Captain Prescott's mother and he retired for a solitary smoke.

CHAPTER XX

Mrs. Prescott made vivid and compelling those days, those things, which Katie had a little while before had the fancy of so easily slipping away from. She made them things which wove themselves around one, or rather, things of which one seemed an organic part, from which one could no more pull away than the tree's branch could pull away from the tree's trunk.

In her presence Katie was claimed by those things out of which she had grown, claimed so subtly that it seemed a thing outside volition. Mrs. Prescott did not, in any form, say things were as they were; it was only that she breathed it.

How could one combat with words, or in action, that rooted so much deeper than mere words or action?

She was a slight and simple looking lady to be doing anything so large as stemming the tide of a revolutionary impulse. She had never lost the girlishness of her figure—or of her hands. So much had youth left her. Her face was thin and pale, and of the contour vaguely called aristocratic. It was perhaps the iron gray hair rolling back from the pale face held the suggestion of austerity. But that which best expressed her was the poise of her head. She carried it as if she had a right to carry it that way.

It was of small things she talked: the people she had met, people they knew whom Katie knew. It was that net-work of small things she wove around Katie. One might meet a large thing in a large way. But that subtle tissue of the little things!

They talked of Katie's mother, and as they talked it came to Katie that perhaps the most live things of all might be the dead things. Katie's mother had not been unlike Mrs. Prescott, save that to Katie, at least, she seemed softer and sweeter. They had been girls together in Charleston. They had lived on the same street, gone to the same school, come out at the same party, and Katie's mother had met Katie's father when he came to be best man at Mrs. Prescott's wedding. Then they had been stationed together at a frontier post in a time of danger. Wayne had been born at that post. They had been together in times of birth and times of death.

Mrs. Prescott spoke of Worth, and of how happy she knew Katie was to have him with her. She talked of the responsibility it brought Katie, and as they talked it did seem responsibility, and responsibility was another thing which stole subtly up around her, chaining her with intangible—and because intangible, unbreakable—chains.

Mrs. Prescott wanted to know about Wayne. Was he happy, or had the unhappiness of his marriage gone too deep? "Your dear mother grieved so about it, Katie," she said. "She saw how it was going. It hurt her."

"Yes," said Katie, "I know. It made mother very sad."

"I am glad that her death came before the separation."

"Oh, I don't know," said Katie; "I think mother would have been glad."

"She did not believe in divorce; your mother and I, Katie, were the old-fashioned kind of churchwomen."

"Neither did mother believe in unhappiness," said Katie, and drew a longer breath for saying it, for it was as if the things claiming her had crowded up around her throat.

Mrs. Prescott sighed. "We cannot understand those things. It is a strange age in which we are living, Katie. I sometimes think that our only hope is to trust God a little more."

"Or help man a little more," said Katie.

"Perhaps," said Mrs. Prescott gently, "that giving more trust to God would be giving more help to man."

"I'm not sure I get the connecting link," said Katie, more sure of herself now that it had become articulate.

Mrs. Prescott put one of her fine hands over upon Katie's. "Why, child, you can't mean that. That would have hurt your mother."

For the moment Katie did not speak. "If mother had understood just what I meant—understood all about it—I don't believe it would." A second time she was silent, as it struggled. "And if it had"—she spoke it as a thing not to be lightly spoken—"I should be very deeply sorry, but I would not be able to help it."

"Why, child!" murmured her mother's friend. "You're talking strangely. You—the devoted daughter you always were—not able to 'help' hurting your mother?"

Katie's eyes filled. It had become so real: the things stealing around her, the thing in her which must push them back, that it was as if she were hurting her mother, and suffering in the consciousness of bringing suffering. Memory, the tenderest of memories, was another thing weaving itself around her, clinging to her heart, claiming her.

But suddenly she leaned forward. "Would I be able to *help* being myself?"she asked passionately.

Mrs. Prescott seemed startled. "I fear," she said, perplexed by the tears in Katie's eyes and the stern line of her mouth, "that we are speaking of things I do not understand."

Katie was silent, agreeing with her.

Mrs. Prescott broke the silence. "The world is changing."

And again agreeing, Katie saw that in those changes friends bound together by dear ties might be driven far apart.

"Katie," she asked after a moment, "tell me of my boy and your friend." There was a wistful, almost tremulous note in her voice. "You have sympathy and intelligence, Katie. You must know what a time like this means to a mother."

Katie could not speak. It seemed she could bear little more that night. And she longed for time to think it out, know where she stood, come to some terms with herself.

But forced to face it, she tried to do so lightly. She thought it just a fancy of Harry's. Wasn't he quite given to falling in love with pretty girls?

His mother shook her head. "He cares for her. I know. And do you not see, Katie, that that makes her about the biggest thing in life to me?"

Katie's heart almost stood still. She was staggered. Through her wretchedness surged a momentary yearning to be one of those people—oh, one of those *safe* people—who never found the peep-holes in their enclosure!

"Tell me of her, Katie," urged her mother's friend. "Harry seems to think she means much to you. Just what is it she means to you?"

For the moment she was desperate in her wondering how to tell it. And then it happened that from her frenzied wondering what to say of it she sank into the deeper wondering what it *was*. What it was—what in truth it had been all the time—Ann meant to her.

Why had she done it? What was that thing less fleeting than fancy, more imperative than sympathy, made Ann mean more than things which had all her life meant most?

Watching Katie, Mrs. Prescott wavered between gratification and apprehension: pleased that that light in Katie's eyes, a finer light than she had ever known there before, should come through thought of this girl for whom Harry cared; troubled by the strangeness and the sternness of Katie's face.

It was Katie herself Mrs. Prescott wanted—had always wanted. She had always hoped it would be that way, not only because she loved Katie, but because it seemed so as it should be. She believed that summer would have brought it about had it not been for this other girl—this stranger.

Katie's embarrassment had fallen from her, pushed away by feeling. She was scarcely conscious of Mrs. Prescott.

She was thinking of those paths of wondering, every path leading into other paths—intricate, limitless. She had been asleep. Now she was awake. It was through Ann it had come. Perhaps more had come through Ann than was in Ann, but beneath all else, deeper even than that warm tenderness flowering from Ann's need of her, was that tenderness of the awakened spirit—a grateful song coming through an opening door.

It had so claimed her that she was startled at sound of Mrs. Prescott's voice as she said, with a nervous little laugh: "Why, Katie, you alarm me. You make me feel she must be strange."

"She is strange," said Katie.

"Would you say, Katie," she asked anxiously, "that she is the sort of girl to make my boy a good wife?"

Suddenly the idea of Ann's making Harry Prescott any kind of wife came upon Katie as preposterous. Not because she would be bringing him a "past," but because she would bring gifts he would not know what to do with.

"I don't think of Ann as the making some man a good wife type. I think of Ann," she tried to formulate it, "as having gone upon a quest, as being ever upon a quest."

"A—quest?" faltered Mrs. Prescott. "For what?"

"Life," said Katie, peering off into the darkness.

Mrs. Prescott was manifestly disturbed at the prospect of a daughter-in-law upon a quest. "She sounds—temperamental," she said critically.

"Yes," said Katie, laughing a little grimly, "she's temperamental all right."

They could not say more, as Ann and Wayne were coming toward them across the grass.

And almost immediately afterward the Osborne car again stopped before the house. It was Mr. Osborne himself this time, bringing the

Leonards, who had been dining with him. They had stopped to see Mrs. Prescott.

Katie was not sorry, for it turned Mrs. Prescott from Ann. Like the football player who has lost his wind, she wanted a little time counted out.

But she soon found that she was not playing anything so kindly as a game of hard and fast rules.

It seemed at first that Ann's ride had done her good. She seemed to have relaxed and did not give Katie that sense of something smoldering within her. Katie sat beside her, an arm thrown lightly about Ann's shoulders — lightly but guardingly.

Neither of them talked much. Mrs. Prescott and Mrs. Leonard were "visiting"; the men talking of some affairs of Mr. Osborne's. He was commending the army for minding its own business—not "butting in" and trying to ruin business the way some other departments of the Government did. The army seemed in high favor with Mr. Osborne.

Suddenly Mrs. Leonard turned to Katie. She was a large woman, poised by the shallow serenity of self-approval.

"I do feel so sorry for Miss Osborne," she said. "Such a shocking thing has occurred. One of the girls at the candy factory—you know she's trying so hard to help them—has committed suicide!"

Mrs. Prescott uttered an exclamation of horror. Katie patted the shoulder beside her soothingly, understandingly, and as if begging for calm. Even under her light touch she seemed to feel the nerves leap up.

Mr. Osborne turned to them. "Poor Cal, she'd better let things alone. What's the use? She can't do anything with people like that."

"It's the cause of the suicide that's the disgusting thing," said Colonel Leonard.

"Or rather," amended his wife, "the lack of cause."

"But surely," protested Mrs. Prescott, "no girl would take her life without—what she thought was cause. Surely all human beings hold life and death too sacred for that."

"Oh, do they?" scoffed Mrs. Leonard. "Not that class. I scarcely expect you to believe me—I had a hard time believing it myself—but she says she committed suicide—she left a note for her room-mate—because she was 'tired of not having any fun!'"

The hand upon Ann's shoulder grew fairly eloquent. And Ann seemed trying. Her hands were tightly clasped in her lap.

"Why, I don't know," said Wayne, "I think that's about one of the best reasons I can think of."

"This is not a jesting matter, Captain Jones," said Mrs. Leonard severely.

"Far from it," said Wayne.

"Think what it means to a girl like Caroline Osborne! A girl who is trying to do something for humanity—to find the people she wants to uplift so trivial—so without souls!"

"It is hard on Cal," agreed Cal's father.

"Though perhaps just a trifle harder," ventured Wayne, "on the girl who did."

"Well, what did she do it for?" he demanded. "Come now, Captain, you can't make out much of a case for her. Mrs. Leonard's word is just right—trivial. She said she was tired of things. Tired—tired—tired of things, she put it. Tired of walking down the same street. Tired of hanging her hat on the same kind of a peg! Now, Captain—if you can put up any defense for a girl who kills herself because she's tired of hanging her hat on a certain kind of peg! Well," he laughed, "if you can, all I've got to say is that you'd better leave the army and go in for criminal law."

"Why didn't she walk down some other street," he resumed, as no one broke the pause. "If it's a matter of life and death—a person might walk down some other street!"

"And I've no doubt," said Captain Prescott, "that if it were known her life, as well as her hat, hung upon it—she might have had a different kind of peg."

They laughed.

"Oh, of course, the secret of it is," pronounced the Colonel, "she was a neurotic."

For the first time Katie spoke. "I think it's such a fine thing we got hold of that word. Since we've known about neurotics we can just throw all the emotion and suffering and tragedy of the world in the one heap and leave it to the scientists. It lets *us* out so beautifully, doesn't it?"

"Oh, but Katie!" admonished Mrs. Prescott. "Think of it! What is the world coming to? Going forth to meet one's God because one doesn't like the peg for one's hat!"

Katie had a feeling of every nerve in Ann's body leaping up in frenzy. "*God?*" she laughed wildly. "Don't drag *Him* into it! Do you think *He* cares"—turning upon Mrs. Prescott as if she would spring at her—"do you think for a minute *He* cares—*what kind of pegs our hats are on!*"

CHAPTER XXI

Katie's memory of what followed was blurred. She remembered how relieved she was when Ann's laugh—oh the memory of that laugh was clear enough!—gave way to sobbing. Sobbing was easier to deal with. She said something about her friend's being ill, and that they would have to excuse them. She almost wanted to laugh—or was it cry?—herself at the way Harry Prescott was looking from Ann to his mother. After she got Ann in the house she went back and begged somebody's pardon—she wasn't sure whose—and told Colonel Leonard that of course he could understand it on the score of Ann's being a neurotic. She was afraid she might have said that rather disagreeably. And she believed she told Mrs. Prescott—she had to tell Mrs. Prescott something, she looked so frightened and hurt and outraged—that Ann had a form of nervous trouble which made it impossible for her to hear the name of God.

The hardest was Wayne. She came to him on the porch after the others had gone—they were not long in dispersing. "Wayne," she said, "I'm sorry to have embarrassed you."

His short, curt laugh did not reveal his mood. It was scoffing—contemptuous—but she could not tell at what it scoffed. He had not turned toward her.

"I'm sorry," she repeated. "Ann will be sorry. She's so—"

He turned upon her hotly. "Katie, quit lying to *me*. I know there's something you're not telling. I've suspected it for some time. Now don't get off any of that 'nervous trouble' talk to me!"

She stood there dumbly.

It seemed to enrage him. "Why don't you go and look after her! What do you mean by leaving her all alone?"

So she went to look after her.

Ann looked like one who needed looking after. Her eyes were intolerably bright. It seemed the heat behind them must put them out.

She was walking about the room, walking as if something were behind her with a lash.

"You see, Katie," she began, not pausing in the walking—her voice, too, as though a whip were behind it—"it was just as I told you. It was just as I tried to tell you. There are two worlds. There's no use trying to put me in yours. See what I bring you! See what you get for it! See what—"

She stood still, rocking back and forth as she stood there. "It was too much for me to hear her talking about *God!* That was a little too much! *My* father was a minister!" And Ann laughed.

A minister was one thing Katie had not thought of. Even in that moment she was conscious of relief. Certainly the ministry was respectable.

But why should it be "too much" for the daughter of a minister to hear anything about God?

"Ann," she began quietly, "I don't want to force anything. If you want to be alone I'll even take my things and sleep somewhere else. But, Ann, dear, if you could tell me a little I wouldn't be so much in the dark; I could do better for us both."

Ann did not seem to notice what she was saying. "She was tired of things! She was tired of things! Tired of hanging her hat on the same kind of peg! Why it's awful—it's awful, I tell you—to always be hanging your hat on the same kind of peg!

"She was tired of not having any fun! Oh so tired of not having any fun! Why you don't care what you do when you get tired of not having any fun!

"Then people laugh—the people who have all the fun. Oh they think it's so funny!—the people who don't have to hang their hats on any kind of peg. So trivial. So—what's that nervous word? Katie—you're not like the rest of them! Why, you seem to *know*—just know without knowing."

"But it's hard for me," suggested Katie. "Trying to know—and not knowing."

Ann was still walking about the room. "I was brought up in a little town in Indiana. You see I'm going to tell you. I've got to be doing something—and it may as well be talking. Now how did I start? Oh yes—I was brought up in a little town in Indiana. Until three years ago, that was where I lived. Were you ever in a little town in Indiana?"

Katie replied in the negative.

"Maybe there are little towns in Indiana that are different. I don't know. Maybe there are. But this one-in this one life was just one long stretch of hanging your hat on exactly the same kind of peg!

"It was so square—so flat—so dingy—oh, so dreadful! It didn't have anything around it—as some towns do—a hill, or a river, or woods. Around it was something that was just nothing. It was just walled in by the nothingness all around it.

"And the people in it were flat, and square, and dingy. And the things around them were just nothing. They were walled in, too, by the nothingness all around them."

Then the most unexpected of all things happened. Ann smiled. "Katie, I'd like to have seen you in that town!"

"I'm afraid," said Katie, "that I would have invented a new kind of peg."

The smile seemed to have done Ann good. She sat down, grew more natural.

"When I try to tell about my life in that town I suppose it sounds as though I were making a terrible fuss about things. When you think of children that haven't any homes-that are beaten by drunken fathers—starved—overworked-but it was the nothingness. If my father only had got drunk!"

Katie smiled understandingly.

"Katie, you've a lot of imagination. Just try to think what it would mean never to have what you could really call fun!"

Katie took a sweep back over her own life—full to the brim of fun. Her imagination did not go far enough to get a real picture of life with the fun left out.

"Oh, of course," said Ann, "there were pleasures! My father and the people of his church were like Miss Osborne—they believed it was one of the underlying principles of life—only they would call it 'God's will'—that all must have pleasure. But such God-fearing pleasure! I think I could have stood it if it hadn't been for the pleasures."

"Pleasures with the fun left out," suggested Kate.

"Yes, though fun isn't the word, for I don't mean just good times. I mean—I mean—"

"You mean the joy of living," said Katie. "You mean the loveliness of life."

"Yes; now your kind of religion—the kind of religion your kind of people have, doesn't seem to hurt them any."

Katie laughed oddly. "True; it doesn't hurt us much."

"My father's kind is something so different. The love of God seems to have dried him up. He's not a human being. He's a Christian."

Katie thought of her uncle—a bishop, and all too human a human being. She was about to protest, then considered that she had never known the kind of Christian—or human being—Ann was talking about.

"Everything at our church squeaked. The windows. The organ. The deacon's shoes. My father's voice. The religion squeaked. Life squeaked.

"I'll tell you a story, Katie, that maybe will make you see how it was. It's about a dog, and it's easy for you to understand things about dogs.

"Some one gave him to me. I suppose he was not a fine dog—not full-blooded. But that didn't matter. *You* know that we don't love dogs for their blood. We love them for the way they look out of their eyes, and the way they wag their tails. I can't tell you what this dog meant to me—something to love—something that loved me—some one to play with—a companion—a friend—something that didn't have anything to do with my father's church!

"He used to feel so sorry when I had to sit learning Bible verses. Sometimes he would put his two paws up on my lap and try to push the Bible away. I loved him for that. And when at last I could put it away he would dance round me with little yelps of joy. He warmed something in me. He kept something alive.

"And then one day when I came home from a missionary meeting where I had read a paper telling how cruelly young girls were treated by their parents in India, and how there was no joy and love and beauty in their lives, I—" Ann hid her face and it was a drawn, grayish face she raised after a minute—"Tono was not there. I called and called him. My father was writing a sermon. He let me go on calling. I could not understand it. Tono always came running down the walk, wagging his tail and giving his little barks of joy when I came. It had made coming home seem different from what it had ever seemed before. But that day he was not there watching for me. My father let me go on calling for a long time. At last he came to the door and said—'Please stop that unseemly noise. The dog has been sent away.' 'Sent *away*?' I whispered. 'What do you mean?' 'I mean that I have seen fit to dispose of him,' he answered. I was trembling all over. 'What right had you to dispose of him?' I wanted to know. 'He wasn't your dog—' The answer was that I was to go up to my room and learn Bible verses until the Lord chastened my spirit. Then I said things. I would *not* learn Bible verses. I *would* have my dog. It ended"—Ann was trembling uncontrollably—"it ended with the rod being unspared. God's forgiveness was invoked with each stroke."

She was digging her finger nails into her palms. Katie put her arms around her. "I wouldn't, Ann dear—it isn't worth while. It's all over now. Wouldn't it be better to forget?"

"No, I want to tell you. Some day I may try to tell you other things. I want this to try to explain them. Loving dogs, you will understand this—better than you could some other things.

"The dog had been given away to some one who lived in the country. It was because I had played with him the Sunday morning before and had been late to Sunday-school."

Her voice was dry and hard; it was from Katie there came the exclamation of protest and contempt.

"No one except one who loves dogs as you do would know what it meant. Even you can't quite know. For Tono was all I had. He—"

Katie's arm about her tightened.

"I could have stood it for myself. I could have stood my own lonesomeness. But what I couldn't stand was thinking about him. Nights I would wake up and think of him—out in the cold—homesick—maybe hungry—not understanding—watching and waiting—wondering why I didn't come. I couldn't keep from thinking about things that tortured me. This man was a deacon in my father's church. From the way he prayed, I knew he was not one to be good to dogs.

"And then one afternoon I heard the little familiar scratch at the door. I rushed to it, and there he was—shivering—but oh so, so glad! He sprang right into my arms—we cried and cried together—sitting there on the floor. His heart had been almost broken—he had grieved—*suffered*. He wasn't willing to leave my arms; just whimpering the way one does when a dreadful thing is over—licking my face—you know how they do—you know how dear they are.

"Now I will tell you what I did. Holding him in my arms, my face buried in his fur—I made up my mind. The family would be away for at least an hour. I would give him the happiest hour I knew how to give him. One hour—it was all I had the power to give him. Then—because I loved him so much—I would end his life."

Katie's face whitened. "I carried out the plan," Ann went on. "I gave him the meat we were to have had for supper. I had him do all his little tricks. I loved him and loved him. I do not think any little dog ever had a happier hour.

"And then—down at a house in the next block I saw my father—and the man he had given Tono to. The man was coming to our house for supper. Our time was up.

"I can never explain to any one the way I did it—the way I felt as I did it. There was no crying. There was no faltering. It seemed that all at once I understood—understood the hardness of life—that things *are* hard—that things have *got* to be done. Then was when it came to me that you've got to harden yourself—that it's the only way.

"I filled a tub with water—I didn't know any other way to do it. Tono stood there watching me. I took a bucket. I took up the dog. I hugged him. I let him lick my face. Though I live to be very old, Katie, and suffer very much, I can never forget the look in his eyes as I put him in the water and held him to put down the bucket. There are things a person goes through that make perfect happiness forever impossible. There are hours that stay."

The face of the soldier's daughter was wet. "I love you for it, Ann," she whispered. "I love you for it. It was strong, Ann. It was fine."

"I wasn't very strong and fine the minute it was over," sobbed Ann. "I fainted. They found me there. And then I screamed and laughed and said I was going to kill all the dogs in the world. I said—oh, dreadful things."

"They should have understood," murmured Kate.

"They didn't. They said I was wicked. They said the Evil One had entered into me. They said I must pray God to forgive me for having killed one of his creatures! Me—!

"Of course it ended in Bible verses. Is it so strange I *loathed* the Bible? And every morning I had to hear myself prayed for as a wicked girl who would harm one of God's creatures. The Almighty was implored not to send me to Hell. 'Send me there if you want to,' I'd say to myself on my knees, 'Tono's not in Hell, anyway.'"

Ann laughed bitterly. "So that's why I'm a sacrilegious, blasphemous person who doesn't care much about hearing about God. I associate Him with thin lips that shut together tight-and people who make long prayers and break little dogs' hearts—and with boots—and souls—that squeak. I can't think of one single thing I ever heard about Him that made me like Him."

"Oh, Ann dear!" protested Katie shudderingly.

"Try not to think such things. Try not to feel that way. You haven't heard everything there is to hear about God. You haven't heard any of it in the right way."

"Perhaps not. I only know what I have heard." And Ann's face was too white and hard for Katie to say more.

"And your mother, dear? Where was she all this time? Didn't she love you—and help?"

"She died when I was twelve. She'd like to have loved me. She did some on the sly—in a scared kind of way."

Katie sat there contemplating the picture of Ann's father and mother and Ann—*Ann*, as child of that union.

"I think she died because life frightened her so. In a year my father married again. *She* isn't afraid of anything. She's a God-fearing, exemplary woman. And she always looks to see if you have any mud on your shoes."

After a moment Ann said quietly: "I hate her."

"So would I," said Katie, and it brought the ghost of a smile to Ann's lips, perhaps thinking of just how cordially Katie would hate her.

"And then after a while you left this town?" Katie suggested as Ann seemed held there by something.

"Yes, after a while I left." And that held her again.

"I was fifteen when I—freed Tono from life," she emerged from it. "It was five years later that you—stopped me from freeing myself. Lots of things were crowded into those five years, Katie—or rather into the last three of them. I had to be treated worse than Tono was treated before it came to me that I had better be as kind to myself as I had been to my dog. Only I," Ann laughed, "didn't have anybody to give me a last hour!"

"But you see it wasn't a last hour, after all," soothed Katie. "Only the last hour of the old hard things. Things that can never come back."

"Can't they come back, Katie? Can't they?"

Katie shook her head with decision. "Do you think I'd let them come back? Why I'd shut the door in their face!"

"Sometimes," said Ann, "it seems to me they're lying in wait for me. That they're going to spring out. That this is a dream. That there isn't any Katie Jones. Some nights I've been afraid to go to sleep. Afraid of waking to find it a dream. There's an awful dream I dream sometimes! The dream is that this is a dream."

"Poor dear," murmured Katie. "It will be more real now that we've talked."

"I used to dream a dream, Katie, and I think it was about you. Only you weren't any one thing. You were all kinds of different things. Lovely things. You were Something Somewhere. You were the something that was way off beyond the nothingness of Centralia."

"The something that didn't squeak," suggested Katie tremulously.

"Something Somewhere. You were both a waking and a sleeping dream. I knew you were there. Isn't it queer how we do—know without knowing? My father used to talk about people being 'called.' Called to the ministry—called to the missionary field—called to heaven. Well maybe you're called to other things, too. Maybe," said Ann with a laugh which sobbed, "you're even 'called' to Chicago."

The laugh died and the sob lingered. "Only when you get there—Chicago doesn't seem to know that it had called you.

"My Something Somewhere was always something I never could catch up with. Sometimes it was a beautiful country—where a river wound through a woods. Sometimes it was beautiful people laughing and dancing. Sometimes it was a star. Sometimes it was a field of flowers—all blowing back and forth. Sometimes it was a voice—a wonderful far-away voice. Sometimes it was a lovely dress—oh a wonderful gauzy dress—or a hat that was like the blowing field of flowers. Sometimes—this was the loveliest of all—it was somebody who loved me. But whatever it was, it was something I couldn't overtake.

"And you mustn't laugh, Katie, when I tell you that the thing that made me think I could catch up with it was a moving-picture show!

"It came to Centralia—the first one that had ever been there. I heard the people next door talking about it. They said there were pictures of things that really happened in the great cities—oh of kings and queens and the president and millionaires and automobile races and grand weddings; that the pictures went on just like the happenings went on; that it was just as if the pictures were alive; that it was just like being there.

"Oh, I was so excited about it! I was so excited I could hardly get ready.

"You see ever since Tono had died—two years before, I had kept that idea that things were hard. That the thing to do was to be hard. I dreamed about things that were lovely—the Something Somewhere things—but as far as the real things went I never changed my mind about them. You mustn't let them into your heart. They just wanted to get in there to hurt you.

"Now I forgot all about that. These pictures were dreams made real. They had caught up with the Something Somewhere. And I was going to see them.

"But I didn't—not that day. I was so happy that my father suspected something. And he got it out of me and said I couldn't go. He said that the things that would be pictured would be the wickedness of the world. That I was not to see it.

"But I made up my mind that I would see the wickedness of the world." Ann paused, and then said in lower voice: "And I have—and not just in pictures."

She seemed to be meeting something, and she answered it. "But just the same," she made answer defiantly, "I'd rather see the wickedness of the world than stay in the nothingness of the world!

"The pictures were to be there a week. I thought of nothing else but how I could see them. The last day there was a thimble-bee. I went to the thimble-bee—said I couldn't stay—and went to the pictures.

"Katie, that moving-picture show was proof. Proof of the Something Somewhere. And in my heart I made a vow—it was a *solemn* vow—that I would find the things that moved in the pictures.

"And there was music—such music as I had never heard before, even though it came out of a box. They had the songs of the grand opera singers. And as I listened—I tell you I was called!—I don't care how silly it sounds—I was called by the voices that had sung into that box. For this was real—if the life hadn't been there it couldn't have been caught into the pictures and the box. It proved—I thought—that all the lovely things I had dreamed were true. I had only to go and find them. People were walking upon those streets. Then I could walk on those streets. And those people were laughing—and talking to each other. Everybody seemed to have friends. Everybody was happy! And all of that really *was*. The pictures were alive. Alive with the things that there were out beyond the nothingness of Centralia.

"The man played something from an opera and showed pictures of beautiful people going into a beautiful place to listen to that very music. He said that the very next night in Chicago those people would be going into that place to listen to those very voices.

"Katie, I don't believe you'll laugh at me when I tell you that my teeth fairly chattered when first it came to me that I must be one of those people! It was something all different from the longing for fun—oh it was something big—terrible—it *had* to be. It was the same feeling of its having to be that I had about Tono.

"Though probably that feeling would have passed away if it hadn't been for my father. He came there and found me, and—humiliated me. And after we got home—" Ann was holding herself tight, but after a moment she relaxed to say with an attempted laugh: "It wasn't all being 'called.' Part of it was being driven.

"Then there was another thing. The treasurer of the missionary society came that night with some money—eighteen dollars—I was to send off the next day. It was that money started me out to find my Something Somewhere."

"Oh *Ann!*" whispered Katie, drawing back. "But of course," she added, "you paid it back just as soon as you could?"

"I *never* paid it back! If I had eighteen *million* dollars, I'd *never* pay it back! I *like* to think of not paying it back!"

Katie's face hardened. "I can't understand that."

"No," sobbed Ann, "you'd have to have lived a long time in nothingness to understand that—and some other things, too." She looked at her strangely. "There's more coming, Katie, that you won't be able to understand."

Katie's face was averted, but something in Ann's voice made her turn to her. "I think it was wrong, Ann. There's no use in my pretending I don't. I *can't* understand this. But maybe I can understand some of the other things better than you think."

"I left at six o'clock the next morning," Ann went back to it when she was calmer. "And at the last minute I don't think I would have had the courage to go if my father hadn't been snoring so. How silly it all sounds!

"And the only reason I got on the train was that it would have taken more courage to go back than to go on.

"Katie, some time I'll tell you all about it. How I felt when I got to Chicago. How it seemed to shriek and roar. How I seemed just buried under the noise. How I walked around the streets that day—frightened almost to death—and yet, inside the fright, just crazy about it. And how green I was!

"Nothing seemed to matter except going to grand opera. I didn't even have sense enough to find a place to stay. I thought about it, but didn't know how, and anyhow the most important thing was finding the things that moved in the pictures—and sang in the box.

"I saw a woman go up to a policeman and ask him where something was and he told her, so I did that, too. Asked him where you went to hear grand opera. And he pointed. I was right there by it.

"I heard some people talking about going in to get tickets.
So I thought I had better get a ticket.
"But they didn't have any. They were all gone.

"When I came out I was almost crying. Then a smiling man outside stepped up to me and said he had tickets and he'd let me have one for ten dollars. I was so glad he had them! Ten dollars seemed a good deal—but I didn't think much about it.

"Then I had my ticket and just two dollars left.

"But that night at the opera I didn't know whether I had two dollars, or no dollars, or a thousand dollars. At first I was frightened because everybody but me had on such beautiful clothes. But soon I was too crazy about their clothes to care—and then after the music began—

"Oh, Katie! Suppose you'd always dreamed of something and never been able to catch up with it. Suppose you'd not even been able to really dream it, but just dream that it was, and then suppose it all came—No, I can't tell you. You'd have to have lived in Centralia—and been a minister's daughter.

"My heart sang more beautifully than the singers sang. 'Now you have found it! Now you have found it!' my heart kept singing.

"When all the other people left I left too—in a dream. For it had passed into a dream—into a beautiful dream that was going to shelter it for me forever.

"I stood around watching the beautiful people getting into their carriages. And I couldn't make myself believe that it was in the same world with Centralia.

"Then after a while it occurred to me that all those people were going home. Everybody was going home.

"At first I wasn't frightened. Something inside me was singing over and over the songs of the opera. I was too far in my dream to be much frightened.

"Then all at once I got—oh, so tired. And cold. And so frightened I did not know what to do. My dream seemed to have taken wings and flown away. All the beautiful laughing people had gone. It was just as if I woke up. And I was on the strange streets all alone. Only some noisy men who frightened me.

"I hid in a doorway till those men got by. And then I saw a woman coming. She was all alone, too. She had on a dress that rustled and lovely white furs, and did not seem at all frightened.

"I stepped out and asked her to please tell me where to go for the night.

"Some time I'll tell you about her, too. Now I'll just tell you that it ended with her taking me home with her to stay all night. She made a lot of fun of me—and said things to me I didn't understand—and swore at me—and told me to 'cut it' and go back to the cornfields—but I was crying then, and she took me with her.

"She kept up her queer kind of talk, but I was so tired that the minute I was in bed I went to sleep.

"The next morning she told me I had got to go back to the woods. I said I would if there were any woods. But there weren't. She laughed and said more queer things. She asked me why I had come, and I told her. First she laughed. Then she sat there staring at me—blinking. And what she said was: 'Poor little fool. Poor little greenhorn.'

"She asked me what I was going to do, and I said work, so I could stay there and go to the opera and see beautiful things. She asked me what kind of a job I was figuring on and told me there was only one kind would let me in for that. I asked her what it was and she said it was *her* line. I asked her if she thought I was fitted for it, and she looked at me—a look I didn't understand at all—and said she guessed the men she worked for would think so. I asked her if she'd say a good word to them for me, and then she turned on me like a tiger and swore and said—No, she hadn't come to that!

"It was a case of knowing without knowing. I was so green that I didn't know. And yet after a while I did. As I look back on it I appreciate things I couldn't appreciate then, thank her for things I didn't know enough to thank her for at the time.

"She was leaving that day for San Francisco. She gave me ten dollars, and told me if I had any sense I'd take it and go back to prayer-meeting. She said I might do worse. But if I didn't have any sense—and she said of course I wouldn't—I was to be careful of it until I got a job. She told me how to manage. And I was to read 'ads' in the newspaper. She told me how to try and get in at the telephone office. She had been there once, she said, but it 'got on her nerves.'

"She told me things about girls who worked in Chicago—awful things. But I supposed she was prejudiced. The last things she said to me was—'The opera! Oh you poor little green kid—I'm afraid I see your finish.'

"But I thought she was queer acting because she led that queer kind of a life."

Ann had paused. And suddenly she hid her face in her hands, as if it was more than she could face. Katie was smoothing her hair.

"Katie, as the days went on it was just as hard to believe that the world of the opera was the same world I was working in—right there in the same city—as it had been the first night to believe it was the same world as Centralia. I learned two things. One was that the Something Somewhere was there. The other that it was not there for me.

"The world was full of things I couldn't understand, but I could understand—a little better—the woman who wore the white furs.

"Oh Katie, you get so tired—you get so dead—all day long putting suspenders in a box—or making daisies—or addressing envelopes—or trying to remember whether it was apple or custard pie—

"And you don't get tired just because your back aches—and your head aches—and your hands ache—and your feet ache—you get tired—that kind of tired—because the city doesn't care how tired you get!

"I often wondered why I went on, why any of them went on. I used to think we must be crazy to be going on."

She was pondering it—somberly wistful. "Though perhaps we're not crazy. Perhaps it's the—call. Katie, what is it? That call? That thing that makes us keep on even when our Something Somewhere won't have anything to do with us?"

Katie did not reply. She had no reply.

"At last I got in the telephone office. That's considered a fine place to work. They're like Miss Osborne; they believe it is one of the fundamental principles of life that all must have pleasures. But they were like the pleasures of Centralia—not God-fearing, exactly, but so dutiful. They didn't have anything to do with 'calls.'

"The real pleasures were going over the wire. It was my business to make the connections that arrange those pleasures. A little red light would flash—sometimes it would flash straight into my brain—and I'd say 'Number, please?'—always with the rising inflection. Then I'd get the connection and Life would pass through the cords. That was the closest I came to it—operating the cords that it went through. There was a whole city full of it—beautiful, laughing, loving Life. But it was on the wire—just as in Centralia it had been in the pictures—and in the box. And oh I used to get so tired—so tight—operating the cords for Life. Sometimes when I left my chair the whole world was one big red light. And at night they danced dances for me—those little red lights."

She brushed her hand before her eyes as if they were there again and she would push them away. "Katie," she suddenly burst forth, "if you ever do pray—if you believe in praying—pray sometimes for the girl who goes to Chicago to find what you call the 'joy of living.' Pray for the pilgrims who go to the cities to find their Something Somewhere. And whatever you do, Katie—whatever you do—don't ever laugh at the people who kill themselves because they're tired of not having any fun!"

"But wasn't there *any* fun, dear?"Katie asked after a moment.

Ann did not speak, but looked at Katie strangely. "Yes," she said. "Afterwards. Differently."

They were silent. Something seemed to be outlining itself between them.
Something which was meaning to grow there between them.

"There came a time," said Ann, "when all of life was not going over the wire."

And still Katie did not speak, as if pushed back by that thing shaping itself between them.

"Your Something Somewhere," said Ann, very low, "doesn't always come in just the way you were looking for it. But, Katie, if you get *very* tired waiting for it—don't you believe you might take it—most any way it came?"

It was a worn and wistful face she turned to Katie. Suddenly Katie brushed away the thing that would grow up between them and laid her cheek upon Ann's hair. "Poor child," she murmured, and the tears were upon Ann's soft brown hair. "Poor weary little pilgrim."

CHAPTER XXII

Ann remained in her room all of the next day. Katie encouraged her to do so, wishing to foster the idea of illness.

It did not need much fostering. She had not gone back to those old days without leaving with them most of her newly accumulated vitality. But it was weakness rather than nervousness. Talking to Katie seemed to have relieved a pressure.

It was Katie who was nervous. It was as if a battery within her had been charged to its uttermost. She was in some kind of electric communication with life. She was tingling with the things coming to her.

So charged was she with new big things that it was hard to manage the affairs of her household as old things demanded they be managed that day. She told Mrs. Prescott again how sorry she and Ann were that Ann had given way. Mrs. Prescott received it with self-contained graciousness. Her one comment was that she trusted when her son decided to marry he would content himself with a wife who had not gone upon a quest.

Katie smiled and agreed that it might get him a more comfortable wife.

The son himself she tried to avoid. That thing which had tried to shape itself between her and Ann still remained there, a thing without body but vaguely outlined between Ann and all other things.

They had not drawn any nearer to it. They let the story rest at the place where all of life had not been going over the wire.

And Katie told herself that she understood. That Ann was to be judged by the Something Somewhere she had formed in her heart rather than by whatever it was life had tardily and ungenerously and unwisely brought her.

That Ann might still cling to a Something Somewhere—a thing for which even yet she would keep the heart right—was suggested that afternoon when Katie told her of Captain Prescott.

She had not meant to tell her. She tried to think she was doing it in order to know how to meet Harry, but had to admit finally that she did it for no nobler reason than to see how Ann would take it.

She took it most unexpectedly. "I am sorry," she said simply, "but I do not care at all for Captain Prescott. I—" She paused, coloring slightly as she said with a little laugh: "We all like to be liked, don't we, Katie? And with me—well it meant something just to know I could be liked—in that nice kind of way. It helped. But that's all—so I hope he doesn't care very much for me. Though if he does," concluded Ann sagely, "he'll get over it. He's not the caring sort."

The words had a familiar sound; after a moment she remembered them as what he had said that night of the "Don't You Care" girls.

While she would have been panic-stricken at finding Ann interested, she was more discomfited than relieved at not finding her more impressed. "To marry into the army, Ann," she said, "is considered very advantageous."

Ann was lying there with her face pillowed upon her hand. She turned her large eyes, about which just then there were large circles, seriously, it would even seem rebukingly, upon Katie. "If I ever should marry," she said, "it will be for some other reason than because it is 'advantageous.'"

Katie felt both rebuked and startled. Most of the girls she knew—girls who had never worked in factories or restaurants or telephone offices, or had never thought of taking their own lives, had not scorned to look upon marriages as advantageous.

Nor, for that matter, had Katie herself.

Ann's superior attitude toward marriage turned Katie to religion. As the niece of a bishop she was moved to set Ann right on things within a bishop's domain. And underlying that was an impulse to set her right with herself.

"Ann," she said, "if somebody said to you, 'I starve you in the name of Katie Jones,' wouldn't you say, 'Oh no you don't. Starve me if you want to, but don't tell me you do it in the name of Katie Jones. She doesn't want people starved!'"

"I could say that," said Ann, "because I know you, and know you don't want people starved. But if I'd never heard anything about you except that I was to be starved in your name—"

"I should think even so you might question. Didn't it ever occur to you that God had more to do with your Something Somewhere than He did with things done in His name in Centralia?"

"Why, Katie, how strange you should think of that. For I thought of it—but I supposed it was the most wicked thought of all."

"How strange it would be," said Katie, "if He had more to do with the 'call' than with the God-fearing things you were called from."

For an instant Ann's face lighted up. But it hardened. "Well, if He had," she said, "it seems He might have stood by me a little better after I was 'called.'"

Katie had no reply for that, so she turned to her uncle, the Bishop.

"Well there's one place where you're wrong, Ann; and that is that religion is incompatible with the love of dogs. You know my uncle—my mother's brother—is a bishop. I don't know just how well uncle understands God, but if he understands Him as well as he does dogs then he must be well fitted for his office. I don't think in his heart uncle would have any respect for any person—no matter how religious—or even how much they subscribed—who wouldn't appreciate the tragedy of losing one's dog. Uncle has a splendid dog—a Great Dane; they're real chums. He often reads his sermons to Caesar. He says Caesar can stay awake under them longer than some of the congregation. I once shocked, but I think secretly delighted uncle, by saying that he rendered to Caesar the things that were Caesar's and to God what Caesar left. Well, one dreadful day someone stole Caesar. They took him out of town, but Caesar got away and made a return that has gone down into dog history. Poor uncle had been all broken up about it for three days. He was to preach that morning. My heart ached for him as he stood there at his study window looking down the street when it was time to go. I knew what he was hoping for—the way you go on hoping against hope when your dog's lost. And then after uncle had gone, and just as I was ready to start myself, I heard the great deep bark of mighty Caesar! You may know I was wild about it—and crazy to get the news to uncle. I hurried over to church, but service had begun. But because I was bursting to tell it, and because I appreciated something of what it would mean to talk about the goodness of God when you weren't feeling that way, I wrote a little note and sent it up. I suppose the people who saw it passed into the chancel in dignified fashion thought it was something of ecclesiastical weight. What it said was, 'Hallelujah—he's back—safe and sound. K—.'

"It was great fun to watch uncle—he's very dignified in his official capacity. He frowned as it was handed him, as if not liking the intrusion into holy routine. He did not open it at once but sat there holding it rebukingly—me chuckling down in the family pew. Then he adjusted his glasses and opened it—ponderously. I wish you could have seen his face! One of our friends said he supposed it read, 'Will give fifty thousand.' He quickly recalled his robes and suppressed his grin, contenting himself with a beatific expression which must have been very uplifting to the congregation. I think

I never saw uncle look so spiritual. And I know I never heard him preach as feelingly. When he came to the place about when sorrow has been upon the heart, and seemed more than the heart could bear, but when the weight is lifted, as the loving Father so often does mercifully lift it—oh I tell you there were tears in more eyes than uncle's. I had my suspicions, and that night I asked, 'Uncle, did you preach the sermon you meant to preach this morning?' And uncle—if he weren't a bishop I would say he winked at me—replied, 'No, dear little shark. I had meant to preach the one about man yearning for Heaven because earth is a vale of tears.' I'm just telling you this yarn, Ann, to make you see that religion doesn't necessarily rule out the love of dogs."

"It's a nice story, and I'm glad you told me," replied Ann. "Only my father would say that your uncle had no religion."

Katie laughed. "A remark which has not gone unremarked. Certainly he hasn't enough to let it harden his heart. As I am beginning to think about things now it seems to me uncle might stand for more vital things than he does, but for all that I believe he can love God the more for loving Caesar so well."

They were quiet for a time, thinking of Ann's father and Katie's uncle; the love of God and the love of dogs and the love of man. Many things. Then Ann said: "Naturally you and I don't look at it the same way. I see you were brought up on a pleasant kind of religion. The kind that doesn't matter."

That phrase started the electric batteries within Katie and the batteries got so active she had to go for a walk.

In the course of the walk she stopped at the shops to see Wayne. She wanted to know if he would let Worth go into the country for a week with Ann. An old servant of theirs—a woman who had been friend as well as servant to Katie's mother—lived on a farm about ten miles up the river and it had been planned that Worth—and Katie, too, if she would—go up there for a week or more during the summer. It seemed just the thing for Ann. It would get her away from Captain Prescott and his mother, and from Major Darrett, who was coming in a few days. Katie believed Ann would like to be away from them all for about a week, and get her bearings anew. And Katie herself would like to be alone for a time and get her bearings, too, and make some plans. In one way or other she was going to help Ann find her real Something Somewhere. Perhaps she would take her to Europe. But until things settled down, as Katie vaguely put it, she thought it just the thing for Ann to have the little trip with Worth.

Wayne listened gravely, but did not object. He was quiet, and, Katie thought, not well. She suggested that working so steadily during the hot weather was not good for him.

He laughed shortly and pointed through the open door to the shops where long rows of men were working at forges—perspiration streaming down their faces.

But instead of alluding to them he asked abruptly: "How is she today?"

"Tired," said Katie. "She didn't sleep well last night."

Something in the way he was looking at her brought to Katie acute realization of how much she cared for Wayne. He was her big brother. She had always been his little sister. They were not giving to thinking of it that way—certainly not speaking of it—but the tenderness of the relationship was there. Consciousness of it came now as she seemed to read in Wayne's look that she hurt him in withholding her confidence, in not having felt it possible to trust even him.

She broke under that look. "Wayne dear," she said unevenly, "I don't deny there is something to tell. I'd like to tell you, if I could. If ever I can, I will."

His reply was only to dismiss it with a curt little nod.

But Katie knew that did not necessarily mean that he was feeling curt.

She was drawn back to the open door from which she could see the long double line of men working steadily at the forges.

"What are those men doing?" she asked.

"Forging one of the parts of a rifle," he replied.

It recalled what the man who mended the boats had said of the saddles: that the first war those saddles would see would be the war over the manufacture of them. Would he go so far as to say the first use for the rifles—?

Surely not. He must have been speaking figuratively.

But something in the might of the thing—the long lines of men at work on rifles to be used in a possible war—made the industrial side of it seem more vital and more interesting than the military phase. This was here. This was real. There was practically no military life at the Arsenal—not military life in the sense one found it at the cavalry post. That had made it seem, from a military standpoint, uninteresting. But here was the real life—over in what the women of the quarter vaguely called "the shops," and dismissed as disposed of by the term.

Suddenly she wondered what all those men thought about God. Whether either the hard blighting religion of Ann's father, or the aesthetic comfortable religion of her uncle "mattered" much to them?

Were the things which "mattered" forging a religion of their own?

But just what were those things that mattered?

A young man had entered and was speaking to Wayne. After a second's hesitation Wayne introduced him to Katie as Mr. Ferguson, who was helping him.

He had an open, intelligent face—this young mechanic. He did not seem overwhelmed at being presented to Captain Jones' sister, but merely replied pleasantly to her greeting and was turning away.

But Katie was not going to let him get away. If she could help it, Katie was not going to let any one get away who she thought could tell her anything about the things which were perplexing her—all those things pressing closer and closer upon her.

"Do many of these men go to church?" she asked.

He appeared startled. Katie's gown did not suggest a possible tract concealed about it.

"Why yes, some of them," he laughed. "I don't think the majority of them do."

Then she came right out with it. "What would you say they look upon as the most important thing in life?"

He looked startled again, but in more interested way. "Higher wages and shorter hours," he said.

"Are you a socialist?" she demanded.

It came so unexpectedly and so bluntly that it confused him. "Why, Katie," laughed her brother, "what do you mean by coming over here and interviewing men on their politics?"

"What made you think I was a socialist?" asked Ferguson.

"Because you had such a quick answer to such a big question, and seemed so sure of yourself. I'm reading a book about socialists. They don't seem to think there is a particle of doubt they could put the world to rights, and things are so intricate—so confused—I don't see how they can be so sure they're saying the final word."

"I don't know that they claim to be saying the final word, but they do know they could take away much of the confusion."

Katie was thinking of the story she had heard the night before. "Do you think socialism's going to remove all the suffering from the world? Reach all the aches and fill all the empty places? Get right into the inner things that are the matter and bring peace and good will and loving kindness everywhere?"

She had spoken impetuously, and paused with an embarrassed laugh. The young mechanic was looking at her gravely, but his look was less strange than Wayne's.

"I don't think they'd go that far, Miss Jones. But they do know that there's a lot of needless misery they could wipe out."

"They're out and out materialists, aren't they? Everything's economic—the economic basis for everything in creation. They seem very cocksure that getting that the way they want it would usher in the millennium. You said the most important thing in life to these men was higher wages and shorter hours. I don't blame them for wanting them—I hope they get them—but I don't know that I see it as very promising that they regard it as the most important thing in life. To do less and get more is not what you'd call a spiritual aspiration, is it?" she laughed. "This is what I mean—it's not the end, is it?"

"Socialists wouldn't call it the end. But it's got to be the end until it can become the means."

"Yes, but if you get in the habit of looking at it as an end, will there be anything left for it to be a means to?"

"Why yes, those spiritual aspirations you mention."

"Unless by that time the world's such an economic machine it doesn't want spiritual aspirations."

"Well Heaven help the working man that's got them in the present economic machine," said Ferguson a little impatiently.

She, too, moved impatiently. "Oh I don't know a thing about it. It's absurd for me to be talking about it."

"Why I don't think it's at all absurd, only I don't think you see the thing clear to the end, and I wish you could talk to somebody who sees farther than I do. I'm new to it myself. Now there's a man doing a lot of boat repairing up here above the Island. I wish you could talk to him. He'd know just what you mean, and just how to meet you."

"Oh, would he?" said Katie. "What's his name?"

"Mann. Alan Mann."

"Why, Katie," laughed Wayne, "it must be that he's that same mythical creature known as the man who mends the boats."

"Yes," said Katie, "I fancy he's the very same mythical creature."

"My little boy talks about him," Wayne explained.

"Yes, he's the same one. I've seen him talking to your little boy and one of the soldiers. He's a queer genius."

"In what way is he a queer genius?" asked Katie.

"Why—I don't know. He's always got a way of looking at a thing that you hadn't seen yourself." He looked up with a little smile from the tool he was trying to adjust. "I'd like to have you tell him you were worrying about socialism hurting spiritual aspirations."

"Would he annihilate me?"

"No, he wouldn't want to annihilate you, if he thought you were trying to find out about things. He'd guide you."

"Oh—so he's a guide, is he? Is he a spiritual or an economic guide?" she laughed.

"I think he might combine them," he replied, laughing too.

"He must be remarkable," said Kate.

"He is remarkable, Miss Jones," gravely replied the admirer of the man who mended the boats. "I wish you could have heard him talking to a crowd of men last Sunday."

"Dear me—is he a public speaker?"

"Yes—in a way. And he writes things."

Katie wanted to ask what things, but they were cut short by the entrance of Captain Prescott. It was curious how his entrance did cut them short. She smiled to herself, wondering what he would have thought of the conversation.

He followed her to the door and inquired for Miss Forrest. His manner was constrained, but his eyes were begging for an explanation. He looked unhappy, and Katie hurried away from him. It seemed she could not bear to have any more unhappiness come pressing against her, even the unhappiness she was confident would pass away.

In her mood of that day it seemed to Katie that the affairs of the world were too involved for any one to have a solution for them. Life surged in too fiercely—too uncontrollably—to be contained within a formula.

As she continued her walk, winding in and out of the wooded paths, awe spread its great wings about her at thought of the complexity and the fathomlessness of the relationships of life. She had but a little peep into them, but that peep held the suggestion of limitlessness.

Because a lonely girl in a barren little town in Indiana had dreamed dreams which life would not deliver to her, life now was beating in upon Katie Jones. Because Ann had been foiled in her quest for happiness, sobering shadows were falling across the sunny path along which Katie had tripped. Did life thwarted in one place take it out in another? Because Ann could not find joy was it to be that Katie could not have peace? Had Ann's yearning for love been the breath blowing to flame Katie's yearning for understanding? Because Ann could not dream her way to realities did it mean that Katie must fight her way to them?

They were such big things—such resistless things—these wild new things which were sweeping in upon her. With the emotion of the world surging in and out like that how could any one claim to have a solution for the whole question of living?

She seemed passing into a country too big and too dark for her of the sunny paths. She needed a guide. She grew lonely at thought of how badly she needed her guide.

She turned for comfort to thought of the things she would do for Ann. She would pay it back in revealing to Ann the beauty of the world. She would assume the responsibility of the Something Somewhere. Perhaps in fulfilling a dream she would find a key to reality.

She found pleasure in the vision of Ann in the old world cathedrals. How wisely they had builded—builders of those old cathedrals—in expressing religion through beauty. At peace in the beauty of form, might Ann not find an inner beauty? She believed Ann's nature to be an intensely religious one. How might Ann's soul not flower when she at last saw God as a God of beauty?

Thus she soothed herself in building a future for Ann. Sought to appease those surgings of life with promise that Ann should at last find the loveliness of life.

But in the end it led to a terrifying vision. A vision of thousands upon thousands of other dreamers of dreams whose soul stuff might be slowly ebbing away in long dreary days of putting suspenders in boxes. Of thousands of other girls who might be growing faint in operating the wires for life. Oh, she had power to fill Ann's life—but would that have power to still for her the mocking whispers from the dreams which had died slow deaths in all the other barren lives? Even though she took Ann from the crowd to a far green hill of happiness, would not Katie herself see from that far green hill all the other girls "called" to life, going forth as pilgrims with the lovely love-longing in their hearts only to find life waiting to seize them for the work of the woman who wore the white furs?

A sob shook Katie. The woe of the world seemed surging just beneath her—rising so high that it threatened to suck her in.

But because she was a fighter she mastered the sob and vowed that rather than be sucked in to the woe of the world she would find out about the world. Certainly she would sit apart no longer. She would study. She would see. She would live.

Life had become a sterner and a bigger thing. She would meet it in a sterner and bigger way. To understand! That was the greatest thing in life.

That passion to understand grew big within her. How could she hope to go laughing through a world which sobbed? How turn from life when she saw life suffering? Why she could not even turn from a little bird which she saw suffering!

There was a noble wistfulness in her longing to talk again with the man who mended the boats.

CHAPTER XXIII

In temporary relaxation from the stress of that mood she was glad to see her friend Major Darrett.

He did not suggest the woe of the world. Because the big new things had become—for the moment, at least—too much for her, there was rest in the shelter of the small familiar things.

So much of the unknown had been beating against her that she was glad for a little laughing respite in the known.

He stood for a world she knew how to deal with. In that he seemed to offer shelter; not that he would be able to do it for long.

He always roused a particular imp in Katie which wanted to be flirtatious. She found now, with a certain relief, that the grave things of life had not exterminated that imp. She would scarcely have felt acquainted with herself had it perished.

And because she was so pleased to find it alive she let it grow very live indeed.

Ann and Worth had been gone for five days. Ann had seemed to like the idea of going. She said she would be glad to be alone for a time and "rest up," as she vaguely put it. Katie told her that when she came back they would make some plans; and she told her she was not to worry about things; that everything was going to be all right.

Ann received it with childlike trust. She seemed to think that it was all in Katie's hands, to accept with a child's literalness that Katie would not let the old things come back, that she would "shut the door in their face."

Other things were in Katie's hands that day: preparations for a big dinner they were giving that night.

It was for some cavalry people who were stopping there. And in addition to the cavalry officers and their wives there was a staff officer from Washington who was valuable to Wayne just then. Katie was anxious that the dinner be a success. She was glad Major Darrett was there. He went a long way toward assuring its success.

And Zelda Fraser was with the party. Katie had seen her for a moment that morning, and would see her again at night. She was stopping with Caroline Osborne, whom she had known at school.

Zelda did not suggest the woe of the world. Neither did she suggest the dreams of the world.

It was early in the afternoon and the Major and Katie were having a conference. He was acquainted with the palate of the visiting staff officer, and was assuring Katie that she was on the way to his good graces.

They had gone into the library, where Katie was arranging flowers. He offered a suggestion there, too. He had an intuitive knowledge of such things, seemed to be guided by inner promptings as to which bowl should hold the lavender sweet peas and which the pink ones.

Though Katie disputed his judgment, glad to be on ground where she could dispute with assurance. They argued it hotly, as if sweet peas were the most vital things in the world. It was good to be venting all one's feeling on things so tangible and knowable as sweet peas.

Her dinner safe in the hands of experts, Katie made herself comfortable and told her friend the Major that she wished now to be put in a brilliant mood. That a brilliant mood was the one thing the skilled laborers in possession of her house could not furnish.

He gallantly defied any laborer in the world to be so skilled as to get Katie out of a brilliant mood.

She told him that was silly, that she had grown very stupid.

He challenged her to prove it.

Katie felt very much at home with him; not merely at home with him the individual, but comfortably at home with the things he represented. It gave her a nice homelike feeling to be flirting with him.

And flirting with him herself, she grew interested in all those others who had flirted with him—she knew they were legion. She seemed to see them off there in the background—a lovely group of spoiled darlings. She did not suppose many of them were much the worse for having flirted with Major Darrett. Suddenly she laughed and told him she regarded him as one of the great educators of the age. He wanted to know in what way he was a great educator. Katie would not tell him. There ensued a gay discussion from which she emerged feeling as if she had had a cocktail.

And looking that way; looking, at least so he seemed to think, from the manner in which he leaned forward regarding her—most attractive, her cheeks so pink, her eyes dancing a little dance of defiance at him, and on her lips a mocking little smile, more sophisticated than any smile he had ever seen before on Katie's lips. "Katie of the laughing eyes" —he had once called her. She was leaning back lazily, a suggestion of insolence in her assurance. As she leaned back that way he marked the lines of her figure as he had never marked them before. He had previously thought of Katie as a good build for golf. Now that did not seem to express the whole of it—and Katie seemed to know it would not express the whole of it. And in summarizing Katie as having a good build for golf he had not properly appraised Katie's foot. It was thrust out now from her very short skirt as if Katie were quite willing he should know it for a lovely foot. And her arm, which was hanging down from the side of the chair, seemed conscious of being something more than a good arm for golf.

She looked so like a child, and yet so lurkingly like a woman. It gave him a new sense of Katie. It blew the warm breath of life over an idea he had had when he came there.

He had just come from Zelda Fraser, having had luncheon at the Osbornes'. He had once thought Zelda stimulating. Now she did not seem at all stimulating in comparison with Katie. She was too obvious. That lurking something in Katie's eyes, that mysterious smile she had, made Katie seem subtle.

If this were to be added to all her other charms—

Katie had always seemed delightfully daring in an innocent sort of way. It seemed now she might be capable of being subtle in a sophisticated way. He had always thought of Katie as romping. A distinguished and quite individual form of romping. She even had a romping imagination. He loved her for her merriness, for her open sunniness. That had been an impersonal love, not very different from the way he might have loved a sister. In fact he had more than once wished Katie were his little sister instead of Wayne's.

He did not wish that now.

She became too fascinating and too desirable in her mysterious new complexity. There was zest in discovering Katie after he had known her so long.

And her eyes and her smile seemed jeering at him for having been such a long while in discovering her.

He wanted to kiss her. That mocking little smile seemed daring him to kiss her. And yet he did not dare to. It seemed part of Katie's lovely new complexity that she could invite and forbid at one and the same time.

Now Zelda could not have done more than the inviting—and so many could invite.

He rose and stood near her. "Katie, you don't mean to marry Prescott, do you?"

She clapped her hands above her head and laughed like a child immensely tickled about something.

He laughed, too, and then asked to be informed what he was laughing at.

"Oh, you're just laughing because I am," laughed Katie.

"Then may I ask, mysterious one, what you're laughing at?"

"Oh I'm laughing at a tumble I once took. 'Twas such a tumble."

"I'd like to tumble to the tumble."

"You would like it. You'd love it."

"I hadn't thought," said the Major, "that when I asked if you meant to marry Prescott I was classifying with the great humorists of all time."

"And I hadn't thought," she returned, "that when I thought Prescott meant to marry me I was classifying with the great tumblers of all time!"

Suddenly she stopped laughing. "No, I don't mean to marry Harry, and I can further state with authority that Harry doesn't mean to marry me."

The laughter went from even her eyes—thinking, perhaps, of whom Harry did mean to marry.

But she was not going to let herself become grave. If she grew quiet she would know again about the woe of the world—surging right underneath. The only way not to know it was underneath was to keep merrily dancing away in one's place on top of it. She made a curious little gesture of flicking something from her hand and whistled a romping little tune.

He stood there surveying her. "It wouldn't do at all for you to marry Prescott, Katie. He's a likeable enough fellow, but with it all something of a duffer."

"Just what kind of man," asked Katie demurely, "would you say I had better marry?"

He sat down in a chair nearer her. "Just what kind of man would you like to marry?"

"How do you know," she asked, still demurely, "that I would like to marry any?"

"Oh you must have a guide, Katie. You must be guided through this wicked world."

She bit her lip and turned away when he told her she must have a guide.

But she turned back, and seriously. "Is it a wicked world?"

With that he ventured to pat the hand now lying on the arm of the chair so near him. "Well you'll never know it, if it is. We'll keep it all from you, Katie. You're safe."

Katie pulled her hand away petulantly. "If there's anything I don't want to be," she said, "it's safe."

That seemed to amuse him. "I only meant," he laughed, "safe from the great outer world."

"Tell me," said Katie, "what's in the great outer world?"

He sat there smiling at her as one would smile at a dear inquisitive child.

"Have you made many excursions into the great outer world?" she asked boldly.

"Oh yes," he replied lightly, "I've been something of an explorer. All men, you know, Katie, are born explorers. Though for the most part I must say I find our own little world the more attractive."

Then he surprised her. "Katie, would you think a man a brute to propose to a girl on the day she was giving an important dinner?"

But right there she pulled herself in. "No more tumbles!" thought Katie.

"It would seem rather inconsiderate, wouldn't it? Such a man wouldn't seem to have a true sense of values."

"Well, dinner or no dinner, the man I have in mind has a true sense of values. He has a true sense of values because he knows Katherine Wayneworth Jones for the most desirable thing in all the world."

It did surprise her, and the surprise grew. None of them had thought of Major Darrett as what they called a marrying man.

And on the heels of the surprise came a certain sense of triumph. Katie knew that any of the girls in what he called their little world would be looking upon it as a moment of triumph, and there was triumph in gaining what others would regard as triumph.

"How old are you, Katie?" he asked.

She told him.

"Twenty-five. And I'm forty-one. Is that prohibitive?"

She looked at him, thinking how lightly the years had touched him—how lightly, in all probability, they would touch him. He had distinctly the military bearing. He would have that same bearing at sixty. And that same charm. He was one to whom experience gave the gift of charm more insidiously than youth could give it.

Life would be more possible with him than with any man she knew within the enclosure. If one were to go dancing and smiling and flirting through the world Major Darrett would be the best possible man to go with.

As she looked at him, smiling at her half tenderly and half humorously, life with Major Darrett presented itself as such an attractive thing that there was almost pain in the thought of not being able to take it.

For deep within her she never questioned not being able to take it. But for the moment—

"You see, Katie," he was saying, "I would be the best possible one for you to be married to, because you could go right on having flirtations. Of course I needn't tell you, Katie dear, that you're a flirt. The trouble with your marrying most fellows would be that they wouldn't like it."

"And of course," she replied, "I would be a good one for you to marry because having my own flirtations I wouldn't be in a position to be critical about yours."

He laughed quite frankly.

Katie leaned back and sat there smiling at him, that new baffling smile he found so alluring.

"But do you know, Katie, I think, for a long time, anyway, we could keep busy flirting with each other."

"And we would keep all the busier," she said, "knowing that the minute we stopped flirting with each other one of us would get busy flirting with somebody else."

He laughed delightedly. "Katie, where did you learn it was very fetching to say outrageous things so demurely?"

"Tell me," said Katie, more seriously, "why do you want to marry?"

"Until about an hour ago I wanted to marry—oh for the most bromidic of reasons. Just because, in the natural course of events, it seemed the next thing for me to do. I'll even be quite frank and confess I had thought of you in that bromidic version of it. Had thought of it as 'eminently suitable'—also, eminently desirable. We'd like to do the same things. We'd get on—be good fellows together. But now I want to marry—and I want to marry *you*—because I think you're quite the most fascinating thing in all the world!"

Lightly and yet seriously he spoke of things—of his own prospects. She knew how good they were. Of where and how they would probably live;—a pleasant picture it was he could draw. It would mean life along the sunny paths. And very sunny indeed it seemed they would be—if possible at all. Certainly one would never have to explain any of one's jokes to Major Darrett.

For just a moment she let herself drift into it. And knowing she was drifting, and not knowing it was for just the moment, he rose and bent over her chair.

"Katie," he whispered, and there was passion in his voice, "I think I can make you fall in love with me."

The little imp in Katie took possession. And something deeper than the little imp stirred vaguely at sound of that thing in his voice. She raised her face so that it was turned up to him. "You think you could? Now I wonder."

"Oh you wonder, do you—you exasperating little wretch! Well just give me a chance—"

But suddenly he was standing at attention, his face colorless. Katie jumped up guiltily, and there leaning against the door—all huddled down and terrible looking—was Ann.

"Why, Katie," she whispered thickly—"*Katie*! But you told me—you *promised* me—that you would *shut the door in his face*."

CHAPTER XXIV

It took her a number of seconds to get the fact that they must know each other.

And even then she could get no grip on the situation. She was too shaken by having jumped—as though she were some vulgar housemaid!

And why was Ann looking like that! She looked dreadful—huddled up that way as if some one was going to beat her!

"Why you can't know each other," said Katie wildly. "How could you know each other? Where would you know each other? And if you *do* know each other,"—turning upon him furiously—"need we all act like thieves?"

He tried to speak, but seemed unable to. He had lost command of himself, save in so far as standing very straight was concerned.

She wished Ann would stand up! It gave her such an awful sense of shame to see Ann huddled like that.

"Katie," Ann whispered, "you told me—"

"I never told you I'd shut the door in Major Darrett's face!" said Katie harshly. "And what are you talking about? What does this all mean?"

He had recovered himself. "Why it merely means, Katie, that we— as you surmised—at one time—knew each other. The—the acquaintance terminated—not pleasantly. That's all. A slight surprise for the moment. No harm done."

Then Ann did stand straight. "It means," she said shrilly, "that if I had never known him"—pointing at him—"you would never have found me there." She pointed down toward the river. "Oh no, no harm done, of course—No harm done—"

"Please let us try and keep very quiet," said Katie coldly. "It is—it is vulgar enough at best. Let us be as quiet—as decent as we can."

Ann crouched down again as though struck.

Then Katie laughed, bitterly. "Why really, it's quite as good as a play, isn't it? It's quite a scene, I'm sure."

"It needn't be," said he soothingly, and relaxing a little. "I own I was startled for the moment, and—discomfited. But you were quite right—we'll go into no hysterics. What I can't understand"—looking from one to the other—"is what she's doing *here*."

Katie's head went up. "She's here, I'll have you know, as my friend. Just as you're here as my friend."

She thought Ann was going to fall, and her heart softened a little. "Suppose you go up to my room, Ann. Lie down. Just—just lie down. Keep quiet. Why did you come home? Is something wrong?"

Ann whispered that Worth had a sore throat. She had a chance to come down in an automobile. She thought she had better. She was sorry she had.

"All right," said Katie. "It's all right. Just go lie down. I'll look after Worth—and you—in a minute."

Ann left the room and Katie turned to the Major. "Well?"

"You're so sensible, Katie," he said hurriedly, "in feeling the thing to do is make no fuss about things. Nothing is to be gained—But for God's sake, Katie, what is she doing here? Where did *you* know her?"

"Oh you tell first," said Katie, smiling a hard smile. "You tell where you found her, then I'll tell where I found her."

"Really—really," he said stiffly, "I must refuse to discuss such a matter with *you*. I can only repeat—she has no business here."

"Then pray why have you any business here?"

He flushed angrily. But restrained himself and said persuasively: "Why, Katie, she's not one of us."

"She's one of *me*," said Katie. "She's my friend."

"I can only say again," he said shortly, "that she has no business to be."

"As I am to be kept so safe from the wicked world," said Katie stingingly, "I presume it is not proper you discuss the matter with me. I take it, however, that she was one of those 'excursions' into the great outer world?"

"Well," he said defiantly, "and what if she was? She was willing to be, I guess. She wasn't knocked down with a club."

"Oh, no! Oh, my no! That wouldn't be your method. And when one is tired of exursions—I suppose one is at perfect liberty to abandon them—?"

"Nonsense! You can't trump up anything of that sort. She wasn't 'abandoned.' She left in the night."

He colored. "I beg your pardon. But as long as we're speaking frankly—"

"Oh pray," said Katie, "let's not be overly delicate in this delicate little matter!"

"Very well then. Her coming was her own choice. Her going away was her own choice. I can see that I have no great responsibility in the matter."

"Why how clever you must be," said Katie, all the while smiling that hard smile, "to be able to argue it like that."

He was standing there with folded arms. "I think I was very decent to her. All things considered—in view of the nature of the affair—I consider that I was very decent."

Katie laughed. "Maybe you were. I found her in the very act of committing suicide."

He paled, but quickly recovered himself. "That was not my affair. There must have been—something afterward."

"Maybe. I'm sure I don't know. But you were the beginning, weren't you?" Suddenly she buried her face in her hands. "Oh I didn't think—I didn't think it could get in here! It's everywhere! It's everywhere! It's *getting* me!"

"Katie—dear Katie," he murmured, "don't. We'll get you out of this. You wanted to be kind. It was just a mistake of yours. We'll fix it up. Don't cry." And he put an arm about her.

She stood before him with clenched hands, eyes blazing.

"Don't touch me! Don't you touch me!" And she left him.

In the hall Nora stopped her to say there were not enough champagne glasses. She made no reply. Champagne glasses—!

She looked after Worth. Then she went to Ann.

"Well, Ann," she began, her voice high pitched and unsteady, "this is about the limit, isn't it?"

"Oh Katie," moaned Ann, "you told me—you told me— you understood. Why, Katie—you must have known there was some one."

"Oh I knew there was some one, all right," said Katie, her voice getting higher and higher, her cheeks more and more red—"only I just hadn't figured, you see, on its being some one I knew! Why how under the sun," she asked, laughing wildly, "did you ever meet Major Darrett?"

"I—I'll try to tell you," faltered Ann miserably. "I want to. I want to make you understand. Katie!—I'll die if you don't understand!"

She looked so utterly wretched that Katie made heroic effort to get herself under control—curb that fearful desire to laugh. "I will try," she said quietly as she could. "I *will* try."

"Why, Katie," Ann began, "does it make so much difference—just because you know him?"

"It makes all the difference! Can't you see—why it makes it so vulgar."

Ann threw back her head. "Just the same—it wasn't vulgar. What I felt wasn't vulgar. Why, Katie," she cried appealingly, "it was my Something Somewhere! You didn't think that vulgar!"

"Oh no," laughed Katie, "not before I knew it was Major Darrett! But tell me—I've got to know now. What is it? Where did you meet him? Just how bad is it, anyhow?"

It must have been desperation led Ann to spare neither Katie nor herself. "I met him," she said baldly, "one night as I was standing on the corner waiting for a car. He had an automobile. He asked me to get in it—and I did. And that—began it."

Katie stepped back from her in horror, the outrage she felt stamped all too plainly on her face. "And you call *that* not vulgar? Why it was *common*. It was *low*."

Then Ann turned. "Was it? Oh I don't know that you need talk. I wouldn't say much—if I were you. I guess I saw the look on his face when I came in. Don't think for a minute I don't know that look. *You got it there.* And let me tell you another thing. Just let me tell you another thing! Whatever I did—whatever I did—I know I never had the look you did when I came in! I never had that look of fooling with things!"

Katie was white—powerless—with rage. "*You* dare speak to *me* like that!" she choked. "You—!"

And all control gone she rushed blindly from the room.

CHAPTER XXV

She had no idea how long she had been walking. She was conscious of being glad that there was so big a place for walking, that walking was not a preposterous thing to be doing. She passed several groups of soldiers. They were reassuring; they looked so much in the natural order of things and gave no sign of her being out of that order.

Though she knew she was out of it. It was dizzying—that feeling of having lost herself. She had never known it before.

After she had walked very fast for what seemed a long time she seemed able to gather at least part of her forces back under control.

That blinding sense of everything being scattered, of her being powerless, was passing.

And the first thing sanity brought was the suggestion that Ann, too, might be like that. Once before Ann had been "scattered" that way—oh she understood it now as she had not been able to do then. And perhaps Ann would have less power to gather herself back—

She grew frightened. She turned toward home, walking fast as she could—worried to find herself so far away.

Major Darrett stepped out from the library to speak to her, but she hurried past him up the stairs.

Ann was not in the room where she had left her.

She looked through the other rooms. She called to her.

Then it must be—she told herself—all the while fear growing larger in her heart—that Ann, too, had gone out for a walk.

"Worth," she asked, grotesquely overdoing unconcern, "where's Miss Ann? Has she gone for a walk?"

"Why, Aunt Kate, she was called away."

"Called *away?*" whispered Katie. "Called where?"

"She said she was called away. She's gone."

"But she's coming back? When did she say, dear," she pleaded, "that she would be back?"

"I don't know, Aunt Kate. She felt awful bad because she had to go. She came and kissed me—she kissed me and kissed me—and said she hated to leave me—but that she had to go. She kept saying she had to."

In the hall was Nora. "Nora," asked Katie, standing with her back to her, "what is it about Miss Forrest?"

"She was called away, Miss Kate. A telegram. I didn't see no boy—"

"They must have 'phoned it," said Katie sharply.

"Yes'm. I didn't hear the 'phone. But I was busy. I'm so upset, Miss Kate, about them champagne glasses. We've telephoned over the river—"

"Never mind the champagne glasses! What about Miss Forrest? How did she go? When did she go?"

"She went in Mr. Osborne's automobile. Miss Osborne sent you some beautiful flowers, Miss Kate. Oh they're just lovely!"

"Oh, I don't care anything about flowers! You say Ann went in the machine?"

"Yes'm. She told the chauffeur—he brought the flowers—that big colored man, you know, Miss Kate—that she was called away, and would he take her to the station. And he said sure he would—and so they went. But, Miss Kate—it's most five o'clock—what will we do about those two champagne glasses!"

"Merciful heavens, Nora! Stop talking about them! I don't care what you do about them!"

She went down to the library. "Look here," she said to the Major, "what is this? What have you done? Where's Ann gone?"

"I don't know a thing about it. I went over to the office—an appointment—and when I came back—hurried back because I was worried about you—I saw her going away in the Osborne car."

"And never tried to stop her?"

"See here, Katie. Why should I stop her? Best thing you can do is let her go."

"Do you know—do you know," choked Katie—"that she may kill herself?"

He laughed. "Oh I guess not. Calm down, Katie. She had her wits about her, all right. I heard her tell the man to drive her to the station. She had sense enough to take advantage of the car, you see. I guess she knows the ropes. Don't think she has much notion of killing herself."

"Oh you don't. Much you know about it! You with your fine noble understanding of life!" She turned away, sobbing. "What shall I do? What *shall* I do?"

But in a moment she stopped. "The thing for me to do," she said, "is telephone the Osbornes' chauffeur."

Which she did. Yes, he had taken the young lady to the station. He didn't know where she was going. He just pulled in to the station and then pulled right out again—she told him there was nothing more to do. He didn't believe she bought a ticket. He saw her walking out to get a train. No, he didn't know what train. There were two or three trains standing there.

"What can I do?" Katie kept murmuring frantically.

Suddenly her face lighted. She sat there thinking for a moment, then called her brother's office. Wayne, she was glad to find, was not there. She asked if she might speak to Mr. Ferguson.

"Mr. Ferguson," she said, "this is—this is Captain Jones' sister. I want for a very particular—a very imperative reason—to speak at once to the—to your friend—that man—why the man that mends the boats, you know. Could you get word for him to come here—here, to my house—right away? Tell him it's very—oh *very* important. Tell him Miss Jones says she—needs him."

Ferguson said it was just quitting time. He'd go up there on his wheel. He thought he could find him. He would send him right down.

She admired the way he controlled what must have been his astonishment.

The man who mended the boats would come. He would know what to do. He would help her. She would keep as calm as she could until he got there.

But surely—surely—Ann wouldn't go away and leave her without a word! Ann couldn't be so cruel as to let her worry like that. Why of course—Ann had left a note for her.

So she looked for the note—tossed everything in the room topsy-turvey. Even looked in the closet.

Again she heard Nora in the hall. "Nora," she said, and Katie's face was white and pleading, "didn't Miss Ann say anything about leaving me a note?"

"Why yes, Miss Kate—yes—sure she did. I was so upset about them champagne glasses—"

"Well, where is it? Oh, hurry, Nora. Tell me."

"Why it's in the desk, Miss Kate. She said you was to look in the desk."

She ran to it with a sob. "Nora, how could you let me—"

Nora was saying again that she was so worried about the champagne glasses—

The desk, of course, would be the last place one would think of looking for a note!

She found, and with trembling fingers smoothed out the note; it had been crumpled rather than folded. It was brief, and so written she could scarcely read it.

"You see, Katie, you *can't*—you simply *can't*. So I'm going. When you come back, you won't want me to. That's why I've got to go now. I'd tell you—only I don't know. I'll get a train—just any train. I can't write. Because for one thing I haven't time—and for another if I began to say things I'd begin to cry—and then I wouldn't go. I've got to keep just this feeling—the one I told you about its *having* to be—

"Katie, you're not like the rest of your world, but it is your world—and see what you get when you try to be any different from it!

"Oh Katie—I didn't think I'd be leaving like *this*. I didn't think I'd ever say to you—"

There it ended.

"Miss Kate," Nora said, "Major Darrett wants to know if he may speak to you in the library."

She went down mechanically.

"Now, Katie," he began quietly and authoritatively, "there are several orders you must give, several things you must attend to, in relation to your dinner. Things seem a little disorganized, and it's getting late, and it won't do, you know, to get these people upset. Now Nora tells me that through some complication or other you're two champagne glasses short."

Katie was staring at him. "And is *that* all that matters? Two champagne glasses short! And here a life—Why what kind of people are we?"

"Katie," he said, his voice well controlled, "we're just that kind of people. No matter what's at stake—no matter what we're thinking about things—or about each other—the thing we've got to do now—you know it—and you're going to do it—is go ahead with this affair."

"I'm not going to have it! Why what do you think I'm made of? I won't. Telephone them. Call it off. I tell you I can't."

"Katie, you think you can't, and yet you know you will. I know exactly what you're made of. I know what your father was made of. I know what your mother was made of. I know that no matter what it costs *you*—you'll go on as if nothing had occurred. Now will you telephone Prescott, or shall I? Ask him about the glasses. And if he can't do anything for you you'll have to call up Zelda at Miss Osborne's and tell the girls they can't come unless they each bring a glass. I'll do it if you want me to. They'll think it a great lark, you know, having to bring their own glasses or getting no champagne."

"Yes," whispered Katie, "they'll think it a great lark. For that matter—everything's a great lark."

She sank to a chair. Her tears were falling as she said again that everything was a great lark. He paid no attention to her but went to the telephone.

But the tears were interrupted. "Miss Kate," said Nora, "can you come and look at the table a minute? They want to know—"

She dried her eyes as best she could and went and looked at the table.

She kept on looking at things—doing things—until she heard the bell.

"If that's some one for me, Nora," she said, "show him in here, and don't interrupt me while he's here." She passed into a small room they used as a den.

He came to her there. And when she saw that it was indeed he she broke down.

"Something is the matter?" he asked gently. "You wanted me? You sent for me?"

She raised her head. "Yes. I sent for you. I need you."

It was evident she needed some one. He would scarcely have known her for Katie—so white, so shaken. "I'm glad you sent for me," he said simply. "Now won't you tell me what I can do?"

"She's gone," whispered Katie.

"Where?"

"I don't know—I don't know where. Away. On a train. Some train. Any train. Somewhere. I don't know where. I thought—oh you'll find her for me—won't you? You *will* find her—won't you?"

She had stretched out her hands, and he took them, holding them strongly in both of his. "Don't you want to tell me what you know? I can't help you unless you tell me."

Briefly she told him—wrenched the heart out of it in a few words. "You see, I failed," she concluded, looking up at him with swimming eyes. "The very first thing—the very first test—I failed. I wanted to do so much—thought I understood so well—oh I was so proud of the way I understood! And then just the minute it came up against *my* life—"

Her head went down to her hands, and because he was holding them it was upon his hands rather than hers it rested, Katie's head with its gold brown hair all disorderly.

"Don't," he whispered, as she seemed breaking her heart with it. "Why don't you know all the world's like that? Don't you know we all can be fine and free until it comes up against *our* lives?"

"I was so *hard*!" she sobbed.

"Yes—I know. We are hard—when it's our lives are touched. Don't cry, Katie." He spoke her name timidly and lingeringly. "Isn't that what life is? Just one long thing of trying and failing? But going on trying again! That's what you'll do."

"If you can find her for me! But I never can hold up my head again—never believe in myself—never do anything—why I never can laugh again—not really laugh—if you don't find her for me."

A curious look passed over his face with those last words. "Well if that's the case," he said, with a strange little laugh of his own, "I've got to find her."

They talked of things. He would go to the station. He would do what he could. If he thought anything to be gained by it he would go on to Chicago. He had to go in a few days anyhow, he explained, to see about some work, and if it didn't seem a mere wild goose chase he would go that night.

The change in Katie, the life which came back to her eyes, rewarded him.

"I'd go with you to the station," she said, "only we're giving a big dinner to-night."

She thought his face darkened. "Oh yes, I know. But that's the kind of person I am. We go on with the dinner—no matter what's happening. It's—our way."

He seemed to be considering it as a curious phenomenon. "Yes, I know it is. And you can't help that either, can you? So you're going to be very festive in this house to-night?"

"Oh *very* festive in this house to-night. Some army people are here from Washington. We're going to have a gorgeous dinner, and I'm going to wear a gorgeous gown and drink champagne and try and smile myself into the good graces of a man who can do things for my brother and be—oh *so* clever and festive."

He looked at her as if by different route he had come again to that thing of pitying her; only along this other route the quality of the pity had changed and there was in it now a tender sadness. "It's not so simple a matter for you, is it—this 'being free'? You're of the bound, too, aren't you? And you've become conscious of your chains. There's all the hope and all the tragedy of it in that." He took an impulsive step toward her and smiled at her appealingly, a little mistily, as he said: "Only please don't tell me you're not going to laugh any more."

CHAPTER XXVI

As a matter of fact Katie did laugh a great deal that night. At least it passed for laughter, and the man who was worth cultivating for Wayne seemed to find it most attractive. It was evident to them all that Katie was getting on famously with him.

It was well that she was, for Wayne himself seemed making little headway. Before dinner Katie had told him briefly that Ann had come down with Worth (whose sore throat didn't seem serious, after all) and then had been called away. She said she couldn't talk about it then; she would tell him later.

But though they had a quiet host they had a vivid and a brilliant hostess. Those who knew Katie best, Mrs. Prescott in particular, kept watching her in wonderment. She had never known Katie to vie with Zelda Fraser in saying those daring things. Katie, though so merry, had seemed a different type. But to-night Katie and Zelda and Major Darrett kept things very lively.

Katie was telling her distinguished guest the tale of the champagne glasses. "Just fancy," she said, "here was I, giving a dinner for you—and it looked as if somebody would have to turn teetotaler or drink out of the bottle! After I finally got it straightened out I told Zelda she must keep her hand as much as possible on the stem of her glass so it would not be noted she was drinking from gothic architecture and the rest of us from classic."

"And you may have observed," blithely observed Zelda, "that keeping my hand on the stem of my glass is an order I am not loathe to obey—be it any old architecture."

They laughed. Zelda was the daughter of a general, and could say very much what she pleased and be laughed at as amusing.

It came to Katie in what large measure they all could do very much as they pleased. It was a game they played, and great liberty was accorded them in that game so long as they took their liberty in accordance with the prescribed rules of that game. But they guarded their own privileges with an intolerance for all those outside their game who would take privileges of their own. That—labeled a respect for good form—was in reality their method of self-defense.

She looked at Zelda Fraser—Zelda with her bold black eyes, her red cheeks which she made still redder—and her *hair*—as long as people were "wearing" hair Zelda wore a little more than any one else. Nothing about her suggested anything so redeeming as a quest for Something Somewhere. No veiled splendor of a dream hovered tenderly over Zelda. Watching her as she bantered with Major Barrett it grew upon Katie as one of the grotesque things of the world that Zelda should be within and Ann without.

Major Barrett had remained. It was Ann who had gone. Yet it was Ann had dreamed the dream. He who had made the "excursion" despoiling the dream. It was Ann had been "called." He who had preyed upon—cheated—that call.

Yet she had not sent him away. She was too much in the game for that. She had not seemed to have the power. Certainly she had not had the wit nor the courage. He had remained and taken command. She had done as he told her.

He was smiling approvingly upon her now, manifestly proud of the way Katie was playing the game.

Seeing it as a thing to win his approval she could with difficulty continue it. She was thankful that the dinner itself had drawn to a close.

Later, on the porch, Caroline Osborne asked for Ann. Zelda and Major Darrett and Harry Prescott were in the group at the time.

"You mean she is not coming back?" she pursued in response to Katie's statement that Ann had been called away.

"I don't know," said Katie. "I'm afraid not."

"Who is she, Katie?" Zelda asked.

"No one you know."

Zelda turned to Prescott. "You know her?"

"Yes," he said. His voice told Katie how hard he was finding it just then to play the game.

"Like her?"

"Yes," he replied.

Zelda threw back her head in an impertinent way of hers that was called engaging. "Love her?"

He stepped nearer Katie, as if for protection. His smile was a dead smile.

"Really, Zelda," said Katie, in laughing protest.

"I just wondered," said Zelda, "if she was going to marry into the army."

Katie saw Major Darrett's smile.

"If she did," she said, "the army would gain something that might do it good."

Major Darrett was staring at her speechlessly. Harry gratefully. "You're very fond of her?" said Caroline Osborne in her sweet-toned way.

"Very," said Kate in way less sweet.

"Too bad we missed her," said Zelda, "especially if she would do us good. Now Cal here's going in for doing good, too. Only she's not trying to do it to the army. She's doing it to the working people."

"Get the distinction," laughed the Major.

"I must get hold of some stunt like that," said Zelda. "The world's getting stuntier and stuntier." She turned to Major Darrett. "Whom do you think I could do good to?"

"Me," he said, and they strolled laughingly away together.

A few minutes later Katie found herself alone with Captain Prescott.

"Katie," he asked pleadingly, "where has Ann gone?"

"She's been called away, Harry. She's—gone away."

"But won't she be back?"

Katie turned away. "I don't know. I'm afraid not."

"Katie," he besought, "won't you help me? Won't you tell me where I can find her? I know—something's the matter. I know—something's strange. But I want to see her! I want to find her!"

> "I want to see her!—I want to find her!"—It invaded the
> chamber in Katie's heart she would keep inexorably shut.
> She dared not speak.

But he was waiting, and she was forced to speak. "Harry, I'm afraid you'll have to forget Ann," she said unsteadily. "I'm afraid you'll have to—" Because she could not go on, sure if she did she would not be able to go on with the evening, she laughed. "I'll tell you what you do," she said briskly. "Marry Caroline Osborne. She's going to have heaps of money and will go in for philanthropy. 'Twill be quite stunty. Don't you see, even Zelda thinks it stunty?"

He stepped back. "I had thought, Katie,"—and his voice pierced her armor—"that you were kind."

She dared not let in anything so human as a hurt. "Well that's where you're wrong. I'm not kind," she said harshly.

"So I see," he answered unsteadily.

But of a sudden the fact that he had been drawn to Ann drew her irresistibly to him. He had been part of all those wonderful days—days of dream and play, or waking and wondering. She remembered that other night they had stood on the porch speaking of Ann—the very night she had become Ann. That fact that he had accepted her as Ann—cared for her—made it impossible to harden her heart against him. "Oh Harry," she said, voice shaking, "I'm sorry. So sorry. It's my fault—and I'm sorry. I didn't want you to be hurt. I didn't want—anybody to be hurt."

Some one called to him and he had to turn away. She stepped into the shadow and had a moment to herself.

What did it *mean*—she wondered. That one was indeed bound hand and foot and brain and heart and spirit?

What had she done save prove that she could do nothing?

Ann had been driven away. And in her house now were Zelda Fraser and Caroline Osborne and Major Darrett and all those others who were not dreamers of dreams. And the dream betrayed—she felt one with *them*.

For she had turned the dream out of doors with Ann: the wonderful dream which sheltered the heart of reality, dream through which waking had come, from which all the long dim paths of wondering had opened—dream through which self had called.

And what was there left?

A house of hollow laughter was left—of pretense—"stunts"—of prescribed rules and intolerance with all breakers of rules even though the breakers of rules were dreamers of dreams.

With a barely repressed sob she remembered what Ann had said in her story of her dog. "I could have stood my own lonesomeness. But what I couldn't stand was thinking about him.... I couldn't keep from thinking things that tortured me."

It was that gnawed at the heart of it.... How go to bed that night without knowing that Ann had a bed? She had loved Ann because Ann needed her, been tender to her because Ann was her charge. She yearned for her now in fearing for her. More sickening than the pain of having failed was the pain of wondering where Ann would get her breakfast. Tears which she had been able to hold back even under the shame of her infidelity came uncontrollably with the simple thought that she might never do Ann's hair for her again.

It seemed to Katie then that the one thing she could not do was go back to her guests.

A boy was coming on a bicycle. He had a letter for Katie.

She excused herself and went to the little room to read it—the same little room where they had been that afternoon.

It was but a hurried note. He had found nothing at the station except that the Chicago train was probably there at the time. Doubtless she had taken it. He had taken a chance and wired the train asking her to wire Katie immediately. That was all he could think of to do. He was taking the night train for Chicago—not that he knew of anything to do there, but perhaps she would like to feel there was some one there. He would have to go soon anyhow—might as well be that night. He would be there three or four days. He told Katie where to address him. He would do anything she asked.

He advised her, for the time, to remain where she was. Probably word would come to her there. She might be able to do more from there than elsewhere. It was not even certain Ann had gone to Chicago—by no means certain. And even if she had—how find her there if she did not wish to be found?

At the last: "I suppose you're very gay at your dinner just now. That must be tough business—being gay. Don't let it harden your heart—as gayety like that could so easily do. And remember—you're *going on!* You're not a quitter. And it's only the quitters stop when they fall down."

Below, shyly off in one corner, written very lightly as if he scarcely dared write it, she found: "You don't know what a wonderful thing it is to me just to know that you are in the world."

Katie went back to her guests with less gayety but more poise.

Major Darrett had remained for a good-night drink with Wayne. He came out to Katie as she was going up stairs.

"I was proud of you, Katie," he said.

"I take no pride in your approval!"

"You made a great hit, Katie."

"Not with myself."

"Katie," he suddenly demanded, "what were you up to? I can't get the run of it. For heaven's sake, what did you mean?"

"You wouldn't understand," she murmured wearily, for she was indeed so very weary then.

"Well, I'm afraid I wouldn't. I don't want to be harsh—when you've had such a hard day, but it looks to me as if you broke the rules."

"What rules?"

"Our rules. You didn't play the game fair, Katie—presenting her here. I never would have done that."

"No," she said, "I know. You put what you call the rules of life so far above life itself."

"And look here, Katie, what's this about Prescott? I'm not going to have him hurt. If he doesn't know the situation, and has any thought of marrying her—why I'm in honor bound to tell him."

That fired her. "Oh you are, are you? Well if your honor moves you to that I'll have a few things to say about that same 'honor' of yours! To our distinguished guest of this evening, for instance," she laughed.

He lost color, but quickly recovered himself. "Oh come now, Katie, you and I are not going to quarrel."

"No, not if you can help it. That wouldn't be your way. But do you know what I think of the 'game' you play?"

She had gone a little way up the stairs, and was standing looking back at him. Her eyes were shining feverishly.

"I think it's a game for cheats."

He did go colorless at that. "That's not the sort of thing you can say to a man, Katie," he said in shaking voice.

"A game for cheats," she repeated. "The cheats who cheat with life—and then make rules around their cheating and boast about the 'honor' of keeping those rules. You'd scorn a man who cheated at cards. Oh you're very virtuous—all of you—in your scorn of lesser cheats. What's cards compared with the divinest thing in life!"

"I tell you, I played fair," he insisted, his voice still unsteady.

"Why to be sure you did—according to the rules laid down by the cheats!"

Wayne came upon her upstairs a little later, sobbing. And sobbingly she told the story—her face buried too much of the time for her to see her brother's face, too shaken by her own sobs to mark how strange was his breathing. Wayne did not accuse her of not having played a fair game. He said almost nothing at all, save at the last, and that under his breath: "We'll move heaven and earth to get her back!"

His one reproach was—"Oh Katie—you might have told *me*!"

CHAPTER XXVII

But they did not get her back. July had passed, and August, and most of September, and they had not found Ann.

Heaven and earth were not so easily moved.

Katie had tried, and the man who mended the boats had tried, and Wayne, but to no avail.

There had come the one letter from her—letter seeking to save "Ann" for Katie. It was a key to Ann, but no key to her whereabouts save that it was postmarked Chicago.

Those last three months had impressed Katie with the tragic indefiniteness of the Chicago postmark.

She had spent the greater part of the summer there, at a quiet little hotel on the North Side, where she was nominally one of a party of army women. That was the olive branch to her Aunt Elizabeth on the chaperone question. For her own part, she had seen too many unchaperoned girls in Chicago that summer to care whether she was chaperoned or not.

Her army friends thought Katie interested in some work which she did not care to talk about. They thought it interesting, though foolhardy to let it bring those lines. Katie was not a beauty, they said among themselves, and could not afford lines. Her charm had always been her freshness, her buoyancy and her blitheness. Now if she lost that—

Wayne had been there from time to time. It was but a few hours' ride from the Arsenal, and his detail to his individual work gave him considerable liberty.

He, too, had more "lines" in September than he had had in June. That they attributed to his "strenuousness" in his work, and thought it to be deplored. After all, the department might throw him down—who knew what it might not do?—and then what would have been the use? For a man who did not have to live on his pay, Captain Jones was looked upon as unnecessarily serious.

But Katie suspected that it was not alone devotion to military science had traced those lines. It surprised her a little that they should have come, but to Katie herself it was so vital and so tragic a thing that it was not difficult to accept the fact of its marking any one who came close to it. After that night at the dance there had several times stirred a vague uneasiness, calling out the thought that it was a good thing Wayne was, as she loosely thought it, immune. But even that uneasiness was lost now in sterner things.

She had never gone into her reasons for looking upon her brother as "immune." It was an idea fixed in her mind by her association with his unhappiness with Clara. Knowing how much he had given, she thought of him as having given all. Her sense of the depth of his hurt had unanalyzed associations with finality, associations intrenched by Wayne's growing "queerness."

It could not be said, however, that that queerness had stood in the way of his doing all he could. Some of the best suggestions had come from him. And Katie had reasons for suspecting he had done some searching of his own which he did not report to her.

She knew that he was worried about her, though he understood too well to ask her to give up and turn back to her own life.

Her gratitude to Wayne for that very understanding made her regret the more her inability to be frank with him about the man who mended the boats. She had had to tell him at first that he was helping, but Wayne had seemed to think it so strange, had appeared so little pleased with the idea, that she had not seen it as possible to make a clean breast of it. She told him that she had talked with him about Ann—that was because he had seen her, knew more about it than she did. And that she had talked with him again the day Ann left, thinking he might have seen her. That Wayne had not liked. "You should have sent for me," he said. "Never take outsiders into your confidence in intimate matters like that."

And what she had not found it possible to try to make clear to him was that the man who mended the boats seemed to her anything but an outsider.

And if he had not seemed so in those days of early summer, he seemed infinitely less so now. She talked with him of things of which she could not talk with anyone else. In those talks it was all the rest of the people of the world who were the outsiders.

He had been there several times during the summer. Katie knew now that he did not mean to spend all his life mending boats. He was writing a play; it was things in relation to that brought him to Chicago. Katie wanted to know about the play, but when she asked he told her, rather shortly, that he did not believe she would like it. He qualified it with saying he did not know that anyone would like it.

When he was there he went about with her as she looked for Ann.

Every day she pursued her search, now in this way, now in that. That search brought her a vision of the city she would have had in no other way. It was that vision, revealed, interpreted, by her anxiety for Ann brought the sleepless nights and the ceaseless imagery and imaginings which caused her army friends to wish that dear Katie would marry before she, as they more feelingly than lucidly put it, lost out that way.

She thought sometimes of Ann's moving picture show, showing her the things of which she had dreamed. All this, things seen in her search, had become to Katie as a moving picture show. It moved before her awake and asleep; "called" to her.

She would stand outside the stores as the girls were coming out at night. Stores, factories, all places where girls worked she watched that way. By the hundreds, thousands, she saw them filling the city's streets as through the long summer one hot day after another drew to a close. Often she would crowd into the street cars they were crowding into, rush with them for the elevated trains, or follow them across the river and see them disappear into boarding-house and rooming-house, those hot, crowded places waiting to receive them after the hot, crowded day. Sometimes she would go for lunch to the places she saw them going to—always searching, and as she searched, wondering, and as she wondered, sorrowing.

She came to know of many things: of "dates"—vulgar enough affairs many of them appeared to be. But she no longer dismissed them with that. She always wondered now if the sordid-looking adventure might not be at heart the divine adventure. Things which she would at one time have called "common" and turned from as such she brooded over now as sorry expression of a noble thing. And then she would go home to her friends at night and sometimes they would seem the moving-picture show—their pleasures and standards—the whole of their lives. And she sorrowed that where there was setting for loveliness the setting itself should so many times absorb it all, and that out on the city's streets that tender fluttering of life for life, divine yearning for joy that joy might give again to life, should find so many paths to that abyss where joy could be not and where the life of life must go. There were days which showed all too brutally that many were "called" and few were saved.

Thus had she passed the summer, and thus it happened that she did not have in September all the freshness and the gladness that had been her charm in May.

Though to the man waiting for her that afternoon she had another and a finer charm. Life had taken something from her, but she had wrested something from life.

"I could have had a job," she said, and smiled.

But the smile was soon engulfed. "And there was a girl who needed it, she told me how she was 'up against it,' and through some caprice she didn't get it. Needing it doesn't seem to make a bit of difference. If anything, it works the other way."

She had read in the paper that morning that the chorus was to be "tried out" for a new musical comedy. Thinking that Ann, too, might have read that in the paper, she went.

She had been seeing something of chorus girls as well as shop girls. She went to all the musical comedies and sat far front and kept her glasses on the chorus. More than once she had stood near stage doors as they were coming out. Seeing them so, they were not a group of chorus girls; they were a number of individuals, any one of whom might be Ann, more than one of whom might be fighting the things Ann had fought, seeking the things Ann had sought. It was that about the city that *got* her. It was a city full of individuals, none of whom were to be dismissed as just this, or exactly that. She challenged all groupings, those groupings which seemed formed by the accidents of life and so often made for the tragedy of life.

She was talking to him about chorus girls; announcing her discovery that they were just girls in the chorus. "I was once asked to define army people," she laughed, "and said that they were people who entered the army—either martially or maritally. Now I find that chorus girls are girls who enter the chorus. Even their vocabularies can't disguise them, and if that can't—what could?

"Though there are different kinds of chorus girls," she reflected. "Some wanted to be somewhere else. Some hope to be somewhere else. And some swaggeringly make it plain that they wouldn't be anywhere else if they could. I'd hate to have to say which kind is the most sad."

"Katie," he said—he never spoke her name save in that timid, lingering way—"don't you think you're rather over-emphasizing the sadness?"

Two girls passed them, laughing boisterously. "Perhaps so. I suppose I am. And yet nothing seems to me sadder than some of the people who would be astonished at suggesting sadness."

That afternoon they were going to the telephone office. Katie had been there early in the summer, to the central office and all the exchanges, but wanted to go again. And Mann said he would like to go with her and see what the thing looked like.

The officials were cordial to them at the telephone office, seeming pleased to exhibit and explain. And it seemed that with their rest rooms and recreation rooms, their various things to contribute to comfort and pleasure, their pride was justified.

But when they were in the immense room where several hundred girls were sitting before the boards, rest rooms and recreation rooms did not seem to *reach*. They walked behind a long row, their guide proudly calling attention to the fact that not one of those girls turned her head to look at them. He called it discipline—concentration. Katie, looking at the tense faces, was thinking of the price paid for that discipline. Many of the girls were very young, some not more than sixteen. They preferred taking them young, said the guide; they were easier to break in if they had never done anything else.

There was not the shadow of a doubt that they were being "broken in." So clearly was that demonstrated that Katie wondered what there would be left for them to be broken in to after they had been thoroughly broken in to that. Walking slowly behind them, looking at every girl as a possible Ann, she wondered what they would have left for a Something Somewhere. She remembered the woman who wore the white furs saying it "got on her nerves" and wondered what kind of nerves they would be it wouldn't "get on." The thing itself seemed a mammoth nervous system, feeding on other nervous systems, lesser sacrificed to greater.

Her fancy reached out to all the things that at that instant were going through those cords. Plans were being made for dinner, for motoring that evening, for many pleasant, restful things. Many little red lights, with many possible invitations, were insistently dancing before tired eyes just then. They seemed endless—those demands of life—demands of life before which other demands of life were slowly going down.

She and Mann were alone for the minute. "And yet," she turned to him, after following his glance to a girl's tense, white face, "what can they do? The company, I mean. One must be fair. They pay better than most things pay, seem more interested in the girls. What more can we ask?"

"Well, what would you think," he suggested, "of 'asking' for a system more interested in conserving nervous systems than in producing millionaires?

"Why, yes," he added, "in view of the fact that it has to make a few men rich, perhaps they are doing all they can. I don't doubt that they think they are. But if this were a thing that didn't have to produce wealth—then it wouldn't need to endanger health. Don't you think that in this nerve-blighting work four or five hours, instead of eight, would be a pretty good day's work for girls just out of short clothes?"

"It would seem so," sighed Katie, as she left the room filled with girls answering calls—girls looking too worn to respond to any "call" life might have for them.

Though when, a little later, they stood in the doorway watching a long line of them passing out into the street it was amazing how ready and how eager they seemed for what life had to offer them. They all looked tired, but many appeared happy—determined that all of life should not be going over the wire. It seemed to Katie the most wonderful thing she knew of that girls from whom life exacted so much could remain so ready—so happily eager—for life.

There was one thing to which she had made up her mind. Amid the confusion of her thinking and the sadness of her spirit one thing she saw as clear. There was something wrong with an arrangement of life which struck that hard at life. The very fact that the capacity for life persisted through so much was the more reason for its being a thing to be cherished rather than sacrificed.

"Let's walk up this way," she was saying; "walk over the river. The bridge is a good place just now."

Katie's face was white and tense as some of the faces they had left behind "No," he said impetuously. "Let's not. Let's do something jolly!"

She shook her head "I have a feeling we're going to find her to-night."

Katie was always having that feeling. But as she looked then he had not the heart to remind her of the many times it had played her false.

Many girls passed them on the bridge, but not Ann. "I can never make up my mind to go," she said. "I always think I ought to wait till the next one comes round the corner."

A girl who appeared to be thinking deeply passed them, turning weary eyes upon them in languid interest.

"I wonder *what*," Katie exclaimed. "What she's thinking about," she explained. "Maybe she's come to the end of her string—and if she has, hundreds of thousands of people about her—oh I think it's terrible"—her voice broke—"the way people are crowded so close together—and held so far apart. Everybody's *alone*. Nobody *knows*."

For a second his hand closed over hers as it rested on the railing of the bridge, as if he would bear some of the hurt for her, that hurt she was finding in everything.

Despite the extreme simplicity of her dress she looked out of place standing on that bridge at that hour; he was thinking that she had not lost her distinction with her buoyancy.

Her face was quivering. "Katie," it made him ask, "don't you think you'd better—quit?"

She turned wet eyes upon him reproachfully. "From *you*?"

"But is any—individual—worth it?"

"Oh I suppose no 'individual' is worth much to you," she said a little bitterly.

There was a touch of irony in the tender smile which was his only response.

They stood there in silence watching men and women come and go—solitary and in groups—groups tired and groups laughing—groups respectable and groups questionable—humanity—worn humanity—as it crossed that bridge.

She recalled that first night she had talked with him—that first time a hot day had seemed to her anything more than mere hot day, that night on the Mississippi—where distant hills were to be seen. She remembered how she had looked around the world that night to see if it needed "saving." It seemed a long time ago since she had not been able to see that the world needed saving.

That was the night the man who mended the boats told her she had walked sunny paths. She looked up at him with a faint smile, smiling at the fancy of his being an outsider.

It seemed, on the other hand, that all the hopes and fears in all the hearts that were passing them were drawing them together. There had been times when she had had a wonderful sense of their silences holding the sum of man's experiences.

"You must go home," he was saying decisively.

"Home? Where? To my uncle's? That's where I keep the trunks I'm not using."

She laughed and brushed away a tear. "You know in the army we don't have homes."

"Well you have temporary homes," he insisted, as each moment she seemed to become more worn. "You know what I mean. Go back to your brother's."

"He'll be ordered from there very soon. There'll not be a place there for me much longer."

He did not seem to have reckoned with that. His face changed. "Then where will you go, Katie?" he asked, very low. "What will you do?"

She shook her head. "I don't know. I don't know where I'll go—and I don't know what I'll do."

They stood there in silence, drawn close by thought of separation.

"Shall we walk on?" she said at last. "I've lost the feeling that we're going to find Ann to-night."

And so, still silently, they walked on.

But when, after a moment, he looked at her, it was to see that she was making heroic effort to control the tears. "Katie!" he murmured, "what is it?"

"We're giving up," she said, and could not say more.

"Why no we're not! It's only the method we're giving up. This way of doing it. You've tried this long enough."

"But what else is there? Just looking. Just keeping on looking—and hoping. Just the chance. What other method is there?"

"We'll find some other," he insisted, not willing, when she looked like that, to speak his fears. "There'll be some other way. But you can't keep on this way—dear."

There was another silence—a different one: silence which opened to receive them at the throb in his voice as he spoke that last word.

He had to go back that night. "Well?" he asked gently, as they neared her hotel.

"I'll be down in a couple of days," replied Katie, not steadily.

"And you'll be there a little while, won't you," he asked wistfully, "before you go—you don't know where?"

"Yes," she said, turning her eyes upon him for just an instant, "a little while—before I go—I don't know where."

But though she was going—she didn't know where—though she was giving up—seemed conquered—through all the uncertainty and the sadness there surged a strange new joy in their hearts as, very slowly, they walked that final block.

At the door, after a moment's full silence, she held out her hand. "And you'll be down there—mending boats?"

He nodded, his eyes going where words had not ventured.

"And you'll—come and see me?" she asked shyly. "You don't mean, do you,"—looking away, as if with scarcely the courage to say it—"that I'm to 'stop'—everything?"

"No, Katie," he said, and his voice was shaking, "I think you must know I do not mean you are to—stop everything."

As they lingered for a final moment, they were alone—far out in the sweet wild new places of the spirit; and all that man had ever yearned for, all joy that had been given and all joy denied seemed as a rich sea—fathomless sea—swelling just beneath that sweet wild new thing that had fluttered to consciousness in their hearts.

CHAPTER XXVIII

The new life in her heart gave her new courage that night to look out at life. She faced what before that she had evaded consciously facing.

Perhaps they would not find Ann at all. Perhaps Ann had given up—as they were giving up. Perhaps Ann was not there to be found.

It was her fight against that fear had kept her so much in the crowds. Ann was there. She had only to find her. Leaving the crowds seemed to be admitting that Ann was not in them; for if she really felt she was in them, surely she would not consent to leaving them.

That idea of Ann's not being there was as a shadow which had from time to time crept beside her. In the crowds she lost it. There were so many in the crowds. Ann, too, was in the crowds. She had only to stay in them and she must find her.

Now she was leaving them; and it was he who understood the crowds was telling her to leave them. Did *he* think she was not there? Why had she not had the courage to press it? There was so much they should have been talking of in those last blocks—and they had talked of nothing.

But the new warmth flooded Katie's heart at thought of having talked of nothing. What was there to talk about so important as talking of nothing? In a new way it drew her back to the crowds; the crowds that talked so loudly of many unlovely things in order to still in their hearts that call for the loveliness of talking of nothing.

It gave her new understanding of Ann. Ann was one who must rest in the wonder of talking of nothing. It was for that she had gone down. The world had destroyed her for the very thing for which life loved her—Katie joining with the world.

She would not have done that to-night. To-night, in the face of all the world, she must have joined with life.

She wondered if all along it was not the thing for which she had most loved Ann. This shy new thing in her own heart seemed revealing Ann. It was kin to her, and to Katie's feeling for her.

Many times she had wondered why she cared so terribly, would ask herself, as she could hear her friends asking if they knew: "But does it matter so much as all this?"

She had never been able to make clear to herself why it mattered so much—mattered more than anything else mattered. None of the reasons presenting themselves on the surface were commensurate to the depth of the feeling. To-night she wondered if deep below all else might not lie that thing of Ann's representing life, her failure with Ann meaning infidelity to life.

It turned her to Ann's letter;—she had not had the courage to read it for a number of days.

"Katie," Ann had written, "I'm writing to try and show you that you were not all wrong. That there was something there. And I'm not doing it for myself, Katie. I'm doing it for you.

"If I can just forget I'm writing about myself, feel instead that I'm writing about somebody you've cared for, believed in, somebody who has disappointed and hurt you, trying to show you—for *your* sake—if I don't mind being either egotistical or terrible for the sake of showing you—

"It's not *me* that matters, Katie—it's what you thought of me. That's why I'm writing.

"I never could talk to you right. For a long time I couldn't talk at all, and then that night I talked most of the night I didn't tell the real things, after all. And at the last I told you something I knew would hurt you without telling you the things that might keep it from hurting, without saving for you the things you had thought you saw. I don't know why I did that—desperate, I suppose, because it was all spoiled, frantic because I was helpless to keep it from being spoiled. And then I said things to *you*—that must show—And yet, Katie, as long as I'm trying to be honest I've got to say again, though all differently, that I was surprised—shocked, I suppose, at something in the way you looked. It's just a part of your world that I don't understand. It's as I told you—we've lived in different worlds. Things—some things—that seem all right in yours—well, it's just surprising that you should think them all right. In your world the way you do things seems to matter so much more than what you do.

"I've gone, Katie, and as far as I'm concerned it's what has to be. You see you couldn't fit me in. The only thing I can do for you now is to—stay gone. You'll feel badly—oh, I know that—but in the end it won't be as bad as trying to fit me in, trying to keep it up. And I can't have you doing things for me in another way—as you'd want to—because—it's hard to explain just what I mean, but after I've been Ann I couldn't be just somebody you were helping. It meant too much to me to be Ann to become just a girl you're good to.

"What I'd rather do—want this letter to do—is keep for you that idea of Ann—memory of her.

"So that's why I want to tell you about some things that really were Ann. I haven't any more right to you, but I want you to know you have some right to her.

"I told you that I was standing on the corner, and that he asked me to get in the automobile, and that I did, and that that—began it. It was true. It was one way to put it. I'll try and put it another way.

"It isn't even fair to him, putting it that way. You know, of course, that he's not in the habit of asking girls on corners to go with him. I think—there at the first—he was sorry for me. I think it was what you would call an impulse and that being sorry for me had more to do with it than anything else.

"And I know I wasn't fair to myself when I put it that way; and you weren't fair to me when you called it common and low. That's what I want to try and show you—that it wasn't that.

"It was in the warm weather. It had been a hot, hard day. Oh they were all hot, hard days. I didn't feel well. I made mistakes. I was scolded for it. I quarreled with one of the girls about washing my hands! She said she was there before I was and that I took the bowl. We said hateful things to each other, grew furious about it. We were both so tired—the day had been so hot—

"Out on the street I was so ashamed. It seemed *that* was what life had come to.

"That afternoon I got something that was going over the wire. You get so tired you don't care what's going over the wire—you aren't alive enough to care—but I just happened to be let in to this—a man's voice talking to the girl he loved. I don't remember what he was saying, but his voice told that there were such things in the world—and girls they were for. One glimpse of a beautiful country—to one in a desert. I don't know, perhaps that's why I talked that way to the other poor girl who was tired—perhaps that's why I went in the automobile.

"I had to ride a long way on the street car to get where I boarded. I had to stand up—packed in among a lot of people who were hot and tired too— the smell so awful—everything so *ugly*.

The Visioning A Novel | 197

"I had to transfer. That's where I was when I first saw him—standing on the corner waiting for the other car.

"Something was the matter—it was a long time coming. I was so tired, Katie, as I stood there waiting. Tired of having it all going over the wire.

"He was doing something to his automobile. I didn't pay any attention at first—then I realized he was just fooling with the automobile—and was looking at me.

"And then he took my breath away by stepping up to me and raising his hat. I had never had a man raise his hat to me in that way—

"And then he said—and his voice was low—and like the voices in your world are—I hadn't heard them before, except on the wire—'I beg pardon—I trust I'm not offensive. But you seem so tired. You're waiting for a car? It doesn't appear to be coming. Why not ride with me instead? I'll take you where you want to go. Though I wish'—it was like the voice on the wire—and for *me*—'that you'd let me take you for a ride.'

"Katie, *you* called him charming. You told about the women in your world being in love with him. If he's charming to them—to you—what do you suppose he seemed to me as he stood there smiling at me—looking so sorry for me—?

"He went on talking. He drew a beautiful picture of what we would do. We would ride up along the lake. There would be a breeze from the lake, he said. And way up there he knew a place where we could sit out of doors under trees and eat our dinner and listen to beautiful music. Didn't I think that might be nice?

"Didn't I think it might be—*nice*? Oh Katie—you'd have to know what that day had been—what so many days—all days—had been.

"I looked down the street. The car was coming at last—packed—men hanging on outside—everybody looking so hot—so dreadful. 'Oh you mustn't get in that car,' he said.

"Beautiful things were beckoning to me—things I was to be taken to in an automobile—I had never been in an automobile. It seemed I was being rescued, carried away to a land of beautiful things, far away from crowded street cars, from the heat and the work that make you do things you hate yourself for doing.

"*Was* it so common, Katie? So low? What I felt wasn't—what I dreamed as we went along that beautiful drive beside the lake.

"For I dreamed that the city of dreadful things was being left behind. The fairy prince had come for me. He was taking me to the things of dreams, things which lately had seemed to slip out beyond even dreams.

"It was just as he had said—A little table under a tree—a breeze from the lake—music—the lovely things to eat and the beautiful happy people. Of course I wasn't dressed as much as they were, so we sat at a little table half hidden in one corner—Oh I thought it was so wonderful!

"And he saw I thought it wonderful and that interested him, pleased him. Maybe it was new to him. I think he likes things that are new to him. Anyhow, he was very gentle and lovely to me that night. He told me I was beautiful—that nothing in the world had ever been so beautiful as my eyes. You know how he would say it, the different ways he would have of saying it beautifully. And I want to say again—if it seems beautiful to you—Why, Katie, I had never had anything.

"Going home he kissed me—

"When I went home that night the world was all different. The world was too wonderful for even thoughts. Too beautiful to believe it could be the world.

"I was in the arms of the wonderful new beauty of the world. Something in my heart which had been crouching down afraid and cold and sad grew warm and live and glad. Life grew so lovely; and as the days went on I think I grew lovely too. He said so; said love was making me radiant—that I was wonderful—that I was a child of love.

"Those days when I was in the dream, folded in the dream, days before any of it fell away, they were golden days, singing days—days there are no words for.

"We saw each other often. He said business kept him away from Chicago much of the time. I didn't know he was in the army; I suppose now he belonged in some place near there. And I think you told me he was not married. He said he was—but was going to be divorced some day. But I didn't seem to care—didn't think much about it. Nothing really mattered except the love.

"Then there came a time when I knew I was trying to keep a door shut— keep the happiness in and the thoughts out. It wasn't that I came to think it was wrong. But the awful fear that wanted to get into my heart was that it was *not* beautiful.

"And it wasn't beautiful because to him it wasn't beautiful. It was only—what shall I say—would there be such a thing as usurping beauty? That was the thought—the fear—I tried and tried to push away. I see I can't tell it; no matter how much we may want to tell everything—no matter how willing we are—there are things can't be told, so I'll just have to say that things happened that forced the door open, and I had to know that what to me was—oh what shall I say, Katie?—was like the prayer at the heart of a dream—didn't, to him, have anything to do with dreams, or prayers, or beautiful, far-away things that speak to you from the stars.

"And having nothing to do with them, he seemed to be pushing them away, crowding them out, hurting them.

"I haven't told it at all. I can't. But, Katie, you're in the army, you must admire courage and I want you to take my word for it when I tell you I did what it took courage to do. I think you'd let me live on in your heart as Ann if you knew what I gave up—and just for something all dim and distant I had no assurance I'd ever come near to. For oh, Katie—when you love love—need it—it's not so easy to let go what's the closest you've come to it. Not so easy to turn from the most beautiful thing you've known—just because something *very far away* whispers to you that you're hurting beauty.

"I didn't go back. One night my Something Somewhere called me away—and I left the only real thing I had—and I didn't go back. I don't know—maybe I'm overestimating myself—perhaps I'm just measuring it by the suffering—but it seems to me, Katie, that you needn't despise yourself when loneliness can't take you back to the substitutes offered for your Something Somewhere. Something in you had been brave; something in you has been faithful—and what you've actually *done* doesn't matter much in comparison with that.

"I've been writing most of the day. It's evening now, and I'm tired. I was going to tell more. Tell you of things that happened afterward—tell you why you found me where you did find me. But now I don't believe I want to tell those things. They're too awful. They'd hurt you—haunt you. And that's not what I want to do. What I want is to make you understand, and if the part I've told hasn't done that—

"'I think it was to save Ann you were going to give up
Verna,' you said. Oh Katie—how did you know? How *do*
you know?

"And then you called to me. You weren't sick at all—were you, Katie? Oh I soon guessed that it was the wonderful goodness of your heart—not the disease of it—caused that 'attack.'

"Then those beautiful days began. I wanted to talk about what those days meant—what you meant—what our play—our dream meant. Things I thought that I never said—how proud I was you should want to make up those stories about me—how I wanted to *be* the things you said I was—and oh, Katie dear, the trouble you got me into by loving to tell those stories—telling one to one man and another to another! I'd never known any one full of *play* like you—yet play that is so much more than just play. Sometimes a picture of Centralia would come to me when I'd hear you telling about my having lived in Florence. Sometimes when I was listening to stories of things you and I had done in Italy I'd see that old place where I used to put suspenders in boxes—! Katie, how strange it all was. How did it happen that things you made up were things I had dreamed about without really knowing what I was dreaming? How wonderful you were, Katie—how good—to put me in the things of my dreams rather than the things of my life. The world doesn't do that for us.

"It seems a ridiculous thing to be mentioning, when I owe you so many things too wonderful to mention—but you know I do owe you some money. I took what was in my purse. I hope I can pay it back. I'm so tired just now it doesn't seem to me I ever can—but if I don't, don't associate it with my not paying back the missionary money!

"Katie, do you know how I'd like to pay you back? I'd like to give you the most beautiful things I've ever dreamed. And I hope that some of them, at least, are waiting somewhere—and not very far off—for you. How I used to love to hear you laugh—watch you play your tricks on people—so funny and so dear—

"Now that's over. Katie, I don't believe it's all my fault, and I know it's not yours. It's our two worlds. You see you *couldn't* fit me in.

"I used to be afraid it must end like that. Yet most of the time I felt so secure—that was the wonder of you—that you could make me so beautifully secure. And your brother, Katie, have you told him? I don't care if you do, only if you tell him anything, won't you try and make him understand everything? I couldn't bear it to think he might think me—oh those things I don't believe you really think me.

"If you don't see me any more, you won't think those things. It's easier to understand when things are all over. It's easier to forgive people who are not around. After what's happened I couldn't be Ann if I were with you. That's spoiled. But if *I* go—I think maybe Ann can stay. For both our sakes, that's what I want.

"'Twas a lovely dream, Katie. The house by the river—the big trees—the big flag that waved over us—the pretty dresses—the lovely way of living—the dogs—the men who were always so nice to us—Last night I dreamed you and Worth and I were going to a wedding. That is, it started out to be a wedding—then it seemed it was a funeral. But you were saying such funny things about the funeral, Katie. Then I woke up—"

The letter broke off there.

CHAPTER XXIX

The next morning Katie did something which it had been in her mind to do for some time. She went to Centralia.

It was not that she expected Centralia to furnish any information about Ann. It was hard to say just why she was so certain Ann had not gone back to Centralia. The conviction had something to do with her belief in Ann.

Centralia, however, might be an avenue to something. Furthermore, she wanted to see Centralia. That was part of her passion for seeing the thing as a whole, realizing it. And she had a suspicion that if anything remained to forgive Ann it would be forgiven after seeing Centralia.

And back of all that lurked the longing to tell Ann's father what she thought of him.

Katie was in a strange mood that day. She had read Ann's letter many times, but had never finished it with that poignantly personal heartache of the night before. It was as if she were not worthy that new thing which kept warm in her own heart. For she had been hostile to the very thing from which the warmth in her own heart drew. The sadness deepened in the thought that the great hosts of the world's people sheltered joy in their own hearts and hardened those very hearts against all to whom love came less fortunately than it had come to them. How could there be 'hope for the world, no matter what it might do about its material affairs, while heart closed against heart like that, while men and women drew their own portions of joy and shut themselves in with them, refusing to see that they were one with all who drew, or would draw. It seemed the most cruel, the most wrong thing of all the world that men—and above all, women—should turn their most unloving face upon the face of love.

Of which things she thought again as she passed various Centralias and wondered if there were Anns longing for love in all those unlovely places.

She came at last, after crossing a long stretch of nothingness, to the town where Ann had lived, town from which she had gone forth to hear grand opera and find the loveliness of life. But as she stepped from the train and approached a group of men lounging at the station it came to her that

"Ann's father," particularly as Ann had not been Ann in Centralia, was a somewhat indefinite person to be inquiring for.

After a moment's consideration she approached the man who looked newest to his profession and asked how many churches there were in Centralia. Thereupon one man beat open retreat and all viewed her with suspicion. But the man of her choice was a brave man and ventured to guess that there were four.

One of his comrades held that there were five. A discussion ensued closing with the consensus of opinion in favor of the greater number.

Then Katie explained her predicament; she wanted to find a man who was a minister in Centralia and she didn't know his name. Reassured, they gathered round interestedly. Was he young or old? Katie cautiously placed him in the forties or fifties. Then they guessed and reckoned that it couldn't be either the Reverend Lewis or that new fellow at the Baptist. Was he— would she say he was one to be kind of easy on a fellow, or did she think he took his religion pretty hard?

Katie was forced to admit that she feared he took it hard. With that they were agreed to a man that it must be the Reverend Saunders.

She was thereupon directed to the residence of the Reverend Saunders. Right down there was a restaurant with a sign in the window "Don't Pass By." But she was to pass by. Then there was the church said "Welcome." No, that was not the Reverend Saunders' church. It was the church where she turned to the right. She could turn to the left, but, on the whole, it would be better to turn to the right—It would all have been quite simple had it not been for the fullness of the directions.

She took it that the fullness of their directions was in proportion to the emptiness of their lives.

As she walked slowly along she appreciated what Ann had said of the town's being walled in by nothingness—the people walled in by nothingness. Her two blocks on "Main Street" showed her Centralia as a place of petty righteousness and petty vice. There was nothing so large and flexible as the real joys of either righteousness or unrighteousness.

Nor was Centralia picturesquely desolate. It had not that quality of hopelessness which lures to melancholy. New houses were going up. The last straw was that Centralia was "growing."

And it was on those streets that a lonely little girl with deep brown eyes and soft brown hair had dreamed of a Something Somewhere.

As she turned in at the residence of the Reverend Saunders Katie was newly certain that Ann had not come back to Centralia. It seemed the one disappointment in Ann she was not prepared to bear would be to find that she had returned to the home of her youth.

Katie had been shown into the parlor. She was sitting in a rocking chair which "squeaked"—her smartly shod foot resting on a pale blue rose—the pale blue rose being in the carpet. The carpet also squeaked—or the papers underneath it did. On the table beside her was a large and ornate Bible, an equally splendid album, and something called "Stepping Heavenward."

Oh no—Ann had not come back. She knew that before she asked.

Ann's father was a tall, thin man with small gray eyes. "Thin lips that shut together tight"—she recalled that. And the kind of beard that is unalterably associated with self-righteousness.

It was clear he did not know what to make of Katie. She was wearing a linen suit which had vague suggestions of the world, the flesh, and the devil. She had selected it that morning with considerable care. Likewise the shoes! And the angle of the quill in Katie's hat stirred in him the same suspicion and aggression which his beard stirred in her.

Thus viewing each other across seas of prejudice, separated, as it were, by all the experiences of the human race, they began to speak of Ann and of life.

"I am a friend of your daughter's," was Katie's opening.

It startled him, stirring something on the borderland of the human. Then he surveyed Katie anew and shut his lips together more tightly. It was evidently just what he had expected his daughter to come to.

"And I came," said Katie, "to ask if you had any idea where she was."

That reached even farther into the border-country. He sat forward—his lips relaxed. "Don't *you* know?"

"No—I don't know. She was living with me, and she went away."

That recalled his own injury. He sat back and folded his arms. "She was living with *me*—and she went away. No, I know nothing of her whereabouts. My daughter saw fit to leave her father's house—under circumstances that bowed his head in shame. She has not seen fit to return, or to give information of her whereabouts. I have tried to serve my God all my days," said the Reverend Saunders; "I do not know why this should have been visited upon me. But His ways are inscrutable. His purpose is not revealed."

"No," said Katie crisply, "I should say not."

He expressed his condemnation of the relation of manner to subject by a compression of both eyes and lips. That, Katie supposed, was the way he had looked when he told Ann her dog had been sent away.

"Did you ever wonder," she asked, with real curiosity, "how in the world you happened to have such a daughter?"

"I have many times taken it up in prayer," was his response.

Katie sat there viewing him and looking above his head at the motto "God Is Love." She wondered if Ann had had to work it.

It was the suggestion in the motto led her to ask: "Tell me, have you really no idea, have you never had so much as a suspicion of why Ann went away?"

"Who?" he asked sharply.

"Your daughter. Her friends call her Ann."

"Her name," said he uncompromisingly, "is Maria."

Katie smiled slightly. Maria, as he uttered it, squeaked distressingly.

"Be that as it may. But have you really no notion of why she went away?"

She was looking at him keenly. After a moment his eyes fell, or rather, lifted under the look. "She had a good home—a God-fearing home," he said.

But Katie did not let go her look. He had to come back to it, and he shifted. Did he have it in him remotely, unavowedly, to suspect?

It would seem so, for he continued his argument, as if meeting something. He repeated that she had a good home. He enumerated her blessings.

But when he paused it was to find Katie looking at him in just the same way. It forced him to an unwilling, uneasy: "What more could a girl want?"

"What she wanted," said Katie passionately, "was life."

The word spoken as Katie spoke it had suggestion of unholy things. "But God is life," he said.

Suddenly Katie's eyes blazed. "God! Well it's my opinion that you know just as little about *Him* as you do about 'life.'"

It was doubtless the most dumbfounded moment of the Reverend Saunders' life. His jaw dropped. But only to come together the tighter. "Young woman," said he, "I am a servant of God. I have served Him all my days."

"Heaven pity Him!" said Katie, and rocked and her chair squeaked savagely.

He rose. "I cannot permit such language to be used in my house."

Katie gave no heed. "I'll tell you why your daughter left. She left because you *starved* her.

"Above your head is a motto. The motto says, 'God Is Love.' I could almost fancy somebody hung that in this house as a *joke*!

"You see you don't know anything about love. That's why you don't know anything about God—or life—or Ann.

"In this universe of mysterious things," Katie went on, "it so happened—as you have remarked, God's ways are indeed inscrutable—that unto you was born a child ordained for love."

She paused, held herself by the mystery of that.

And as she contemplated the mystery of it her wrath against him fell strangely away. Telling him what she thought of him suddenly ceased to be the satisfying thing she had anticipated. It was all too mysterious.

It grew so large and so strange that it did not seem a matter the Reverend Saunders had much to do with it. Telling him what she thought of him was not the thing interesting her then. What interested her was wondering why he was as he was. How it had all happened. What it all meant.

Her wondering almost drew her to him; certainly it gave her a new approach. "Oh isn't it a pity!" was what Katie said next. And there was pain and feeling and almost sympathy in her voice as she repeated, "Isn't it a pity!"

He, too, spoke differently—more humanly. "Isn't—what a pity?"

"That we bungle it so! That we don't seem to know anything about each other.

"Why I suppose you *didn't* know—you simply didn't have it *in* you to know—that the way she needed to serve God was by laughing and dancing!"

He was both outraged and drawn. He neither rebuked nor agreed. He waited.

"You see it was this way. You were one thing; she was another thing. And neither of you had any way of getting at the thing that the other was. So you just grew more intolerant in the things *you* were, and that, I suppose, is the way hearts are broken and lives are spoiled."

Her eyes had filled. It had drawn her back to her mood of the morning. "Doesn't it seem to you," she asked gently of the Reverend Saunders, "that it's just an awful pity?"

The Reverend Saunders did not reply. But he was not looking at Katie's quill or Katie's shoes. He was looking at Katie's wet eyes.

And Katie, as they sat there for a moment in silence, was not seeing him alone as the Reverend Saunders. She was seeing him as product of something which had begun way back across the centuries, seeing far back of the Reverend Saunders that spirit of intolerance which had shaped him—wrung him dry—spirit which in the very beginning had lost the meaning of those words which hung above the Reverend Saunders' head.

It seemed a childish thing to be blaming the Reverend Saunders for the things the centuries had made him.

Indeed, she no longer felt like "blaming" any one. Sorrow which comes through seeing leaves small room for blame.

Katie did not know as much about the history of mankind as she now wished she did—as she meant to know!—but there did open to her a glimpse of the havoc wrought by the forerunners of the Reverend Saunders—of all the children of love blighted in the name of a God of love.

She had risen. And as she looked at him again she was sorry for him. Sterility of the heart seemed a thing for pity rather than scorn. "I'm sorry for you," she spoke it. "Oh I'm sorry for us all! We all bungle it! We're all in the grip of dead things, aren't we? Do you suppose it will ever be any different?"

And still he looked, not at the quill or the shoes, but the eyes, eyes which seemed sorrowing with all the love sorrows of the centuries. "Young woman," he said uncertainly, "you puzzle me."

"I puzzle myself," said Katie, and wiped her eyes and laughed a little, thinking of the scornful exit she had meant to make after telling him what she thought of him.

She retraced her steps and waited for two hours at the station, reconstructing for herself Ann's girlhood in Centralia and thinking larger thoughts of the things which spoiled girlhoods, the pity of it all. And it seemed that even self-righteousness was not wholly to blame. Katie felt a little lonely in losing her scorn of "goodness." She had so enjoyed hating the godly. If even they were to be gently grouped with the wicked as more to be pitied than hated, then whom would one hate?

Did knowing—seeing—spoil hating? And was all hating to go when all men saw?

At the last minute she had a fight with herself to keep from going back and refunding the missionary money! The missionary money worried Katie. She wanted it paid back. But she saw that it was not her paying it back would satisfy her. She even felt that she had no right to pay it back.

CHAPTER XXX

She returned to Chicago to find that her uncle was in town. He had left a message asking her to join him for dinner over at his hotel.

It was pleasant to be dining with her uncle that night. The best possible antidote she could think of for Ann's father was her dear uncle the Bishop.

As she watched him ordering their excellent dinner she wondered what he would think of Ann's father. She could hear him calling Centralia a God-forsaken spot and Ann's father a benighted fossil. Doubtless he would speak of the Reverend Saunders as a type fast becoming obsolete. "And the quicker the better," she could hear him add.

But she fancied that the Reverend Saunderses of the world had yet a long course to run in the Centralias of the world. She feared that many Anns had yet to go down before them.

At any rate, her uncle was not that. To-night Katie loved him anew for his delightful worldliness.

Though he was not in his best form that night. He was on his way out to Colorado for the marriage of his son. "There was no doing anything about it," he said with a sigh. "My office has made me enough the diplomat, Katherine, to know when to quit trying. So I'm going out there—fearful trip—why it's miles from Denver—to do all I can to respectablize the affair. It seemed to me a trifle inconsiderate—in view of the effort I'm making—that they could not have waited until next month; there are things calling me to Denver then. Now what shall I do there all that time?—though I may run on to California. But it seems my daughter-in-law would have her honeymoon in the mountains while the aspens are just a certain yellow she's fond of. So of course"—with his little shrug Katie loved—"what's my having a month on my hands?"

"Well, uncle, dear uncle," she laughed, "hast forgotten the days when nothing mattered so much as having the leaves the right shade of yellow?"

"I have not—and trust I never will," he replied, with a touch of asperity; "but I feel that Fred has shown very little consideration for his parents."

"But why, uncle? I'm strong for her! She sounds to me like just what our family needs."

He gave her a glance over his glasses—that delighted Katie, too; she had long ago learned that when her uncle felt occasion demand he look like a bishop he lowered his chin and looked over his glasses.

"Well our family may need something; it's the first intimation I've had, Katherine, that it's in distress—but I don't see that a young woman who votes is the crying need of the family."

"She's in great luck," returned Katie, "to live in a State where she can vote."

He held up his hands. "*Katie? You?*"

"Oh I haven't prowled around this town all summer, uncle, without seeing things that women ought to be voting about."

He stared at her. "Well, Katie, you—you don't mean to take it up, do you?"

He looked so unhappy that she laughed. "Oh I don't know, uncle, what I mean to 'take up,' but I herewith serve notice that I'm going to take something up—something besides bridge and army gossip."

She looked at him reflectively. "Uncle, does it ever come home to you that life's a pretty serious business?"

"Well I hadn't wanted it to come home to me tonight," he sighed plaintively. "I'm really most upset about this unfortunate affair. I had thought that you, Katie, would be pleasant."

"Forgive me," she laughed. "I can see how it must disturb you, uncle, to hear me express a serious thought."

He laughed at her delightedly. He loved Katie. "You've got the fidgets, Katie. Just the fidgets. That's what's the matter with the whole lot of you youngsters. It's becoming an epidemic—a sort of spiritual measles. Though I must say, I hadn't expected you to catch it. And just a word of warning, Katie. You've always been so unique as a trifler that one rather hates to see you swallowed up in the troop of serious-minded young women. I was talking to Darrett the other day—charming fellow, Darrett—and he held that your charm was in your brilliant smile. I told him I hadn't thought so much about the brilliant smile, but that I knew a good deal about a certain impish grin. Katie, you have a very disreputable grin. You have a way of directing it at me across ponderous drawing-rooms that I wish you'd stop. It gives me a sort of—'Oh I am on to you, uncle old boy' feeling that is most—"

"Disconcerting?"

"Unreverential."

He looked at her, humorously and yet meditatively—fondly. "Katie, why do you think it's so funny? Why does it make you want to grin?"

"You know. Else you wouldn't read the grin."

"But I don't know. Nobody else grins at me."

"Oh don't you think we're a good deal of a joke, uncle?"

"Joke? Who?—Why?"

"Us. The solemnity with which we take ourselves and the way the world lets us do it."

He laughed. Then, as one coming back to his lines: "You have no reverence."

"No, neither have you. That's why we get on."

He made an unsuccessful attempt at frowning upon her and surveyed her a little more seriously. "Katie, do you know that the things you say sometimes puzzle me. They're queer. They burrow. They're so insultingly knowing, down at the root of their unknowingness. I'll think—'She didn't know how "pat" that was'—and then as I consider it I'll think—'Yes, she did, only she didn't know that she knew.' I remember telling your mother once when you were a little girl that if you were going to sit through service with your head cocked in that knowing fashion I wished she'd leave you at home."

Katie laughed and cocked her head at him again, just to show she had not forgotten. Then she fell serious.

"Uncle, for a long time I only smiled. I seemed to know enough to do that. Do you think you could bear it with Christian fortitude if I were to tell you I'm beginning now to try and figure out what I was smiling at?"

He shook his head. "'Twould spoil it."

He looked at his niece and smiled as he asked: "Katie dear, are you becoming world weary?" Katie, very smart that night in white gown and black hat, appealed to him as distinctly humorous in the role of world weariness.

"No," returned Katie, "not world weary; just weary of not knowing the world."

Afterward in his room they chatted cheerfully of many things: family affairs, army and church affairs. Katie strove to keep to them as merely personal matters.

But there were no merely personal matters any more. All the little things were paths to the big things. There was no way of keeping herself detached. Even the seemingly isolated topic of the recent illness of the Bishop's wife led full upon the picture of other people she had been seeing that summer who looked ill.

Her uncle was telling of a case he had recently disposed of, a rector of his diocese who was guilty of an atheistic book. He spoke feelingly of what he called the shallowness of rationalism, of the dangers of the age, beautifully of that splendid past which the church must conserve. He told of some lectures he himself was to deliver on the fallacies of socialism. "It's honeycombing our churches, Katherine—yes, and even the army. Darrett tells me they've found it's spreading among the men. Nice state of affairs were we to have any sort of industrial war!"

It was hard for Katie to keep silence, but she felt so sadly the lack of assurance arising from lack of knowledge. Well, give her a little time, she would fix that!

She contented herself with asking if he anticipated an industrial war.

The Bishop made a large gesture and said he hoped not, but he felt it a time for the church to throw all her forces to safeguarding the great heritage of the country's institutions. He especially deplored that the church itself did not see it more clearly, more unitedly. He mentioned fellow bishops who seemed to be actually encouraging inroads upon tradition. Where did they expect it to lead?—he demanded.

"Perhaps," meekly suggested Katie, "they expect it to lead to growth."

"Growth!" snorted the Bishop. "Destruction!"

They passed to the sunnier subject of raising money. As regards the budget, Bishop Wayneworth was the church's most valued servant. His manner of good-humored tolerance gave Mammon a soothing sense of being understood, moving the much maligned god to reach for its check book, just to bear the friendly bishop out in his lenient interpretation of a certain text about service rendered in two directions.

He was telling of a fund he expected to raise at a given time. If he did, a certain capitalist would duplicate it. The Bishop became jubilant at the prospect.

And as they talked, there passed before Katie, as in review, the things she had seen that summer—passed before her the worn faces of those girls who night after night during the hot summer had come from the stores and factories where the men of whom her uncle was so jubilantly speaking made the money which they were able to subscribe to the church. She thought of her uncle's church; she could not recall having seen many such faces in the pews of that church. She thought of Ann—wondered where Ann might be that night while she and her uncle chatted so cheerfully in his pleasant room at his luxurious hotel. She tried to think of anything for which her uncle stood which would give her confidence in saying to herself, "Ann will be saved." The large sum of money over which he was gloating was to be used for a new cathedral. She wondered if the Anns of her uncle's city would find the world a safer or a sweeter place after that cathedral had been erected. She thought of Ann's world of the opera and world of work. Was it true—as the man who mended the boats would hold—that the one made the other possible—only to be excluded from it? And all the while there swept before her faces—faces seen in the crowd, faces of those who were not finding what they wanted, faces of all those to whom life denied life. And then Katie thought of a man who had lived & long time before, a man of whom her uncle spoke lovingly in his sermons as Jesus the Christ, the Son of the living God. She thought of Ann's father—how far he had gone from a religion of love. Then came back to her lovable uncle. Well, what of him?

Charm of personality, a sense of humor, a comfortable view of living (for himself and his kind) did not seem the final word.

"Uncle," Katie asked quietly, "do you ever think much about Christ?"

In his astonishment the Bishop dropped his cigar.

"What a strange man he must have been," she murmured.

"Kindly explain yourself," said he curtly.

"He seemed to think so much about people. Just people. And chiefly people who were down on their luck. I don't believe he would have been much good at raising money. He had such a queer way of going around where people worked, talking with them about their work. If he were here now, and were to do that, I wonder if he'd help much in 'stemming the rising tide of socialism' What a blessing it is for our institutions," Katie concluded, "that he's not anywhere around."

The Bishop's hand shook. "I had not expected," he said, "that my own niece, my favorite niece—indeed, the favorite member of my family—was here to—revile me."

"Uncle—forgive me! But isn't it bigger than that thing of being members of the same family—hurting each other's feelings? Oh uncle!" she burst forth, no longer able to hold back, "as you stand sometimes at the altar don't you hear them moaning and sobbing down underneath?"

He looked at her sharply, with some alarm.

"Oh no," she laughed, "not going crazy. Just trying to think a little about things. But don't you ever hear them, uncle? I should think they might—bother you sometimes."

"Really, Katherine," he said stiffly, "this is most—annoying. Hear whom moaning and sobbing?"

"Those people! The worn out shop girls and broken down men and women and diseased children that your church is built right on top of!"

Not the words but the sob behind them moved him to ask gently: "Katie dear, what is it? What's the trouble?"

Her eyes were swimming. "Uncle—it's the misery of the world! It's the people who aren't where they belong! It's the lives ruined through blunders—it's the cruelty—the needless *cruelty* of it all." She leaned forward, the tears upon her cheeks. "Uncle, how can you? You have a mind—a kind heart. But what good are they? If you believe the things you say you believe—oh you think you believe them—but you don't seem to connect them. Here to-night we've been talking about the forms of the church—finances of the church—and humanity is in *need*, uncle—bodily need—and oh the *heart* need! Why don't you go and see? Why you've only to look! What are your puny little problems of the church compared with people's lives? And yet you—cut off—detached—save in so far as feeding on them goes—claim to be following in the footsteps of a man who followed in *their* footsteps—a man who went about seeing how people lived—finding out what troubled them—trying—" She sank back with a sob. "I didn't mean to—but I simply *can't understand it*. Can't understand how you *can*."

She hid her face. *Those faces*—they passed and passed.

He had risen and was walking about the room. After a moment he stopped and cleared his throat. "If I didn't think, Katherine, that something had happened to almost derange you, I should not have permitted you to continue these ravings."

She raised her head defiantly. "Truths people don't want to hear are usually disposed of as ravings!"

"Now if I may be permitted a word. Your indictment is not at all new, though your heat in making it would indicate you believed yourself to be saying something never said before—"

"I know it's been said before! I'm more interested in knowing how it's been answered."

"You have never seemed sufficiently interested in the affairs of the church, Katherine, for one to think of seriously discussing our charities with you—"

"Uncle, do you know what your charities make me think of?"

He had resumed his chair—and cigar. "No," he said coldly, "I do not know what they make you 'think of.' I was attempting to tell you what they were."

"I know what they are. The idea that comes to my mind has a rather vulgar—"

"Oh, pray do not hesitate, Katherine. You have not been speaking what I would call delicately."

"Your charities are like waving a scented handkerchief over the stockyards. Or like handing out after-dinner mints to a mob of starving men."

"You're quite the wrong end there—as is usual with you agitators," he replied comfortably. "We don't give them mints. We give them soup."

"*Giving* them soup—even if you did—is the mint end. Why don't you give them jobs?"

He spread out his hands in gesture of despair. "What a bore a little learning can make of one! My dear niece, I deeply regret to be compelled to inform you that there aren't 'jobs' enough to go around."

"Why aren't there?"

"Why the obvious reason would seem, Katie," he replied patiently, "that there are too many of them wanting them."

"And as usual, the obvious reason is not it. There are too many of you and me—that's the trouble. They don't have the soup because they must furnish us the mints." It was Katie who had risen now and was walking about the room. Her cheeks were blazing. "I tell you, uncle, I feel it's a disgrace the way we live—taking everything and doing nothing. I feel positively cheap about it. The army and the church and all the other useless things—"

"I do not agree with you that the army is useless and I certainly cannot permit you to say the church is."

"You'll not be able to stop other people from saying it!"

He seemed about to make heated reply, but instead sank back with an amused smile. "Katie, your learning sounds very suspiciously as though it were put on last night. I feel like putting up a sign—'Fresh Paint—Keep Off.'"

"Well at any rate it's not mouldy!"

"At college I roomed with a chap who had a way of discovering things, getting in a fine glow of discovery over things everybody else had known. He would wake me out of a sound sleep to tell me something I had heard the week before."

"And it's trying to be waked out of a sound sleep, isn't it, uncle?" she flashed back at him.

It ended with his kindly assuring her that he was glad she had begun to think about the problems of the world; that no one knew better than he that there was a social problem—and a grave one; that men of the church had written some excellent things on the subject—he would send her some of them. Indeed, he would be glad to do all in his power to help her to a better understanding of things. He was convinced, he said soothingly, that when she had gone a little farther into them she would see them more sanely.

CHAPTER XXXI

Katie was back home; or, more accurately, she was back at Wayne's quarters, where they could perhaps remain for a month or two longer.

And craving some simple, natural thing, something that could not make the heart ache, she went out that afternoon to play golf. The physical Kate, Katie of the sound body, was delighted to be back playing golf. Every little cell sang its song of rejoicing—rejoicing in emancipation from the ill-smelling crowds, return to the open air and the good green earth.

It seemed a saving thing that they could so rejoice.

Katie was reading the little book on man's evolution which the man who was having much to do with her evolution had—it seemed long ago—sent her in the package marked "Danger." She had finished the book about women and was just looking through the one on evolution on the day Caroline Osborne's car had stopped at her door. That began a swift series of events leaving small place for reading. But when, that last day they were together in Chicago, she asked him about something to read, he suggested a return to that book. There seemed wisdom and kindness in the suggestion. The story of evolution was to the mind what the game of golf was to the body. With the life about her pressing in too close there was something freeing and saving in that glimpse of herself as part of all the life there had ever been. Because the crowds had seemed the all—were suffocating her—something in that vastness of vision was as fresh air after a stifling room. It was not that it did away with the crowds—made her think they did not matter; they were, after all, the more vital—imperative—but she had more space in which to see them, was given a chance to understand them rather than be blindly smothered by them.

For a number of years Katie had known that there was such a thing as evolution. It had something to do with an important man named Darwin. He got it up. It was the idea that we came from monkeys. The monkey was not Katie's favorite animal and she would have been none too pleased with the idea had it not been that there was something so delicious about solemn people like her Aunt Elizabeth and proper people like Clara having come from them. She was willing to stand it herself, just because if she came from them they did, too. She had assumed all along that she believed in Darwin and that people who did not believe in him were benighted. But the chief reason she had for believing in him was that the church had not believed in him. That was through neither malice nor conviction as regards the church, but merely because it was exciting to have some one disagreeing with it. It had thrilled her as "fearless," She had always meant to find out more about evolution, she had a hazy idea that there was a great deal more to it than just the fact of having come from monkeys, but she led such a busy life — bridge and things—that there was never time and so it remained a thing she believed in and was some day going to find out about.

Now she was furious with herself and with everybody connected with her for having lived so much of her life shut out from the knowledge— vision—that made life so vast and so splendid. It was like having lived all one's life in sight of the sea and being so busy walking around a silly little lake in a park that there was no time to turn one's face seaward. She wondered what she would think of a person who said the little toy lake kept her so busy there was never a minute to turn around and take a good look at the sea!

Katie had always loved the great world of living things—the fishes and birds—all animals—all things that grew. They had always called to her imagination—she used to make up stories about them. She saw now that their real story was a thousand-fold more wonderful—more the story—than anything she had been able to invent. She would give much to have known it long before. She felt that she had missed much. There was something humiliating in the thought of having lived one's life without knowing what life was. It made one seem such a dead thing. Now she was on fire to know all about it.

She smiled as it suggested to her what her uncle had said a few days before of the fresh paint. She supposed there was some truth in it, that one who was conserving the past must find something raw and ludicrous in her state of mind. Her passion to fairly devour knowledge would probably bring to many of them the same amused smile it had brought to her uncle. But it was surprising how little she minded the smile. She was too intent on the things she would devour.

Her glimpse into this actual story of life brought the first purely religious feeling she had ever known. It even brought the missionary fervor, which, as they sat down to rest, she exercised upon Worth, who had been proudly filling the office of caddy. She told him that she was going to tell him the most wonderful fairy story there had ever been in the world. And the thing that made it most wonderful of all was that, while it was just like a fairy story in being wonderful, it was every bit true. And then she told him a little of the great story of how one thing became another thing, how everything grew out of something else, how it had been doing that for millions of years, how he was what he was then because through all those years one thing had changed, grown, into something else.

As she told it it seemed so noble a thing to be telling a child, so much purer and more dignified—to say nothing of more stimulating—than the evasive tales of life employed in the attempt to thwart her childish mind.

Worth was upon her with a hundred questions. *How* did a worm become something that wasn't a worm? Did it know it was going to do it? And why did one worm go one way and in a lot of million years be a little boy and another worm go another way and just never be anything but a worm? Did she think in another hundred million years that little bird up there would be something else? Would *they* be anything else? And why—?

She saw that she had let herself in for a whole new world of whys. One thing was certain: if she were to remain with Worth she would have to find out more about evolution. Her knowledge was pitifully incommensurate to his whys.

But it was beautiful to her the way his mind reached out to it. He was lying on his stomach, head propped up on hands, in an almost prayerful attitude before an ant hill. Did she think those little ants knew that they were alive? Would they ever be anything else? He wanted to be told more stories about things becoming other things, seemed intoxicated with that idea of the constant becoming.

"But, Aunt Kate," he cried, "mama told me that God made me!"

"Why so He did, Worthie—that is, I suppose He did—but He didn't just make you out of nothing."

He lay there on the grass in silence for a long time, looking at the world about him—thinking. After a while he was singing a little song. This was the song:

"Once I was a little worm—
Long—long—ago."

Katie smiled in thinking how scandalized Clara would be to have heard the story just told her son, story moving him to sing a vulgar song about having been a horrid little worm. It would be Clara's notion of propriety to tell Worth that the doctor brought him in his motor car and expect his mind, that wonderful, plastic little mind of his, to be proper enough to rest content with that lucid exposition of the wonder of life.

The time was near for Clara's six months of Worth to begin. Katie had promised she would bring him to her wherever she was; and Clara was in Paris and meaning to remain there. It meant that Worth would spend the winter in Paris, away from them; from time to time—as the custom of the city dictated—he would be taken for perfunctory little walks in the *Bois* and would be told to "run and play" if he asked indelicate questions concerning the things of life.

> In the light of this story of the ways of growth the arrangement about Worth seemed an unnatural and a brutal thing.

She did not believe that, as a matter of fact, Clara wanted Worth. The maternal passion was less strong in Clara than the passion for *lingerie*. But she wanted Worth with her for six months because that kept him from Wayne and Katie for six months and she knew that they did want him.

The poor little fellow's summer had not been what Katie had planned. Part of the time he had been with his father and part of the time with her— that thing of division again, and as neither of them had been happy any of the time Worth had had to suffer for it. He seemed to have to suffer so much through the fact that grown-up people did not know how to manage their lives.

Suddenly he sat up. "Aunt Kate," he asked, "when's Miss Ann coming back?"

"I don't know, dear."

"Well where *is* she?"

"She's been—called away."

"Well I wish she'd come back. I like Miss Ann, Aunt Kate."

"Yes, dear; we all do."

"She tells nice stories, too. Only they're about fairies that are just fairies—not worms and things that are really so. Do you suppose Miss Ann knows, Aunt Kate, that she used to be a frog?"

Katie laughed and tried to elucidate her point about the frog. But she wondered what difference it might not have made had Ann known that, as Worth put it, she used to be a frog. With Ann, fairy stories would have to be about things not real. All Ann's life it had been so. It suddenly seemed that it might have made all the difference in the world had Ann known that the things most wonderful were the things that were.

Or rather, had the world in which Ann lived cared to know real things for precious things, the desire for life as the most radiant thing that had ever been upon the earth. Ann would have found the world a different place had men known life for the majestic thing it was, seen that back of what her uncle called the "splendid heritage of the country's institutions" was the vastly more splendid heritage of the institution of life. Letting the former shut them from the latter was being too busy with the toy lake to look out at the sea.

Seeing Ann as part of all the life that had ever been upon the earth she became, not infinitesimal, but newly significant. Widened outlook brought deepened feeling. Newly understanding, she sat there brooding over Ann anew, pain in the perfection of her understanding.

But new courage. Life had persisted through so much, was so triumphant. The larger conception lent its glow to the paling belief that Ann would persist, triumph.

"Aunt Kate," Worth burst forth, "let's take the boat and go up and find the man that mends the boats."

Aunt Kate blushed. "Oh no, dearie, we couldn't do that."

"Why we did do it once," argued Worth.

"I know, but we can't do it now."

"I don't see why not."

No, Worth didn't see.

"I just want to ask him, Aunt Kate, if he knows that he used to live in a tree."

"Oh, he knows it," she laughed.

"He knows everything," said Worth.

"Worthie, is that why you like him? 'Cause he knows everything? Or do you like him—just because you like him?"

"I like him because he knows everything—but mostly I like him just because I like him."

"Same here," breathed Aunt Kate.

The man who mended the boats was coming to see her that night. Perhaps golf and evolution should not grow arrogant, after all.

He had been strange about coming; when she talked with him over the 'phone he had hesitated at the suggestion and finally said, with a defiance she could not see the situation called for, that he would like to come. In

Chicago he had once said to her: "There's too much gloom around you now for me to contribute the story of my life. But please remember that that was why I didn't tell it."

She wondered if the "story of his life" had anything to do with his hesitancy in coming to see her. Surely he would have no commonplace notions about "different spheres," though he had mentioned them, and with bitterness. He was especially hostile to the army, had more than once hurt her in his hostility. She would not have resented his attacking it as an institution, that she would expect from his philosophy, but it was a sort of personal contempt for the army and its people she had resented, almost as she would a contemptuous attitude toward her own family.

She had contended that he was unjust; that a lack of sympathy with the ends of the army—basis of it—should not bring him to a prejudiced attitude toward its people. She maintained that officers of the army were a higher type than civilians of the same class. He had told her, almost roughly, that he didn't think she knew anything about it, and she had replied, heatedly, that she would like to know why she wouldn't know more about it than he! In the end he said he was sorry to have hurt her when there was so much else to hurt her, but had not retracted what he had said, or even admitted the possibility of mistake.

It seemed that one of the worst things about "classes" was that they inevitably meant misunderstanding. They bred antagonism, and that prejudice. People didn't know each other.

Considering it now, she wondered, though feeling traitorous to him in the wondering, if the man who mended the boats might shrink from anything so distinctly social as calling upon her.

Their meetings theretofore had been on a bigger and a sterner basis; she had missed a few of the little niceties of consideration, a few of those perfunctory and yet curiously vital courtesies to which she had all her life been accustomed as a matter of course from her army men; but it had been as if they were merely leaving them behind for things larger and deeper, as if their background was the real world rather than world of perfunctory things. From him she had a consideration, not perfunctory, but in the mood of the things they were sharing. That sense of sharing big things, things real and rude, had swept them out of the world of artificial things. Now did he perhaps hold back in timidity from that world of the trivial things?

She put it from her, disliking herself as of the trivial things in letting it suggest itself at all. Expecting him to be just like the men she had known would be expecting the sea to behave like that lake in the park.

That night she put on her most attractive gown, a dress sometimes gray and sometimes cloudy blues and greens, itself like the sea, and finding in Katie a more mysterious quality than her openness would usually suggest. Feeling called upon to make some account to herself for dressing more than occasion would seem to demand, she told herself that she must get the poor old thing worn out and get something new.

But it was not a poor old thing, and the last thing Katie really wanted was to succeed in getting it worn out.

As she dressed she was thinking of Ann's pleasure in clothes. There were times when it had seemed a not altogether likeable vanity. It was understandable—lovable—after having been to Centralia, after knowing. So many things were understandable and lovable after knowing.

She wished she might call across the hall and ask Ann to come in and fasten her dress. She would like to chat with her about the way she had done her hair—all those intimate little things they had countless times talked about so gayly.

She walked over into Ann's room—room in which Ann had taken such pride and pleasure. Ann had loved the things on the dressing-table, she had more than once seen her fairly caressing those pretty ivory things. She wondered if Ann had anything resembling a dressing-table—what she wore—how she managed.

Those were the little worries about Ann forever haunting her, as they would a mother who had a child away from home. New vision of the immensity of life could save her from giving destroying place to that sense of the woe of the world, but a conception of the wonders of the centuries could not keep out the gnawing fear that Ann might not be getting enough to eat.

There was a complexity in her mood of that night—happiness and sadness so close as at times to be indistinguishable—the whole of it making for a sense of the depth of life.

But their evening was constrained. Katie blamed the dress for part of it, vexed with herself for having put it on. She had wanted to be attractive—not suggest the unattainable.

And that was what something seemed suggesting. He appeared less ill at ease than morose. Katie herself, after having been so happy in his coming, was, now that he was there, uncontrollably depressed. They talked of a variety of things—in the main, the things she had been reading—but something had happened to that wonderful thing which had grown warm in their hearts as they walked those last two blocks.

Even the things of which they talked had lost their radiance. What did it matter whether the universe was wonderful or not if the wonderful thing in one's own heart was to be denied life?

From the first, it had been as if the things of which they talked were things sweeping them together, they were in the grip of the power and the wonder of those things, wrung by the tragedy of them, exalted by the hope—in it all, by it all, united. It was as if the whole sea of experience and emotion, suffering and aspiration, was driving, holding, them together.

So it had been all along.

But not tonight. It was now—or at least so it seemed to Katie—as if those forces had let them go. What had been as a great sea surging around their hearts was now just things to talk about.

It left her desolate. And as she grew unhappy, she forced her gaiety and that seemed to put him the farther away.

The two different worlds had sent Ann away; was it, in a way she was unable to cope with, likewise to send him away?

Watts passed through the hall. She saw him glance out at the soldier loweringly and after that he grew more morose, almost sullenly so.

It seemed foolish to talk of one's being free when held by things one could not even see.

It was just when she was feeling so lonely and miserable she wished he would go that the telephone rang and central told her that Chicago was trying to get her.

It was in the manner of the old days that she turned to him and asked what he thought it could be.

The suggestion—possibility—swept them back to the old basis, the old relationship. Katie grew excited, unnerved, and he talked to her soothingly while she waited for central to call again.

They spoke of what it probably was; her brother was in Chicago, Katie told him, and of course it was he, and something about his own affairs. Perhaps he had news of when he would be ordered away. Yes, without doubt that was it.

But there was a consciousness of dissembling. They were drawn together by the possibility they did not mention, drawn together in the very thing of not mentioning it.

As in those tense moments they tried to talk of other things, they were keyed high in the consciousness of not talking of the real thing. And in that there was suggestion of the other thing of which they were not talking. It was all inexplicably related: the excitement, the tenseness, the waiting, the dissembling.

Katie had never been more lovely than as she sat there with her hand on the telephone: flushed, stirred, expectant—something stealing back to her eyes, something both pleading and triumphant in Katie's eyes just then.

The man sitting close beside her at the telephone desk scarcely took his eyes from her face.

When the bell rang again and her hand shook as it took down the receiver he lay a steadying hand upon her arm.

At first there was nothing more than a controversy as to who had the line. In her impatience, she rose; he rose, too, standing beside her.

"Here's your party," said central at last.

Her "party" was Wayne.

But something was still the matter on the line; she could not get what Wayne was trying to tell her.

As her excitement became more difficult to control the man at her side kept speaking to her—touching her—soothingly.

At last she could hear Wayne. "You hear me, Katie?"

"Oh yes—*yes*—what is it?"

"I want to tell you—"

It was swallowed up in a buzzing on the line.

Then central's voice came clear and crisp. "Your party is trying to tell you that *Ann* is found."

"Oh—" gasped Katie, and lost all color—"Oh—"

"Katie—?" That was Wayne again.

"Oh *yes*, Wayne?"

"I have found her. She is well—that is, will be well. She is all right—going to be all right. I'll write it all to-morrow. It's all over, Katie. You don't have to worry any more."

The next instant the telephone was upside down on the table and Katie, sobbing, was in his arms. He was holding her close; and as her sobs grew more violent he kissed her hair, murmured loving things. Suddenly she raised her head—lifting her face to his. He kissed her; and all the splendor of those eons of life was Katie's then.

CHAPTER XXXII

Captain Jones had come down from Fort Sheridan late that afternoon. He had been in Chicago for several days, as a member of a board assembled up at Fort Sheridan. The work was over and he would return to the Arsenal that night.

But he was not to go until midnight. He would have dinner and go to the theater with some of the friends with whom he had been in those last few days.

He wished it were otherwise. He was in no mood for them. He would far rather have been alone.

He had a little time alone in his room before dinner and sat there smoking, thinking, looking at the specks of men and women moving about in the streets way down there below.

He was in no humor that night to keep to the everlasting talk about army affairs, army grievances and schemes, all those things of a world within a world treated as if larger than the whole of the world. The last few days had shown him anew how their hold on him was loosening.

There seemed such a thing as the army habit of mind. Within their own domain was orderliness, discipline, efficiency, subservience to the collectivity, pride in it, devotion to it—many things of mind and character sadly needed in the chaotic world without. But army men lacked perspective; in isolation they had lost their sense of proportion, of relationships. They had not a true vision of themselves as part of a whole. They had, on the other hand, unconsciously fallen into the way of assuming the whole existed for the part, that they were larger than the thing they were meant to serve. Their whole scale was so proportioned; their whole sense of adjustment so perverted.

They lacked flexibility—openness—all-sides-aroundness.

Life in the army disciplined one in many things valuable in life. It failed in giving a true sense of the values of life.

He could not have said why it was those inflated proportions irritated him so. They lent an unreality to everything. They made for false standards. And more and more the thing which mattered to him was reality.

He tried to pull away from the things that thought would lure him into. He had not the courage to let himself think of her tonight.

He feared he had not increased his popularity in the last few days. At a dinner the night before a colonel had put an end to a discussion on war, in which several of the younger officers showed dangerous symptoms of hospitality to the civilian point of view, with the pious pronouncement: "War was ordained by God."

"But man pays the war tax," he had not been able to resist adding, and the Colonel had not joined in the laugh.

He found it wearisome the way the army remained so smug in its assumption that God stood right behind it. When worsted on economic grounds—and perhaps driven also from "survival of the fittest" shelter—a pompous retreat could always be effected to divinity.

It was that same colonel who, earlier in the evening, had thus ended a discussion on the unemployed. "The poor ye have always with you," said the Colonel, delicately smacking his lips over his champagne and gently turning the conversation to the safer topic of high explosives.

He turned impatiently from thought of it to the men and women far down below. He was always looking now at crowds of men and women, always hoping for a familiar figure in those crowds.

With all the baffling unreality there had been around her, she seemed to express reality. She made him want it. She made him want life. Made him feel what he was missing—realize what he had never had.

It seemed that if he did not find her he would not find life.

She, too, had wanted life. Her quest had been for life—that he knew. And he wanted to find her that he might tell her he understood, tell her—what he had never told any one—that all his life he, too, had dreamed of a something somewhere.

And he was growing the farther apart from his army friends because he had come to think of them as standing between.

During the summer he had seen. In the mornings when they were going to work, in the evenings when they were going home, he had many times been upon the streets with the people who worked. He could not any longer regard the enlargement of the army, its organization and problems as the most vital thing in the world. It did not seem to him that what the world wanted was a more deadly rifle. His lip curled a little as he looked down at the men and women below and considered how little difference it made to them whether rifles were improved or not. And so many things did make difference with them—they needed improvements on so many things—that to be giving one's life to perfecting instruments of destruction struck him as a sorry vocation.

It made him feel very distinctly apart.

He knew of no class of men more isolated from the real war of the world than were the men of the army. They were tied up in their own war of competition—competition in preparedness for war. They were frantically occupied in the creation of a Frankenstein. They would so perfect destruction as to destroy themselves. Meanwhile their blood had grown so hot in their war of competition that they were in prime condition for persuading themselves a real war awaited them. This hot blood found its way into much talk of hardihood and strenuousness, vigor, martial virtues, "the steeps of life," "the romance of history"—all calculated to raise the temperature of tax-paying blood. So successful was the self-delusion of the militarist that sanity appeared mollycoddelism.

Their greatest fear was fear of the loss of fear.

And now they were threatened by colorless economists who were mollycoddelistically making clear that the "stern reality" was the giant hallucination.

It seemed rather close to farce.

That night he was going back. Katie, too, had gone. For the first time that summer neither of them would be there. It seemed giving up.

Loneliness reached out into places vast and barren in the thought that both in the things of the heart and the affairs of men he seemed destined to remain apart.

He looked far more the dreamer than the man of warfare as he sat there, his face, which was so finely sensitive as sometimes to be called cold, saddened with the light of dreams which know themselves for dreams alone.

That very first night, night when she had been so shy, he had felt in her that which he called the real thing, which he knew for the great thing, which had been, for him, the thing unattainable. And with all her timidity, aloofness, elusiveness, he had felt an inexplicable nearness to her.

He had found out something about the conditions girls had to meet. His face hardened, then tightened with pain in the thought of those being the conditions Ann was meeting. He did not believe those conditions would go on many days longer if every man had to see them in relation to some one he cared for. "The poor ye have always with you" might then prove less authoritative—less satisfying—as the final word.

And the other conditions—things his sort stood for—Darrett—the whole story—He had come to loathe the words chivalry and honor and all the rest of the empty terms that resounded so glibly against false standards.

Something was wrong with the world and he could not see that improving a rifle was going to go very far toward setting it right.

And there was springing up within him, even in his loneliness and gloom, a passion to be doing something that would help set it right.

An older officer with whom he had been talking that day had spoken lovingly of his father, under whom he had served; spoken of his hardihood and integrity, his manliness and soldierliness. As he thought of it now it seemed to him that just because he *was* his father's son—had in him the blood of the soldier—he should help fight the real battles of the day—the long stern battles of peace.

His father had served, faithfully and well. He, too, would like to serve. But yesterday's needs were not to-day's needs, nor were the methods of yesterday desirable, even possible, for to-day. What could be farther from serving one's own day than rendering to it the dead forms of what had been the real service to a day gone by?

There came a curious thought that to give up the things of war might be the only way to save the things that war had left him. That perhaps he could only transmit his heritage by recasting the form of giving.

Looking out across the miles of the city's roofs, hearing the rumble of the city as it came faintly up to him, watching the people hurrying to and fro, there was something puerile in the argument that men any longer needed war to fill their lives, must have the war fear to keep them from softness and degeneration. Thinking of the problems of that very city, it seemed men need not worry greatly about having nothing to fight for, no stimulus to manhood.

Men and women! Those men and women passing back and forth and all the millions of their kind, they were what counted. The things that mattered to them were the things that mattered. Their needs the things to fight for.

So he reflected and drifted, brushing now this, now that, in thought and fancy.

Weary—lonely—he dreamed a dream, dream such as the weary and the lonely have dreamed before, will dream again. Too utterly alone, he dreamed he was not alone. Heart-hungry, he dreamed of love. He dreamed of Ann. He had dreamed of her before, would dream of her again. Dream of her, if for nothing else, because he knew she had dreamed of love; because she made him know that it was there, because, unreasoningly, she made him hope.

Her face that night at the dance—that night in the boat, when they had talked almost not at all, had seemed to feel no need for talking—things remembered blended with things desired until it seemed he could feel her hair brush his face, feel her breath upon his cheek, her arms about his neck—vivid as if given by memories instead of wooed from dreams.

But the benign dream became torturing vision—vision of Ann with hands held out to him—going down—her wonderful eyes fearful with terror.

It was that which dreaming held for him.

And it seemed that he—he and his kind—all of those who stood for the things not real were the thing beating Ann down.

Dreams gone and vision mercifully falling away there came a yearning, just a simple human yearning, to know where she was. He felt he could bear anything if only he knew that she was safe.

The telephone rang. He supposed it was some of his friends—something about the hour for dining.

He would not answer. Could not. Too sick of it all—too sore.

But it kept ringing, and, habit in the ascendency, he took down the receiver.

It was not a man's voice. It was a woman's. A faint voice—he could scarcely catch it.

And could with difficulty reply. He did not know the voice, it was too faint, too far-away, but a suggestion in it made his own voice and hand unsteady as he said: "Yes? What is it?"

"Is this—Captain Jones?"

The voice was stronger, clearer. His hand grew more unsteady.

"Yes," he replied in the best voice he could muster. "Yes—this is Captain Jones. Who is it, please?"

There was a silence.

"Tell me, please," he managed to say. "Is it—?"

The voice came faintly back, "Why it's—Ann."

The keenest joy he had ever known swept through him. To be followed by the most piercing fear. The voice was so faint—so unreal—what if it were to die away and he would have no way to get it back!

It seemed he could not hold it. For an instant he was crazed with the sense of powerlessness. He felt it must even then be slipping back into the abyss from which it had emerged.

Then he fought. Got himself under command; sent his own voice full and strong over the wire as if to give life to the voice it seemed must fade away.

"Ann," he said firmly, authoritatively, "listen to me. No matter what happens—no matter what's the matter—I've got something you must hear. If we're cut off, call up again. Will you do that? Are you listening?"

"Yes," came Ann's voice, more sure.

"I've got to see you. You hear what I say? It's about Katie. You care a little something for Katie, don't you, Ann?"

It was a sob rather than a voice came back to him.

"Then tell me where I can find you."

She hesitated.

"Tell me where you're living—or where I can find you. Now tell me the truth, Ann. If you knew the condition Katie was in—"

She gave him an address on a street he did not know.

"Would you rather I came there? Or rather I meet you down town? Just as you say. Only I *must* see you tonight."

"I—I can't come down town. I'm sick."

His hand on the receiver tightened. His voice, which had been almost harsh in its dominance, was different as he said: "Then I'll come there— right away."

There was no reply, but he felt she was still there. "And, Ann," he said, very low, and far from harshly, "I want to see you, too."

There was a little sob in which he faintly got "Good-bye."

He sank to a chair. His face was buried in his hands. It was several minutes before he moved.

CHAPTER XXXIII

Children seemed to spring up from the sidewalk and descend from the roofs as his cab, after a long trip through crowded streets with which three months before he would have been totally unfamiliar, stopped at the number Ann had given. All the way over he had been seeing children: dirty children, pale-faced children, children munching at things and children looking as though they had never had anything to munch at—children playing and children crying—it seemed the children's part of town. The men and women of tomorrow were growing up in a part of the city too loathsome for the civilized man and woman of today to set foot in. He was too filled with thought of Ann—the horror of its being where she lived—to let the bigger thought of it brush him more than fleetingly, but it did occur to him that there was still a frontier—and that the men who could bring about smokeless cities—and odorless ones—would be greater public servants than the men who had achieved smokeless powder. Riding through that part of town it would scarcely suggest itself to any one that what the country needed was more battleships.

The children still waited as he rang an inhospitable doorbell, as interested in life as if life had been treating them well.

He had to ring again before a woman came to the door with a cup in her hand which she was wiping on a greasy towel.

She looked very much as the bell had sounded.

She let him in to a place which it seemed might not be a bad field for some of the army's boasted experts on sanitation. It was a place to make one define civilization as a thing that reduces smell.

Several heads were stuck out of opening doors and with each opening door a wave stole out from an unlovely life. Captain Wayneworth Jones, U. S. Army, dressed for dining at a place where lives are better protected against lives, was a strange center for those waves from lives of struggle.

"She the girl that's sick?" the woman demanded in response to his inquiry for Miss Forrest.

He replied that he feared she was ill and was told to go to the third floor and turn to the right. It was the second door.

He hesitated, coloring.

"Would you be so kind as to tell her I am here? I think perhaps she may prefer to see me—down here."

The woman stared, then laughed. She looked like an evil woman as she laughed, but perhaps a laughing saint would look evil with two front teeth gone.

"Well we ain't got no *parlor* for the young ladies to see their young men in," she said mockingly. "And if you climbed as many stairs as I did—"

"I beg your pardon," said he, and started up the stairway.

On the second floor were more waves from lives of struggle. The matter would be solemnly taken up in Congress if it were soldiers who were housed in the ill-smelling place. Evidently Congress did not take women and children and disabled civilians under the protecting wing of its indignation.

Wet clothes were hanging down from the third floor. They fanned back and forth the fumes of cabbage and grease. He grew sick, not at the thing itself, but at thought of its being where he was to find Ann.

Though the fact that he was to find her made all the rest of it—the fact that people lived that way—even the fact of her living that way—things that mattered but dimly.

As he looked at the woman in greasy wrapper who was shaking out the wet clothes he had a sudden mocking picture of Ann as she had been that night at the dance.

The woman's manner in staring at him as he knocked at Ann's door infuriated him.

But when the door was opened—by Ann—he instantly forgot all outside.

He closed the door and stood leaning against it, looking at her. For the moment that was all that mattered. And in that moment he knew how much it mattered—had mattered all along. Even how Ann looked was for the moment of small consequence in comparison with the fact that Ann was there.

But he saw that she was indeed ill—worn—feverish.

"You are not well," were his first words, gently spoken.

She shook her head, her eyes brimming over.

He looked about the room. It was evident she had been lying on the bed.

"I want you to lie down," he said, his voice gentle as a woman's to a child. "You know you don't mind me. I come as one of the family."

He helped her back to the bed; smoothed her pillow; covered her with the miserable spread.

Ann hid her face in the pillow, sobbing.

He pulled up the one chair the room afforded, laid his hand upon her hair, and waited. His face was white, his lips trembling.

"It's all over now," he murmured at last. "It's all over now."

She shook her head and sobbed afresh.

His heart grew cold. What did she mean? A fear more awful than any which had ever presented itself shot through him. But she raised her head and as she looked at him he knew that whatever she meant it was not that.

"What is it about Katie?" she whispered.

"Why, Ann, can't you guess what it is about Katie? Didn't you know what Katie must suffer in your leaving like that?"

"I left so she wouldn't have to suffer."

"Well you were all wrong, Ann. You have caused us—" But as, looking into her face, he saw what she had suffered, he was silenced.

She was feverish; her eyes were large and deep and perilously bright, her temples and cheeks cruelly thin. But what hurt him most were not the marks of illness and weakness. It was the harassed look. Fear.

Fear—that thing so invaluable in building character.

Thought of the needlessness of it wrung from him: "Ann—how could you!"

"Why I thought I was doing right," she murmured. "I thought I was being kind."

He smiled faintly, sadly, at the irony and the bitter pity of that.

"But how could you think that?" he pressed. "Not that it matters now—but I don't see how you could."

She looked at him strangely. "Do you—know?"

He nodded.

"Then don't you see? I left to make it easy for Katie."

He thought of Katie's summer. "Well your success in that direction was not brilliant," he said with his old dryness.

Her eyes looked so hurt that he stroked her hand reassuringly, as he would have stroked Worth's had he hurt him. And as he touched her—it was a hot hand he touched—it struck him as absurd to be quibbling about why she had gone. She was there. He had found her. That was all that mattered.

He became more and more conscious of how much it mattered. He wanted to draw her to him and tell her how much it mattered. But he did not—dared not.

"And how did you happen to be so unkind as to call me up, Ann?" he asked with a faint smile.

"I wanted—I wanted to hear about Katie. And I wanted"—her eyes had filled, her chin was trembling—"I was lonesome. I wanted to hear your voice."

His heart leaped. For the moment he was not able to keep the tenderness from his look.

"And I knew you were there because I saw it in the paper. A woman brought back some false hair to be exchanged—I sell false hair," said Ann, with a wan little smile and unconsciously touching her own hair—"and what she wanted exchanged—though we don't exchange it—was wrapped up in a newspaper, and as I looked down at it I happened to see your name. Wasn't that funny?"

"Very humorous," he replied, almost curtly.

"I had been sick all day—oh, for lots of days. But I was trying to keep on. I had lost two other places by staying away for being sick—and I didn't dare—just didn't dare—lose this one. You don't know how *afraid* you get—how frightened you are—when you're afraid you're going to be sick."

The fear—sick fear that fear of sickness can bring—that was in her eyes as she talked of it suddenly infuriated him. He did not know what or whom he I was furious at—but it was on Ann it broke.

He rose, overturning his unsteady chair as he did so, and, seeking command, looked from the window which looked down into a squalid court. The wretchedness of the court whipped his rage. "Well for God's sake," he burst forth, "what did you *do* it for! Of all the unheard of—outrageous—unpardonable—What did you *mean*"—turning savagely upon her—"by selling false hair?"

"Why I sold false hair," said Ann, a little sullenly, "so I could live."

"Well, didn't you know," he demanded passionately, "that you could *live* with *us*?"

She shook her head. "I didn't think I had any right to—after—what happened."

He came back to her. "Ann," he asked gently, "haven't you a 'right to'—if we want you to?"

She looked at him again in that strange way. "Are you sure—you know?"

"Very sure," he answered briefly.

"And do you mean to say you would want me—anyhow?" she whispered.

He turned away that she might not see how badly and in what sense he wanted her. His whole sense of fitness—his training—was against her seeing it then.

The pause, the way she was looking at him when he turned back to her, made restraint more and more difficult. But suddenly she changed, her face darkening as she said, smolderingly: "No—I'm not *that* weak. If I can't live—I'll *die*. Other people make a living! Other girls get along! Katie would. Katie could do it."

She sat up; he could see the blood throbbing in her neck and at her temples. She was gripping her hands. She looked so frail—so helpless.

"But Katie is strong, Ann," he said soothingly.

"Yes—in every way. And I'm not." She turned away, her face twitching. "Why I seem to be just the kind of a person that has to be taken care of!"

He did not deny it, filled with the longing to do it.

"It's—it's humiliating."

He would at one time have supposed that it would be, should be; would have held to the idea that every man and woman ought be able to make a living, that there was something wrong with them if they couldn't. But not after the things he had seen that summer. The something wrong was somewhere else.

"And yet you don't know," Ann was saying brokenly, "how hard it is. You don't know—how many things there are."

She turned to him impetuously. "I want to tell you! Then maybe it will go. I couldn't tell Katie. But I don't know—I don't know why—but I could tell you anything."

He nodded, not clear-eyed, and took one of her hands and stroked it.

Her cheeks grew more red; her eyes glitteringly bright. "You see—it's *men*—things like—that's what makes it hard for girls."

He pressed her hand more firmly, though his own was shaking.

"Katie told you—Katie must have told you about—the first of it—" She faltered. He drew in his breath sharply and held it for an instant. "And after that—" She turned upon him passionately. "*Do* they know? *Does* it make a difference?"

He did not get her meaning for an instant and when he did it brought the color to his face; he had always been a man of great reserve. But Ann seemed unconscious. This was the reality that realities make.

He shook his head. "No. You only imagine."

"No, I don't imagine. They pretend. Pretend they know."

He gritted his teeth. So those were the things she had had to meet!

"They lie," he said briefly. "Bluff." And for an instant he covered his eyes with her hand.

"You see after—after that," she went on, "I couldn't go back to the telephone office. I don't know that I can explain why—but it seemed the one thing I couldn't do, so—oh I did several things—was in a store—and then a girl got me on the stage—in the chorus of 'Daisey-Maisey.' I thought perhaps I could be an actress, and that being in the chorus would give me a chance."

She laughed bitterly. "There are lots of silly people in the world, aren't there?" was her one comment on her mistake.

"That night—the last night—" she told it in convulsive little jerks—"the manager said something to me. *He* pretended. And when he saw how frightened I was—and how I loathed him—it made him furious—and he said things—vowed things—and he kissed me—and oh he was so *terrible*—his face—his lips—"

She hid her face, rocking back and forth. He sat on the bed beside her, put his arm around her as he would around Katie or Worth, holding her tenderly, protectingly, soothingly, his own face white, biting his lips.

"He vowed things—he claimed—I knew I couldn't stay with the company. I was even afraid to stay until it was over that night. I had a chance to run away—Oh I was so *frightened*." She kept repeating—"I was so *frightened*.

"I can't explain it—you'd have to see him—his *lips* his thick, loose awful lips!"

"Ann," he whispered. "Please, dear—don't talk about it—don't think about it!"

"But I want it to go away! I don't want to be alone with it. I want somebody to know. I want *you* to know."

"All right," he murmured. "All right. I want to hear." His whole body was set for pain he knew must come.

Ann's eyes were full of terror, that terror that lives after terror, the anguish of terror remembered. "It's awful to be alone with awful thoughts," she whispered. "To be shut in with something you're afraid of."

"I know—I know," he soothed her. "But you're going to tell me. Tell *me*. And then you'll never be alone with it again."

"I've been afraid so much," she went on sobbingly. "Alone so much—with things that frightened me. That night I was alone. All alone. And afraid. You see I went and went and went. Just to be getting *away*. And at last I was out in the country. And then I was afraid of *that*. I went in something that seemed to be a barn. Hid in some hay—"

He gripped her arm as if it were more than he could stand. His face was colorless.

"I almost went crazy. Why I think I *did* go crazy—with fear. Being alone. Being afraid."

He looked away from her. It seemed unfair to her to let himself see her like that—her face distorted—unlovely—in the memory of it.

"When it came daylight I went to sleep. And when I woke up—when I woke up—" She was laughing and sobbing together and it was some time before he could quiet her. "When I woke up another man was bending over me—an old man—so *old*—so—

"Oh, I suppose it was just that he was surprised at finding me there. But I thought—I hadn't got over the night before—

"So again I went. Just went. Just to get away. And that was when I saw it was life I'd have to get away from. That there wasn't any place in it for me. That it meant being alone. Afraid. That it was just *that*—those thick awful lips—that old man's eyes—Oh no—no—not that!"

She was fighting it with her hands—trying to push it away. It took both tenderness and sternness to quiet her.

"So I hurried on,"—she told it in hurried, desperate way, as if fearful she would not get it all told and would be left alone with it. "To find a way. A place. I just wanted to find the way—the place—before anything else could happen. I thought all the people who looked at me *knew*. I thought there was nothing else for me—I thought there was something wrong with me—and when I remembered what I had wanted—I hated—hated them.

"I saw water—a bridge. On the bridge I looked down. I was going to—but I couldn't, because a man was looking up at me. I hated him, too." She paused. "Though I've thought of it since. It was a queer look. I believe that man *knew*. And wanted to help me.

"But I didn't want to be helped. Nothing could help. I just wanted to get away—have it over. So I hurried on—across your Island—though I didn't know—just looking for a place—a way. Just to have it all over."

She changed on that, relaxed. Her eyes closed. "To have it all over," she repeated in a whisper. She opened her eyes and looked up at him. "Doesn't that ever seem to you a beautiful thing?"

His eyes were wet. "Not any more," he whispered. "Not now."

"Then again I saw water—the other side of the Island." She went back to it with an effort, exhausted. "I ran. I wanted to get there. Have it all over—before anything else could happen. I couldn't *look*—but I kept saying to myself it would only be a minute—only a minute—then it would be all over—not so bad as having things happen—being alone—afraid—"

She shuddered—drew back—living it—realizing it. Her visioning—realizing—had gone on beyond her words, beyond the events. She was shuddering as if the water were actually closing over her. But again she was called back by Katie's voice and that look he felt he should not be seeing went as a faint smile formed on her lips. "Then Katie. Katie calling to me. Dear Katie—pretending.

"I didn't want to go. I thought it was just something else. And oh how I wanted to get it all over!" She sobbed. "But I saw it was a girl. Sick. I wasn't able to help going—and then—Well, you know. Katie. How she fooled me. And saved me."

She looked up at him, again the suggestion of a smile on her colorless lips. "Was there ever anybody in the world so wonderful—so funny—as Katie?

"But at first I couldn't believe in her. I thought it must be just something else." She stopped, looking at him. "Why I think it wasn't till after I met *you* I felt sure it couldn't be—"

His arm about her tightened. He drew her closer to him. He was shaken by a deep sob.

And so she rested, lax, murmuring about things that had happened, sometimes smiling faintly as she recalled them. The terror had gone, as if, as she had known, telling it to him had freed her. That twisted, unlovely look which he had tried not to see, loving her too well to wish to see it, had gone. She was worn, but lovely. She was resting. At peace.

And so many minutes passed when she would not speak—resting, rescued. And then she would whisper of little things that had happened and smile a little and seem to drift the farther into the harbor of security into which she had come.

He saw that—exhausted, protected, comforted—she was going to fall asleep. His heart was all tenderness for her as he held her, adoring her, sorrowing over her, guarding her. "I haven't really slept all summer," she murmured at last, and after a few minutes her breathing told that sleep had come.

But when, in trying to unfasten her collar—he longed to be doing some little thing for her comfort—he took his hand from hers, she started up in alarm and he had to put it back, reassuring her, telling her that she was not alone, that nothing could ever harm her again.

An hour passed. And in that hour things which he would have believed fixed loosened and fell. It was all shaken—the whole of his thinking. It could never be the same again. Old things must go. New things come.

Watching Ann, yearning over her, sorrowing, adoring, he saw life as what life had done to her. Saw it as the thing she had found.

He watched the curve of her mouth. Her beautiful bosom rising and falling as she slept. The lovely line of her throat, the blood throbbing in her throat, her long lashes upon her cheek, that loveliness—beauty— that sweetness and tenderness—and *what it had met*. She, so exquisitely fashioned for love—needful of it—so perfect—so infinitely to be desired and cherished—and *what she had found*. He writhed under a picture of that old man bending over her—of that other man—bully, brute—thick awful lips snatching at her as a dog at meat. And then still another man. That first man. Darrett. *His* friend. *His* sort. The man who could so skillfully use the lure of love to rob life—

As he thought of him—his charm, cleverness—how that, too, had been pitted against her—starved, then offered what she would have no way of judging—close to her loveliness, conscious of her warmth, her breath, the superb curves of her lovely body—thinking of what Darrett had found— taken—what he had left her *to*—there were several minutes when his brain was unpiloted, a creaking ship churning a screaming sea.

And now? Had it killed it in her? Taken it? If he were to kiss her in the way he hungered to kiss her would it wake nothing more than that sick terror in her wonderful eyes? That thought became as a band of hot steel round his throat. Was it *gone*? How could she be sleeping that way with her hand in his—his face so close to her—if there remained any of that life-longing that had been there for Darrett to find?

Life grew too cold, too gray and misshapen in that thought to see it as life. It could not be. It was only that she was exhausted. And her trust in him.

At least there was that. Then he would make her care for him by caring for her—caring for her protectingly, tenderly, surrounding her with that sea of tenderness that was in his heart for her. Life would come back. He would woo it back. And no matter how the flame in his own heart might rage he would wait upon the day when he could bring the love light to her eyes without even the shadow of remembering of fear.

So he yearned over her—sorrowing, hoping. And life was to him two things. What life had done to Ann. What life would be with Ann. He wanted to let himself touch his lips lightly to her temple—so close to him. But he would not—fearing to wake the fear in her, vowing to wait till love could come through a trust that must cast fear forever from the heart.

Passion melted to tenderness; the tenderness flooding him in thought of the love he would give her.

That same night he had her taken to a hospital. It was the only way he could think of for caring for her, and she was far enough from well to permit it. He left her there, again asleep, and cared for. Then returned to his hotel and telephoned Katie. It was past daylight before sleep came to him.

CHAPTER XXXIV

Once again Katie was donning the dress which had the colors of the sea. She was wearing it this time, not because she must get the poor old thing worn out, but because she had been asked to wear it. "By Request" she was saying to herself, with a warm smile, as she shook out its folds.

As Nora was fastening it for her she saw her own face in the mirror and tried to twist it about in some way. It seemed she would have to make some explanation to Nora for looking like that.

It had been a day of golden October sunshine without, and within Katie's heart a day of such sunshine as all her years of sunshine had never brought. She had not felt like playing golf, or like reading about evolution; body and mind were filled with a gladness all their own and she had taken a long walk in and out among the wooded paths of her beautiful Island and had been filled with thoughts of many beautiful and wonderful things. Of the past she had thought, and of the future, and most of all of the living present: the night before, and that evening, when he was coming to see her again and would have things to tell her.

He had wanted to tell them then—some of the things about himself which he said she must know and which he gave fair warning would hurt her, "Then not to-night," she had said.

And now the happiness was too great, filled her too completely and radiantly for her to fear the pain of which she had been warned. She was fortified against all pain.

Wayne's finding Ann seemed to throw the gate to happiness wide open to her, giving her, not only happiness, but the right to it. She smiled in thinking how, again, it was Ann who opened a door.

If Ann had never come she would not—in this way which had made it all possible—have known her man who mended the boats. The experience with Ann was as a bridge upon which they met. It was because of Ann they could walk so far along that bridge.

The adventure, and what had come to seem the tragedy of the adventure, was over. It turned her back to those first days of play—the pretending which had led to realizing, the fancies which had been paths to realities.

They would not go on in just that way; some other way would shape itself; she and Wayne would talk of it, make some plan for Ann. She could plan it better after the letter she would have from Wayne the next day telling of finding Ann.

It was a new adventure now. The great adventure. But it was because she had ventured at all that the great adventure was offered her.

Her venturing had led her to the crowds. She was not forgetting the crowds. She would go back to them. It could not be otherwise. There was much she wanted to do, and so much she wanted to know. But she would go back to them happy, and because happy, wiser and stronger.

In myriad ways life had beckoned to her, promised her, as with buoyant step and singing heart she walked sunny paths that golden October afternoon.

Later she had stopped to see Mrs. Prescott, and she, as she so often did, talked of Katie's mother. Katie was glad to be talking of her mother, and, as they also did, of her father. It brought them very near, so close it was as if they could know of the beautiful happiness in their child's heart. They talked of things which had happened when Katie was a little girl, making herself as the little girl so real, visualizing her whole life, making real and dear those things in which her life had been lived.

As she thought of it again that night, after she was dressed and was waiting, hurt did come in the thought of his feeling for the army. She must talk to him again about the army, make him see that thing in it which was dear to her.

Though could she? She did not seem able to tell even herself just what there was in her feeling for the army.

Instead of arguments, came pictures—pictures and sounds known from babyhood: Men in uniform—her father in uniform, upon his horse—dress parade—the flag—the band—from reveille to taps things familiar and dear swept before her.

It would seem to be the picturesque in it which wove the spell; but would her throat have tightened, those tears be springing to her eyes at a thing no deeper than the picturesque? No, in what seemed that fantastic setting were things genuine and fine: simplicity, hospitality, friendship, comradeship, loyalty, courage in danger and good humor in petty annoyances.

Those things—oh yes, together with things less admirable—she knew to be there.

She got out her pictures of her father and mother; her father in uniform—that gentle little smile on her mother's face. She thought of what her mother had endured, of what hosts of army women had endured, going to outlandish spots of the earth, braving danger and doing without cooks! She was proud of them, proud to be of them.

She lingered over her father's picture. A soldier. Perhaps he was of a vanishing order, but she hoped it would be long—very long—before the things to be read in his face vanished from the earth.

Through memories of her father there many times sounded the notes of the bugle—now this call, now that, piercing, compelling, sounding as *motif* of his life, thing before which all other things must fall away. She seemed to hear now the notes of retreat—to see the motionless regiment—then the evening gun and the band playing the Star Spangled Banner and the flag—never touching the ground—coming down for the night. She answered it in the things it woke in her heart: those ideals of service, courage, fidelity which it had left her.

She would talk to him—to Alan (absurd she should think it so timidly—so close in the big things—so strange in some of the little ones)—about her father and mother. To make them real to him would make him see the army differently. It hurt her to think of his seeing it as he did, hurt her because she knew how it would have hurt them. To them, it had been the whole of their lives. They had not questioned; they had served. They had given it all they had.

And that other thing there was to tell her—? Was that, too, something that would have hurt them? She hoped not. It seemed she could bear the actual hurt to herself better than thought of the hurt it would have been to them.

But when the bell rang and she heard his voice asking for her a tumult of happiness crowded all else out.

She was shyly radiant as she came to him. As he looked at her, it seemed to pass belief.

But when he dared, and was newly convinced, as, his arms about her he looked down into her kindling face, his own grew purposeful as well as happy, more resolute than radiant. "We will make a life together," he said, as if answering something that had been in his thoughts. "We will beat it all down."

An hour went by and he had not told the story of his life, life itself too mysterious, too luring, too beautiful. Whenever they came near to it they seemed to hold back, as if they would remain as they were then. Instead, they told each other little things about themselves, absurd little things, drawing near to each other by all those tender little paths of suddenly remembered things. And they lingered so, as if loving it so.

It was when Katie spoke of her brother that he was swept again into the larger seriousness. Looking into her tender face, his own grew grave. "You know, Katie—what I told you—what I must tell you—"

"Oh yes," said Katie, "there was something, wasn't there?" But she put out her hand as if to show there was nothing that could matter. He took the hand and held it; but he did not grow less grave.

"Katie," he asked, "how much do you really care for the army?"

It startled her, stirring a vague fear in her happy heart.

"Why—I don't know; more than I realize, I presume." She was silent, then asked: "Why?"

He did not reply; his face had become sober.

"You are thinking," she ventured, "that your feeling for it is going to be—hard for me?"

He nodded; he was still holding her hand tightly, as if to make sure of keeping it.

"You see, Katie," he went on, with difficulty, "I have reason for that feeling."

"What do you mean?" she asked sharply.

"I have tried not to show you that I knew anything—in a personal way—about the army."

Her breath was coming quickly; her face was strained. But after a moment she exclaimed: "Why—to be sure—you were in the Spanish War!"

"No," said he with a hard laugh, "I am nothing so glorious as a veteran."

He felt the hand in his grow cold. She drew it away and rose; turned away and was picking the leaves from a plant.

But she found another thing to reach out to. "Well I suppose"—this she ventured tremulously, imploringly—"you went to West Point—and were—didn't finish?"

"No, Katie," he said, "I never went to West Point."

"Well then what did you do?" she demanded sharply.

He laughed harshly. "Oh I was just one of those fools roped in by a recruiting officer in a gallant-looking white suit!"

"You were—?" she faltered.

"In the ranks. One of the men." The fact that she should be looking like that drove him to add bitterly: "Like Watts, you know."

She stood there in silence, held. The radiance had all fallen from her. She was looking at him with something of the woe and reproach of a child for a cherished thing hurt.

"Why, Katie," he cried, "*does* it matter so? I thought it was only when we were *in* that we were so—impossible."

But she did not take the hands he stretched out. She was held.

It drove him desperate. "Well if *that's* so—if to have been in the army at all is a thing to make you look like *that*—Heaven knows," he threw in, "I don't blame you for despising us for fools!—But I don't know what you'll say when I tell you—"

"When you tell me—what?" she whispered.

"That I have no honorable discharge to lay at your feet. That I left your precious army through the noble gates of a military prison!"

She took a step backward, swaying. The anguish which mingled with the horror in her face made him cry: "Katie, let me tell you! Let me show you—"

But Katie, white-faced, was standing erect, braced for facing it. "What for? What did you do?"

Her voice was quick, sharp; tenseness made her seem arrogant. It roused something ugly in him. "I knocked down a cur of a lieutenant," he said, and laughed defiantly.

"You *struck*—an officer?"

"I knocked down a man who ought to have been knocked down!"

"*Struck*—your superior officer?"

"Katie," he cried, "that's your way of looking at it! But let me tell you—let me show you—"

But she had turned from him, covered her face; and before Katie there swept again those pictures, sounds: her father's voice ringing out over parade ground—silent, motionless regiment; the notes of retreat—those bugle notes, piercing, compelling, thing before which all other things must fall away—evening gun and lowered flag—

She lifted colorless face, shaking her head.

"*Katie!*" he cried. "Our life—*our* love—*our* life—"

She raised her hand for silence, still shaking her head.

"Won't you—*fight* for it?"he whispered. "*Try?*"

She kept shaking her head. "Anything else," she managed to articulate. "Anything else. Not this. You don't understand. Can't. Never would." Suddenly she cried: "Oh—*go away!*"

For a moment he stood there. But her face was locked against appeal. Colorless, unsteady, he turned and left her.

Katie put out her hand. Her father—her father in uniform, it had been so real, it seemed he must be there. But he was not there. Nothing was there. Nothing at all. As the front door closed she started forward, but there sounded for her again the notes of the bugle—piercing, compelling, thing before which all other things must fall away. "Taps," this time, as blown over her father's grave, soldiers' heads bowed and tears falling for a fine soldier who would respond to bugle calls no more.

CHAPTER XXXV

Paris was in one of her gray moods that January afternoon. Everything was gray except the humanity. Emotion never seemed to grow gray in Paris. From her place by the window in Clara's apartment Katie was looking down into the narrow street, the people passing to and fro. Two men were shaking hands. They would stop, then begin again. They had been doing that for the last five minutes. They seemed to find life a very live thing. So did the *femme de menage* and her soldier, who also had been standing over there for the last five minutes. Katie did not want to look longer at the *femme de menage* and her soldier, so she turned her chair a little about and looked more directly at Clara.

Clara was in gray mood, too. Only Clara differed from the streets in that it was the emotion was gray; the *robe de chambre* was red.

So were Clara's eyes. "It's not pleasant, Katie," she was saying, "having to remain here in Paris for these foggy months—with all one's friends down on the Riviera."

"No," said Katie grimly, "life's hard."

Clara's tears flowed afresh. "I've often thought *you* were hard, Katie. It's because you've never—*cared.* You've never—suffered."

Katie smiled slightly, again looking out the window at the *femme* and her soldier, who were as contented with the seclusion offered by a lamp-post as though it were seclusion indeed. As she watched them, "hard"did not seem the precise word for something in Katie's eyes.

"You see, Katie," Clara had resumed, as if her woe gave her the right to rebuke Katie for the lack of woe, "you've always had everything just the way you wanted it."

"Just exactly," said Katie, still looking at the *femme de menage.*

"Your grandfather left you all that money, and when you want to do a thing all you have to do is do it. What can you know of the real sorrows and hardships of life?"

"What indeed?" responded Katie briskly.

"And your heart has never been touched—and I don't believe it ever will be," Clara continued spitefully—Katie seemed so complacent. "You have no real feeling. You're just like Wayne."

Katie laughed at that and looked at Clara; then laughed again, and Clara flushed.

"Speaking of Wayne," said Katie in off-hand fashion, "he's been made a major."

She watched Clara as she said it. There were things Katie could be rather brutal about.

"I'm sure that's very nice," said the woman who had divorced Wayne.

"Yes, isn't it? And other things are going swimmingly. One of those things he used to be always puttering over—you may remember, Clara, mentioning, from time to time, those things he used to be puttering around with—has been adopted with a whoop. A great fuss is being made over it. It looks as though Wayne was confronted with something that might be called a future."

"I'm sure I'm very glad," said Clara, "that somebody is to have something that might be called a future. Certainly a woman with barely enough to live on isn't in much danger of being confronted with one."

Katie made no apology to herself for the pleasure she took in "rubbing it in." She remembered too many things too vividly.

"It's pretty hard," said Clara, "when one has a—duty to society, and nothing to go on."

Katie was thinking that society must be a very vigorous thing, persisting through all the "duties" people had to it.

She smiled now in seeing that the thing which had brought her to Clara that day was in the nature of a "duty to society" and that in her case, too, a duty to society and a personal inclination moved happily together.

Katie was there that afternoon to buy Worth.

So she put it to herself in what Clara would have called her characteristically brutal fashion.

She was sure Worth could be had for a price. She had that price and she believed the psychological moment was at hand for offering it.

The reason for its being the psychological moment was that Clara wanted to join a party at Nice and did not have money enough to buy the clothes which would make her going worth while. For there was a man there—an American, a rich westerner—whom Clara's duty to society moved her to marry.

That was Katie's indelicate deduction from Clara's delicate hints.

And Katie wanted Worth. It wasn't wholly a matter of either affection or convenience. It had to do, and in almost passionate sense, with something which was at least in the category with such things as duties to society. Worth seemed to her too fine, too real, to be reared by a "truly feminine woman," as Clara had been known to call herself. Clara's great idea for Worth was that he be well brought up. That was Clara's idea of her duty to society. And it was Katie's notion of her duty to society to save him from being too well brought up.

The things she had been seeing, and suffering, in the past year made her feel almost savagely on the subject.

Katie had been there since October. Clara had magnanimously permitted Worth to remain with his Aunt Kate most of the time, with the provision that Katie bring him to her as often as she wanted him. This was unselfish of Clara, and cheaper.

Clara's alimony was not small, but neither were her tastes. Indeed the latter rose to the proportions of duties to society.

Katie knew it was as such she must treat them in the next half hour. She must save the "maternal instinct" Clara was always talking about—usually adding that it was a thing which Katie, of course, could not understand—by taking it under the sheltering wing of the "child's good."

Katie knew just how to reach the emotions which Clara had, without outraging too much the emotions she persuaded herself she had.

So she began speaking in a large way of life, how hard it was, how complicated. How they all loved Worth and wished to do the best thing for him, how she feared it must hurt the child's personality, living in that unsettled fashion, now under one influence, now under another. She spoke of Clara's own future, how she had *that* to think of and how it was hard she be so—restricted. She drew a vivid picture of what life might be if Clara didn't "provide for the future"—she was careful to use no phrase so raw to truly feminine ears as "make a good marriage." And then, rather curtly when it came to it, tired of the ingratiating preamble, she asked Clara what she would think of relinquishing all claim on Worth and taking twenty thousand dollars.

Clara tried to look more insulted by the proposition than invited by the sum. But Katie got a glimmer of that look of greed known to her of old.

She went on talking. She was sure every one would think it beautiful of Clara to let Worth go to them just because they had a better way of caring for him, just because it was for the child's good. Every one would know how it must hurt her and admire her for the sacrifice. And then Katie mentioned the fact that the matter could be closed immediately and Clara start at once for Nice and perhaps that itself would "mean something to the future."

From behind Clara's handkerchief—Clara's tears were in close relation to Clara's sense of the fitness of things—Katie made out that life seemed driving her to this, but that it hurt her to think so tragic a thing should be associated with so paltry a sum.

"It's my limit," said Katie shortly. "Take it or leave it."

Amid more sobs Katie got that all the Jones family were heartless, that life was cruel, but that she was willing to make any sacrifice for her child's good.

"Then I'll go down and get him," said Katie, rising.

Clara's sobs ceased instantly. "Get who?"

"My lawyer. I left him down there talking to the *concierge*."

"Katie Jones—how *could* you!"

"Oh she looks like a decent enough woman," said Katie. "I don't think it will hurt him any."

"Katie, you have grown absolutely—*vulgar*. And so *hard*. You have no fineness—no intuition—nothing feminine about you. And how dared you bring your lawyer here to me? What right had you to assume I'd do this?"

"Why I knew you well enough, Clara, to believe you would be willing to do it—for your child's good."

Clara looked at her suspiciously and Katie hastened to add that she brought him because she wanted to pay ten thousand francs on account and she thought Clara might want to get the disagreeable business all settled up at once so she could hurry on to Nice before those friends of hers got over to Algiers, or some place where Clara might not be able to go after them.

Clara again looked suspicious, but only said it was inconsiderate of Katie to expect her to receive a lawyer with her poor eyes in that condition.

But when Katie returned with him Clara's eyes were a softer red and she managed to extract from the interview the pleasure of showing him that she was suffering.

As she watched the transaction, Katie felt a little ashamed of herself. Not because she was doing it, but because she had known so well how to do it. But with a grimace she banished her compunctions in the thought of its being for the child's good, and hence a duty to society.

Less easy to banish was the hideous thought that she might have been able to get him for less!

By the time the attorney had gone Clara seemed to be looking upon herself as one hallowed by grief; she was in the high mood of one set apart by suffering. In her eyes was something which she evidently felt to be a look of resignation. In her hand something which she certainly felt to be an order for ten thousand francs.

The combination first amused and then irritated Katie. It was exasperating to have Clara giving herself airs about the grief which was to make such a sorry cut in Katie's income.

Clara, in her mellowed mood, spoke of the past, why it had all been as it had. She was even so purged by suffering as to speak gently of Wayne. "I hope, Katie—yes, actually hope—that Wayne will some time find it possible to care, and be happy."

And when Katie thought of how much Wayne had cared, why he had not been happy, it grew more and more difficult to treat Clara as one sanctified by sorrow.

It gave her a fierce new longing for the real, the real at all costs, a contempt for all that artifice and self-delusion which made for the things at war with the real.

She had enough malice to entertain an impulse to strip Clara of her complacency, take away from her her pleasant cup of sorrow, make her take one good look at herself for the woman she was rather than the woman she was flaunting. But she had no zest for it. What would be the use? And, after all, self-deception seemed a thing one was entitled to practice, if one wished.

What Katie wanted most was to get out into the air.

CHAPTER XXXVI

To get out into the air was the thing she was always wanting in those days, or at least for the last two months it had been so. At first she had been too wretched to be conscious of needing anything.

But Katie was not built for wretchedness; everything in her was fighting now for air, what air meant to spirit and body.

It was in the sense of the spirit that she most of all wanted to get out into the air, out into a more spacious country than the world Clara suggested, out where the air was clear and keen and where there were distances more vast than those which would shut her in.

For she had looked into a larger country. Allegiance to the smaller one could not be whole-hearted.

She wondered if it were true she was getting hard. Something in her did seem hardening. At any rate, something in her was wanting to fight, fight for air, fight, no matter who must be hurt in the struggle, for that bigger country into which she had looked, those greater distances, more spacious sweeps. Sometimes she had a sense of being in a close room, and nothing in the world was so dreadful to Katie as a close room, and felt that she had but to open a door and find herself out where the wind would blow upon her face. And the door was not bolted. It was hers to open, if she would. There were no real chains. There were only dead hands, hands which live hands had power to brush away. And the room was made close by all those things which they of the dead hands had loved, things which they had served, things which, for them, had been out in the open, not making the air unbearable in a close room. And when she wanted to tell them that she must get out of the room because it was too close for her, that she could no longer stay with things which shut out the air, it seemed they could not understand—for they were dead, but they could look at her with love and trust, those hands, which could have been so easily brushed away, as bolts on the door of the room holding the things they had left for her to guard.

And they were proud, and their trusting eyes seemed to say they knew she would not make all their world sorry for them.

She walked slowly across Pont du Carrousel, watching the people, the people going their many ways, meeting their many problems, wondering if many of them had well loved hands, either of life or death, as bolts upon the doors which held them from more spacious countries, holding them so securely because they could be so easily brushed away. It was people, people of the crowds, who saved her from a sense of isolation her own friends brought: for she was always certain that in the crowds was some one else who was wondering, longing, perhaps a courageous some one who was fighting.

Paris itself had fought, was fighting all the time. She loved it anew in the new sense of its hurts and its hopes. And always it had laughed. She felt kinship to it in that. Seeming so little caring, yet so deeply understanding. The laughter-loving city had paid stern price that its children might laugh. It seemed to her sometimes that one could love and hate Paris for every known reason, but in the end always love for the full measure it gave. She stood for a moment looking at the spire of Sainte Chapelle, slender as a fancy, yet standing out like a conviction; watching the people on the busses, the gesticulating crowds—blockades of emotion, the men on the Quai rummaging among the book-stalls for possible treasures left by men who had loved it long before, looking at the thanks in stone for yesterday's vision of to-morrow, and everywhere cabs—as words carrying ideas— breathlessly bearing eager people from one vivid point to another in the hurrying, highly-pitched, articulate city.

It interested her for a time, as things that were live always interested Katie. The city's streets had always been for her as waves which bore her joyously along. But after a time, perhaps just because she was so live, it made her unbearably lonely.

The things they might do together in Paris! The things to see—to talk about.

And still filled with her revolt against Clara's self-delusions, she asked of herself how much the demand of her spirit to soar was prompted by the hunger of her heart to love.

She could not say. She wondered how many of the world's people would be able to say. How many of the spacious countries would have been gained had men been fighting only for their philosophies, pushed only by the beating of wings that would soar. But did that make the distances less vast? Less to be desired? Though visioning be child of desiring—was the vision less splendid, and was not the desire ennobled?

Her speculations were of such nature as to make her hurry home to see whether there was American mail.

A certain letter which sometimes came to her was called "American mail." All the rest of the American mail which reached Paris was privileged to be classed with that letter.

Katie had come over in October with her Aunt Elizabeth, who felt the need of recuperation from the bitter blow of her son's marriage. Katie, too, felt the need of recuperation—she did not say from what, but from something that made her intolerant of her aunt's form of distress. Her aunt said that Katie was changing: growing unsympathetic, hard, unfeminine. She thought it was because she did not marry. It would soften her to care for some one, was the theory of her Aunt Elizabeth.

She had remained in order to be with Worth; and, too, because there seemed nothing to go back to. Mrs. Prescott had come over to be for a time with a niece who was studying music, and she and Katie were together. Now the older woman was beginning to talk of wanting to go back; she was getting letters from Harry which made her want to see him. The letters sounded as though he were in love again.

And Katie was getting letters herself, letters to make her want to see the writer thereof. They, too, sounded as if written by one in love. With things as regards Worth adjusted, Katie would be free to go with her friend, and she was homesick. At least that was the non-committal name she gave to something that was tugging at her heart.

But—go home to what? For what?

Her vision had not grown any clearer. It was only that the "homesickness" was growing more acute.

And that night's mail did not fill her with a yearning to become an expatriate.

In addition to the "American mail" there was a letter from Ann. That evening after Worth was asleep and Mrs. Prescott had gone to her room, Katie reread both letters, and a number of others, and thought about a number of things.

Wayne had undertaken the supervision of Ann. In his first letter, that unsatisfactory letter in which he gave so few details about finding Ann, he had said quite high-handedly that he was going to look after things himself. "I think, Katie," he wrote, "that with the best of intentions, your method was at fault. I can see how it all came about, but it is not the way to go on. It was too unreal. The time of make-believe is over. Ann is a real person and should work out her life in a real way, her own way, not following your fancyings. She must be helped until she gets stronger and more prepared.

You've had the thing come too tragically to you to see it just right, so I'm going to step in and I want you to leave things to me."

So Wayne had "stepped in" and was lending Ann the money to study stenography. Katie had made a wry face over stenography, which did not have a dream-like or an Ann-like sound—but a very Wayne-like one!—but had entered no protest; at that time she had been too dumbly miserable to enter protest about anything.

Wayne seemed to her curt and rather unfeeling about the whole thing, insisting, somewhat indelicately, she thought, on the point that Ann be prepared to earn her own living and that there be no more nonsense about her. She hoped he was kinder with Ann than he sounded in his letters about her.

Ann was in New York. Wayne had said, and Katie agreed with him, that Chicago was not the place for her to start in anew. She had gone through too many hard things there. And Katie was glad for other reasons. With Wayne in Washington, she would have no more occasion to be in the middle-west and Ann would be too far away in Chicago.

But Katie was looking desperately homesick at that thought of having no more occasion to be in the middle-west.

The man who mended the boats was still out there, mending boats and finishing his play, which she knew now was to be about the army. One reason he had wanted to mend boats there was that he might know some of the men who worked in the shops at the Arsenal, interested in that relation of labor to militarism.

For two months Katie had heard nothing from him. In those first months he, too, seemed helpless before it, seemed to understand that Katie's feeling was a thing he could not hope to understand—much less, change.

Then there rose in him the impulse to fight, for her, against it all, stir her to fight.

"Katie," he wrote in that first letter, letter she was re-reading that night, "we have seen two sides of the same thing. Our two visions, experiences, have roused in us two very different emotions. Does that mean it must kill for us what we have said is the biggest emotion—experience—the greatest joy and brightest hope life has brought us?

"We're both bound by it. I by the hurt it's brought me, you by the happiness; I by the hate it roused, you by the love that lingers round it. Are we going to make no efforts to set ourselves free? Are we so much of the past that the institutions of the past and the experiences and prejudices of those institutions can shut us out from the future and from each other?

"Katie, you have the rich gift of the open mind. I don't believe that, lastingly, there's anything you'll shut out as impossible to consider. Your eyes say it, Katie—say they'll look at everything, and just as fairly as they can. Oh they're such honest, fearless, just eyes—so wise and so tender. And it was I—I who love them so—brought that awful look of hurt to those wonderful eyes. Katie—I want to spend all of my life keeping that hurt look from those dear eyes!

"You're asked to do a hard thing, dear Katie. It's cruel it should be *you* so hard a thing is asked of. Asked to look at a thing you see through the feeling of a lifetime as though seeing it for the first time. To look at all you've got to push aside things you regarded as fixed. I suppose every one has something that to him seems the things unshakable, something he finds it terrifying to think of moving. All your traditions, all your love and loyalty cling round this thing which it seems to you you can't have touched. But Katie, as you read these pages won't you try to think of things, not as you've been told they were, but just as they seem to you from what you read? Think of them, not in the old grooves, but just as it comes in to you as the story of a life?

"You'll try to do that for me, won't you, dear fair-minded, loving-spirited Katie?

"I was a country boy; lived on a farm, got lonesome, thought about things I had nobody to talk to about, read things and wanted more things to read, part the dreamer and part the great husky fellow wanting life, adventure, wanting to see things and know things—most of all, experience things. I want to tell you a lot about it sometime. I can't let go the idea that there is going to be a sometime. Just because there's so much to tell, if nothing else. And, Katie, *isn't* there something else?

"No way to begin the story of one's life!

"Then I went away from home. To see the world. Try my fortune. Experience. Adventure. That was the call.

"And the very first thing I fell in with that recruiting officer in the white suit. I can see just how that fellow looked. Get every intonation as he drew the glowing picture of life in the army

"The army sounded good. The army was experience, adventure, with a vengeance. A life among men. A chance. He told me that an intelligent fellow like me would soon be an officer. Of course I agreed perfectly I was an intelligent fellow, impressed with army intelligence in picking me for one. Why I could see myself as commander-in-chief in no time!

"There's the cruelty of it, Katie. The expectation they rouse to get you— the contemptuous treatment after they've got you. The difference between the army of the 'Men Wanted For the Army' posters and the army those men find after those posters have done their work.

"Remember your telling me about visiting at Fort Riley when you were quite a youngster? The good time you had?—how gay it was? How charming your host was? As nearly as I can figure it out, I was there at the same time, filling the noble office of garbage man. Now, far be it from me, believing in the dignity of all labor, to despise the office of garbage man. I can think of conditions under which I would be quite happy to serve my country in that capacity. But having enlisted because of the noble figure of a soldier carrying a flag, I grew pretty sore at the 'Damn you, we've got you' manner in which I was ordered to carry things—well, not to be too indelicate let us merely say things less attractive than the flag.

"It's not having to peel potatoes and wash dishes; it's seeming to be despised for doing it that stirs in men's hearts the awful soreness that makes them deserters.

"In our regiment men were leaving right along. Our company had a particularly bad record on desertions. Our captain, a decent fellow, was away most of the time and the lieutenant in command was a cur. I'd find a more gentle word for him if I could, but I know none such. Army men talk a great deal about discipline. But there's a difference between discipline and bullying. This fellow couldn't issue an order without making you feel that difference.

"He had a laugh that was a sneer. It wasn't a laugh, just a smile; a smile that sneered. He couldn't pass a crowd of men cutting grass without making their hearts sore.

"I don't say he's the typical army man. I don't doubt that there are men high in the army who, if all were known, would despise him as much as the men in his company did. But I do say that if there were not a good many a good deal like him more than fifty thousand young men of America would not have deserted from the United States army in the past twelve years.

"There was a fellow in our company I had been particularly sorry for. He wasn't a bad sort at all; he was more dazed than anything else; didn't understand the army manner; the army snobbishness. This lieutenant couldn't look at him without making him sullen.

"One day he told him to do a loathsome thing, then stood there with that sneering smile watching him do it. Well, he did it, all right; that's what *gets* you, that powerlessness under what you know for injustice. But that night he left.

"I knew he was going. He wanted me to go with him. I don't know why I didn't. I don't blame men for deserting. But for my own part, it would only be two years more; I used to say to myself, 'You got into this. You'll see it through.'

"They caught him, brought him back the next day. I happened to be there at the time. So did our spick and span lieutenant. The man who had been caught—or boy, rather, for he was but that—was anything but spick and span. His clothes were torn and muddy, his face dirty and bloody—it had been scratched by something. He knew what he was in for. Court martial and imprisonment for desertion. We knew what *that* meant.

"He was a sorry, unsoldierly sight. Gone to pieces. Unnerved. All in. His chin was quivering. And then the little lieutenant came along, starting out for golf. He stood in front of him and looked him up and down—this boy who had been caught. Boy who would be imprisoned. And as he looked at him he laughed; or smiled rather, that smile that was a sneer.

"He stood there continuing to smile—torturing him with that smile he couldn't do a thing about—this boy who was down; this fellow who was all in. That was when I struck him in the face and knocked him down.

"The penalty for that, as I presume I need not tell an army girl, is death. 'Or such other punishment as a court martial may direct.'

"The thing directed in my case was imprisonment at Fort Leavenworth for five years. Most of the men in that prison would say, 'Give me death.'

"I'd better not say much about it. Something gets hot in my head when I begin to talk about it. If you were with me—your cooling hand, your steadying eyes—I could tell you about it. 'If you were with me'! I find that a very arresting phrase, Katie.

"Those were black years. Cruel years. Years to twist a man's soul. They took something from me that will not be mine again. I remember your telling how Ann said there were things to make perfect happiness forever impossible. She was right. There *are* hours that stay.

"I went into the army just an adventurous boy. I came from it an embittered man. My experience with it made me suspect all of life. I was more than unhappy. I was sullen. I *hated*—and I wanted to get even. Oh it was a lovely spirit in which I went forth a second time to meet the world.

"I don't know what might not have happened, I think I was right in line to become a criminal, like so many of the rest of them who have served time at Leavenworth—I don't suppose the United States has any finer school anywhere than its academy for criminals at Fort Leavenworth—had it not been for a man I met.

"I got a job in a garage. I had always been pretty good at mechanical things and knew a little about it. And there I met this man—and through him came salvation.

"I don't know, Katie, maybe socialism will not save the world. I don't see how it can miss it—but be that as it may, I know it has saved many a man's soul. I know it saved mine.

"This fellow—an older man with whom I worked—talked to me. He saw the state I was in, won my confidence and got my story. And then he began talking to me and gave me books. He got me to come to his house instead of the places I was going to, saying nothing against the other places, but just making his things so much more attractive. We used to talk and argue and gradually other things fell away just because there was no room for them.

"You know I had loved books—read all I could get—but didn't seem to get the right ones. Well, after I had served time breaking clay I didn't care anything about books—too sore, too dogged, too full of hate. But the love for the books came back, and through the books, and through this friend, came the splendid saving vision.

"Vision of what the world might be—world with the army left out, with all that the army represented to me vanished from the earth. With men not ruling and cursing other men; but working together—the world for all and all for the world. And the thing that saved me was that I saw there was something to work for—something to believe in—look at—think about— when old memories of the guard knocking me down with the butt of his gun would tear into my soul and bring me low with the hate they roused.

"And so I began again, Katie dear, that sense of things as they might be—that vision—taking some of the sting from what I had suffered from things as they were. I stopped hating and cursing; I began thinking and dreaming. There came the desire to *know*. I tore into books like a madman. I couldn't go on hating my fellow-men because I was too busy trying to find out about them. And so it happened that there were things more interesting to think about than the things I had suffered in the army; I was carried out of myself—and saved.

"I wish I could talk to some of those other fellows! Some of those boys who ran away from the army, not because they were criminals and cowards, but just because they didn't know what to make of things. I wish I could talk to some of those men who dug clay with me at Fort Leavenworth—men who went away cursing the government, loathing the flag, hating all men, and who have nothing to take them out of it. I wish I could take them up with me to the hill-top and say—'There! Don't look at the little pit down below! Look out! Look wide!'

"Katie—you aren't going to save men by putting them at back-breaking work under brutalized guards. You aren't going to redeem men by belittling them. You're going to save them by making them *see*. And the crime of our whole system of punishments is that it does all in its power, not to make them see, but to shut them out from seeing...."

In the letters which followed he told her other things, things he had done, the work he hoped to do, what he wanted to do with his life. Told it with the simplicity of sincerity, the fine seriousness untainted with the self-consciousness called modesty.

He believed he could work with men; things he had already done made him believe he could do more, bigger things. He wanted to help fight the battles of the people who worked; not with any soldier of fortune notion, but because he was one of those people, because he had suffered as one of those people, and believed he saw their way more clearly than the mass of them were seeing it.

And he wanted to write about men; had some reason for believing he could. He was hoping that his play would open the way to many other things; it looked as though it were going to be put on.

He told of his feeling for it. "More than a showing up and a getting even, though there *is* that. It will be no prancing steed and clanking saber picture of the army. More digging of clay than waving of the flag. I see significant things arising from that survival of autocracy in a democracy, an interesting study in the bitter things coming out of the relation of the forms and habits of a vanishing order to the aspirations and tendencies of a forming one. And in that bending of spirit to form, the army codes and standards making for the army habit of mind, the army snobbishness and narrowness. The things that shape men, until a given body of men have particular characteristics, particular limitations. You said that if you loved them for nothing else you would love army people for their hospitality. But in the higher sense of that beautiful word they are the least hospitable of people. Their latch string of the spirit is not out. Their minds are tight—fixed. They have not that openness of spirit and flexibility of mind that make for wider visioning.

"And it's not that they haven't, but why they haven't, brings one to the vein.

"Yes, I got the article you sent me, written by your army friend, eloquent over the splendid things war has done for the human race, the great things it has bred in us. Well if the 'war virtues' aren't killed by an armed peace, then I don't think we need worry much about ever losing them. It's the people at war for peace who are going to conserve and utilize for the future the strong and shining things which days of war have left us. Men who must base their great claim on what has been done in the past are not the men to shape the future—or even carry the heritage across the bridge. War is now a faithful servant of capitalism. Its glorious days are over. It's even a question whether it's longer valuable as a servant. It may lose its job before its master loses his. In any case, it goes with capitalism; and if the good old war virtues are to be saved out of the wreck it's the wreckers will save them!

"Which is not what I started out to say. This play into which I'm seeking to get the heart of what I've lived and thought and dreamed is not the impersonal thing this harangue might make it sound. I trust it's nothing so bloodless as a study of economic forces or picture of the relationship of old things to new. It's that only as that touches a man's life, means something to that life. It's about the army because this man happens, for a time, to be in the army—it's what the army does to him that's the thing.

"Though it seems to me a pretty dead thing in these days. Life itself is a dead thing with you gone from it."

In the letter she received that night he wrote: "Katie, is it going to spoil it for us? Can it? *Need* it? We who have come so close? Have so much? Are outlived things to push us apart? That seems *too* bitter!

"Oh don't think that I don't *see*. The things it would mean giving up. The wrench. And, for what?—your friends would say. At times I wonder how I *can*—ask it, hope for it. Then there lives for me again your wonderful face as it was when you lifted it to me that first time. *You*—and I grow bold again.

"I don't say you wouldn't suffer. I don't say there wouldn't be hurts, big hurts brought by the little things arising from lives differently lived. I know there would be times of longing for things gone. For the sunny paths. For it couldn't be all sunny paths with me, Katie. Those years in the dark will always throw their shadow.

"Then, how dare I? Loving you—laughing, splendid you—how can I?

"Because I believe that you love me. Remembering that light in your eyes, knowing *you*, I dare believe that the hurts would be less than the hurt of being spared those hurts.

"I can hear your friends denouncing me. Hear their withering arguments, and I'll own that at times they do wither. But, Katie, I just can't seem to *stay* withered!

"You're such an upsetting person, dear Katie. To both heart and philosophy. It's not possible to hate a world that Katie's in. World that didn't spoil Katie. And if there are many of the *you*—oh no other real you!— but many who, awakened, can fight as you can fight and love as you can love—wouldn't it be a joke on us revolutionists if we were cheated out of our revolution just by the love in the hearts of the Katies?

"Well, nobody would be so happy in that joke as would the defrauded revolutionists!

"You make me wonder, Katie, if perhaps it isn't less the vision than the visioning. Less the thing seen than that thing of striving to see. Make me feel the narrowness in scorning the trying to see just because not agreeing with the thing seen. Sometimes I have a new vision of the world. Vision of a world visioning. Of the vision counting less than the visioning.

"Those moments of glow bear me to you. Persuade me that our visions must be visioned together.

"Life's all empty without you. The radiance is not there. In these days light comes only through dreams, and so I dream dreams and see visions.

"Dreams of *us*—visions of the years we'd meet together. And you are not bowed and broken in those visions, Katie. You're very strong and buoyant—and always eager for life—and always tender. No, not *always* tender. Sometimes fighting! Telling me I don't know what I'm talking about. It's a splendid picture of Katie fighting—eyes shining, cheeks red.

"And then at the very height of her scorn, Katie happens to think of something funny. And she says the something funny in her inimitable way. Then she laughs, and after her laugh she's tender again, and says she loves me, though still maintaining I didn't know what I was talking about!

"And in the visions there are times when Katie is very quiet. So still. Hushed by the wonder of love. Then Katie's laughing eyes are deep with mystery, Katie's face seems melted to pure love, and from it shines the light that makes life noble.

"In these days of a fathomless loneliness I dare not look long upon that vision.

"Do you ever hear a call, dear heart? A call to a freer country than any country you have known? Call to a country where the things which bind you could bind no more? And if in fancy you sometimes let yourself drift into that other country, am I with you there? Do you ever have a picture of our venturing together into the unknown ways—daring—suffering—rejoicing—*growing*? Sometimes sunshine and sometimes storm—but always open country and everwidening sky-line. Oh Katie—how splendid it might be!"

She read and re-read it, dreaming and picturing. And at length there settled upon her that stillness, that pause before life's wonder and mystery. Her eyes were deep. The light that makes life noble glorified her tender face.

She broke from it at last to look for a card they had there giving dates of sailings.

CHAPTER XXXVII

They would get in late that afternoon. Off on the horizon was a hazy mass which held the United States of America, as sometimes the haze of a dream may hold a mighty truth.

Katie and Mrs. Prescott were having a brisk walk on deck. They paused and peered off at that mist out of which New York must soon shape itself.

"Just off yonder's your country, Katie," the older woman was saying. "Soon you'll see the flag flying over Governor's Island. Will it make you thrill?"

"It always has," replied Katie.

Mrs. Prescott stole a keen look at her, seeing that she was not answered. They had had some strange talks on that homeward trip, talks to stir in the older woman's mind vague apprehensions for the daughter of her old friend. It did not seem to Mrs. Prescott what she called "best" that a woman—and particularly an unmarried one—should be doing as much thinking as Katie seemed to be doing. She wished Katie would not read such strange books; she was sure Walt Whitman, for one, could not be a good influence. What would happen to the world if the women of Katie's class were to—let down the bars, she vaguely and uneasily thought it. And she was too fond of Katie to want her to venture out of shelter.

"Well it ought to, Katie dear. I don't know who has the right to thrill to it, if you haven't. Doesn't it make you think of those sturdy forefathers of yours who came to it long ago, when it was an unknown land, and braved dangers for it? Your people have always fought for it, Katie. There would be no country had not such lives as theirs been given to it."

Katie was peering off at the faint outlines which one moment seemed discernible in the mist and the next seemed but a phantom of the imagination, as the truth which is to stand out bold and incontestable may at first suggest itself so faintly through the dream as to be called a phantom of the imagination. "True," she said. "And fine. And equally true and fine that there's just as much to fight for now as there ever was."

"Oh yes," murmured Mrs. Prescott, "we must still have the army, of course."

"The fighting's not in the army," said Katie, to herself rather than to her friend.

The older woman sighed. "I'm afraid I don't understand you, Katie." After a pause she added, sadly: "Something seems happening in the world that is driving older people and younger people apart."

Katie turned to her affectionately. "Oh, no."

But more affectionately than convincingly. Mrs. Prescott looked at her wistfully: so strong, so buoyant, so fearless and so fine; she felt an impulse to keep her, though for what—from what—she would not have been able to say.

"Katie dear," she said gently, "I get a glimpse of what you mean in there still being things to fight for. You mean new ideas; new things. I know you're stirred by something. I feel your enthusiasm; it shines from your face. Enthusiasm is a splendid thing in the young, Katie. In any of us. New things there always are to fight for, of course. But, dear Katie—the old things? Those beautiful *old* things which the generations have left us? Things fought for, tested, mellowed by our fathers and mothers, and their fathers and mothers? Aren't they a little too precious, too hardly won, too freighted with memories to be lightly cast aside?"

Katie looked at her friend's face, itself so incontestably the gift of the generations. It made vivid her own mother's face, and that her own struggle. "I don't think," she said tremulously, "that you are justified in saying they are 'lightly' cast aside."

They were silent, looking off at the land which was breaking through the mists, responding in their different ways to the different things it was saying to them.

"It seems to me," Mrs. Prescott began uncertainly, "that it is not for women—particularly women to whom they have come as directly as to you and me—to cast them off at all. We seem to be in strange days. Days of change. To me, Katie, it seems that the work for the women—*our* women—is in preserving those things, dear things left to us, holding them safe and unharmed through the destroying days of change."

She had grown more sure of herself in speaking.

The last came staunchly.

"It seems," she added, "that it would be enough for us to do. And the thing for which we are best fitted."

Katie was silent; she could not bear to say to her friend—her mother's friend—that it did not seem to her enough to do, or the thing for which she was best fitted.

She was the less drawn to the idea because of a face she could see down in the steerage: face of an immigrant girl who was also turning eager face, not to the land for which her forefathers had fought, but to that which would be the land of her descendants.

She had seen her there before, face set toward the land into which she was venturing. She had become interested in her. She seemed so eager. And thinking back to the things seen in her search for Ann, other things she had been reading of late, a fear for that girl—pity for her—more than that, sense of responsibility about her grew big in Katie.

It made it seem that there was bigger and more tender work for women than preserving inviolate those things women had left. As she drew near the harbor of New York she was more interested in the United States of America as related to that girl than as associated with her own forefathers who had fought for it long before.

And as it had been for them to fight in the new land, it seemed that it was for her, not merely to cherish the fact of their having fought, not holding that as something apart—something setting her apart, but to fight herself; not under the old standards because they had been their standards, but under whatsoever standards best served the fight. It even seemed that the one way to keep alive those things they had left her was to let them shape themselves in whatever form the new spirit—new demands—would shape them.

Mrs. Prescott was troubled by her silence. "Katie dear," she said, "you come of a long line of fine and virtuous women. In these days when everything seems attacked—endangered—*that*, at least—that thing most dear to women—most indispensable—must be held inviolate. And by such as you. Wherever your ideas may carry you, don't let *that* be touched. Remember that the safety of the world for women goes, if you do."

It turned Katie to Ann. Safety *she* had found. Then again she looked down at the immigrant girl—beautiful girl that she was. And wondered. And feared.

She turned to Mrs. Prescott with a tear on her eyelashes and a smile a little hard about her lips. "Would you say that 'fine and virtuous women' have succeeded in keeping the world a perfectly safe place for women?"

Mrs. Prescott was repelled, but Katie did not notice. She was looking with a passionate sternness off at New York. "Let *anything* be touched,"she spoke it with deep feeling. "I say *nothing's* too precious to be touched—if touching it can make things better!"

Mrs. Prescott had gone below. Katie feared that she had wounded her, and was sorry. She had not been able to help it. The face of that immigrant girl was too tragically eager.

They were almost in now, close to Governor's Island, over which the flag was flying. It gripped her as it had never done before.

"Boy," she said to Worth, perched on a coil of rope beside her, "there's your country. Country your people came to a long time ago, and fought for, and some of them died for. And you'll grow up, Worth, and *you'll* fight for it. Not the way they fought; it won't need you to fight for it that way; *they* did that—and now that's done. But there will be lots for you to fight for, too; harder fights to fight, I think, than any they fought. You'll fight to make it a better place for men and women and little children to live in. Not by firing guns at other men, Worth, but by being as wise and kind and as honest and fair as you know how to be."

It was her voice moved him; it had been vibrant with real passion.

But after a moment the face of the child of many soldiers clouded. "But won't I have *any* gun 'tall, Aunt Kate?" he asked wistfully.

She smiled at the stubborn persistence of militarism. "I'm afraid not, dear. I hope we're not going to have so many guns when you're a man. But, Worth, if you don't have the gun, other little boys will have more to eat. There are lots of little boys and girls in the world now haven't enough to eat just because there are so many guns. Wouldn't you rather do without the gun and know that nobody was going hungry?"

"I—guess so," faltered Worth, striving to be magnanimous but looking wistful.

"But, Aunt Kate," he pursued after another silence, "what's father making guns for—if there aren't going to be any?"

Katie's smile was not one Worth would be likely to get much from. "Ask father," she said rather grimly. "I think he might find the question interesting."

Worth continued solemn. "But, Aunt Kate—won't there be anybody 'tall to kill?"

"Why, honey," she laughed, "does it really seem to you such a gloomy world—world in which there will be nobody to kill? Don't worry, dear. The world's getting so interesting we're going to find lots of things more fun than guns."

"Maybe," said Worth, "if I don't have a gun you'll get me an air-ship, Aunt Kate."

"Maybe so," she laughed.

"The man that mends the boats says I'll have an air-ship before I die, Aunt Kate."

She gave Worth a sudden little squeeze, curiously jubilant at the possibility of his having an air-ship before he died. And she viewed the city of sky-scrapers adoringly—tenderly—mistily. "Oh Worthie," she whispered, "isn't it *lovely* to be getting home?"

CHAPTER XXXVIII

She found it difficult to adjust herself to the Ann who had luncheon with her the next day. The basis of their association had shifted and it had been too unique for it to be a simple matter to appear unconscious of the shifting.

She had not seen Ann since the day they said the cruel things to each other. Wayne had thought it best that way, saying that Ann must have no more emotional excitement. She had acquiesced the more readily as at the time she was not courting emotional excitement for herself.

And now the Ann sitting across the table from her was not the logical sequence of things experienced in last summer's search for Ann. She was not the sum of her thoughts about Ann—visioning through her, not the expression of the things Ann had opened up. It was hard, indeed, to think of her as in any sense related to them, at all suggestive of them.

An Ann radiating life rather than sorrowing for it was an Ann she did not know just what to do with.

And there was something disturbing in that rich glow of happiness. She did not believe that Ann's something somewhere could be stenography. Yet her radiance—the deep, warm quality of it—suggested nothing so much as a something somewhere attained. It seemed to Katie rather remarkable if the prospect of soon being able to earn her own living could make a girl's eyes as wonderful as that.

There was no mistaking her delight in seeing Katie and Worth. And a sense of the old relationship was there—deep and tender sense of it; but something had gone from it, or been added to it. It was not the all in all.

Truth was, Ann was more at home with her than she was with Ann.

After luncheon they went up to Katie's room for a little chat. Katie talked about stenography and soon came to be conscious of that being a vapid thing to be talking about.

"What pretty furs," she said, in the pause following the collapse of stenography.

That seemed to mean more. "Yes, aren't they lovely?" responded Ann, with happy enthusiasm. "They were my Christmas present—from Wayne."

The way Ann said Wayne—in the old days she had never said it at all—led instantly, though without her knowing by what path, to that strange fear of hers in finding Ann so free from fear.

Ann was blushing a little: the "Wayne" had slipped out so easily, and so prettily. "He thought I needed them. It's often so cold here, you know."

"Why certainly one needs furs," said Katie firmly, as if there could be no question as to *that*.

Katie's great refuge was activity. She got up and began taking some dresses from her trunk.

Then, just to show herself that she was not afraid, that there was nothing to be afraid about, she asked lightly: "What in the world brings Wayne up to New York so much?"

Ann was affectionately stroking her muff. She looked up at Katie shyly, but with a warm little smile. There was a pause which seemed to hover over it before she said softly: "Why, Katie, I think perhaps I bring him up to New York."

Everything in Katie seemed to tighten—close up. She gave her most cobwebby dress a perilous shake and said in flat voice: "Wayne's very kind, I'm sure."

Ann did not reply; she was still stroking her muff; that smile which hovered tenderly over something had not died on her lips. It made her mouth, her whole face, softly lovely. It did something else. Made it difficult for Katie to go on pretending with herself.

Though she made a last stand. It was a dreadful state of affairs, she told herself, if Ann had been so absurd as to fall in love with Wayne—*Wayne*—just because he had been kind in helping her get a start.

She followed that desperately. "Oh yes, Wayne's really very kind at heart. And then of course he's always been especially interested in you, because of me."

Ann looked up at her. The look kept deepening, sank far down beneath Katie's shallow pretense.

"Well, Katie," Ann began, with the gentle dignity of one whom life has taken into the fold, "as long as we seem into this, I'd rather go on. Wayne said I was to do just as I liked about telling you. Just as it happened to come up. But I think you ought to know he is not interested in just the way you think." She paused before it, then said softly, with a tremulous pride: "He cares for me, Katie—and wants to marry me."

"He can't do that! He *can't do that!*"

It came quick and sharp. Quick and sharp as fire answering attack.

She sat down. The sharpness had gone and her voice was shaking as she said: "You certainly must know, Ann, that he can't do that."

So they faced each other—and the whole of it. It was all opened up now.

"It's very strange to me," Katie added hotly, "that you wouldn't know that."

It seemed impossible for Ann to speak; the attack had been too quick and too sharp; evidently, too unexpected.

"I told him so," she finally whispered. "Told and told him so. That you would feel—this way. That it—couldn't be. He said no. That you felt—all differently—after last summer. And I thought so, too. Your letters sounded that way."

Katie covered her eyes for a second. It was too much as if the things she was feeling differently about were the things she was losing.

"And when you want to be happy," Ann went on, "it's not so hard to persuade yourself—be persuaded." She stopped with a sob.

"I know that," was wrung wretchedly from Katie.

"And since—since I *have* been happy—let myself think it could be—it just hasn't seemed it *could* be any other way. So I stopped thinking—hadn't been thinking—took it for granted—"

Again it wrung from Katie the this time unexpressed admission that there was nothing much easier than coming to look upon one's happiness as the inevitable.

"And Wayne kept saying," Ann went on, sobs back of her words, "that all human beings are entitled to work out their lives in their own way. You believed that, he said. And I—I thought you did, too. Your letters—"

"No," said Katie bitterly, "what I believed was that *I* was entitled to work out *my* life in my own way. Wayne got his life mixed up with mine."

The laugh which followed them was more bitter, more wretched than the words.

She had persuaded herself the more easily that she was entitled to work out her life in her own way because she had assumed Wayne would be there to stand guard over the things left from other days. He was to stay there, fixed, leaving her free to go.

She could not have explained why it was that the things she had been thinking did not seem to apply to Wayne.

The thing grew to something monstrous. There whirled through her mind a frenzied idea as to what they would do about sending Major Barrett a wedding announcement.

Other things whirled through her mind—as jeers, jibes, they came, a laugh behind them. A something somewhere was very commendable while it remained abstract! Having a fine large understanding about Ann had nothing to do with having Ann for a sister-in-law! "Calls" were less beautiful when responded to by one's brother! *This* (and this tore an ugly wound) was what came of helping people in their quests for happiness.

It was followed by a frantic longing to be with Mrs. Prescott—in the shelter of her philosophy, hugging tight those things left by the women of other days. Frightened, outraged, her impulse was to fly back to those well worn ways of yesterday.

But that was running away. Ann was there. Ann with the radiance gone; though, for just that moment, less stricken than defiant. There was something of the cunning of the desperate thing cornered in the sullen flash with which she said: "You talked a good deal about wanting me to be happy. Used to think I had a right to be. When it was Captain Prescott—"

It was unanswerable. The only answer Katie would be prepared to make to it was that she didn't believe, all things considered, it was a thing she would have said. But doubtless people lost nice shades of feeling when they became creatures at bay fighting for life.

And seemingly one would leave nothing unused. "I want you to know, Katie, that I paid back that money. The missionary money. You made me feel that it wasn't right. That I—that I ought to pay it back. I earned the money myself—some work there was for me to do at school. I wanted to—to buy a white dress with it." Ann was sobbing. "But I didn't. I sent back the money."

Katie was wildly disposed to laugh. She did not know why, after having worried about it so much, Ann's having paid back the missionary money should seem so irrelevant now. But she did not laugh, for Ann was looking at her as pleadingly, as appealingly, as Worth would have looked after he had been "bad" and was trying to redeem it by being "good."

With a sob, Ann hid her face against her muff.

Seeing her thus, Katie made cumbersome effort to drag things to less delicate, less difficult, ground.

"Ann dear," she began, "I—oh I'm *so* sorry about this. But truly, Ann, you wouldn't be at all happy with Wayne."

Ann raised her face and looked at her with something that had a dull semblance to amusement.

"You see," Katie staggered on, "Wayne hasn't a happy temperament. He's morose. Queer. It wouldn't do at all, Ann, because it would make you both wretchedly unhappy."

She found Ann's faint smile irritating. "I ought to know," she added sharply, "for I've lived in the house with him most of my life."

"You may have lived in the house with him, Katie," gently came Ann's overwhelming response. "You've never understood him."

Katie openly gasped. But some of her anger passed swiftly into a wondering how much truth there might be in the preposterous statement. Wayne as "immune" was another idea jeering at her now. And that further assumption, which had been there all the while, though only now consciously recognized, that Wayne's knowing Ann's story, made Ann, to Wayne, impossible—

Living in the same house with people did not seem to have a great deal to do with knowing their hearts.

"Wayne," Ann had resumed, in voice low and shaken with feeling, "has the sweetest nature of any one in this world. He's been unhappy just because he hadn't found happiness. If you could see him with me, Katie, I don't think you'd say he had an unhappy nature—or worry much about our not being happy."

Katie was silent, driven back; vanquished, less by the words than by the light they had brought to Ann's face.

And what she had been wanting—had thought she was ready to fight for—was happiness—for every one.

"Of course I know," Ann said, "that that's not it." That light had all gone from her face. It was twisted, as by something cruel, blighting, as she said just above a whisper: "There's no use pretending we don't know what it is."

She turned her face away, shielding it with her muff.

It was all there—right there between them—opened, live, throbbing. All that it had always meant—all that generations of thinking and feeling had left around it.

And to Katie, held hard, it was true, all too bitterly true, that she came of what Mrs. Prescott called a long line of fine and virtuous women. In her misery it seemed that the one thing one need have no fear about was losing the things they had left one.

But other things had been left her. The war virtues! The braving and the fighting and the bearing. Hardihood. Unflinchingness. Unwhimperingness.

Those things fought within her as she watched Ann shaken with the sobs she was trying to repress.

Well at least she would not play the coward's part with it! She brought herself to look it straight in the face. And what she saw was that if she could be brave enough to go herself into a more spacious country, leaving hurts behind, she must not be so cowardly, so ignobly inconsistent as to refuse the hurts coming to her through others who would dare. Through the conflict of many emotions, out of much misery, she at last wrenched from a sore heart the admission that Wayne had as much right to be "free" as she had. That if Ann had a right to happiness at all—and she had always granted her that—she had a right to this. It was only that now it was she who must pay a price for it. And perhaps some one always paid a price.

"Ann?"

Ann looked up into Katie's colorless, twitching face.

"I hope you and Wayne will be very happy." It came steadily, and with an attempted smile.

The next instant she was sobbing, but trying at the same time to tell Ann that sisters always acted that way when told of their brothers' engagements.

CHAPTER XXXIX

She did not see her brother until evening. "Katie," he demanded sharply, "have you been disagreeable to Ann?"

She shook her head. "I haven't meant to be, Wayne."

Her face was so wretched that he grew contrite. "You're not pleased?"

"Why, Wayne, you can scarcely expect me to be—wholly pleased, can you?"

"But you always seemed to understand so well. I"—he paused in that constraint there so often was between them in things delicately intimate—"I've never told you, Katie, how fine I thought you were. So big about it."

"It's not so difficult," said Kate, with a touch of her old smile, "to be 'big' about people who aren't marrying into the family."

It seemed that he, too, was not above cornering her. "You know, Katie, it was your attitude in the beginning that—"

"Just don't bother calling my attention to that, Wayne," she said sharply. "Please credit me with the intelligence to see it for myself."

Then she went right to the heart of it. "Oh Wayne—think of Major Barrett's *knowing*."

The dull red that came quickly to his face told how bitterly he had thought of it, though he only said quietly: "Damn Barrett."

"But you can't damn him. Suppose you were to be stationed at the same place!"

He laughed shortly. "Well that, at least, is something upon which I can set your fears at rest."

She looked up quickly. "What do you mean?"

"I mean, Katie, that my army days are over."

She stared at him. "I don't understand you."

"It shouldn't be so difficult to comprehend. I have resigned my commission."

"Wayne," she asked slowly, "what do you mean?"

"Just what I say. That I have resigned my commission. That I am out of the army."

It made it seem that the whole world was whirling round and round and that there was nothing to take hold of. "But you can't do that. Why your whole life is there—friends—traditions—work—future."

"Not my future," he said briefly.

His calm manner made it the more bewildering. "Wayne, I don't see how you can—in such a light manner—give up such a big thing!"

He turned upon her in manner less calm. "What right have you to say that it is done in a 'light manner'!"

The words had a familiar sound and she recalled them as like something she had said to Mrs. Prescott the day before; just the day before, when she had been so sure of things, and of herself.

"But where is your future then, Wayne?" she asked appealingly. "We know, don't we, how hard it is for army men to find futures as civilians?"

"I'm going into the forest service."

Katie never could tell why, for the moment, it should have antagonized, infuriated her that way. "So that's it. That's what got—a poetic notion! And I suppose," she laughed scornfully, "you're going into the ranks? What is it they call them? Rangers? Starting in at your age—with your training—to 'work from the bottom up'—is that it?"

"No," he replied coldly, "that is not it. You have missed it about as far as you could. I have no such picturesque notion. I am doing no such quixotic thing. I value my training too highly for that. It should be worth too much to them. I don't even scorn personal ambition, or the use of personal pull, so you see I'm a long way from a heroic figure. I know I've a brain that can do a certain type of thing. I know I'm well equipped. Well, so far as the equipment goes, my country did it for me and I mean to give it back; only I've got to do it in my own way."

"Why, Katie," he resumed after a pause, "I never was more surprised in my life than to find you so out of sympathy with this. I knew what most people would think of it, but I quite took it for granted that you would understand."

"It seems a little hard," replied Katie with a tearful laugh, "to understand the fine things other people do. And, Wayne, I'm so afraid it will lead to disappointment! Aren't you idealizing this forest service? Remember Fred's tales of how it's almost strangled by politics. And you know what that means. Let us not forget Martha Matthews!"

It was a relief to be laughing together over a familiar thing. Martha Matthews was the daughter of a congressman from somewhere—Katie never could remember whether it was Texas or Wyoming. She had been asked to "take her up" at one time when the army appropriation bill was pending and Martha's father did not seem to realize that the country needed additional defense. But when Martha discovered that army people were "perfectly fascinating—and *so* hospitable"Martha's parent suddenly awakened to the grave dangers confronting his land. Katie had more than once observed a mysterious relationship between the fact of the army set being fashionable in Washington and the fact that the country must be amply protected, further remarking that army people were just clever enough to know when to be fascinating.

"No," he came back to it in seriousness, "I don't think I have many illusions. I know it's far from the perfect thing, but I see it as set in the right direction. It seems to me that that, in itself, ought to mean considerable. It's the best thing I know of—for what I have to offer. Then I want to get out of cities for awhile—get Ann away from them." He paused over that and fell silent. "Osborne offered me a job," he came back to it with a laugh. "Seemed to think I was worth a very neat sum a year to his company—but that was scarcely my notion. In fact I doubt if I would have so much confidence in the forest service if it weren't for his hatred of it. You can judge a thing pretty well by the character of its enemies. Then I'm enough the creature of habit to want to go on in a service; I'm schooled to that thing of the collectivity. But I'll be happier in a service that—despite the weak spots in it—is in harmony with the big collectivity—rather than hopelessly discordant with it. And perhaps it needs some more or less disinterested fellows to help fight for it," he added with a touch of embarrassment, as if fearing to expose himself.

He had come close enough to self-betrayal for Katie, despite her fear and confusion, to feel proud of him as he looked then.

"Wayne," she asked, "have you felt this way a long time? Out of sympathy with the army?"

He did not at once reply, thinking of the night he had sat beside Ann, night when the whole world was shaken and things he had regarded as fixed loosened and fell. Just how much had been loosening before that— some, he knew—just how much would have more or less insecurely held its place had it not been for that night, he was not prepared to say—even to himself.

"Longer than I knew, I think," he came back to Katie. "One night last fall I went to a dinner and they drank our toast." He repeated it, very slowly. "'My country—may she always be right—but right or wrong—my country.'

"I used to have the real thrill for that toast. That night it almost choked me. That 'right or wrong' is a spirit I can thrill to no longer. I'm more interested in getting it right.

"Though I'll own it terrified me, just as it seems to you, to feel it slipping from me. Recently I had occasion to go up to West Point and I spent a whole day deliberately trying to get back my old feeling for things—the whole business that we know so well and that I used to love so much.

"And, in a way, I could; but as for something gone. That day up at the Point was one of the saddest of my life. I still loved the trappings. They still called to me. But I knew that, for me, the spirit was dead.

"Oh I have no sensational declarations to make about the army. I wouldn't even be prepared to say what I think about disarmament. It's more complex than most peace advocates seem to see. I only know that the army's not the thing for me. I can't go on in it, simply because my feeling for it is gone."

He had been speaking slowly and seriously; his head was bent. Now he looked up at her. "It was at the close of that day—day up at West Point—that I resigned my commission. And if you had seen me that night, Katie, I doubt if you would reproach me with 'doing it lightly.'"

The marks of struggle had come back to his face with the story of it.
They told more than the words.

"Forgive me," she said in her impetuous way. "No, I didn't know. How awful it is, Wayne, that we *don't* know—about each other."

She was forced to turn away; but after a moment controlled herself and turned back to add: "Wayne dear, I think you're right. I'm proud of you."

"Oh, I'm entitled to no halo," he hastened to say. "It's the fellow who would do it without an income might be candidate for that."

"But you *would* do it without an income, Wayne," she insisted warmly.

"I don't know. How can I tell whether I would or not?

"And you'll be good to Ann?" he took advantage of her mood to press, as though that were the one thing she could do for him. "You know, how much she needs you, Katie."

The Visioning A Novel | 279

"I shall certainly want to be good to Ann," she murmured. "Though I don't think she needs me much—any more."

Something about her went to his heart. "Why, Katie—we all need you."

She shook her head; there were tears, but a smile with them. "Not much, Wayne. Not now. I'm not—indispensable. Though pray why should one wish to be anything so terrifying as indispensable?"

"Will you take Worth?" she asked after a little while. "He goes—with you and Ann?"

"We want him. And Katie, we want you. We're to go to Colorado and fight the water barons," he laughed. "Aren't you coming with us?"

She shook her head. "Not just now. I want to flit round in the East a little first. Be gay—renew my youth," she laughed, choking a little.

She drew him to talk of his hopes. "I'll fess up, Katie," he said, when warmed to it by her sympathy, "that I fear I do have rather a poetic notion about it. I want to *do* something—something that will count, something set in the direction of the future. And I like the idea of going back to that old frontier—place where I was born—and where mother went through so much—and where father fought—and because of which he died. And serving out there now in a way that is just as live—just as vital—as the way he served then."

He paused; they were both thinking of their father and mother, of how they might not have understood, of the sadness as well as the triumph there is in change, that tug at the heart that must so often come when the new generation sees a little farther down the road than older eyes can see, the ache in hearts left behind when children of a new day are called away from places endeared by habit into the incertitude and perhaps the danger of ways unworn.

"Life seems too fine a thing, Katie, to spend it making instruments of destruction more deadly. It's not a very happy thought to think of their being used; and it's not a very stimulating one to think of their not being. In either case, it doesn't make one too pleased with one's vocation. And life seems a big enough thing," he added, a little diffidently, "to try pretty hard to get one's self right with it."

He did not understand the way Katie was looking at him as she replied: "Yes, Wayne; I know that. I've been thinking that myself."

Something moved her to ask: "Wayne, do you think you would have done it, if it had not been for Ann?"

"I think," he replied quietly, "that possibly that is still another thing I have to thank her for." His face and voice gave Katie a sharp sense of loneliness, that loneliness which came in seeing how poorly she had understood him, how little people knew each other.

They talked of a number of things before he suddenly exclaimed: "Oh Katie, I must tell you. That fellow—what's his name? Mann? The mythical being known as the man who mends the boats is a fellow you'll have to avoid, should you ever see him again—which of course is not likely."

She had turned and was looking out at the lights in the street below. "Yes?"

"Who do you suppose the scoundrel *is*?"

"I'm sure I don't know," she faltered.

"A military *convict*. Attacked an officer. Served time at Leavenworth."

Katie was intent upon the lights down below.

"And what do you suppose he was prying around the Island for?"

"I'm sure I have no idea," she managed to say.

"Going to write a *play*—a play about the *army*! Now what do you think of that? Darrett found out about it. Oh just the man, you see, to write a play about the army! And some sensationalists here are going to put it on. It's the most damnable insolence I ever heard of! They ought to stop it."

"Oh, I don't know," said Katie, still absorbed in the cabs down below; "a man has a right to use his experiences—in a play."

"Well a fine view he'll give of it! It's the most insufferable impertinence I ever knew of!"

She turned around to ask oddly: "Why, Wayne, why all this heat? You're not in the army any more."

"Well, don't you think I'm not *of* it, when an upstart like that turns up to rail at it!"

"But how do you know he'll rail?"

"Oh he'll rail, all right. I know his type. But we'll see to it that it's pretty generally understood it's military life as presented by a military *convict*."

"Perhaps you can trust him to make that point clear himself," said Katie rather dryly.

"The *coward*. The *cur*."

She turned upon him hotly. "Look here, Wayne, I don't know why you're so sure you have a right to say that!"

"I'd like to know why I haven't! Attacked an officer without the slightest provocation whatsoever! Some kind of a hot-headed taking sides with a deserter, I believe it was. I suppose this remarkable play is to be a glorification of desertion," he laughed.

"Well," said Katie with an unsteady laugh, "perhaps there are worse things to glorify than desertion."

He stared at her. "Come now, Katie, you know better than that."

But Katie was looking at him strangely. "Wayne," she said quietly, "you're a deserter, yourself."

He flushed, but after an instant laughed. "Really, Katie, you have a positive genius for saying preposterous things."

"In which there may occasionally lurk a little truth. You *are* deserting. Why aren't you?"

"I call that about as close to rot as an intelligent person could come," he replied hotly. "I'm resigning my commission. It's perfectly regular."

"Yes; being an officer and a gentleman, you *can* resign your commission, and have it perfectly regular. Being that same officer and gentleman, you never were mugged—treated as a prospective criminal; no four thousand posters bearing your picture will now be sent broadcast over the country; no fifty dollars is offered lean detectives for your capture; you're in no chance of being thrown into prison and have your government do all in its power to wring the manhood out of you! Oh no—an officer and a gentleman—you resign your commission and go ahead with your life. But you're leaving the army, aren't you? Deserting it. And why? Because you don't like the spirit of it. And yet—though you're too big for it—though it's *time* for you to desert—you're enough bound by it not to let the light of your intelligence fall for one single second on the question of desertion!"

She had held him. He made no reply, looking in bewilderment at her red cheeks and blazing eyes.

Suddenly her face quivered. "Wayne," she said, "I don't use the term as a hard name. I'm not using it in just its technical sense, our army sense. But mayn't desertion be a brave thing? A fine thing? To desert a thing we've gone beyond—to have the courage to desert it and walk right off from the dead thing to the live thing—? Oh, don't mind my calling you a deserter, Wayne," she added, her eyes full of tears, "for the truth is I'd like to be a deserter myself. But perhaps one deserter is enough for a family—and you beat me to it." She laughed and turned back to the cabs.

He wanted to go on with the argument; show her what it was in desertion that army men despised, make the distinction between deserting and resigning. But the truth was he was more interested in the things Katie had said than in the things which could be called in refutation.

And Katie puzzled him; her heat, feeling, not only astonished but worried him a little. She was standing there now beating a tattoo on the window pane. He wondered what she was thinking about. The experience as to Ann revealed Katie to him as having thought about things he would not have dreamed she was thinking about. What in the world did she mean by saying she'd like to be a deserter herself? One of her preposterous sayings—but it was true that considerable truth had often lurked at the heart of Katie's absurd way of talking.

Watching her, he was drawn to thought of her attractiveness and that made him wonder whom Katie would marry. He had always been secretly proud of his sister's popularity; it seemed she should make a brilliant marriage. Live brilliantly. It was the thing to which she was adapted. Katie was unique. Distinctive. Secretly, unadmittedly, he was very ambitious for her. And with a little smile he considered that seemingly Katie was just shrewd enough to be ambitious for herself. She had steered her little bark safely past the place where she would be likely to marry a lieutenant. Was she heading for a general?

So he reflected with humor and affection, watching Katie beat the tattoo on the window.

Thought of what some one had said of her as the army girl suggested something that changed his mood, bringing him suddenly to his feet. "Katie," he demanded, "how much did you ever talk to this fellow? You don't think, do you, that he was trying to get you for his 'army girl'—or some such rot? If I thought that—You don't think, do you, Katie, that that was what he was trying to work you for?"

Katie suddenly raised her hands and pushed back her hair, for the minute covering her eyes. "No, Wayne," she said, "I don't think that was what he was trying to 'work me' for."

And unable to bear more, she told him that she was very tired and asked him to go.

CHAPTER XL

Katie Jones was very gay that winter. She made her home at her uncle's, near Washington, though most of the time she was in Washington itself, with various cousins and friends; there were always people wanting Katie, especially that winter, when she had such unfailing zest for gayety.

They wondered that she should not be more broken up at her brother's absurd move in quitting the army—just at the time the army offered him so much. She seemed to take it very easily; though Katie was not one to take things hard, too light of spirit for that. And they wondered about his marriage to a girl whom nobody but Katie knew anything about. Katie seemed devoted to her and happy in the marriage.

"Why, naturally I am pleased," she said to a group of army people who were inquiring about Wayne's bride. "She is my best friend. The girl I care most about."

Major Darrett was one of the group. Some one turned to him and asked if he had met her when she visited Katie at the Arsenal the summer before. He replied that he had had that pleasure and that she was indeed beautiful and very charming.

Katie hated him the more for having to be grateful to him.

She knew that he was sorry for her and grew more and more gay. She could not talk of it, so was left to disclaim tragedy in frivolity. It was royally disclaimed.

There were a few serious talks with older army men, men who had known her father and who were outraged at Wayne's leaving the army when he was worth so much to it and it to him. In her efforts to make them see, she was forced to remember what the man who mended the boats said of their lack of hospitality. They were unable to entertain the idea of there being any reason for a man's leaving the army when he was being as well treated in it as Wayne was. Katie's explanations only led them to shake their heads and say: "Poor Wayne."

It was impossible to bury certain things in her, for those were the things she must use in defending Wayne. And in defending him, especially to her uncle, she was forced to know how far those things were from being decently prepared for burial. She was never more gay than after one of her defenses of her brother.

The winter had passed and it was late in April, not unlike that May day just the year before when she had first seen her sister-in-law. Try as she would she could not keep her thoughts from that day and all that it had opened up.

She had received a letter from her sister-in-law that morning. It was hard to realize that the writer of that letter was the Ann of the year before.

Her thoughts of Ann led seductively to the old wonderings which Ann had in the beginning opened up. She wondered how many of the people with whom things were all wrong, people whom good people called bad people, were simply people who had been held from their own. She wondered how many of those good people would have remained good people had life baffled them, as it had some of the bad people. The people whom circumstances had made good people were so sure of themselves. She had observed that it was from those who had never sailed stormy waters came the quickest and harshest judgments on bad seamanship in heavy seas.

Ann had met Helen and did not seem to know just what to think about her. "She's nice, Katie," she wrote, "but I don't understand her very well. She has so many strange ideas about things. Wayne thinks you and she would get on famously. She doesn't seem afraid of anything and wants to do such a lot of things to the world. I'm afraid I'm selfish; I'm so happy in my own life—it's all so wonderful—that I can't get as excited about the world as Helen does."

And yet Ann would not have found the world the place she had found it were it the place Helen would have it. But Ann had found joy and peace—safety—and was too happy in her own life to get excited about the world—and thought Helen a little queer!

That was Ann's type—and that was why there were Anns.

Ann was radiant about the mountains and their life in them. "Helen said it about right, Katie. They're hard on the hair and the skin—but good for the soul!" They would be for the summer in one of the most beautiful mountain towns of Colorado and wanted Katie to come and bring Worth. Wayne had consented to leave him for a time with Katie at their uncle's. That Katie knew for a concession received for staying in New York with Ann until after her marriage.

She believed she would go. She was so tired of Zelda Fraser that she would like to meet Helen. And she would like the mountains. Perhaps they would do something for *her* soul—if she had not danced it quite away. She was getting very wretched about having to be so happy all the time.

She was on her way to Zelda's that afternoon, Zelda having asked her to come in for a cup of tea and a talk. A whiff of some new scandal, she supposed. That was the basis of most of Zelda's "talks."

Though possibly she had some things to tell about Harry Prescott's approaching marriage to Caroline Osborne. Katie had been asked to be a bridesmaid at that wedding.

"While we have known each other but a short time," Caroline had written in her too sweet way, "I feel close to you, Katie, because it was through you Harry and I came together. Then whom would we want as much as you! And as it is to be something of an army wedding, may I not have you, whom Harry calls the 'most bully army girl' he ever knew?"

Mrs. Prescott had also written Katie the glad news, saying she was happy, believing Caroline would make Harry a good wife. Katie was disposed to believe that she would and was emphatically disposed to believe that Mr. Osborne would make Harry a good father-in-law. Katie's knowledge of army finances led her to appreciate the value of the right father-in-law for an officer and gentleman who must subsist upon his pay.

But she had made an excuse about the wedding, in no mood to be a bridesmaid, especially to a bride who would enter the bonds of matrimony on the banks of the Mississippi, just opposite a certain place where boats were mended.

She walked on very fast toward Zelda's, trying to occupy the whole of her mind with planning a new gown.

But Zelda had more tender news to break that day than that of a new scandal. "Katie," she approached it, in Zelda's own delicate fashion, "what would you think of Major Darrett and me joy-riding through life together?"

"I approve of it," said Katie, with curious heartiness.

"Some joy-ride, don't you think?"

"I can fancy," laughed Katie, "that it might be hard to beat. I think," she added, "that he's just the one for you to marry. And I further think, Zelda, that you're just the one for him to marry."

Zelda looked at her keenly. "No slam on either party?"

"On the contrary, a sort of double-acting approval," she turned it with a laugh.

"Then as long as your approval has a back action, so to speak, I cop you out right now, Katie, for a bridesmaid."

"Don't," said Katie quickly. "No, Zelda, I'm not—suitable."

"Why not?"

"Oh, too old and worn," she laughed. "Bridesmaids should be buds."

"Showing up the full-blowness of the bride? Don't you think it!"

"So you hastened to get me!"

"Come now, Katie, you know very well why I want you. Why wouldn't I want you? Anyhow," she exposed it, "father wants you. Father thinks you're so nice and respectable, Katie."

"And so, for that matter," she added, "does my chosen joy-rider."

"I'm not so sure of his being particularly impressed with my respectability," replied Katie.

"He's always been quite dippy about you, Katie. I don't know how I ever got him."

Zelda spoke feelingly of the approaching nuptials of her old school friend. "Cal's considerable of a prissy, but take it from me, Harry Prescott will see that all father's money doesn't pour into homes for the friendless— so there's something accomplished. Heaven help the poor fellow who must live on his pay," sighed Zelda piously.

Major Darrett, too, was to be congratulated on his father-in-law. Just the father-in-law for a man ambitious to become military attache.

It was nice, Katie told herself as she walked away, to know of so many weddings. She insisted upon asserting to herself that she was glad all her friends were getting on so famously.

Though if Zelda persisted, she would have to go West earlier than she had planned. She could not regard Ann's sister-in-law as suitable person for attendant at Major Darrett's wedding. That would be a little *too* much like playing the clown at a masked ball.

The image was suggested by seeing one of those grotesque figures across the street. He was advertising some approaching festivity. With the clown was a monkey. He put the monkey down on the sidewalk and it danced obediently in just the place where it was put down.

Suddenly it seemed to Katie that she was for all the world like that monkey—dancing obediently in the place where she was put down, not asking about the before or after, just dutifully being gay. That monkey did not know the great story about monkeys; doubtless he was even too degraded by clowns to yearn for a tree. He only danced at the end of the string the clown held—all else shut out.

She—shutting out the before and after—was that pathetically festive little monkey; and society was the clown holding the string—the whole of it advertising the tawdry thing the clown called life.

Only *she* knew that there were trees. She had danced frantically in seeking to forget them, but the string pulled by the clown fretted her more and more.

She could not make clear to herself why it had seemed that if Wayne were to be "free," she could not be; it was as if all the things she had worked out for herself had been appropriated by her brother. Everybody could not go into more spacious countries! There were some who must stay behind and make it right for the deserters.

Wayne's marrying Ann had turned her back to familiar paths. It had terrified her. There seemed too much involved, too little certainty as to where one would find one's self if one left the well-known ways.

She had been put in the position of the one hurt just when she had been steeled to bring the hurt. It gave her a new sense of the hurts—uncertainty as to the right to deal them.

And probably no monkey would dance more obediently than the monkey who had run away and been frightened at a glimpse of the vastness of the forest.

She would have to remain and explain Wayne, because she felt responsible about Wayne. It was her venturings had found what had led Wayne to venture—and, in the end, go. How could she outrage the army as long as Wayne had done so?

So it had seemed to Katie in her hurt and bewilderment. And the bewilderment came chiefly because of the hurt. It appalled her to find it did hurt like that.

But it was spring—and she knew that there were trees!

She paused and watched a gardener removing some debris that had covered a flower bed. It was spring, and there were new shoots and this gardener was wise and tender in taking the old things away, that the new shoots might have air. Katie could see them there—and tender green of them, as he lifted the old things away that the growing things might come through. The gardener did not seem to feel he was cruel in taking the dead things away. As a good gardener, he would scout the idea of its being unkind to take them away just because they had been there so long. What did that matter, the wise gardener would scornfully demand, when there were growing things underneath pushing their way to the light?

And if he were given to philosophizing he might say that the kindest thing even to the dead things was to let the new things come through. Thus life would be kept, and all the life that had ever been upon the earth perpetuated, vindicated, glorified.

It seemed to Katie that what life needed was a saner gardener. Not a gardener who would smother new shoots with a lot of dead things telling how shoots should go.

She drew a deep breath, lifted her face to the sky, and *knew*. Knew that she herself had power to push through the dead things seeking to smother her. Knew that if she but pushed on they must fall away because it was life was pushing them away.

She walked on slowly, breathing deep.

And swinging along in the April twilight she had a sense of having already set her face toward a more spacious country. And of knowing that it had been inevitable all the time that she should go. The delay had been but the moment's panic. Her life itself mattered more than what any group of people thought about her life.

Spring!—and new life upon the earth. It was that life itself, not the philosophy men had formulated for or against it, was pushing the dead things away. It was not even arrested by the fear of displacing something.

She had held herself back for so long that in the very admission that she longed to see him there was joy approaching the sweetness of seeing him. A long time she walked in the April twilight—knowing that it was spring— and that there was new life upon the earth.

Harry Prescott would be married within two weeks. It seemed nothing was so important as that she witness that ceremony. Dear Harry Prescott, who would be married on the banks of the Mississippi, close by a certain place where boats were mended.

CHAPTER XLI

It was hard for Katie to contain her delight in Wayne's generosity when she found he had left his launch with Captain Prescott. "Now wasn't that just sweet of father?" she exulted to Worth as they walked together down to the little boat house.

Worth was more dispassionate. "Y—es; but why wouldn't he, Aunt Kate? Where would he take it?"

"Well, but it's just so nice, dearie, that it's here."

"You going out in it?" he demanded.

Katie looked around. Some soldiers and some golfers in the distance, but like the day Ann had come upon the Island, no one within immediate range.

"Watts says she's running like a bird, Aunt Kate. Somebody was out this morning and somebody's going again this afternoon."

"Maybe she won't be here for them to take!"

"You going to take it, Aunt Kate?" he pressed excitedly.

"Well, I don't just *know*, Worth." She looked up the river. She could see a part of the little island where she had once pulled in to ask about the underlying principles of life, but not being able to see the other side of it, how could she be sure whether a launch ride was what she wanted or not?

"Father says we mustn't go in it alone, Aunt Kate. Shall I see if we can get Watts?"

"N—o; that's not exactly the idea," said Aunt Kate, stepping into the launch.

"Goin', Aunt Kate?"

"Why—I don't know. I thought I'd just *sit* in it a little while."

So Worth joined her for the delightful pastime of just sitting in it for a little while.

"I'd rather like to find out whether it's in good condition." She turned to Worth appealing. "It seems we ought to be able to tell father whether they're taking good care of it, doesn't it, Worth?"

"I guess I'll go and get Watts."

"I don't know why, but I don't seem able to get up a great deal of enthusiasm for that idea." Her fingers were upon the steering wheel, longingly. Eyes, too, were longing. Suddenly she started the engine. "We'll just run round the head of the Island," she said.

So they started up the river—the river as blue and lovely as it had been that day a year before when she had cheated it, and had begun to see that life was cheating her.

"Worth," she asked, "what is there on the *other* side of that little island?"

"Why, Aunt Kate—why on the other side of it is the man that mends the boats."

"Oh, that so? Funny I never thought of that.

"But I suppose," she began again, "he wouldn't be very likely to be there mending boats now?"

"Why yes, Aunt Kate, he might be."

"You heard anything about him, Worth?"

"Yes sir; Watts says he has cut him *out*. He says he's *on* to him."

"That must be a bitter blow," said Aunt Kate. "Watts getting *on* to one—and cutting one out.

"Watts say anything about whether he was still mending boats?" she asked in the off-hand manner people adopt for vital things.

"Why I guess he is, 'cause he made a speech last week—oh there was a whole *lot* of men—and he just *sowed seeds of discontentment.*"

"Such a busy little sower!" murmured Aunt Kate lovingly.

She knew that he was there, or at least had been there the week before, for just as she was leaving her uncle's she had received a note from him. They had not been writing to each other since the brief letter she had sent him the day after receiving the announcement of her brother's engagement. This note had been written to tell her no special thing; simply because, he said, after trying his best for a number of weeks, he was not longer able to keep from writing. He wrote because he couldn't help it. He had determined to love her too well to urge her to do what, knowing it all, she evidently felt could not hold happiness for her. But the utter desolation of life without her had crumbled the foundation of that determination.

In the note he said that his boat-mending days were about over. They would not have lasted that long only he had had no heart for other things.

But the letter gave Katie heart for other things! Its unmistakable wretchedness made her superbly radiant.

"Why, Worthie," she exclaimed, "just see here! Here's the very place where we landed that other time."

"Oh yes, Aunt Kate—it's still here."

She smiled; he could not have done better had he been trying.

"Now I wonder if I could make that landing again. I was proud of the way I did that before. I don't suppose I could do it again."

That baited him. "Oh yes, I guess you could, Aunt Kate. You just try it."

She demonstrated her skill and then they once more enjoyed the delightful pastime of just sitting in the launch.

Katie's eyes were misty, her lips trembled to a tender smile as she finally turned to him. "Worth dear, will you do something for your Aunt Kate?"

"Sure I will, Aunt Kate." Suddenly he guessed it. "Want me to get the man that mends the boats?"

She nodded.

"I'll *try* and get him for you, Aunt Kate."

"Try pretty hard, Worthie."

He started, but turned back. "What'll I tell him, Aunt Kate?"

The smile had lingered and the eyes were wonderfully soft just then. "Tell him I'm here again and want to find out some more about the underlying principles of life."

"The—now what is it, Aunt Kate?"

"Well just say life," she laughed tremulously. "Life'll do."

She found it hard to keep from crying. There had been too much. It had been too long. It was not with clear vision she looked over at the big house where Harry Prescott's wedding feast would be served on the morrow.

It seemed that about half of her life had passed before Worth came back—alone.

Pretense fell away. "Didn't you get him?"

"Why, Aunt Kate, there's another man there. But don't you feel so bad, Aunt Kate," he hastened. "We will get him, 'cause that other man is going to tell him."

"Oh, he—then he is here?"

"Oh yes, he's here. He's just over at the shop."

"I see," said Aunt Kate, very much engaged with something she appeared to think was trying to get in her eye.

"But, Worth," she asked, when she had blinked the gnat away, "what did you tell this other man?"

"Why, I just told him. Told him you was here and wanted the *other* man that mended the boats. The first man. The big man, I said. He knows who I mean."

"I should hope so," she murmured.

"But what did you tell him I wanted to see him *for*?" she asked, suddenly apprehensive.

Worth had sat down and begun upon a raft. "Why, I just told him. Told him you had come to find out some more about life."

"*Worth!* Told that to a *strange* man!"

"But I guess he didn't know what I meant, Aunt Kate. He's one of those awful dumb folks that talk mostly in foreign languages. I think he's some kind of a French Pole—or *something*."

She breathed deeper. "Oh, well perhaps one's confidences would be safe—with a French Pole."

"So he knows you want him, Aunt Kate, but he don't know just what you want him for."

"Yes; that's quite as well, I think," said Aunt Kate.

The other half of her life had almost passed when again there were footsteps—very hurried footsteps, these were.

It was not the French Pole, though some one who did not seem at home with the English tongue, some one who stood there looking at her as if he, too, wanted to cry.

Worth was the self-possessed member of the party. "Hello there," he said; "it's been a long time since we saw you, ain't it?"

"It seems to me to have been a—yes, a long time," replied the man who mended the boats, never taking his eyes from Katie.

Saying nothing more, he pulled in her boat, secured it. Held out his hand to help her out—forgot to let go the hand when her feet were upon firm earth. Acted, Worth thought, as though he thought somebody was going to *hurt* her.

A steamboat was coming down the river. And Worth!—a much interested Worth. The man who mended the boats did not seem to find his surroundings all he could ask.

"I want to show you this island," he began. "It's really quite a remarkable island. You know, I've been *wanting* to show it to you. There's a stone over here—quite—quite an astonishing stone. And a flower. Queer. Really an astounding flower. I don't believe you ever saw one like it."

"Pooh!" said Worth, starting on ahead. "I bet *I've* seen one like it."

"Say—I'll tell you what I'll bet *you*. I'll bet you two dollars and a quarter you can't get that raft done before we get back!"

"Well I'll just bet *you* two dollars and a *half* that I *can*!"

"It's a go!"—and Aunt Kate and the man who mended the boats were off to find the astonishing stone and the astounding flower, Worth calling after them: "Now you try to keep him, Aunt Kate. Keep him as long as you can."

It was after she had succeeded in keeping him long enough for considerable headway to have been made in raft-construction that he exclaimed: "Katie, will you do something for me?"

Her eyes were asking what there could be that she would not do for him.

"Then *laugh*, Katie. Oh if you could know how I've longed to hear you *laugh* again."

She did laugh, but a sob overtook the laugh. Then laughed again and ran away from the sob. But the laugh was sweeter for the sob.

"You *will* laugh, Katie, won't you?" he asked with an anxiety that touched deep things.

"Why there'll be days and days when I shan't do anything else!" Then her laughing eyes grew serious. "Though just a little differently, I think. I've heard the world sobbing, you know."

"But a world that is sobbing needs Katie's laughing." He drew her to him with something not unlike a sob. "I need it, I know."

There was a wonderful sense of saving herself in knowing again that the world was sobbing. What she could have borne no longer was drowning the world's sobs in the world's hollow laughter.

"Katie," he cried, after more time had elapsed without finding either the astonishing stone or the astounding flower, "here's a little sunny path! I want you to walk in it."

Laughingly he pushed her over into the narrow strip of sunshine, where there was just room for Katie's feet.

But Katie shook her head. "What do I care about sunny paths, if I must walk them alone?" And laughing, too, but with a deepening light in her eyes, she held out her hand to him.

But it was such a narrow sunny path; there was not room for two.

So Katie made room for him by stepping part way out of the sunshine herself. Smiling, but eyes speaking for the depth of the meaning, she said: "I'd rather be only half in the sunshine than be—"

"Be what, Katie?" he whispered.

"Be without you."

"Katie," he asked passionately, "you mean that if walking together we can't always be all in the sunshine—?"

"The thing that matters," said Katie, "is walking together."

"Over roads where there might be no sunshine? Rough, steep roads, perhaps?"

"Whatever kind, of roads they may be," said Katie, with the steadiness and the fervor of a devotee repeating a prayer.

They stood there as shadows lengthened across sunny paths, thinking of the years behind and the years ahead, now speaking of what they would do, now folded in exquisite silences.

And after the fashion of happy lovers who must hover around calamities averted, he exclaimed: "Suppose Ann had never come!"

It sent her heart out in a great tenderness to Ann: Ann, out in her mountains, and happy. Nor was the tenderness less warm in the thought that Ann would join with Wayne and the others in deploring. Ann, who was within now, would, Katie knew, grieve over her going without.

But that was only because Ann did not wholly understand. Everything the matter with everybody was just that they did not wholly understand. She grew tender toward all the world.

There rose before her vision of a possible day when all would understand; when none would wish another ill or work another harm; when war and oppression and greed must cease, not because the laws forbade them, but because men's hearts gave them no place.

"I see it!" she whispered unconsciously.

Her face was touched with the fine light of visioning. "See what—dear Katie? Take *me* in."

"The world when love has saved it!" She remembered their old dispute and her arms went about his neck as she told him again: "Why 'tis *love* must save the world!"

He held her face in his two hands as if he could not look deeply enough. And as he looked into her eyes a nobler light was in his own.

"As it has saved us," he whispered.

They grew very still, hushed by the wonder of it. In their two hearts there seemed love enough to redeem the world.

"Yes, my boy, and the air was rushing out of it with tremendous force. It was a mere crack, and took a long time to open sufficiently for a man to pass in. But there, don't talk about it. We have passed through as terrible an experience as you, and it has nearly killed the Major."

Gwyn passed the greater part of the next twenty-four hours in sleep, and then woke up, and was very little the worse. He rose and went to Joe, who snatched at his hand, and then nearly broke down; but, mastering his emotion, he too insisted upon getting up; and soon after the two lads went on to the Major's, where the old officer was lying back in an easy-chair.

"Hah!" he cried, as he grasped the boys' hands; "now I shall be able to get better. This has nearly killed me, Joe, my boy; but I've been coming round ever since they found you."

"Tell us how it all was, father," said Joe, as he sat holding the Major's hand in his. "Colonel Pendarve always put me off when I asked him, and told me to wait."

"I'm ready to do the same, my boy, for it has been very horrible. But, thank heaven, only one life has been lost!"

"Has one man been drowned?" cried Gwyn, excitedly. "I thought everyone was saved."

"One man is missing, Gwyn—that man Dinass. They say he was hanging about the mine that day, and he has not been seen since, and I'm afraid he went down unnoticed. Oh, dear; I wish we had not engaged in this wild scheme; but it is too late to repent, and the poor fellow will never be found."

"Not when the mine is pumped out again, father?" said Joe.

"Pumped out? That will never be, my boy. The water must have broken into one of the workings which ran beneath the sea, and unless the breach could be found and stopped it would be impossible."

"Don't leave me for very long," said the Major, after they had sat with him some time; "but go for a bit—it will do you good."

The two lads went straight away to the mine, where the engineer was busy cleaning portions of the machinery, but ready enough to leave off and talk to them.

"Want to get my engines in good order, sir, so that they'll sell well, for they'll never be wanted again. Nay, sir, that mine'll never be pumped out any more. Sea's broke in somewhere beyond low-water mark. It's all over now."

"Do you think Tom Dinass was below?" said Gwyn.

"Yes, poor fellow. He's a man I never liked; but there, he never liked me. No one saw him go down, but he's never been seen since."

They left the silent mine—only so short a time back a complete hive of industry—and went on to Harry Vores' cottage, where the owner was busy gardening, and Sam Hardock was seated in the doorway sunning himself, but ready to try and rise on seeing the two lads, though he sank back with a groan.

"How are you, gen'lemen? How are you?" he cried cheerily. "Very glad to see you both about; I can't manage it yet. Water's got in my legs; but the sun's drying it out, and as soon as I can walk I'm going to see about that bit of business. You know."

"There drop it, Sam, old man," said Vores, who had left his gardening to come up and shake hands. "Glad to see you gentlemen. Been down by the mine? Looks sad, don't it, not to have the smoke rising and the stamps rattling?"

"Don't you interrupt," said Hardock. "I want to talk to the young masters about him. Have you told the guv'nors what I said about Tom Dinass?"

"'Course they haven't," said Vores. "He's got a crotchet in his head, gentlemen, that poor Tom Dinass made a hole, and let in the sea-water."

"Crotchet? Ah, I know, and so do they. I say he did it out o' spite."

"How?" said Vores, with a grim smile at the visitors.

"I don't say how," replied Hardock; "but if we knew we should find he sunk dinnymite somehow and fired it over one of the old workings."

"Struck a match and held it under water, eh?"

"Don't you talk about what you don't understand," said Hardock, sternly. "You ask the young gentlemen here if shots can't be fired under water with 'lectric shocks, or pulling a wire that will break bottles of acid and some kinds of salts."

"Well, if Tom Dinass did that," said Vores, sharply, "I hope he blew himself up as well; but it's all a crank of yours, old man. Tom Dinass never did that. Let the poor fellow alone where he lies, somewhere at the bottom of the mine."

"Ah, you'll see," said Hardock—"You give my dooty to your fathers, young gentlemen, and tell them I'd be glad to see them if they'd look in on me. I'd come up to them, as in dooty bound, but my legs won't go. I s'pose it's rheumatiz. I want to hear what they'll say."

"Do you think the mine can be pumped dry again, Sam?" said Gwyn, suddenly, "so as to get to work once more?"

"Do I think I could dive down among the breakers with a ginger-beer cork and a bit o' wire, and stop up the hole? No, I don't, sir. That mine—the richest nearly in all Cornwall—is dead, and killed by one man out o' spite."

Vores caught Gwyn's eye, gave him a peculiar look, and tapped his forehead; but Hardock caught the movement.

"Oh no, I arn't, Harry Vores. I'm no more cracked than you are; but I won't quarrel, for you and your wife have been very good to me, and you did a brave thing when you come down that hole and got us out."

"Yah!" cried Vores, "such stuff. Why, anyone would have done it. You would for me. There, I don't mean you're mad—only that you've got that crook in your mind about Tom Dinass. Well, it's a blessing the poor fellow had neither wife nor child to break their hearts about him."

Chapter Fifty Two
The General Wind-Up

The days wore on, and the Colonel and Major shook their heads at Sam Hardock when he made his accusation as to the cause of the catastrophe; while the captain went about afterward in an aggrieved way, for he could get no one to believe in his ideas. The Colonel and his partner took the advice of an expert, and in a short time it was announced that no effort would be made to pump the mine dry, a few hours' trial by way of test proving that the water could not be lowered an inch.

The work-people were all liberally paid off, and began to disperse, finding work at different mines; and after several consultations, the Colonel and his old brother officer being quite of the same mind, an interview was held with a well-known auctioneer, and the whole of the machinery was announced for sale.

Just about this period, without saying anything at home, Gwyn and Joe, who had passed a good deal of time beneath the cliffs at low-water, to try and find out anything suggestive of an attempt being made to destroy the mine by an explosive—finding nothing, however, but a few places where the rocks had been chipped down by the point—determined to examine the spot from which they had escaped by the help of Vores.

The latter being consulted, expressed his willingness to go, and Sam Hardock was asked to accompany them, but he shook his head.

"No," he said, "my legs are all right again; but there aren't nothing to be got by it, and I should advise you all not to go."

But another actor in the late adventures expressed his willingness to be of the party, and tore off at full speed one morning when, well provided with candles, matches and magnesium wire, they started off, following the edge of the cliff, till, about a mile west of the mine, Grip seemed to take a plunge into the sea and disappear.

"Knows his way again," said Vores, laughing; and upon the spot where the dog had disappeared being reached, a way down for some forty or fifty feet was found, close by which a narrow opening, with the debris lying about as the pieces had been chipped, met the eye.

On approaching this, Grip made his appearance, barking loudly, and then turned and went in again.

"Will you go first, sir?" said Vores; and Gwyn led, candles being lit as soon as they were a little way in.

They followed the descent for the most part on all-fours, and lastly by creeping and pushing the lanthorns on in front, till at last the long, low, sloping cavern was reached where so terrible a time had been passed.

The floor was littered with broken stones, the result of the shot that was fired, and for a few moments Gwyn knelt there listening, expecting to hear the hiss and roar of the wind dislodged by the pressure of the water; but the only sound heard was the rustling and panting of those who were following; and as soon as Joe was out they went together to the descent into the mine.

Here there was no way down farther than about twenty feet; then the water lay calm, smooth and black.

"It was higher than this when we were here, Joe," exclaimed Gwyn.

"Yes, right over the floor."

"Pressed up by the confined air, perhaps, gentlemen," said Vores; and with this explanation they had to be content.

"But about how high above the sea are we here, Vores?" said Gwyn.

"No height at all, sir. According to my calculation, as we came down, we are about sea-level, and the mine must be full."

They returned, bringing a few crystals as mementoes of their adventure; and that evening, when the Major was at the Cove house, Gwyn was about to bring the specimens out and relate where they had been that day, when the servant announced the comma of two visitors, and Messrs Dix and Brownson, the solicitors, who seemed to be now on the most friendly terms, were shown in.

Their visit was soon explained. They had seen the announcement, they said, of the sale, and they thought it, would be a pity to remove all the machinery, as it was in position for carrying out the working of the mine.

Finally, they were there for the purpose of making the Colonel a liberal offer for the estate, house, mine, machinery, everything, as it stood.

Mr Dix was the chief speaker; and when he had finished, and stood smilingly expectant that the Colonel would jump at the offer, he was somewhat taken aback by the reply,—

"But I do not want to sell my estate. This has been my home, sir, for years."

"But as you wish to sell the machinery, my dear sir," said Mr Dix, "surely you would not mind parting with the mine now?"

"Indeed, but I should," said the Colonel.

"Then you will try and clear it, and commence work again?"

"Never, sir," said the Colonel, emphatically.

"Surely, then, you would not hinder others from adventuring upon what may prove a failure, but who are still willing to try?"

"Indeed, but I would, sir," said the Colonel. "The machinery will be sold for what it will fetch, and then I shall return to my old, calm, peaceful life."

"But, my dear sir," began Mr Brownson.

"Pray do not argue the matter, sir," said the Colonel, and at last the two solicitors went disappointed away. But in the three weeks which elapsed before the auction, four more applications were made, still without result, and then came the sale, months of work, and at last the whole of the appliances of the mine that could be got at were swept away.

It was about three months later that, one evening, the Major sat at a round table over which Colonel Pendarve presided, with divers books before him and a carefully-drawn-up balance-sheet, which he proceeded to read; Mrs Pendarve, Gwyn and Joe Jollivet being the other listeners. It was full of details, vouchers for all of which were in the books.

But Major Jollivet stopped him.

"Look here, Pendarve," he said; "the weather is going to change, or I have one of my fever fits coming on, so I don't want to be bothered. Look here, I joined you in this speculation, and it has turned out unfortunate. I trust you in every way, and I know that everything you have done is for the best. So just tell me in plain figures what is the amount of the deficit, and I will draw you a cheque for one-half. If it's too big a pull, Joe, you will have to go to work, and I into a smaller house. Now, then, please let me know the worst."

"Glad you take it so well," said the Colonel, frowning, and coughing to clear his voice, while Mrs Pendarve looked very anxious, and the lads exchanged glances.

"Ahem!" coughed the Colonel again. "Well, sir, in spite of the very favourable returns made by the mine, our expenses in commencing, for machinery, and the months of barren preparation, we are only—"

"Will you tell me the worst?" cried the Major, angrily.

"I will," said the Colonel; "the worst is, that after all we have paid and received, we now have standing in the bank the sum of twelve hundred pounds odd, which, being divided by two, means just over six hundred pounds apiece."

"Loss?" cried the Major.

"Gain," said the Colonel. "We worked the mine for the boys, so that money will just do for their preparation for the army, for they're fitter for soldiers than miners after all."

The Major had risen to his feet, and stood with his lips trembling.

"Am I dreaming?" he said.

"No, my dear old friend; very wide awake."

"Then I have not lost?"

"No; gained enough to pay well for Joe's education, and I stand just the same. Now, boys, a good training with an army coach, and then Sandhurst. What do you say?"

"Hurrah!" cried the boys in a breath; and when they repeated it their fathers joined in.

About a month later Grip was loose in the garden, and seeing some one approach, Gwyn rushed at the dog, seized him by the collar, and chained him up before turning back to meet—Tom Dinass, who was coming up to the house.

"You here—alive?" cried Gwyn.

"Seems like it, sir," said the man, grinning. "That there dorg's as nasty and savage as ever. Guv'nor in?"

"Yes, I'm here, sir," said the Colonel, who had seen the man approach. "Then you were not drowned in the mine?"

"Oh, no, I warn't drowned in the mine."

"Well, what is your business?"

"Would you mind taking me in where we sha'n't be heard?"

"No, sir; you can speak out here. I don't suppose you have anything to say that my son may not hear."

"Oh, very well, then, sir, it's this here. Old Dix—Loyer Dix—sent me here, ever so long ago, to spy out and report on your mine, and I did; and both Dix and Loyer Brownson, as they're partners now, finding it a likely spec, wanted to buy it, but you wouldn't sell, and worked it yourself."

"Well, sir, what of that?"

"Oh, only that they were disappointed, and they became friends after, and sent me here to get took on and report everything."

"Ah, I see," said the Colonel, quietly; "a spy in the camp."

"Yes, sir," said the man, grinning.

"And you reported everything to them?"

"Yes, sir, o' course; they paid me to, and so I did."

"And took our money, too!" said Gwyn, indignantly.

"Oh, but I worked for that, Mr Gwyn, sir, and worked hard."

"Exactly," said the Colonel, smiling; and seeing that it was apparently taken as a good joke, Dinass grinned widely.

"Then they got more and more disappointed as they found out what a prize they'd let slip through their fingers; and at last got so wild that, when I went to report to 'em one Sunday, they asked me if I couldn't do something to spoil your game."

"On a Sunday, eh?" said the Colonel.

"Oh, yes, it was on a Sunday, sir. So I said I'd try and think it out; and at last I did, and went and told 'em I thought I could let the water in and spoil the mine, and then they'd be able to buy it cheap."

"And what did they say?"

"Oh, they both coughed and rubbed their hands, and said it would be too shocking a thing to do, and that I should be bringing myself under the law, and all on in that way, pretending like to make me feel that they didn't want me to do it, but egging me on all the time."

"Ah, I see," said the Colonel, while Gwyn's teeth gritted together with rage.

"I wasn't going to shilly-shally, so I ast 'em downright if I should do it, and 'Oh, dear no,' says they, they couldn't think of such a thing; and little Dix says, 'Of course, as we promised, if we had succeeded in buying the mine for our company through your reports we should have given you the situation of captain of the working and a hundred pounds; but we couldn't think of encouraging such criminal ideas as those you 'mulgated. Let me see,' he says, 'it was to be a hundred pounds, warn't it?'

"'Yes,' I says, 'it was.'

"'Exactly,' he says, 'but we haven't got the mine, so we wish you good-morning,' which was like renewing the offer in an underhanded way. So I come back and did it."

"How?" burst in Gwyn.

"Easy enough, sir. Found out where the highest gallery ran, stuck a big tin o' stuff over it, and set it off with a little 'lectric machine on the rocks. I knowed everybody would soon get out."

"Oh!" ejaculated Gwyn.

"Be quiet, my boy. Very clever and ingenious, Mr Dinass; and we thought you were drowned."

"Me, sir? No, I knew a trick worth two of that."

"But may I ask why you have come to me now after ruining our property?"

"Why, because they've chucked me over, sir. They say I insult them by thinking they would ever do such a thing. That was when I went and asked 'em for my money. Last thing was, when I told 'em it was their doing, and they set me at it, they said I were trying to blackmail 'em—that they never thought I meant such a thing, and that if I warn't off they'd hand me over to the police."

"Exactly like them," said the Colonel.

"Yes, sir, just like 'em. I call it mean, and I told 'em so, and that if they threatened me I'd speak out and let people know the truth. And I says at last, 'I give you a month to think over it; and if you don't give me my hundred pounds then, I shall blow the whole business, and how do you like that?'"

"And what did Mr Dix say?"

"'Brownson,' he says, 'send for a policeman at once.'"

"Yes, just what he would say," said the Colonel, while Gwyn wished fervently he had not tied up Grip.

"Yes, sir, that's what he said; but I give 'em rope, and I've been again and again; and last time they let me see that all the blame should be on me and none on them, for no one would believe that loyers like them could do wrong, while everyone would think bad of me. Last of all they ordered me off, and after thinking it over a bit I've come to you, sir."

"What for?" said the Colonel.

"Why, for you to go to law with them for spoiling your mine. You've only got to start it, and I'll come and swear to it all, and you can get them transported. Don't you be afraid, sir; I'll come and speak out, and then—"

"I'm to give you a hundred pounds, I suppose?"

"Well, sir," said the man, grinning, "I must have it out o' some one. But don't you be afraid; I'll bring it home to 'em sharp. Now what do you say?"

"This," cried the Colonel; "I'm too old, and my son is too young, to horsewhip such a scoundrel as you are. Be off my premises at once, sir; and if you dare to come here again, old as I am, or young as he is, we'll try."

"What?" cried Dinass, in a bullying tone.

"Gwyn, my boy," said the Colonel, calmly, "go and unloose Grip."

The words acted like magic, and they never saw Tom Dinass again, for in consultation with his old partner and friend it was decided that nothing was to be gained by a prosecution. The mining was over, they were as happy without it, and life was not long enough to punish scoundrels who had lost already in their nefarious game.

"But, oh!" cried Gwyn, "I only wish he had stopped till I had let loose Grip."